THE LAST DEAD GIRL

"Dolan's seemingly effortless prose sets off dialogue that surprises and delights, and his intricate plot is simply dazzling: a twisting, shifting labyrinth of events, characters, and motivations."

—Booklist (starred review)

"Dolan's writing is excellent . . . The twists and turns flow effortlessly . . . Chilling."

—Forbes

"Mr. Dolan's characters are human enough to catch you off guard, and he makes the actions of even the creepiest ones believable."

—The Wall Street Journal

"Dolan plays out the complications with a spider's patience."

—Kirkus Reviews

VERY BAD MEN

"Harry Dolan knows how to write a book that grabs you."

—The Arizona Republic

"*Very Bad Men* is . . . a neat technical achievement [and] a nuanced piece of fiction."

—Tom Nolan, The Wall Street Journal

"A riveting crime novel . . . Relentless pacing, a wry sense of humor, and an engaging protagonist add up to another winner for Dolan."

—Publishers Weekly

continued . . .

"The rare crime novel with something for everyone who reads crime fiction." —*Kirkus Reviews* (starred review)

"Unless you're clairvoyant, you will be blindsided at least four times in this slowly unraveling story of an oddly normal, single-minded killer . . . Simply great storytelling." —*San Antonio Express-News*

"Dolan is exceptionally good at keeping the pacing going, using strong, well-developed, colorful characters, brisk dialogue, and seemingly endless plot twists. It's easily one of the year's best mysteries." —*Lansing State Journal*

"[A] cleverly plotted, hard-boiled tale . . . Dolan's knack for layering his narrative with nods to the genre's form . . . and allusions to other mysteries and manuscripts . . . adds to the reader's pleasure." —*Minneapolis Star Tribune*

"Dolan makes sure that both the characters and dialogue stay rough around the edges, just like the scenery of northern Michigan, giving *Very Bad Men* a satisfyingly realist bite." —*Mystery Scene Magazine*

PRAISE FOR
BAD THINGS HAPPEN

"Great f***ing book, man. I was totally hooked." —Stephen King

"Tightly plotted, sophisticated, and engrossing . . . This is a winner." —Nelson DeMille

"Go along for the thrill ride." —James Patterson

THE LAST
DEAD GIRL

HARRY DOLAN

BERKLEY BOOKS
New York

THE BERKLEY PUBLISHING GROUP
Published by the Penguin Group
Penguin Group (USA) LLC
375 Hudson Street, New York, New York 10014

USA • Canada • UK • Ireland • Australia • New Zealand • India • South Africa • China

penguin.com

A Penguin Random House Company

Berkley trade paperback ISBN: 978-0-425-27382-1

The Library of Congress has cataloged the Amy Einhorn Books hardcover edition of this title as follows:

Dolan, Harry
The last dead girl / Harry Dolan.
p.   cm.
ISBN 978-0-399-15796-7
1. Women college students—Crimes against—Fiction.
2. Rome (N.Y.)—Fiction.   I. Title.
PS3604.O424L37   2014   2013030283
813'.6—dc23

PUBLISHING HISTORY
Amy Einhorn Books hardcover edition / January 2014
Berkley trade paperback edition / October 2014

PRINTED IN THE UNITED STATES OF AMERICA

10 9 8 7 6 5 4 3 2 1

Cover photograph © Caras Ionut / Trevillion Images.
Cover design by David J. High, highdzn.com.

To my brother, Terry,
and my sister, Michelle

THE LAST DEAD GIRL

1

Rome, New York
The last night of April, 1998

They put me in a room with white tile on the walls and a pair of
long fluorescent lights glaring down from the ceiling. The lights
let out a slow, crackling hiss. I had a cut on my temple. It had
stopped bleeding, but now it itched. I tried to ignore it.

They left me there alone. Nothing in the room but a wooden table
and two chairs with metal frames and padded seats. I sat in a chair,
held my hands above the surface of the table. The right one trembled—
faintly, but you could see it. I thought about what could be causing it:
more than one thing, but I knew part of it was anger. I made a fist and
the trembling stopped.

An hour passed. There was no clock, but they had let me keep my
watch. They'd taken everything else—Swiss Army knife, keys, everything I had in my pockets.

I got up and circled the table under the hiss of the fluorescent
lights. Reached for the cut on my temple. Dried blood. I crossed to
the door and tried the knob. Locked.

I returned to my chair and picked it up. Thought about smashing something. Maybe the lights: they were glass, they would break. Then I could be angry in the dark.

Childish.

I walked another circuit of the room, dragging the chair behind me this time. Slightly less childish. The metal legs made a satisfying screech against the floor.

The door opened and a uniformed cop looked in at me and frowned. I put the chair back where it belonged and sat. The door closed. A few minutes later it opened again and a different cop came in, one I hadn't seen before. Dressed in a gray suit, with a detective's gold shield on a lanyard around his neck.

He sat down across from me.

"Why'd you kill the girl?" he said.

His tone was mild, bored, bureaucratic. I studied his face. He had dark hair cut short, a heavy brow, a long, fleshy nose. His skin was olive and he had gone too long without a shave. He must have been around fifty years old. His eyes looked tired.

"Seriously?" I said.

"Yes. Seriously."

"Does that ever work for you?"

He tipped his head to the side. "Sometimes."

"A cold open like that—'Why'd you kill the girl?'—and then they just confess?"

"You'd be surprised what works."

He turned his chair so he could rest an elbow on the table. Drew a thumb over the stubble along his jaw.

He said, "Why don't you tell me how you think this should go."

I gestured at the tiled walls. "You could leave me waiting here for another hour."

"You're not going to get all wounded on me, are you?" he said, his lip curling in a ghost of a smile. "I don't think you're that delicate. And I've been a little busy."

"You could give me your name."

He rubbed his chin thoughtfully. "That's fair," he said. "I'm Frank Moretti. You're Darrell Malone, but you go by your middle name, David. The girl was Jana Fletcher. Somebody strangled her. She was twenty-five, a law student at Bellamy University. How long did you know her?"

"Ten days."

"That's precise."

I shrugged. "That's how long it was."

"Ten days," he repeated. "That's fast."

"What are you trying to say?"

"Nothing, really. Just that you got close to her in a short time."

"Is that a question?"

"It's an observation. How did you meet her?"

"It was an accident."

He gave me the lip curl again. "Isn't that the way it goes. Sometimes I think life is just one long string of accidents."

"She was in a car accident," I said. "A minor one. I came along and helped her. Gave her a ride home."

"And that was the beginning of your relationship?"

"Yes."

"When did you start sleeping with her?"

The question made me frown. "I'm not sure I want to tell you."

"Why not?"

"Because it's none of your business."

"Actually, it is," Frank Moretti said. "You could say my business is finding out things that are none of my business. Shall I tell you what I found out tonight before I came in here?"

I leaned back in my chair. "Go ahead."

"I found out that you started sleeping with Jana Fletcher ten nights ago. That's an intimate bit of knowledge, but the walls of Jana's apartment are very thin, and her landlady, who lives next door, is very observant."

"Meaning she likes to spy on people."

"She told me you've been there every night since, and you have your own key. That's a minor detail, but it interests me."

"It made things easier," I said. "Jana tended to leave early in the morning. I tend to sleep late. She wanted me to be able to lock up when I left."

Moretti nodded. "I also learned, from a different source, that you're engaged to be married—but not to Jana Fletcher."

"What source told you that?"

"I know a reporter at the *Sentinel*. He looked you up in the archives. They ran the announcement in the local section. Quite a write-up. A lot of fanfare. It got me thinking about the name Malone. There's a library on the campus of the university with the name Austin Malone on it. Also a science lab, and a hospital wing. A relative of yours?"

"My great-grandfather."

"How did he make enough money to get his name on so many things?"

"Exploiting the masses. What does this have to do with Jana?"

"I wonder about the contrast," Moretti said. "I was in her apartment tonight. It's nothing much. Nobody in her family ever got their name on anything."

"What's your point?"

"My point is, she was from the wrong side of the tracks."

I heard myself laugh. A grim little thing, more like a cough.

"'The wrong side of the tracks'? Do people even say that anymore?"

"My point is, maybe that was part of the attraction," said Moretti. "Here's a girl you can impress with your money. She's not like the women you're used to. Maybe she's willing to do things your fiancée won't do. Maybe she likes it rough. Did she ask you to choke her?"

I felt the skin flush along my arms and on the back of my neck. Something sour twisted in the pit of my stomach.

"You're way off."

"Maybe I am," Moretti said, and then went quiet. His tired eyes stared at me. I returned the stare. The fluorescent lights crackled above us. The fingers of my left hand found the cut on my temple and traced it gently.

"You want me to get someone in here?" Moretti said.

His voice was tired like his eyes, and bland. I didn't answer him.

"Someone to look at that cut," he said. "A team of surgeons maybe? You don't want a scar. It might ruin your looks."

I brought my hand down to the table. "You're wasting your time."

He let out a long breath. "I'm trying to understand your relationship with Jana Fletcher. I don't think that's a waste of time."

"You're chasing down the wrong trail. I'm not the one who killed her."

Moretti nodded once to acknowledge my denial.

"Did you ever hit her?"

The thing in my stomach twisted again. "Why would you ask me that?"

"That's not an answer."

"I never hit her."

"But someone did."

No trace of doubt in his tone. He was stating a fact.

"How do you know about that?" I said. But then it came to me: the landlady.

Moretti didn't bother to answer me. "Someone hit Jana Fletcher ten days ago," he said. "Left a mark on her cheek. Ten days. Does that sound familiar?"

"She had that mark the night I met her. I didn't give it to her."

"Who did? Did you ask her?"

"She wouldn't tell me."

"That's convenient."

"It's the truth."

I watched Moretti drum his fingers on the table.

"Here's what I think," he said. "The two of you met and something clicked right away. You fell into bed together. It got a little crazy that first night. You hit her. Maybe you were just playing around, but you hit her harder than you meant to. Hard enough to leave a mark. A woman can forgive something like that, if it happens in the heat of the moment. Or as I said, maybe she liked it rough."

The drumming stopped. "Then tonight, you got carried away," he said. "You put your hands on her throat. You thought she'd like it. Some women do. But you're a strong guy, you went too far. Too much pressure. I'm not saying you did it on purpose. If you tell me it was an accident—"

I felt the muscles of my shoulders tense. Found myself shaking my head.

"I didn't do it. Stop playing games."

"Have I been playing games?"

"You know it wasn't an accident," I said. "I found her. I called 911. I saw what she looked like. No one did that by accident." The memory made me shudder. "You don't really believe I killed her."

"Why shouldn't I?"

"Whoever killed her broke the door in. Why would I do that? I have a key."

"Sometimes people stage crime scenes," Moretti said with a shrug. "They go in with a key. They do something they shouldn't. Then they go back out, lock up, kick the door in. They pretend they found it that way."

The sour thing in my stomach threatened to rise up into my throat. I tried to relax, tried to settle it back down. The room seemed suddenly warm, the white walls sickly.

"No," I said. "I can understand why you'd think that, but you're wrong. You're wasting your time."

"You said that before," he said mildly. "So tell me, how should I be spending my time?"

I closed my eyes, tried to think. I did my best to block everything out, make it all fade away, even the hiss of the lights.

"Someone hit her," I said eventually. "That's the place to start. You need to find him. And there's something else."

"What else?"

I opened my eyes. "You're going to think I'm making it up. But I'm not. If I were making it up, I'd have a better story."

Something passed over his face. A flicker of amusement.

"Why don't you tell me the story you've got."

"There may have been someone watching her," I said. "A week ago. That's what she thought anyway. We never saw anyone. I didn't take it seriously. Not seriously enough."

Moretti drew away from me, skeptical. "So I should be looking for someone you never saw? Someone who may not exist?"

"I think he exists. Probably he's the same one who hit her. You said you went to her apartment tonight."

"Yes."

"In back of the house, there are woods. He might have been watching her from there. I think he might have left something behind."

"What?"

"I went looking," I said. "In the woods. I found it near a fallen tree. But I left it there. Because how could I know if it was his? And what would I have done with it anyway?" My voice was speeding up. I made an effort to slow it down. "But you could look for it. It's bound to be there still. Maybe it would tell you something."

"What are we talking about?" Moretti asked.

"It's a long shot, but maybe it was his and maybe there's something on it. A fingerprint or DNA—"

"What did you find?"

"A stick."

"A stick? You're telling me you found a stick in the woods?"

"A popsicle stick."

2

One week earlier

J ana Fletcher had the dream again, the one where she was
trapped in a dark place underground. There were noises in the
dream—small animals scurrying—and a damp smell. And
there was a door she could never quite reach. A plain door with a
knob made of black metal, vaguely old-fashioned. A door you
wouldn't want to turn your back on, because you couldn't trust it,
because it didn't belong underground. If you turned your back on it,
it might open.

She woke in the night and sat up. Heard the sound of her own
breathing and the bedsprings squeaking with her movement. David
stirred beside her. She felt his hand on the small of her back.

"What's the matter?" Sleepy voice.

"Nothing," she said.

Moonlight in her window. She waited for David to fall back
asleep, then slipped out of bed and found his button-down shirt. She
put it on and walked barefoot to the bathroom. The dream had faded
from her mind. It used to make her heart race, make the air rasp

through her lungs; sometimes she'd need an hour to come down from it. But now the details drifted away from her like wisps of fog.

She lit a candle on the bathroom sink, looked at her face in the mirror. Her skin was neither dark nor white—coffee with cream, her mother used to say. Good, clear skin. It made the bruise on her cheek stand out all the more. Jana appraised it in the candlelight: a rough crescent around her left eye. Deep purple, the color of plums.

A tough thing to explain, because it looked like the kind of bruise you'd get if someone punched you in the face.

She left the candle burning and walked to the kitchen, buttoning David's shirt as she went. She turned the lock of the back door, opened it, and slipped out, letting the screen door close behind her with a soft clap.

She stood on her little brick patio and turned her face up to the night sky—the moon high and half full behind thin clouds. Cool air, maybe sixty degrees. She liked the feel of it on her skin beneath the shirt. No rain for now, but there'd been plenty in the last few days. She knew there would be more.

The clouds drifted past the moon. One of them was shaped like a crescent. Like her bruise.

She'd spent three days with it, and she was finding ways to explain. Because people asked. They were tentative, apologetic—but they asked. A woman in her constitutional law class had asked her what happened, and Jana had blamed it on a fall. Jogging in the park, a shoelace comes untied, and the next thing you know you're sprawling face-first on the ground. Not very plausible, but the woman believed her. Because that was the other thing. People wanted to believe. They wanted a nice, reassuring explanation.

There'd been others. Like the guy behind the counter at the shop where she bought coffee. For him she made up a story about the child of a friend. A toddler. Toddlers play with blocks—clunky wooden ones. They have tantrums, they throw things. The tale told itself.

You should have ducked, the guy said. Jana laughed. Next time she would.

Then there was the manager at the restaurant where she waited tables: a motherly woman, though she wasn't very many years older than Jana. She asked the question with a bit more concern than the others, and Jana answered her more carefully. She invented a softball league, very informal, one game a week. Jana played second base. Someone hit a grounder and it took a bad hop and she didn't get her glove up in time. A softball's not so soft, not really, not when it hits you in the cheek.

A respectable lie, Jana thought. Her favorite part was the bad hop. She had played on the softball team in high school and the coach always warned her to watch out, to stay alert, because sometimes the ball took a bad hop.

The restaurant manager listened with a grave expression. Doubtful.

"Is that the way you want to leave it?" she asked when Jana finished.

"I'm not sure what you mean."

The manager looked sad. "I mean you can trust me, hon. You can say what really happened. You don't have to tell me stories."

And Jana nearly wavered, because of the kindness in the woman's voice. But in the end she said, "It's not a story, it's what happened." She smiled. "I don't have any stories."

The manager sighed and suggested that Jana take some time off, that she come back later in the week, after the swelling went down all the way. Then she could cover the mark with makeup, for the sake of the customers. Bruises are bad for business. It shouldn't be hard to cover up; the manager could show Jana how; she knew some tricks.

And now, in the moonlight, Jana remembered their conversation. She hadn't gone back to the restaurant since, and she wasn't sure if she would. But she didn't regret the lies she'd told. Not the one about the bad hop, or the one about not having any stories.

Because that was a lie too. She had stories.

There was David, for instance. She had met him three nights ago. In the rain, as it happened. She had brought him home to her apartment, half a duplex on a dead-end street. And she had slept with him that first night, something she never did, but he was tall and she liked the shape of his jaw and he had a voice that was just a bit husky, as if he were getting over a cold.

He had strong hands too, but he was smart enough to let her take control. He let her undress him the first time and laid back, his heels hanging off the foot of her bed. His body was lean; she explored it with her hands and her mouth. He got hard, fast, and stayed hard, but he didn't rush her. Finally she kissed his chest and wrapped a hand around him, straddled him, took him inside her, just the tip. Still he waited, let her lead, and she sank herself onto him, all the way, and then she felt those strong hands on her hips, helping her move. And then the bedsprings and his voice saying her name, and she came so hard she moaned, which never happened either.

David. She didn't know much about him, except that he was a year older—twenty-six—and he'd grown up here, in Rome, New York. He'd gone to college somewhere else and had a degree in engineering. She thought he came from money, but she wasn't sure. There was something in the way he spoke, the way he carried himself, a confidence. When he took her out, he paid, no hesitation. On the other hand, his job was inspecting houses for people who wanted to buy them. Not what you'd call a high-powered occupation. He drove a pickup truck—and not a new one, but one that was well broken in. So, mixed signals. She had never seen where he lived.

She didn't know what he thought of her, living in her cheap apartment. Maybe that she came from money too, and was slumming, trying to prove that she could make it on her own.

And he liked her body, her skin; that was part of it, she thought. His own skin was pale; he would get off on the novelty of sleeping with a black girl. Which was funny, because she never thought of herself as a black girl. She had a black father she had never met, and a white mother who had raised her in Geneva, New York, a little town on the shore of Seneca Lake.

David. He was a good story. Jana didn't know how long he would stay around, but he'd been back each night since they met. And if they kept at it, she would have to do something about the bedsprings, because her landlady lived in the other half of the duplex—a respectable elderly woman—and whenever Jana saw her now she got a disapproving look.

She wasn't going to worry about her landlady.

Jana stepped off the bricks of the patio and into the grass. The lawn ran down in a gentle slope until it came to the edge of the woods in the distance. The wet ground yielded beneath her bare feet. The slightest breeze, cool on her body. She had nothing on but David's shirt, and it was thin. She might as well be naked.

A daring thought. Her fingers worked the buttons of the shirt, one by one. She parted it, drew it down off her shoulders, testing herself. Bold Jana. She felt goose bumps on her stomach, her breasts; felt her nipples stiffen in the air.

David inside. So close. She could wake him and bring him out here and lay him down on the grass. She closed her eyes, let it play out in her mind.

Something shifted and she opened her eyes. She drew the shirt up onto her shoulders and hugged it around her. She had a feeling of being watched, a physical sensation, real as the touch of the air on her skin. She thought of her landlady, who had her own brick patio nearby, on the other side of a woodpile and a forsythia bush, but when she went to check there was no one there. She looked off across the lawn, tried to see if there might be some figure in the woods. But all she could see was dark between the trees.

You're scaring yourself, she thought. It's nothing. Too much moonlight and night. Getting a little too daring. Rein it in, Jana.

Nothing.

I rolled onto my side and reached for Jana. Felt only the rumpled sheets. I got up and stood naked in the dim of the room. Looked around for my boxers and slipped them on. Couldn't find my shirt.

I drifted through the apartment, bare feet on old hardwood floors. I didn't worry about tripping over things because the apartment was one of the sparest I had ever seen. No clutter, no clothes strewn around. In fact, Jana Fletcher owned fewer clothes than any other woman I knew: her wardrobe fit easily into a tiny closet and a chest of drawers. She owned precisely four pairs of shoes: sneakers, hiking boots, loafers, heels.

Minimal furniture as well: the chest of drawers, her bed, a night table. A desk in the living room; no sofa, no television. No computer either. When she needed to do research or write a paper, she went to one of the computer labs at the university.

Her desk faced a blank wall. Nearby, there was a small wood-burning fireplace with a shelf over it that served as a mantel. On the shelf sat a long piece of two-by-four in which someone had drilled four shallow holes, each one broad enough to hold a tea-light candle.

The candles were burning now.

The only other object on the mantel was a clay bowl that held a single coin: a quarter. The quarter was strange. Imperfect. Part of it had been worn away so that in the upper left quadrant—right around George Washington's forehead—it came to a point.

No other trinkets. No keepsakes, no vases. Jana had a few books for her classes and a small but eclectic collection of novels, from Alexandre Dumas to Stephen King. She had two houseplants. I could see them now as I stepped through the archway into the kitchen. A cactus and an African violet in twin pots arranged like centerpieces on the kitchen table. A faint glow fell on them from a light above the stove.

The back door of the apartment stood open. I looked through the closed screen door and saw Jana standing outside on the lawn. She wore my shirt, which came down to her knees. I stepped closer to the screen, but I didn't go out, and as I watched she shrugged off the shirt, baring her shoulders and her back. Her dark hair hung down between her shoulder blades. Her body was a sculpture in the moonlight, a figure of blacks and grays. And even though I had known her for only three days, I thought I might be in love with her.

On the night we met, I'd been out driving on a dark road outside Rome.

When people think of upstate New York, they think of farmland and rolling hills. They think of roads that wind like snakes and little towns that never change from one decade to the next. The speed limit goes down to thirty and there's a gas station and a general store and a barn where someone's selling antiques. There's an old lady rocking on a porch and a roadside vegetable stand, and then the limit goes back up to fifty-five and there's nothing to see for miles but fields and trees.

Rome isn't one of those little towns. It's a city. It has good neighborhoods and bad ones. It has businesses that are growing, and others that are dying. It has a history that dates back to the American Revolution. It was the site of the groundbreaking for the Erie Canal in 1817 and the home of a major Air Force base all through the Cold War.

Rome is gray and sprawling like a city, and at night it lights up like a city. On the night I met Jana, I wanted to get away from it. I left my apartment and drove north with no particular destination in mind. I got onto Route 46 and followed it out past the city's edge. After a while I took some random turns and wound up heading west on Quaker Hill Road.

Houses gave way to woods. Beyond the reach of the city lights, the night turned purer. The scenery began to look a little unreal, the way it does sometimes when you're driving through the dark. A light rain began to fall. Not a dangerous rain: just enough to wet the road in front of me, leaving it a sparkling black in the light of my truck's high beams. As if I were driving on obsidian.

There were oak trees along the roadside and when the light washed over them the leaves glittered like gemstones. I remember that. I remember having the thought that I was traveling through a forest of emeralds.

The deer came out of nowhere.

It came bounding from the woods south of the road and it didn't try to cross in front of me; it didn't even come into my lane. I got one clear glimpse of it in the high-beam light and then I overtook it and it was right next to me, leaping along with me like a big friendly dog. It was there beside me shadowy in the dark, and I swear if I had rolled the window down I could have reached out and touched it.

I was driving slow for the rain, but not that slow: maybe forty-five or fifty. I read somewhere once that a deer can run forty miles an hour, but as the seconds ticked by this one kept pace with me.

I never thought of speeding up or slowing down.

We came to a curve and something changed. Maybe the deer had begun to feel the strain or maybe it had decided to let me win. Either way, it slacked off. It was still gamboling along, but it was in my rear-view mirror now, a shadow getting smaller until it was gone in the night.

I let out a breath I'd been holding in. The rain fell in thin lines on the windshield and the wipers swept the lines away. A half mile on, I saw headlights approaching. I clicked the high beams down to low and a car rushed by in the eastbound lane. It was nothing to look at, a beat-up subcompact, but the driver was pushing it hard. I watched the taillights receding in the rearview.

I wondered if the deer was still in the road. It probably wasn't. If it was, the driver would probably see it in time. There was no reason to think something terrible was going to happen, and nothing I could do about it anyway. I didn't need to touch the brakes. I didn't need to start looking for a place to turn around.

I found a little side road that led into some farmer's field. I pulled onto it and backed out again, swinging around so I was heading east. The rain didn't care; it kept on falling. The view was much the same in this direction; the leaves were the same sharp-edged emeralds.

Just when I thought I'd gone far enough and wasn't going to find anything, I rounded a bend and saw lights in the distance. The solid red of taillights, and the lazy blink of hazards.

The subcompact was there on the roadside, unmoving. The deer was there too. And Jana Fletcher.

3

pulled onto the shoulder and stepped out into the rain. In the glow of my headlights, Jana Fletcher walked back from her car to the deer. She was dressed in black. There was something dreamlike in the way she moved. I wondered if she was in shock.

The deer—a white-tailed doe—looked smaller than it had before, probably because it was lying on the ground. It was on its side, with its head resting on the road as on a pillow. Its eyes were open and staring.

Jana crouched beside it and touched the fur of its belly with her fingertips. She didn't look up when I approached.

"Are you all right?"

Her dark hair fell in curls, damp with beads of rain. I was crouching now too, but she still didn't look at me.

"I didn't see it coming," she said.

Her voice sounded soft. I got the sense she was talking to herself.

"I didn't see it, and then it was right there."

"You were driving fast," I said.

Finally she looked up. She had brown eyes. No sign of shock in them; they were clear, intense. "It ran straight at me. It jumped onto the hood of the car. Did you see?"

"No."

"Like it was trying to run right over the car. At first I thought it did. I thought I'd come back here and it would be gone. Into the woods. Do you think it's dead?"

I thought it must be, but I didn't want to say so. I listened to the falling rain and the murmur of my truck's engine.

She turned her attention back to the deer, running her fingers over the fur.

"It's beautiful," she said.

She shifted her hand to the deer's shoulder and the movement put her off-balance. She steadied herself, resting one knee on the ground. As I watched her, I saw things I hadn't noticed before. She had a red bruise on her cheek. It didn't look like something you'd get in a car accident. And her blouse was wide open at the collar. I could see there were two buttons missing.

"What's your name?" I asked her.

She told me, and I told her mine.

"Are you hurt?" I said.

"No."

"What happened to your face?"

She touched the red mark on her cheek as if she had just remembered it.

"It's no big deal."

"Maybe you should go to a hospital."

She braced her hands on her thighs and stood. "I'm not worried about me. I'm worried about the deer. What if it's not dead?"

I got up too. We faced each other across the body of the doe.

"It's not moving."

"It doesn't look injured," she said. "There's no blood."

"It got hit by a car," I said gently. "I think it's hurt in ways we can't see. Internal injuries—"

Jana Fletcher shook her head stubbornly and rain fell from her hair.

"It didn't get hit. I told you, it jumped onto the car."

"I'm sure it seemed that way. Your car rides low to the ground. You hit a deer, the momentum's going to carry it up over the hood."

"I know what I saw."

She looked away from me and stepped around the body of the doe. Bending down, she laid a palm against the creature's rib cage.

I left her there and walked to the front of her car, a blue Plymouth Sundance. No damage to the grille, the headlights unbroken. But there were dents on the hood, and the windshield was shattered on the passenger side—the kind of damage that might well have been caused by a frightened animal trying to scramble over a moving car. I could see bits of safety glass strewn like diamonds over the dash.

When I returned to Jana I found her down on one knee again, stroking the doe's back. Her blouse was wet through from the rain. She must have been feeling the chill of the night air. I got an old nylon jacket from the truck and brought it to her. She thanked me for it, slipped her arms through the sleeves.

"Is there someone you can call?" I said.

"My mother lives in Geneva."

"Maybe someone closer."

"Could you help me?"

"Sure. I'll take you wherever you need to go."

"I meant with the deer," she said. "Could you help me put it in my car?"

I looked at the Plymouth. "You don't want to drive that. Not with the windshield broken."

"In your truck then."

"Where will we go?"

"I know an animal hospital. It's open all night."

She must have read the skepticism in my eyes. She went to her car and came back with a plastic makeup case. Opened it and held the mirror near the nostrils of the doe. A fine mist appeared on the silver glass.

"You see?" she said. "She's breathing. We have to do something for her."

Jana tucked the case away and looked to me to see if I would come through for her. I smiled and shook my head, but I was already making plans. The first step would be to move the truck, get it facing in the other direction, back it up close. Then find something to use as a stretcher. I thought I had a tarp that would work. Move the deer onto the tarp, then lift it into the truck bed.

Jana had her own ideas. She slipped her hands beneath the shoulder of the doe, shifted her feet for leverage, tested the weight.

"Help me out here," she said.

"Hold on."

"She's not that heavy. You'll see."

"Just give me a minute."

She didn't wait. She started to lift. I forgot my plans and hurried to help. Dropping to one knee, I worked my hands beneath the animal's rib cage. Maybe we would have been able to carry the thing that way. Maybe. But just then the doe's eyes blinked. The hind legs scrambled. I fell back in surprise and toppled into the grass by the roadside. Jana did better. She kept her balance.

The doe got her four legs underneath her and turned a tangled circle, her hooves clipping out a drunken rhythm on the wet black of the

road. She skittered toward the broken yellow centerline and lifted her
nose up into the rain, then bounded across with her white tail held high.

I watched her disappear into the woods on the other side. Jana
took a few steps into the road, as if she wanted to follow. She stood at
the yellow line in the rain until I went to bring her back. When I
touched her shoulder she spun around. Her eyes bright.

"Beautiful," she said. "Did you see? Beautiful."

I used my cell phone to call a tow truck for her car, waited with her
until it came, offered to drive her home. She kept very still in the
seat beside me, but I could tell she was wide-awake; I could feel a
keyed-up energy coming from her. I drove under the limit, glancing
at her from time to time, but she kept her focus on the road ahead.

"What were you doing out tonight?" I asked.

A gentle shake of her head. "Don't ruin it."

"What do you mean?"

"We just witnessed a miracle. We don't want to muck it up with a
lot of talk."

"A miracle?"

"What else would you call a resurrected deer?"

I thought "resurrected" might be too strong a word, but then
again I'd been sure the animal was dead. So let her have that one.

"I just wondered where you were coming from, where you were
going."

She grinned without looking my way. "That's a little better. Maybe
we should both take this time to think about where we're coming from
and where we're going."

I laughed, a quiet laugh that trailed off into silence. Jana rode at ease
beside me with her handbag in her lap, along with a green file folder thick

with papers—two items she had retrieved from her car. As we cruised along I looked over once more at her profile. Her features—long nose, high cheekbones—hinted at something foreign and exotic. Which made the red mark on her cheek more of an affront. I had asked her about it once and wanted to ask again, but maybe it was best to let it drop.

Still, I had questions. "I'm curious about what's in that folder," I said.

She graced me with a sidelong look. "Now you're just being nosy."

Her house was tucked away on a cul-de-sac. We reached it near midnight. A sprawling oak tree grew by the driveway and sent out a long, low branch to brush the front window. I pulled in under the tree and she reached over to turn off the ignition.

"You're soaking," she said. "Come in and I'll put your clothes in the dryer."

She went inside without waiting for an answer. I followed. She draped my nylon jacket over a chair and left me in the kitchen. Came back with a big white towel. She held it up and said, "Come here," and I leaned forward so she could work it over my wet hair. She did the same for her own hair, dropped the towel on the floor, and started unbuttoning my shirt.

"I lied," she said softly, looking up into my eyes. "I don't have a dryer."

That was three nights ago. Now through the screen door I watched her standing half naked in the moonlight, my shirt down around her waist. Suddenly she pulled it up and clutched it tight around her. She looked to her right, took a few steps in that direction, came back. She stood looking out toward the woods, her back to me still, and I opened the screen door and went out.

4

Jana heard the door and whirled around. A gasp of breath, hand over her heart, until she realized it was only David. He crossed the patio and came out into the grass, wearing nothing but his skin and his boxers. Worry lined his brow.

"Is something wrong?"

"No," she said. "Just a feeling I had. Like someone was watching me."

He took a few steps toward the woods. "Did you see someone?"

"No. I was just being paranoid. I'm sure there's no one there."

He came back to her and the lines on his brow went away. He took hold of the front of the shirt and pulled her close.

"I'll tell you a secret," he said. "*I* was watching you."

She had a quick flash of a thought: that it wasn't David she'd felt watching her, that it wasn't anyone she would want to meet. She pushed the thought aside and made herself smile.

"Were you now?" she said.

His hands made their way under the shirt and he bent to kiss her.

She thought again of laying him down on the grass, but what she wanted was to go back inside.

He must have had the same idea. She felt his hands trail along her sides and he ducked down and lifted her up, tossing her onto his shoulder. She kicked her legs and laughed, and he spun her around and carried her into the house.

S omeone was watching.

Call him K if you like. That's how he thought of himself at times like this. There were things he wouldn't normally do, like slinking through the woods at night and spying on young lovers. Not his style. But K was different; he had no such inhibitions. Truth be told, K liked that sort of thing.

K had been watching the house for almost two hours. At one point he had crept right up to the bedroom window. Even in the darkness he could see the two of them sleeping in there, and he could tell they were naked under the sheets. He wished he had gotten there sooner, because he felt sure they'd been fucking. He would have liked to see them fuck.

After a few minutes at the window, he crept back to the edge of the woods. He found a spot a dozen feet in, where he could sit on a fallen tree trunk and still have a view of the house. He leaned forward with his elbows on his knees and meditated. That was as close as he could come to a word for it. Meditation was when you sat without moving and tried not to think about anything. Which was a fair description, except that he did move, just a little. He had a wooden stick like you'd find in a popsicle, and he held it in his right hand and twirled it around with his fingers. Call it a nervous tick.

And he was thinking. He couldn't help it. He was thinking about the girl and about what he had to do to her.

And then she came out. As if his thought had drawn her. She came out wearing only a shirt and stood looking at the moon.

K got up from the tree trunk and walked closer to the edge of the woods and thought that this could only be better if she had come out wearing nothing at all. And then it happened, as if his thought had made it happen. The girl opened the shirt, let it fall back off her shoulders, and he could see everything he wanted to see. Her breasts, surprisingly full for a girl her size. The soft plane of her stomach. A little patch of hair, trimmed in the shape of a triangle.

He could take her now, he thought. Sprint across the grass and be on her before she understood what was happening. The very idea gave him an erection hard as steel.

A reckless idea, out of control, impulsive. K was not impulsive. The girl wrapped the shirt around her again, and K believed that this was somehow his doing too. He was being punished for his reckless thoughts.

Then the boyfriend came out, bare-chested, wearing boxers. Tarzan in a loincloth. He could be trouble, K thought. It would be foolish to do anything while he was around.

The boyfriend picked the girl up, surprised her. She let out a squeal of a laugh that carried across the lawn. K watched them retreat into the house. He stayed where he was.

Give them some time, he thought. Then try the bedroom window again. He might see something good.

But he had to be cautious. He couldn't hope to finish the girl tonight. He'd have to wait. And plan. The important thing was not to get caught.

If you did something and didn't get caught, it was just the same as if it never happened.

5

The next morning I made a bad mistake.

Jana was gone by the time I got up—off to one of her classes. She'd left a key and a note asking me to lock the door when I left. I showered and dressed in the clothes I'd worn the night before. The shirt she'd worn. I helped myself to a glass of orange juice from her fridge. Took it out onto the patio in back.

The morning sun had dried the grass, but there was more rain coming. As I walked onto the lawn, I heard the sound of a rake biting into the earth. Jana's landlady was working next door, digging up last year's flower bed, getting ready to plant something new.

The woman was thin, stooped over, ancient. She wore a scarf to cover her hair and a ragged dress that might have come off the back of a medieval peasant. I'd seen her before but she never said a word to me, and she didn't now, even when I wished her good morning. She shot me a dark glance from under her brow.

I turned away from her and looked off at the woods. Thought about the night before—Jana's feeling that she was being watched.

She made light of it after, but there'd been a moment when she seemed genuinely afraid. I had a job scheduled for the afternoon, a home inspection, but for now I was free. I had time for a walk in the woods.

I could have set out straight across the lawn. I'm not sure why I didn't, except that I was feeling the weight of the landlady's disapproval. I was a stranger here, unwelcome. For all I knew, she owned those woods. I had no business traipsing through them.

I polished off the orange juice, took the glass inside, and went out again, this time through the front door, locking up behind me. My truck was parked beneath the oak. I skirted around it, walked east down Jana's little street until I came to a bigger one called Clinton Drive. Three blocks south on Clinton there was a run-down playground: basketball hoops without nets, a baseball field without bases. A sign by the street read CYPRESS PARK.

A few young kids were playing on a rusty swing set. Their mothers talked nearby. I cut across the ball field to the edge of the woods and walked along until I found the beginning of a trail. It wound aimlessly through a floor of wet leaves left over from the fall. Every now and then I saw a candy wrapper or a crushed can—the flotsam left behind by careless teenagers.

The ground began to rise and the trail smoothed out, heading west and north. It came to a ravine with a sharp drop, twenty feet down. The only way across was a narrow footbridge that might have had a railing once but didn't have one now. I crossed it slowly, listening to every pop and creak of the wooden planks.

After the bridge I left the trail and came to the northern border of the woods. I found a spot that overlooked the lawn behind Jana's apartment and saw a bent figure toiling with a rake—the landlady working in her garden. I kept within the cover of the trees so she wouldn't see me. A dozen feet in from the wood's edge I found a fallen trunk with the bark peeling off, a perfect place for someone to sit and watch Jana in the moonlight.

I would have given a lot for a bare patch of mud, a clear set of footprints. But the ground here was covered with the same carpet of leaves, not quite dried by the sun. If there were prints, they were indistinct. Yet there was one plain sign that someone had been here: a broken popsicle stick lying on the ground by the tree trunk. No way to tell how long it had been there or who had left it. Maybe a watcher in the night, or maybe one of the same teenagers who had been careless with soda cans and candy wrappers.

I walked back through the woods the way I'd come. Crossed the bridge. Followed the trail to Cypress Park. The kids had abandoned the swings and were taking turns on a slide. Their mothers supervised. I left the woods and marched through the ball field. None of them paid me any mind. On Clinton Drive a chipmunk scrambled along the top of a hedge, froze when it saw me, watched me go by. When I got back to Jana's duplex I saw a guy in a long tan coat sitting on her landlady's stoop, smoking a cigarette. He stared at me as I walked up the driveway, and when I approached Jana's door he crushed out the cigarette and got up.

"Hey, *kámoš*. You and me, we talk."

I paused with Jana's key in the lock. "Do I know you?"

"You don't know me, I don't know you. That's what we talk about."

He wore a silk shirt under the coat and what looked for all the world like leather pants.

"You're not a tenant," he said, wagging a finger at me. Like I'd done something naughty.

"That's true," I said, "but I know the woman who lives here."

"You shouldn't have a key."

"She let me borrow her spare."

"Maybe you think you live here now, huh?"

"No. I'm visiting."

"You don't live here. She pays rent for one. If there's two, it's more."

"I'm visiting."

"I can't have it. She's already behind."

He had acne scars and greased-back hair, and he spoke with an accent but it seemed to come and go. I thought it might be Eastern European. Czech or Polish.

"You got a key," he said. "Maybe you pay what she owes."

"Who are you?" I said.

He smiled and his teeth were definitely Eastern European. "I'm the landlord, *kámoš*."

I shook my head. "The landlord's a nice old lady. Lives next door."

"That's my grandma. She owns the house, I collect the rent."

He reached into the pocket of his coat and handed me a grubby business card: LANIK RENTALS. SIMON LANIK, LEASING AGENT.

"That's me," he said. "You pay or no?"

"Why should I believe you? Anyone can have a card printed."

"Oh, you can believe me, *kámoš*." He looked over at the other stoop. The old woman was there now, standing with the door half open. "Hey, Nana," he said to her. "This one's real slick."

She put her head down and waved a withered hand in the air, as if she was disgusted with the both of us.

Simon Lanik turned back to me. "You got a key. Good for you. You won't be here long, and the girl won't either. Unless somebody pays."

"How much does Jana owe you?" I asked.

He hesitated just a little, as if he might be padding out the number.

"Three fifty," he said.

"I don't have that much."

"What you got, *kámoš*?"

I brought my wallet out. "Four twenties," I said. "Eighty bucks."

"That's a start," he said, reaching for the bills.

I held them back. Nodded in the direction of the old woman. "I'll give them to her," I said, "and you'll write me a receipt."

He laughed. "Whatever you want, Slick."

I got my receipt and Simon Lanik went away. I went inside. I poured myself a bowl of cereal and thought about whether Lanik might have been responsible for Jana's bruise. I decided he made a poor candidate. I could see him slapping a woman if she fell behind on the rent, but he had written the receipt with his left hand, scribbled it in pencil on the back of his business card. Jana's bruise was on the left side of her face. I thought she must have been hit by someone right-handed.

I took my cereal into the living room and sat at her desk. She had an address book with butterflies on the cover. Names and numbers committed to paper, because she didn't own a cell phone. The person who hit her was probably a man, because men hit women. Probably someone she knew, so his name could be in the book. I paged through it. There were about thirty entries. None of the names jumped out at me, except one. *Roger Tolliver*. Jana had mentioned him. He was one of her law professors, a rising star on the faculty.

I dragged a legal pad across the blotter, picked up a pen, and copied down his name and number. I didn't know what I would do with it. Call him up and ask him if he hit her in the face? Ask him if he hid out in the woods last night, with a popsicle?

I could figure it out later. For now, I copied more names—every man's name I could find in the book. Then I remembered the night I met Jana; I thought of it as the Night of the Doe. She had a file with her that night, a green folder thick with papers.

I'm curious about what's in there, I'd said.

Now you're just being nosy.

I hadn't seen the folder since. But the desk had a file drawer. I opened it and found it stuffed with folders. None of them labeled, but only one of them thick enough to be the one I was looking for. I started to take it out, and that's when I made the bad mistake.

I stopped.

Because Jana Fletcher had trusted me to be alone in her apartment. She had given me a key. And she had made it plain enough that she didn't want to tell me about what happened to her face, or about the contents of this folder.

So I closed the drawer.

I kept the names I'd copied. Tore the page from the pad, folded it, and put it in my pocket. But I didn't do anything with it—not until after she died.

That was Thursday morning, the twenty-fourth of April. In the days that followed I learned some important things about Jana Fletcher.

I learned that she'd been born on the night of the spring equinox, which made her an Aries, though she didn't believe in astrology. I learned that she had broken her arm as a kid—a fall from a rope swing—and that she had once stepped on a rattlesnake, but had been saved by a pair of knee-high leather boots.

I learned that she played tennis, but not well; that she had taken ballet classes; that she had played the part of Rosalind in her high school's production of *As You Like It*.

I learned that she sang with perfect pitch and that her favorite songwriters were Sheryl Crow and Dar Williams.

I learned that she loved dogs—handsome, purebred dogs and mutts from the pound and little yappy excitable dogs with black button eyes and too much fur. She didn't have one of her own, but she couldn't see one on the street without trying to stop and pet it.

I learned that her favorite color was indigo, mainly because she liked the word. I learned that her favorite restaurant was a place called The Falcon on Madison Street near the university, and that she liked to sit in a particular booth in the back—the one with a canoe hanging over it, suspended by wires from the ceiling.

I learned that she lit candles whenever she came home, that she could cook without following a recipe, and that she noticed the smallest of details—like the fact that I had leafed through her address book and copied some of the names on a page from her legal pad.

I found that out a few days later. Sunday night. Cool rain outside, but Jana and I were in her living room, with a fire burning in the fireplace. We had started out on our feet with our clothes on and by degrees wound up naked on the floor. At some point we'd had the good sense to put down blankets and pillows so we wouldn't have to lie on the bare wood.

"I know what you did," she said.

She was beside me with her head resting in the crook of my arm, the flat of her palm over my heart, her right leg wrapped around mine. I wondered what she meant, decided she must be talking about Simon Lanik, about the rent.

I said, "It was no big deal. It was only eighty dollars."

"Not that," she said, propping herself up on an elbow. "Though I know about that too. It was sweet, but you didn't have to. I can handle the Laniks. And I'll pay you back."

I didn't care if she paid me back, but I didn't say it. I said, "All right. What else did I do?"

Jana rolled away from me and got to her feet. Took the legal pad from the desk and brought it down to me. She straddled my waist, held the pad so I could see it.

I had torn away the sheet I'd written on, but the pen had left indentations on the page underneath. She had gone over that page with a blunt pencil, rubbing it lightly over the lines of text, so the indented letters showed up white on a field of gray.

Clever. I had to smile. "Where'd you learn that?" I asked her. "The Hardy Boys?"

"Nancy Drew," she said.

"I can explain."

"You don't need to. You haven't called any of them, have you? You haven't tried to track them down?"

"No. I was tempted. But I thought better of it."

Jana tossed the pad away. "I'm glad. About both things. Glad you were tempted and glad you didn't give in to the temptation." She rested her palms on my shoulders. "I just wanted to have that out in the open."

I reached up to touch the mark on her cheek. "If we're getting things out in the open, we should talk about the other night." The Night of the Doe. "There's something—"

But she was already shaking her head. "Forget about that. It's a stupid thing that happened. It's over." She turned her head so I could see her profile. "Look," she said. "It's fading. In a few more days you won't be able to see it."

"That's not what I meant. There's something else. Something I should tell you. You never asked why I was out driving that night—"

She put her fingers on my lips to silence me.

"Is it important?" she said.

I nodded.

"Is it serious?"

I nodded again.

"I don't want to talk about anything important or serious right now," Jana said. "But I'll make you a deal." She shifted her body, moved her thighs down over my hips. "In a little while, if there's still something you need to tell me, you can tell me."

She took her fingers away from my lips and I didn't say anything, and she brought her hands up to the top of her head and arched her back and I still didn't say anything. She lifted herself and lowered herself down again, and after a little while I forgot there was anything I needed to say.

6

Here's the thing I meant to tell Jana that night: I was engaged to a woman named Sophie Emerson.

We were set to be married in the fall, on a day in late September. There was going to be a carriage, and horses, and doves. The doves would be released at just the right moment, to symbolize whatever it is that you symbolize by releasing doves. The ceremony would take place in a garden on an estate, because Sophie's mother knew someone from her sorority days who had married into an estate. And the mayor would preside, because Sophie's father knew someone else who knew the mayor.

Sophie kept a binder with all the details: a guest list for the rehearsal dinner, another for the ceremony itself, a third for the reception after; a set list for the band; menus from the caterers and brochures from the carriage company and the dove people. And on and on. When one binder filled up, she got another. She kept them on the coffee table in our apartment.

"I can tell what you're thinking," she'd say to me. "You didn't know what you were getting into. But why not? A little spectacle won't hurt you, and my parents can afford it. It's mostly for them."

"Really?" I'd say, teasing her. "We're doing this for them?"

"And for me," she'd say, breaking into a smile. "I'm only getting married once, and by god I'm having horses."

O n the night I met Jana, the Night of the Doe, Sophie and I had known each other for six months; we'd been living together for three.

We lived in an apartment not far from Rome Memorial Hospital, where Sophie spent most of her time. She was a surgical intern. The first time I saw her she was dressed in a set of blue scrubs; she wore cat's-eye glasses and had her hair gathered up in a clip. A cross between a doctor and a sexy librarian.

She was about to make an offer on a house and she had hired me to do the inspection. The place she had picked out was in a fine neighborhood and had a lot of surface charm, but there was mold in the basement and some substandard wiring and a furnace that wouldn't last another winter.

I walked her through and gave her my report.

"That sounds bad," she said.

"The good news is, it can all be fixed," I told her.

"What's the bottom line? Would I be crazy to buy this house?"

"That's up to you."

"I think I'd be crazy," she said. "What about these cabinets?"

We had ended our tour in the kitchen.

"What about them?" I said.

"I think they're hideous. Do you think they're hideous?"

"That's not really my area."

"And the walls," she said. "Too beige."

"A lot of people do that on purpose. Neutral colors. Makes the house easier to sell."

"Way too beige. I'd have to get someone in here to paint."

"Painting's easy," I said. "You could do it yourself."

Sophie laughed. "Like I'd have time to paint. I'd hardly have time to live here." She turned a circle in the center of the kitchen, as if she were having one last look. "There's no way I'm buying this house," she said. "Do you want to get a drink?"

You know what I was worried about?" Sophie Emerson said. "The lawn."

She'd left it to me to pick the bar and we wound up in a dive on Dominick Street. A hangout for tradesmen, the kind of place my father would have gone to.

"Houses have lawns," said Sophie. "You have to mow them. And water them. And kill the weeds. You have to plant things and trim them and cut them down and put them in a paper sack and haul them to the curb."

She took a sip from her margarita. She had asked for a cosmopolitan, but the bartender vetoed that idea.

"But it sounds like the lawn would be the least of my worries," she said. "Mold and bad wiring and all the rest. I'm not ready to deal with that stuff."

I picked at the label on my beer. "Why do you want to buy a house in the first place?" I asked her.

She didn't answer me right away. She took her glasses off and rubbed her eyes.

"You'll laugh," she said.

"No, I won't."

"Maybe you won't. But you'll think less of me. I wanted a house because of Brad Gavin."

Brad Gavin turned out to be someone she worked with, another intern at the hospital.

"You've seen those shows," she said. "On TV. About young doctors."

I nodded.

"They're always competing," she said. "Who can get the best fellowship. Who can perform the trickiest procedures. Who can scrub in for the most surgeries. Right?"

"Right."

"Well, all that's true. Only it doesn't end there. Doctors are competitive about everything. Even little things. Who's got the newest cell phone. Who can shoot a better game of pool. And no matter what it is, Brad Gavin is always the one to beat."

"And he bought a house."

"Exactly. And I thought: Why should he be the one with the house? I could get a house." She put her glasses on and looked at me over the rim of her margarita. "You think less of me now, don't you?"

"No."

"You do, but it's all right. I've got a flaw in my character. But I plan to reform." She took the cat's-eye glasses off again and held them by a stem. "Let me ask you something, David Malone. Does anyone call you Dave?"

"Almost no one."

"I'm gonna call you Dave. But that's not what I meant to ask you." She pushed the margarita aside and leaned close to me across the table. "The glasses," she said. "Do you like me better with them or without them, or does it not matter to you at all?"

Something in her voice, either alcohol or mischief. I was hoping for mischief.

I leaned close, took the glasses from her hand, opened up the stems. Put them on her. I reached to take the clip out of her hair, a dicey maneuver, hard to pull off gracefully. I managed it. Her hair tumbled down. She combed her fingers through it.

"Then it does matter," she said. "Good to know, Dave."

Sophie didn't buy a house. But three months later we got engaged. She gave up the apartment she'd been living in and I gave up mine, and we moved into a bigger one together.

The cabinets in the kitchen were a few years out of date, but they were easy to replace. The walls in the bedroom were unacceptably beige, but I primed them and painted them sky blue. The bedroom windows faced south and had heavy, dusty curtains. We took them down and put up blinds that we could open to let in the light in the morning.

Not that Sophie was there much in the mornings. She worked an intern's hours, a schedule I could never predict. Sometimes she'd climb into our bed just as I was climbing out of it. Sometimes I'd come home in the evening and find her sleeping, a plate of half-eaten takeout on her night table, her clothes in a pile on the floor.

On the twentieth of April, a Sunday, she came home at four in the afternoon and stumbled into bed. She asked me to wake her at eight-thirty so we could share a late dinner. I let her sleep till nine, then went in and sat on the bed—my side—and turned on a lamp. Then music on the clock radio. This was the way I'd learned to wake her: gradually, so she could get used to the idea.

While I waited for the music to do its work, I tidied up my side of the room. Newspapers off the floor, dirty socks into the basket in our walk-in closet. I moved to her side, picked up a bra and panties from the night before, reached for the scrubs she'd been wearing when she came home.

She had her eyes open by then. Still groggy. She said, "You can leave those, Dave. I'll take care of them."

I was checking the pockets, because there was always something in them: a pen, a pad, a sample of some new medication the reps were trying to sell . . .

Sophie was alert now, covers off, out of bed. "Dave, give me those."

. . . a tissue, an empty condom wrapper . . . That was new. Never found one of those before.

She got the scrubs away from me, the wrapper too. She closed her fist around it as if she could make it disappear.

"This was not supposed to happen."

She looked around for her glasses, found them, put them on. It took a few seconds, but it seemed like she needed the delay. I let her have it.

"Dave," she said, "it's not what you think."

Which, when you get right down to it, is something people only say when it's exactly what you think.

I knew the next line, heard myself say it. "Who is he, Sophie?"

"It was one time, I swear. It'll never, ever happen again."

"Sophie—"

"And I'm sorry," she said. "You've got to believe that." And I did. She was trembling. I could see it.

I put my arms around her, but it was no good. I said, "Sophie, tell me who."

"I don't want to," she said. "You'll think less of me."

Which was just enough of a clue to suggest the answer. I didn't want to believe it.

"Not Brad Gavin," I said.

The glasses came off and she held on to me tight. Her face against my neck, her tears on my skin. She didn't say the name. We didn't need to say it again. It had been said.

I got loose from her after a while, and out of the apartment. Into my truck. And that was it; that was the catalyst: looking in Sophie's pockets. It was enough to send me out into the night, to Quaker Hill Road, to my rendezvous with Jana Fletcher. The Night of the Doe.

7

K stayed away from that spot in the woods, the place where he had watched Jana Fletcher standing naked in the moonlight. Because something like that only happens once. You can't recapture it. If you think you can, you're kidding yourself.

Besides, the spot in the woods had its limits. You couldn't see the front of the duplex from there; you couldn't see people coming and going. For that, you needed a better vantage point, and K found one: in the parking lot of a dumpy apartment complex across the street. When he parked in a corner of the lot, he had a perfect view of Jana Fletcher's front door. And he could stay there as long as he wanted. The people who lived in the complex weren't exactly neighborhood-watch types. They weren't going to call the police if they saw a stranger sitting in a parked car.

So he spent some time there. Not crazy, obsessive time. He wasn't watching Jana Fletcher twenty-four hours a day. But he spent enough time to figure out that she generally left her apartment early in the morning and came back in the afternoon. Then she left again in the evening, between seven and eight, driving off in her little blue Plymouth. K assumed she was meeting her boyfriend for dinner, because when she came back the boyfriend would roll in right behind her in his pickup truck. And they would go in together and he would spend the night.

Which meant that K couldn't do it at night, the thing he needed to do. Not with the boyfriend there.

The other thing K discovered was that the neighbor woman seemed to leave the duplex two evenings a week. She'd come out around six-thirty, dolled up in her finest, scarved and bejeweled like a gypsy. She'd hobble over to a big boat of a car and climb in and rattle off down the street. Where she went, K didn't know. Not on a date, not an old crone like that. More likely a bingo game or some kind of church meeting.

Whatever it was, she went every Monday and Wednesday. Or she seemed to. K couldn't be sure; he hadn't been watching very long. But she had gone out two Mondays in a row, and one Wednesday, and tonight would be the second Wednesday.

K knew that tonight would be the test. He had woken up this morning with a sense of purpose, and with an image of Jana Fletcher in his mind, the way she looked in the moonlight. He would be there watching tonight—in the corner of the parking lot—and if the neighbor went out at six-thirty he should have at least a half-hour window during which Jana would be alone in the duplex. K wouldn't need a half hour. He would glide in and glide out. A few minutes and it would be done.

As the morning wore on, he started feeling restless and eager. At noon he got into his car and drove to Jana Fletcher's street. A warm day, sunny, the last day of April. He turned into the lot of the apartment complex, dodging potholes filled with yesterday's rain. He found the corner of the lot and cut the engine. A line of spindly ever-greens in front of him, and in the space between two of them he could see the duplex. Jana's car gone, the boyfriend's pickup parked in the drive.

K wondered if the boyfriend was still asleep in the apartment. That must be the life, he thought: fucking all night, sleeping all day. But not *all* day. If he slept *all* day, he would still be there when Jana got back in the afternoon; he would be there at six-thirty when the old woman left. And that would ruin K's plan. So the boyfriend had to go. K had to make sure of it.

How? He couldn't go over there, knock on the door, tell him to clear out. Nothing as crude as that. But K had other methods. He had the power of his thoughts. He knew the boyfriend's name because it was on the side of his truck: DAVID MALONE. HOME INSPECTIONS. K focused on the duplex across the street, sending his thoughts out to find Malone, to wake him up, to bring him out. K sharpened his focus, aiming it at the front door, willing the door to open. If he con-centrated intensely enough, if he wanted it, then his thoughts could make it happen.

He must have been concentrating hard, because the tap at the window beside him startled him.

K turned to see a woman leaning on his car, her left hand braced on the roof, her face inches from the window. Dyed-blond hair. Nice eyes, though there were shadows underneath them. Full lips colored red. She was asking him a question he couldn't make out. He rolled the window down to hear it.

"You got any cigarettes?"

He shook his head. "Sorry."

"You got money for cigarettes?"

"No money," he said.

"Everybody's got money."

K had no answer for that.

"What are you doing?" the woman asked.

"Nothing. Just passing the time."

"That's cool. That's what I'm doing too. Passing the time."

She went quiet, but she didn't leave. K could smell cigarette smoke on her breath, along with the odor of stale beer. She held a red Solo cup in her right hand. He watched her take a drink from it.

"Do you live here?" he asked her.

"I've got friends who live here," she said. "I come here a lot. Sometimes they let me crash."

"Well, maybe they can help you. I don't give money to people I don't know."

"Yeah, I got that message off you. Loud and clear. Have I seen you before?"

"I'm sure you haven't."

"I think I saw you here the other night. What's your thing? You just come here and sit in your car?"

K started to deny it, then changed his mind. "That's right," he said. "I sit here and concentrate, and my thoughts make things happen."

"No way."

"It's true."

And it was. Across the street, Jana Fletcher's front door opened. David Malone stepped out, bare-chested, carrying his shirt. Tarzan.

"Hey, are you watching that guy?" the woman said. "Is this like a stakeout?"

"Yes," said K. "It's like a stakeout."

"Are you a cop?" the woman said, an edge of suspicion creeping into her voice. "Because I haven't done anything wrong." She paused a beat. "Not yet anyway."

"Are you planning to?"

"Maybe. But if you're a cop, you have to tell me. Otherwise it's entrapment."

"I think you're mistaken," said K.

"No, that's for real. It's like a law."

"I think you may have an imperfect grasp of the law."

Across the street, Malone locked Jana Fletcher's door. He stood on her steps in the sunlight, putting on his shirt.

"I don't think you're a cop," the woman said to K. She raised the red cup to her lips and brought it down again. "Who is that guy?" she said.

"That's Tarzan," said K. "The Ape Man."

"You talk a lotta shit. Anyone ever tell you that?"

Malone buttoned his shirt as he walked to his truck.

"I'm leaving," K said to the woman.

"That's a shame," the woman said, smiling. "I was just warming up to you."

Her teeth weren't bad, K thought. Just not quite straight.

"You want to go for a ride?" he said.

The smile got bigger. "I thought you'd never ask."

The woman wore a sleeveless top and a short skirt. She had fine legs. K admired them when she got in the car, and stole glances at them as he drove along, following Malone. He tried to guess her age and decided she must be in her late twenties or early thirties. Still pretty, but cigarettes and too much sun were beginning to take a toll on the skin of her arms and chest. Her clothes seemed inexpensive, and she carried a cheap leather purse on a long, thin strap. But she wore a ring on her left hand, silver with a purple stone. An amethyst.

"What's your name?" he asked her.

"Jolene," she said.

"Like the song?"

"What song?"

Up ahead, Malone's truck bounced over a set of railroad tracks. K thought about the woman's red Solo cup. He didn't want beer spilled in his car. He held out his hand for the cup and after a second she gave it to him. After they passed over the tracks, he gave it back to her.

"You've never heard that song?" he said.

"Maybe you could sing some. Maybe I'll recognize it."

He tried to think of the words, could only remember the chorus.

"Jolene, Jolene, Jolene, *Jo-leeeeeene.*"

She rested the red cup on her thigh. "That's not much of a song," she said. "You're just saying my name over and over."

"There's more to it," K said.

"It's good though. You have a nice voice. Did you ever sing in a choir?"

Malone's brake lights flared. He made a turn onto the main drag, Erie Boulevard, and headed downtown. K followed.

"I'm messing with you," Jolene said. "About the song."

"I thought you might be," said K.

"It's Dolly Parton. I love that song. I just wanted to see if you'd sing it."

Malone drove past the university and the hospital and pulled into the lot of an apartment complex—an upscale version of the one across from Jana Fletcher's duplex. The pickup truck rolled into a numbered space close to one of the buildings, and K found a space marked VISITOR farther back.

He watched Malone disappear into the building. Impossible to tell which apartment was his. It could be useful to know. There was a row of mailboxes beside the entry door. There might be names on the boxes or there might just be numbers. K could go and check, but he wondered if there might be another way.

"What are we doing here?" Jolene asked him.

"Shhhh," he said.

The building had three stories and each of the units on the top two floors had a balcony. More likely than not, David Malone lived on the second or third floor. Two chances out of three. K believed that if he concentrated, he could make Malone come out onto his balcony.

"How long are we gonna follow this guy?" Jolene asked.

K held up a finger to silence her, and she murmured something that sounded like "You're gettin' to be kind of a drag." But she didn't say anything more. He focused on each balcony in turn, starting on the third floor, working his way left to right, then the second floor, right to left.

He came to the last one with no result and glanced over at Jolene. She was sitting quietly, balancing the red Solo cup on one knee. No hands.

He reached over carefully and picked it up. Held it in his lap while he started over with the balconies. He got through the third floor and halfway through the second before Jolene broke his concentration.

"I don't have germs, you know," she said.

"What's that now?"

She pointed at the red cup. "You can have a drink if you want. You won't catch anything."

"I'm not thirsty," he said.

A bit of movement caught his eye. A car pulling into the space beside Malone's pickup truck.

"Well, maybe I'm thirsty," Jolene said. "Did you ever think of that?"

The woman who got out of the car wore glasses and a doctor's white coat. K watched her go up the steps and into the building.

"Rude to hold on to it," Jolene said, "if you're not even gonna drink it."

K offered the cup to her. "Take it," he said. "Just be careful. Use two hands."

Up on the second floor—all the way on the left—David Malone stepped out onto his balcony. He put a mug of coffee on the railing.

"Two hands," Jolene said. "What am I, a baby?"

"Shhhh," said K.

"Are you shushing me again?" Jolene said. "I don't believe you." She drank from the beer, holding it with two hands. "Oh wow," she said. "Look, it's a guy on a balcony. This is great."

Movement on the balcony, a door sliding, and out came the woman with the glasses. The white coat was gone; she wore blue hospital scrubs. Her hair had been pinned up before, but now it was down. Another beauty, K thought. Maybe Malone had them all over the city.

"Oooooh, hey," Jolene said. "It's two people on a balcony."

K tried to tune her out. He watched the scene unfold. Malone and the woman didn't look happy. They kept their distance from each other. Malone picked up his coffee and took a sip.

"Uh-oh," Jolene said. "He's not using two hands."

8

Sophie Emerson was still wearing the engagement ring I'd bought her. That was the first thing I noticed when she came onto the balcony: the sunlight glinting on the diamond.

"I've missed you," she said.

I sipped my coffee so I wouldn't have to answer her right away. Because there were a couple of answers I could have given. *I've missed you too*—that was one way to go. *I haven't thought of you at all*—that was another. The truth was somewhere in the middle. I'd thought of her, but not enough, not as much as I should have.

We'd been apart for ten days, and though I had visited the apartment on those days, I had always managed to come at times when she was out, working her crazy intern's schedule. She had called my cell phone, three or four times a day at first, then less as time passed. I left the calls unanswered.

"This can't go on," she said.

I put the coffee down. "I know."

"I feel terrible."

"I know that too."

"It hasn't happened again. With Brad. If you're wondering. Or with anyone else. Just to be clear."

"Sophie—"

"And it won't. I promise you. So the question is: Can we work this out? What do I have to do, to get you back here?"

The coffee called to me again, because I needed a delay, an excuse not to answer. I left the mug on the balcony rail.

"I need to tell you something," I said, "about what happened that night." I almost called it the Night of the Doe, but that wouldn't have meant anything to her. For me and Sophie, it was something else. The Night of the Condom Wrapper.

"All right," she said.

"After I left here, I went driving. And I met someone."

"Oh."

"I didn't mean to. It was an accident." I gave her the story, as much of it as she needed: the rain and the deer and the girl.

She listened with a frozen expression, and I thought she wouldn't say anything. But after a time she said, "What's her name?"

"Jana Fletcher."

"And that's where you've been, all these nights? With her?"

"Yes."

Sophie turned away from me and leaned on the railing. I looked at the ring on her finger. The sun was still shining, but it couldn't find the diamond.

"That first night," she said, "when you didn't come home, I got worried. Part of me knew you had a good reason to stay away. You were upset about what happened. But part of me thought that you'd gone out in the dark and the rain and wrapped your truck around a tree. All because of a dumb thing I did."

Sophie chuckled, an unexpected sound. "I actually went in to the hospital, to make sure you weren't there. Then later on, when you didn't come home and didn't call, I got mad. I thought you were acting like a child. But when I saw you today I thought everything might be all right." Her head bowed and her hair obscured her face. "Now you've knocked the wind out of me. Is this how you felt that night, when you found out about Brad?"

"Yes."

"Then I'm sorry I did that to you. You must hate me."

"I don't hate you, Sophie. I was hurt, but I'm past it."

"You are?"

"So you shouldn't blame yourself for it. You shouldn't get bogged down in regret. I don't blame you, and I don't regret it."

Sophie stood up from the railing and faced me. "You don't?"

"No," I said. "I think maybe it was meant to happen. Maybe we had to go through this. If we hadn't, I never would have met her."

Which is not the thing to say to a woman who's wearing your ring.

What happened next—I didn't see it coming. One moment Sophie's hand was resting on the railing, the next it was moving fast. She hit me twice. First with her palm—a light slap that surprised me more than it hurt me. Surprised her too, I think. The second one was more deliberate and had more behind it. She used the back of her hand, and the diamond ring cut a slash on my temple.

What just happened?" Jolene said.

"I don't know," said K.

"It was pretty good though, wasn't it? It picked up at the end."

The balcony was empty now. Malone had gone in through the sliding glass door and the woman had followed him.

K started the car and pulled out of the parking space.

"We're leaving?" Jolene said.

"Nothing more to see."

K waited for a gap in traffic and made a left onto the street. Beside him, Jolene held the red Solo cup between her knees.

"Don't worry," she said. "It's empty."

"It's okay," he told her. "I'm sorry I was rude to you before."

"You're not so bad."

"I want to make it up to you. Take a look in the glove compartment."

"Here?"

"Right. What do you see?"

"I see an owner's manual."

"Underneath."

K heard her digging around.

"A popsicle stick."

"Keep going," he said.

"Wait, are these rolling papers?"

"Getting warmer."

Then a squeal as she pulled out a baggie and held it up. "Jackpot!"

"There you go."

"Oh, you're the best," she said. "The absolute best."

K drove out into the wild. That's how he thought of it. Out on the back roads beyond the edge of the city. He looked for a spot he remembered: a turnout and a broken-down fence made of wooden posts, and an old mule path that ran off under the trees. By the time he found the turnout, Jolene had opened up the baggie and the papers—working smoothly in the moving car—and rolled two thick joints.

They left the car and climbed over the fence, and when they were out of sight of the road Jolene took a lighter from her purse and fired up one of the joints. She held the smoke in her lungs for longer than K would have thought possible, and let it out in a burst of a laugh that tipped her head back and turned her face up to the sky.

The path ran straight and level. They followed it east in the warm afternoon and the only sound they heard was birdsong and their own footsteps. They passed the joint between them until it burned down to a nub, and K thought Jolene would want the second one right away, but she strolled along for a while, humming, taking things in.

There were trees growing on one side of the path, and on the other a channel of water, low and wide and dark. Jolene stopped and looked down into it, as if she were noticing it for the first time.

"What is that?" she said.

"It used to be the Erie Canal," said K.

"No way."

"I promise you."

"I didn't know it was still around," she said. "I thought it was from, like, the eighteen hundreds."

"A lot of it's been filled in, but you can still find pieces of it here and there."

He watched her lean out over the water.

"This path used to be part of it," he said. "Mules would walk along here, towing the barges on the canal."

"I knew that," she said. "We learned it in school. We used to sing a song about it."

"Low bridge," K said. "Everybody down."

"That's the one."

"I've got a mule and her name is Sal," he sang. "Fif-teen miles on the Erie Canal."

"Are you sure you never sang in a choir?"

K laughed. Jolene was still leaning over the water, and he realized she was trying to see her reflection. He took her hand to steady her.

"You don't want to fall in," he said.

I used to sing in a choir," said Jolene. They were walking east again. She kept close to him so that once in a while their arms brushed together.

"It was in high school," she said. "We took a trip once to a competition in New York City. We didn't win. But I remember it was Christmastime and we went to see a show. The Rockettes." She seemed to hesitate, making up her mind how much to tell. "And I decided I wanted to do that, to be a dancer. But my mom said I wasn't tall enough."

K kicked a small stone down the path. "How tall do you have to be?"

"I don't know." The words came out soft and sad.

"I could see you as a dancer," he said. "You've got nice legs."

That cheered her. "You're sweet," she said, taking his arm shyly, as if they were kids and he was walking her home.

"I've been tryin' to figure you out," she said. "I've decided you're some kind of private eye, and you were following that guy today because his wife hired you. You're supposed to catch him cheating. Am I close?"

It was nothing like that, K thought.

"It's something like that," he said.

"So the woman on the balcony, was that the wife or the mistress?"

"I can't really talk about it," K said. "It's confidential."

Looking ahead on the path, he spotted a bullfrog lounging in a patch of sunlight. He stopped short, held Jolene back, pointed it out to her. After a few seconds he took a cautious step forward and the frog hopped to the edge of the canal. Another step and it leapt down into the dark water.

Jolene went to look for it, standing on the side of the path, staring down at the rippling water. K came up behind her.

"It's gone," she said.

K said nothing. He wrapped his arms around her middle and she leaned back into him.

"This is nice," she whispered.

She smelled of cigarette smoke, and pot, but there was something else too. Something sweet. He thought she must have snuck a breath mint from her purse.

"I know why you brought me here," she said.

"Do you?"

"It's a pretty place. Out of the way. Perfect."

"It *is* perfect, isn't it?" said K. "You know, there's something I have to do later and I've been worrying about it all day. I need to relax. And being with you has helped."

"That's cool. That's what I want too, to help you relax. Just the two of us out here, I think we can make that happen. It might be easier if we had a blanket, but we'll make do." She wiggled her bottom into him. "That's what you want, isn't it?"

"Yes."

"I thought so."

He rested his chin on her shoulder. "But I don't know if I should."

"Oh, I think you should."

"It's complicated. There are a lot of things to consider."

"Keep it simple," Jolene said. "Think about the things I can do for you, to get you to relax."

K's hands slipped under her shirt and she drew in the muscles of her stomach. Then she yawned, a big yawn that arched her back. She giggled at the end of it. "Pot does that to me sometimes. Tires me out."

"What else does it do?" K asked. "Does it ever affect your memory?"

"No. It never has."

"What about drinking—does that make you forget?"

She laughed. "How much drinking do you think I've done today?"

K looked down at the still surface of the water. "So you're not going to forget me? You're not going to wake up tomorrow with just the haziest idea of what I look like or where you saw me?"

Jolene rubbed herself against him. "Not a chance," she said. "I'm definitely gonna remember you."

K took one of his arms from her middle, put it around her neck.

"That's what I thought."

9

n the room with the white-tile walls—after Jana Fletcher died, after I found her body—I watched Detective Frank Moretti pinch the bridge of his fleshy nose between his fingertips; I heard him draw a deep breath.

"A popsicle stick?" he said.

"In the woods behind Jana's apartment," I said. "I can show you where."

He laid his palm on the table between us. "Let's not get ahead of ourselves. I need to know everything about her, whatever you can tell me. Start with the day you met and we'll go from there."

And we did. I told him everything I could remember about the Night of the Doe, and the night in the moonlight when Jana thought she was being watched. I told him about Simon Lanik, the landlady's grandson. We talked about every time I'd seen Jana, every place we'd gone together. Sometimes Moretti took notes. Once in a while, one of his colleagues would knock on the door and call him out into the hallway, and I'd hear snatches of their conversation—as the door closed when Moretti left and as it opened when he came back.

We talked about Sophie Emerson too. I would have left her out of it, but Moretti already knew about her—knew we were engaged. And he could see the cut on my temple and wanted to know how it happened. When I told him, he laughed. "You got off easy," he said.

Sophie had regretted hitting me as soon as it happened—at least, she said she was sorry. I don't know if she really was, or should have been. She offered to stitch up the cut for me or drive me to the hospital where someone else could do it. I wound up tending it myself—swabbing it with alcohol in the bathroom of our apartment, covering it with gauze and tape.

At that point, Jana had a few hours left to live, and nothing I did in those hours was any use to her at all.

I slipped out of the apartment without another word to Sophie. Easy enough—it's not as if she wanted to stop me. I ate lunch in a diner downtown. After that, I drove out to a subdivision with an artificial lake and a nine-hole golf course and did a home inspection for an insurance salesman and his pregnant wife. Four bedrooms, three baths, finished basement—all in good shape, apart from a roof that needed to be reshingled.

I collected a check from the insurance salesman, took it to my bank. Stopped for coffee. By then it was going on five o'clock, and I was scheduled to meet Jana for dinner at seven-thirty at The Falcon, the restaurant with the canoe hanging from the ceiling.

That was the plan. But I could've deviated from the plan. I could've gone to her and done the thing I'd been putting off—I could've told her about Sophie.

I went driving instead, to think it over, to plan it out. You could say the cut on my temple had left me skittish about talking to women. Or you could say I was a coward and my cowardice cost Jana her life.

It's hard to remember everywhere I drove—though Frank Moretti wanted me to remember; in the room with the white-tile walls, he questioned me about every detail. I know I went out to Quaker Hill Road. There was nothing to mark the spot where Jana met the deer, except for a few specks of glass from the shattered windshield of her Plymouth.

At seven-thirty I was sitting in our usual booth, the one beneath the canoe. I peeled the tape and gauze from my temple, because I figured however bad the cut might look, it wouldn't be as noticeable as having a white square stuck to my head. I waited.

When Jana didn't show by seven forty-five, I used my cell phone to call her apartment. No answer. I left a message on her machine. At eight o'clock I called again. Same thing.

At ten after eight I finished off the drink I'd ordered and left some money on the table for the waitress. I drove to Jana's apartment—fast, but not too fast. Because on the one hand someone had given her a bruise and maybe spied on her from the woods, but on the other hand I didn't want to overreact. Maybe something unexpected had come up, maybe she had car trouble.

I turned onto her street around eight-thirty and saw her beat-up Plymouth in the drive—with the brand-new windshield, the one the shop had put in after the deer shattered the old one. All the lights in the apartment seemed to be off, but beyond that nothing looked wrong. Even the front door looked normal at first. But when I went to put my key in the lock the door swung inward and I saw that part of the jamb had splintered away.

And I was wrong about the lights. There was a light burning inside. A single tea-light candle on the living room floor, about eighteen inches from Jana's left foot.

I flipped a switch and the overhead light came on, and if there had been any doubt in my mind that Jana was dead, it went away.

She lay on her back with her eyes open, her face tipped toward her right shoulder. I remember thinking that the crescent bruise on her cheek was gone.

(It's fading. In a few more days you won't be able to see it.)

She had other bruises now: ugly ones on her neck where someone had pressed his thumbs into her throat. Her blouse had been torn open. Her jeans and underwear had been pulled down to her knees. Her feet were bare.

The two-by-four from the mantel over the fireplace lay on the floor beside her. It was four feet long—longer than a baseball bat—and she might have used it as a club. I'd like to think she did; I'd like to think she got in at least one good swing at her killer.

If she did, it would explain what happened to the tea-light candles. They would have been burning on the mantel, nestled in the shallow holes drilled into the two-by-four. Now they were scattered across the hardwood floor, three of them extinguished, one still glowing.

I can still recall the scene, but what I can't picture now is the expression on Jana's face, and that's a blessing. I can only remember that it was wrong. Like when you catch a glimpse of someone you know on the street and they don't know you're watching them, and they're miserable or angry or depressed, and you're seeing them in an unguarded moment. They don't look right; they don't look like themselves.

That's not it exactly, but it's close. As close as I can come.

S o you never checked for a pulse," Frank Moretti said.

"No."

"Some people would have."

"I didn't need to," I said. "She was gone."

"And you didn't cover her."

"Cover her?"

"With a sheet or a blanket."

"Should I have done that?"

"It's better you didn't. It tends to screw up the forensics."

"Then why—"

"Because it's something people do," Moretti said. "She's there on the floor, exposed, vulnerable. Someone who cared about her might have been tempted to cover her up."

"Meaning I didn't care about her."

"I haven't said that."

F or what it's worth, I held her hand. I called 911 on my cell phone and knelt beside her to wait, and her hand, when I took it, was neither cold nor warm. It felt empty as a glove, but I held on to it anyway. I'm not sure how long—as long as it took for the first cop to show up.

He was young, a patrolman on traffic duty. I met him at the door and he caught sight of the body right away and brushed past me. I stood in the archway to the kitchen watching the back of him as he looked down at Jana. I think it must have been his first murder. When he finally turned around, his face looked ashen. I stepped backward into the kitchen and gestured toward the sink. I thought he might need it.

He didn't, in the end. He bent over it with his mouth open and gulped air, but that was all. When he straightened up, he wiped his sleeve across his mouth, though it looked dry enough to me.

"You're all right," I told him.

The wrong thing to say, because it reminded him that I'd been there all along. He'd been careless. Who knows what I could've done while he had his back to me? I could've clocked him over the head and swiped his gun and gone for a joyride in his car. He decided to get tough retroactively.

"Put your hands on your head."

"Oh, come on."

"Do it."

He unsnapped his holster and touched the grip of his gun, and I put my hands on my head. When he told me to turn around, I did that too. I was facing the wall beside the archway. I could hear cars pulling into the drive, more cops coming. I felt his hand on the back of my collar, heard him say I had the right to remain silent. He shoved me forward roughly and if I hadn't turned my head I think he would have broken my nose. As it was, the side of my face hit the wall and the impact opened up the cut on my temple.

In the room with the white-tile walls, my fingers kept returning to the cut. It had its own topography: a long, thin ridge. Moretti had given me a Band-Aid to cover it, but it wasn't big enough. I could feel the ends of the cut on either side.

Moretti saw me fussing at it. He closed his notebook and said,

"All right. We'll take a break. Ten minutes. Then we'll start again at the beginning."

"No," I said.

"No?"

"I'm leaving."

The idea amused him. "You're not leaving."

"I've told you everything I know."

"I still have questions."

It was almost three in the morning and I had questions too. Not the kind that could be answered in that room. I was tired and I needed to know where I stood. The only way to find out was to press the issue.

"This has gone on long enough," I said. "You can let me go or you can charge me with something. And I don't think you're going to charge me."

"Why not?" said Moretti.

"Because by now you've had a chance to figure out what time Jana died." I was guessing, but it seemed likely. It was probably the subject of one of his conversations in the hallway. "And if it happened while I was sitting in The Falcon waiting for her, that's something you can verify. You might have done it already."

I was hoping that might be true, but Moretti's reaction—the terse shake of his head—made it clear I wasn't going to be so lucky.

"The medical examiner's best guess is that Jana Fletcher died sometime between six and seven," he said, "which means it happened while you were out driving and thinking. According to your story."

"It's not a story."

"It is until I confirm it."

I shrugged. "You're still not going to charge me. It's too soon. You want to be sure. You don't want to be proven wrong later—when you find out it was someone else. That would be embarrassing—"

"I can live with the embarrassment."

"It would be bad for you, and for the entire police department. You're forgetting who I am. My family's name is on buildings in this city. If you get this wrong, I can make trouble for you."

Moretti frowned. "Are you threatening me?"

"No. I'm done talking to you. If you plan to keep me here, I'll need to call a lawyer."

I sat back and crossed my arms, and he glared at me from under his heavy brow. Up above us, the fluorescent lights hissed—a fitting sound track for our contest of wills. We might have gone on like that for a long time, but someone knocked on the door and Moretti stood up slowly and took his notebook and went out.

He stayed away for twenty minutes. After the first ten, I got up and checked the door (locked) and stretched and paced around the table. I couldn't hear any sound from the hallway, but I figured Moretti was out there talking to someone—maybe about whether I could really cause them trouble if they refused to let me go. I hoped they were talking about that, and I hoped the prospect made them nervous. But I didn't think it would—not if they made any kind of inquiry about my family's connections. Because everything I had said to Moretti was a bluff.

Moretti had been the first to bring up Austin Malone, who had managed to get his name on some buildings at Bellamy University. Austin was my great-grandfather, true enough, and he had been a wealthy man in his day. He had inherited a business from his father: a mill that produced copper wire for telephone lines and copper pipe for plumbing. But a mill is a grubby place, and Austin Malone had no interest in spending time in grubby places. He sold the mill after his father died—to the Revere Copper Company in 1928—and used the money to buy as much prestige and refinement as it could buy.

It bought quite a lot. Austin Malone kept his money out of the stock market and managed to weather the Great Depression and the Second World War. But when he died in 1949, he left behind five sons and three daughters—and a great fortune divided eight ways works out to eight rather modest fortunes. Flash forward two more generations and there was nothing much left, just a name carved into a stone façade here and there, and a comfortable middle-class existence. My father was a building contractor and sent me to college to study engineering. I had relatives with good careers—I even had a cousin who practiced law. But it was tax law, not criminal law. Not the kind that could help me.

So my threat against Frank Moretti was empty talk: I couldn't begin to make any trouble for him. And if he wanted to make trouble for me, there was no one in the Malone clan who could pick up a phone and make it go away.

I don't know if my bluff worked, or if Moretti was an honest cop who didn't want to arrest someone for murder without being sure, but something changed in the twenty minutes he was gone. When he came back into the room the glare had gone out of his eyes and they looked tired again. He had a plastic bag that held my wallet and my phone and my other possessions. He tossed it on the table and held the door for me and said, "You're free to go."

10

The central police station in Rome is in the old courthouse building on North James Street. There are broad steps in front that lead down to a plaza with a pool and a fountain. There are cherry trees planted around the pool, and benches among the cherry trees.

I'd been there before and I knew the fountain was something to see, especially after sundown when they turned on the lights around the pool. But at three in the morning there was no one to appreciate the spectacle: the lights had been dimmed and the water had gone still.

I walked down the courthouse steps and through the plaza, past a sign that read NO LOITERING AFTER DARK. I didn't loiter. I came to the street and thought about my truck, which would still be at Jana's. I could get a cab to take me there, but there were no cabs in sight.

I hiked a block to a bus stop and sat on one end of the bench under the shelter. An elderly black man in a trench coat sat on the other end.

His coat had a tear along the shoulder that had been mended with duct tape.

"Do you know when the next bus comes?" I asked him.

"Somewhere 'round six a.m., I guess."

"Is that the one you're waiting for?"

"Might as well wait for that as wait for anything."

There was a map of the bus routes on the shelter wall, and a quick check confirmed that none of the routes would take me anywhere near Jana's apartment, even if I wanted to wait until six. My back ached from sitting in the white-tile room, and the cut on my temple itched. I was tired. I took out my phone to call a cab, and the display revealed seven missed calls, all of them from Sophie.

I tried to imagine what I might say to her, came up with nothing, put the phone down on the bench. I leaned my head against the plexiglass wall of the shelter and closed my eyes, just to rest them.

The man in the trench coat said, "You got the wrong idea, son, sleepin' in a bus stop. Cops'll roust you for sure."

"I'm not going to sleep."

He laughed. "Think I know what a man looks like when he's 'bout to sleep."

I slept. Had a dream too, though I don't remember much of it. I know there was candlelight in it, and Jana Fletcher, and she was alive.

I woke with the man in the trench coat shaking my shoulder.

"Come on now, son, your ride's here," he said.

I sat up and rubbed my eyes.

"You're a lucky fella," he said. "Ride like that."

I looked around for a cab, then remembered I hadn't called one.

The man in the trench coat was trying to hand me my cell phone.

"I took the liberty of makin' the arrangements," he said. "Figured you wouldn't mind."

On the other side of the street, a car sat by the curb. The hazard lights blinking, the driver's door open. A woman stood by the door. Cat's-eye glasses and her hair gathered in a clip. Sophie.

"Your phone rang while you were sleepin', so I took the liberty," the man in the trench coat said. "Good thing I did, since it was your lady callin'."

Sophie was watching me but she stayed where she was. She didn't cross the street.

"Go on now," the man said. "You'd be a damn fool not to go with a lady like that."

The following afternoon I woke up in my own bed for the first time in ten days.

The blinds were closed but I could see daylight seeping through. I sat up, swept the covers off, planted my feet on the floor. Raised a hand to my temple and felt the stitches Sophie had put there after she brought me home.

She'd been unnaturally calm in the car.

"Seven times I called you," she'd said.

"I'm sorry."

"I heard on the news, about that girl. Local news, eleven o'clock. I didn't know where you were. I called and you didn't answer."

"The cops took my phone."

"I thought you were dead."

"Why would—"

"I thought you were with that girl and you were dead, just like her.

The news didn't mention you, but I thought maybe they wouldn't—maybe they'd wait until the police notified your next of kin. And that's not me, I'm only your fiancée. They'd be trying to call your damn mother in Florida—"

"Sophie, I'm alive."

"Seven times. Finally some detective answered, and he passed me off to some *other* detective, and he wouldn't tell me anything, except that you couldn't come to the phone, you were being questioned."

"That was probably Moretti—"

"So then I knew you were alive, and I was left to wonder if you were a suspect in a murder."

"I'm not."

"Is that why they kept you there half the night?"

"Well, I might be, a little," I said. "But it'll pass. I didn't do it."

Without taking her eyes off the road Sophie made a fist and punched me in the shoulder. She punched me again, harder. And again.

"You didn't do it," she said, echoing me. "Did you think I thought you did it?"

At home she peeled the Band-Aid from my temple and looked at my cut. I hadn't done much to clean it up; there was still dried blood around it.

"What happened?" she asked.

I told her about the young patrolman at Jana's apartment.

"You can't mess with this, Dave. It won't heal properly, and it could get infected."

"Sew it up," I told her.

She arched an eyebrow. "Now you trust me to sew it up?"

"Just do it. You've got stuff here, don't you?"

"I've got a suture kit," she said, "but it'll hurt. I don't have anything to numb it."

"Do it. How bad could it be?"

"Let's find out."

I was all right while she cleaned the cut, with water and with alcohol. Then she got her kit and put the first stitch in, slowly and methodically, tugging on the thread.

"Oh my god, that hurts," I said.

Sophie bit her lip. "Two more."

"Promise?"

"Maybe three."

"Jesus Christ."

"Stop wincing."

"There's a needle," I said, "piercing into my flesh."

"Just imagine what this is doing for me."

She put the last stitch in, tied it off, and snipped the thread.

"Now leave it alone," she said. "And stop letting people shove your face into walls."

I opened the blinds in the bedroom and the daylight didn't kill me, so I went around the apartment and opened all the blinds we had. Sophie was gone, but she'd left me a present: a box of big waterproof bandages on the kitchen table. I brewed coffee and drank a cup. Poured another and took it into the spare bedroom I used as an office.

This was 1998 and I had a computer that took up my entire desk: a monitor as big as a footlocker, a CPU tower, a keyboard and mouse—all connected by a tangle of cables. I booted it up and checked my calendar. I'd slept through a home inspection scheduled for one o'clock, and I had another at five. It was almost four now. Too late to cancel, and I'd have to hurry. I needed a shower and I still had to pick up my truck from Jana's.

I got as far as the doorway before turning back. I returned to the desk, opened the middle drawer, and saw a folded sheet of paper: the list of names I'd copied from Jana's address book. I'd tossed it in there days ago.

Around a dozen names, and only one was familiar: Roger Tolliver, one of Jana's professors. I had his phone number but no address.

I didn't have time to deal with the list, not if I wanted to keep my appointment. I had to choose one or the other.

I wavered and decided I could look up one name and leave the rest for later. Roger Tolliver—that would be the one. I could've used the computer, but those were the days of dial-up Internet. The phone book would be faster.

I found him. *Tolliver, R.* Right where he belonged, between *Tolliver, Paul* and *Tollman, Julia.* And when I found him my choice was made. I forgot about my appointment. Roger Tolliver lived on Quaker Hill Road.

The houses on Quaker Hill Road kept their distance from one another. Most of them were relics from the forties, with stone chimneys and white clapboard. But Tolliver's house was different: new construction, two stories with an attached garage; brick façade in front, vinyl siding everywhere else.

I got there after five, because it took that long to shower and eat and arrange a cab ride to retrieve my truck. I thought Tolliver might be home, but when I knocked I got no answer. Let me revise that: no one came to the door. I did get an answer. Tolliver had a dog—a big, angry, deep-chested dog, from the sound of him. The kind you might see at a prison camp, straining against a leash, baring his teeth, snapping at the air, reminding you that it would be insane to try to escape.

The dog started barking as soon as I knocked and kept it up even when I stepped down from the porch. I went around to the back and pushed through some hedges growing beneath a window, and when I leaned close to the glass I could see him in there. Less wolflike than I had imagined. He was a shepherd, Anatolian, pale tan with a black muzzle. Still barking like a mad thing, like he had caught one of the prisoners cutting a hole in the fence, trying to run.

But it turned out he was the one in a cage. Tolliver kept him in a metal crate, barely big enough for him to turn around—probably to stop him from eating the furniture.

People are careless.

When Roger Tolliver left his house that day, he made sure the doors were locked, front and back. The windows too, at least the ones on the ground floor. But who bothers to check the windows upstairs?

I had a ladder on my truck. I got it out, extended it, leaned it against the front of the garage. Above the garage, a section of the roof sloped up to a pair of windows on the second floor, and I could see that the one on the left was open several inches.

Walking on a sloped roof can be dangerous if you don't have experience. I had plenty. Sometimes when you're doing an inspection, you don't need to climb on the roof; you can see everything you need to see from the ground. But I always go up. The customers like it. You're doing something they wouldn't want to do themselves. It makes them think they're getting their money's worth.

I climbed up, popped the window screen out, raised the sash. Slipped through into what looked like a guest bedroom. Replaced the screen. The dog was barking louder than ever.

I found the stairs and went down to him. Tolliver's house had a great room with a fireplace. There was a stone floor around the hearth, and the dog's crate sat on the stone. I knelt by the crate and let the shepherd sniff the back of my hand, and his barking gave way to a guttural growl—which seemed to be as close as we were likely to come to being friends.

More growling as I backed away from him and crossed to the front door. I unlocked it and went outside, took my ladder down, collapsed it, and returned it to the truck. When I came back in, the dog had forgotten all about our friendship. We were back at the prison camp and he had caught me trying to scale the gate.

I let him bark. I hoped he might wear himself out. Hard to estimate how much time I had before Tolliver got home; college professors make their own schedules. I thought he lived alone, based on what I'd seen so far. There were framed photos on the stairway wall of a man and two young children, a boy and a girl—presumably Tolliver and his son and daughter. No wife in any of the photos. I checked the closet near the entryway and found men's coats, but nothing for a woman or a child. There were toys and games in the closet, packed away, as if Tolliver's kids visited him but didn't live here.

Down to business. I had two reasons for my illegal entry into Roger Tolliver's house, and they were easy to summarize: buttons and popsicle sticks.

I tackled the second one first. Found the refrigerator in Tolliver's kitchen, opened the freezer door. He had frozen pizzas, frozen fish. No popsicles, but he liked ice cream. He had pints of Häagen-Dazs, ice cream sandwiches, ice cream bars.

Ice cream bars on wooden sticks.

Which proved nothing, of course. How many people have ice cream bars in their freezer?

I closed the door and went looking for buttons.

Consider: On the Night of the Doe, when I met Jana Fletcher on Quaker Hill Road, she had a bruise on her cheek. It seemed likely, now, that she got it from her professor, Roger Tolliver. But if I asked him, he could deny it. He could say she already had the bruise when he saw her that night, or that she was never in his house. And I couldn't prove him wrong.

Unless I could find her buttons.

On that night in the rain, Jana had been dressed in black. Her blouse had been open at the collar, with two buttons missing.

I looked for them everywhere in Tolliver's house. I could picture them: milky white like pearls against the black of the blouse. All of Tolliver's carpets were white or off-white, so I found myself crawling over his floors, searching sometimes by touch. The dog barked all the while. I looked between cushions, under furniture. I started on the ground floor and moved up, and when I'd looked in every corner and along every mopboard I came up empty.

Then I thought to look in the closets. I found it in the closet of the guest bedroom—Tolliver's vacuum cleaner.

I detoured to the bathroom at the top of the stairs and grabbed a towel, brought it back, and spread it on the bedroom floor.

Downstairs the dog was going wild. From the sound of it, we had a full-fledged manhunt under way. I pictured soldiers running in black boots, searchlights sweeping over the ground.

I pried the vacuum cleaner open and wrestled the bag free. Used my pocketknife to slice it open. Reached into the gray mass of dirt and dust and hair. Naturally the bag was almost full. I started emptying it one handful at a time, spreading the mess on the towel, searching it with my fingers.

The gray dust floated in the air. I tried not to breathe it. The dog barked. I reached into the bag for another handful and my fingers closed on something flat and round. Somehow the barking grew even louder and more feverish.

My fingers lost their grip on the round thing, and found it again, and the barking moved closer to me, ascending the stairs. My hand pulled free of the bag, and as I brushed the dirt from one of Jana's buttons, I turned to see the dog in the doorway, with Roger Tolliver holding him on a leash.

11

R oger doesn't like you," Roger Tolliver said.

I got to my feet and tried to make sense of that. Either Tolliver had the habit of talking about himself in the third person or—

"The dog's name is Roger," Tolliver said. He tugged on the leash, and the barking gave way to a low growl. "My wife named him. She thought it was a funny joke. Gives you some idea of the marriage. Are you going to put the knife away?"

Last I knew, my pocketknife had been on the floor, but now it was in my hand.

"Are you going to keep hold of the dog?" I asked.

"He probably wouldn't bite you, even if I let him go," Tolliver said. "He'd knock you down, surely. Keep you down, I imagine. He'd put his teeth on you, but he wouldn't bite. You see the distinction?"

I nodded, though I wasn't clear about the distinction. I knew I didn't want to see it demonstrated. The dog barked, showing his teeth. I'm not sure he realized he wasn't going to bite me.

"I'll keep hold of him," Tolliver said. "I haven't called the police yet. I don't know what I'd tell them. That someone broke in in order to savage my vacuum cleaner—but who would believe it?" He patted the dog absently. "How did you get in?"

I glanced at the bedroom window, which was open a few inches, the way I'd found it.

"I used a ladder."

"That's resourceful," Tolliver said. "And if that's your truck in the driveway, then you're David Malone. Which means you're here about Jana. But if you wanted to talk about Jana, I would've welcomed you. I would've let you in through the front door."

I folded my knife and slipped it in my pocket. Then held up Jana's button so he could see. "I'm here about this," I said.

He gathered the leash until he had the dog by the collar. Reached for the button with his free hand. Confusion in his eyes, then recognition.

"Oh, for heaven's sake," he said, offering it back. "Come on, then. We'll talk."

We talked outside. Tolliver had a dog run in his backyard: a patch of ground fifteen feet by sixty, enclosed by a chain-link fence. He led Roger the dog in through the gate and set him free of the leash. I stayed on the other side of the fence.

"I've tried keeping him out here while I'm gone during the day," Tolliver told me. "But if no one's with him he goes crazy."

He looked fairly crazy now, even though Tolliver was with him. The dog dashed from one end of the enclosure to the other, stopping now and then to jump up and put his paws on Tolliver's shoulders. When he did, Tolliver pushed him down again and sent him on his way.

"If he's alone out here for too long, he starts digging under the fence," Tolliver said, and from the state of the ground I could see it was true. "So he's better off inside, in the crate. It keeps him calm."

The dog sprinted to the far end of the run, spun around, and came back. He remembered he didn't like me, barked at me through the fence. Tolliver had brought a sack of toys from the house: rawhide bones and tennis balls. He picked out a ball and tossed it toward the far end. The dog raced after it.

"It's terrible," Roger Tolliver said, "what happened to Jana."

"She was here, a week and a half ago," I said. "On the twentieth. Wasn't she?"

"That's true."

"She left here missing some buttons," I said, "and with a bruise."

"I know. That was Roger's fault."

The dog came back with the ball in his mouth. Tolliver pried it away and tossed it down the length of the run.

"That night was the first time Jana came to the house," he said. "I had the dog in the crate, like I sometimes do when I have company. When Jana saw him locked up, she didn't like it, even after I explained the reason. I let him out and he took to her right away. He's playful, as you can see."

As if on cue, the dog ran up with the ball. Tolliver tried to grab it and the two of them started a tug-of-war.

"He's playful," Tolliver said again, "but he plays rough. And it's worse when there's someone around who really wants to play. Someone who loves dogs. Like Jana."

Roger the dog won the war and lay down to gnaw on the ball.

"You've seen how he runs," Tolliver said. "He's the same way in the house. He'll charge from one room to another and back. That Sunday night, Jana got him all riled up. When he's like that, he's nothing but momentum. She was bending down to pick up one of his toys and he barreled into her. The top of his head collided with her cheek."

Tolliver stood facing me across the chain-link fence. I tried to decide if I believed him.

"What about the buttons?" I asked. "The dog did that too?"

He nodded. "Like I said, Roger plays rough. I couldn't begin to tell you how many missing buttons he's responsible for, how many torn sleeves, how many chewed-up pant legs. I was mortified by the whole thing, but Jana put some ice on her cheek and laughed it off."

He shrugged his shoulders as if the incident embarrassed him, and I looked in his eyes and tried again to decide if he was lying. He had bright, keen eyes and a pleasant face, brown hair that had begun to thin on top but was thick and curly on the sides. He was a couple of inches shorter than me, maybe forty years old, a bit heavy in the middle, though he carried it well enough. His clothes were casual: twill shirt, no tie, khaki pants, Timberland boots.

He didn't look like a man who would make rough passes at his students and rip the buttons from their blouses and slap them around, but looks didn't mean anything. And he was a law professor, which meant he was a lawyer, which meant he was trained to speak persuasively. It was his job to be convincing.

So it was too soon to decide if he was telling the truth. In any case, I had more questions.

"You said that night was the first time Jana came to your house."

"That's right."

"What was she doing here?"

Tolliver turned away from me, looked down at the dog at his feet.

"Well," he said, "that's a long story."

———

H ave you heard of the Innocence Project?" Roger Tolliver asked me. "It sounds familiar," I said.

We were sitting in white plastic chairs on his deck. Roger the dog was trotting from one end of the dog run to the other, watching us, trying to decide how he felt about being left behind.

"It's an organization that tries to help people who've been wrongly convicted, tries to get their sentences overturned," Tolliver said. "That's something lawyers have been doing for a long time, of course. And you don't have to be part of an official organization to do it." He paused, looked away shyly. "Well, for the past few years I've been running my own small-scale Innocence Project at the university."

A big flowerpot sat on the deck by his feet. Nothing growing in it but some clover. I watched him brace one of his boots against the rim.

"We've had some success," he said. "There was a case from the late seventies in Syracuse: a string of sexual assaults against college students by a young Hispanic man. A twenty-year-old named Hector Delgado was convicted after some of the women picked his image out of a photo array. There was DNA recovered at the time—semen and saliva from the perpetrator—but it was never tested. The technology wasn't sophisticated enough back then. We won an appeal two years ago, after the DNA finally got tested and the tests proved it didn't match Hector Delgado. He was released from prison after serving sixteen years.

"The *Syracuse Herald* ran the story, and it got picked up by the Associated Press. *Newsweek* did a feature. They sent a photographer to take my picture. My colleagues at the university still tease me about that. But that kind of publicity helps draw students to the law school—students who want to make a difference."

"Like Jana," I said.

"Exactly," said Tolliver. "I usually don't work with first-year students, but Jana was eager. She joined the project when the new term started, in January. I rely on students to take care of a lot of routine work: basic research on cases, responding to inquiries from prisoners and their family members—people looking for help."

He clasped his hands over his stomach, interlacing his fingers. "The truth is," he said, "we have requests coming in all the time, by phone or letter or e-mail, far more than we can possibly take on. The number of criminal convictions that wind up being overturned in this country is remarkably small, and each appeal takes a huge commitment of time and resources, so you have to be very selective. Some of the students have a hard time understanding that.

"Jana was one of those. She felt drawn to one case in particular, a local case—Gary Dean Pruett. He was convicted of murdering his wife. The evidence was thin, but Pruett made a lousy defendant. He was a high school teacher and he'd been having an affair with one of his former students, which was enough to make him unsympathetic to a jury. His wife, Cathy, had found out about the affair, and he admitted that they had argued about it. But according to him, she just disappeared one Saturday afternoon—drove away and never came back.

"Cathy Pruett was a teacher too, and when the police started looking for her they found her car parked on a street near her school. They found her body three weeks later, dumped in a field on the outskirts of the city. She'd been stabbed and then smothered. Their suspicions fell on Gary Pruett early on, and when they searched *his* car they discovered strands of his wife's hair in the trunk. But that was the only physical evidence they ever found to link him to her death. And it was far from conclusive. Pruett's lawyer argued that the hair had come from a blanket that was also found in the trunk, one that Pruett and his wife had used on a picnic."

"If that was all the evidence they had, how did they convict him?" I asked.

An unexpected smile wrinkled the corners of Tolliver's eyes. "It wasn't all they had," he said. "They had Napoleon."

"Napoleon?"

"Napoleon Washburn, believe it or not. Goes by the nickname Poe." Tolliver looked off westward, where the sun was lowering toward the tops of the trees. "Poe Washburn was a small-time crook," he said. "Shoplifting, petty theft. He was known for stealing bicycles. Then he got picked up for something more serious: he stole a car. He was facing real prison time. He was in the county jail awaiting sentencing—at the same time Gary Pruett was awaiting trial. They were locked up in adjacent cells. Washburn claimed they got to talking one day and Pruett confessed to killing his wife."

"Do you think Washburn was telling the truth?"

"It's hard to say. But the lesson is, if you're suspected of a crime, you should talk to your lawyer and nobody else. Not your best friend, not the police, not some guy you meet in jail. It's a commonsense rule, but people ignore it all the time."

He spread his hands, inviting me to agree. I nodded. I didn't mention that I'd talked to a detective for hours the night before.

"So Washburn testified at the trial about this alleged confession," Tolliver said. "And the jury voted to convict. Now Gary Dean Pruett's serving a life sentence."

"Do you think he's innocent?" I asked.

"I don't know. He claims to be."

"And he turned to you for help—he contacted your Innocence Project?"

The smile came back to Tolliver's eyes. He shook his head. "That's the strange thing," he said. "The bicycle thief called us."

"Washburn?"

Tolliver nodded. "Jana was the one who answered the call—around the middle of February. Apparently, Poe Washburn suffered an attack of conscience. He told her there was no jailhouse confession—he made it up. She did some research on the Pruett case and saw how flimsy it was, and she brought it to me. I told her we'd have to pass."

"Why?"

Tolliver ran a palm over his hair. "Because there are certain realities you have to accept. You can't save everybody. You have to weigh the odds. In most of these cases, when a conviction is overturned, it's because of DNA evidence. It's hard to argue with DNA. If it doesn't match, you've got the wrong guy. But there was no DNA from the perpetrator in the Pruett case. Pruett's wife wasn't sexually assaulted.

"So it comes down to the confession. Suppose Washburn made it up. You have to convince a judge that he lied about it before, but he's telling the truth now. Then you have to prove that without the confession, the jury wouldn't have convicted Gary Pruett. That's not a sure thing. But even if you can prove it, Pruett doesn't walk free, not yet. At best you get him a new trial.

"On top of all that, there's the element of time. Pruett's wife was killed less than two years ago. Pruett was convicted last spring. If he didn't do it, then he's been suffering a terrible injustice. But there are others who've been suffering the same kind of injustice for decades. Time shouldn't matter, but it does. If you can't help everybody, you try to help the ones who've been waiting the longest."

Tolliver took his foot down off the flowerpot and leaned toward me.

"I made all these arguments for Jana, back in February," he said. "She wasn't happy. I couldn't blame her. I'm not happy about it either."

"But she didn't let it go," I said.

"No. That's why she came here, the Sunday before last. To try again to convince me." He frowned. "And she got a black eye for her trouble, because Roger wanted to play."

"But you didn't change your mind?"

"Yes and no," he said, looking down at the deck. "I didn't commit to anything, but I said I'd talk to Poe Washburn. I thought it was the least I could do."

"So you talked to him?"

"On the phone, yes. It didn't go well. When I asked him if he was prepared to swear out an affidavit—to say that he lied about Pruett's confession—he wouldn't give me a straight answer. 'I want to do the right thing,' he told me, 'but it's hard to know what's right. And I need to be sure you're going to look out for me.'"

"What did he mean?" I asked. "Was he afraid of what would happen if he told the truth?"

Tolliver looked up at me. "That was the implication: that there were people who wouldn't like it if he changed his story. But it was also about money. He talked about making a new start. 'I'd have to get out of this city,' he said, 'and that won't come cheap.' Finally I put the question to him bluntly: Did Pruett confess to him or not? 'I'll say what you need me to say,' he told me. 'As long as you're ready to take care of me.'"

Tolliver shrugged. "That was the end of it. I knew he didn't care about helping Gary Pruett. He had called us because he hoped to get something out of it, and he'd be useless as a witness."

I watched Tolliver reach down to the flowerpot and pluck a leaf of clover.

"What did Jana say when you told her?" I asked him.

"I never told her," he said. "I saw her the day before yesterday, and I meant to tell her. But I knew she'd be disappointed. And she was different; she seemed happier than I'd seen her before. When I asked her what happened, she said she met someone. 'What's his name?' I asked. 'David,' she told me. So when I saw your name on the truck outside today, I knew who you were." He rubbed the clover between his fingers, flicked it away. "So here we are, and Jana's gone. Do the police have any leads?"

I thought about how to answer. The only lead I'd been able to give Frank Moretti was a popsicle stick in the woods.

"I don't really know," I said.

Tolliver got up from his chair. Out in the yard, Roger the dog was getting restless. He pawed at the dirt beneath the chain-link fence.

"You should be careful," Tolliver said to me. "The boyfriend's always a suspect."

I might have said the same about the college professor.

He brought out his wallet and handed me a card. "You'll want to steer clear of the police," he said. "Call me if you need anything."

I got up and took the card and wondered about Roger Tolliver. Because he was right: I was a suspect. Yet he seemed not at all suspicious of me. Maybe it was a code among defense lawyers: everyone is presumed innocent. Maybe he trusted Jana's judgment and assumed she wouldn't get involved with someone who would murder her. Or maybe he knew I was innocent because he knew exactly what happened to Jana, because he was the one who put his hands around her throat.

Impossible to tell as we stood on his deck in the sunset light.

"Who do you think killed her?" I asked him.

The question seemed to take him by surprise. "I couldn't begin to guess," he said. "It might have been a random crime. The neighborhood where she was living . . ." He trailed off, as if nothing more needed to be said.

"What about Poe Washburn?" I asked.

He furrowed his brow. "Washburn has no violence in his record. I don't know what his motive would be."

I pressed on. "What about the people Washburn was afraid of?"

"Why would they kill Jana?"

"They wanted Washburn to keep his mouth shut. Jana wanted him to talk."

The idea seemed to bother him. I could see it in his posture, in his eyes. I suppose it might have been an act, but if it was, it was a good one.

"I assumed Washburn was making them up," Tolliver said. "He wanted to justify asking me for money. I didn't believe there was a real threat." The furrows worked their way into his brow again. "Do you think I was wrong?"

12

I drove east on Quaker Hill Road in the last light of the day, past the spot where I met Jana Fletcher on the roadside. I'd left Tolliver without answering his question, but I'd asked him one last question of my own. I wanted to know about the file Jana had with her the night she visited him, the night we met. Tolliver confirmed what I had already guessed: that it held the notes from her research on the Pruett case.

The file had been on my mind since the night before. I remembered it in the white-tile room with Frank Moretti, and even then I thought it might be important. I pictured it: a thick green folder in the drawer of her desk.

I didn't tell Moretti about it.

I knew if I told him he would take it. It would probably be logged into evidence, and I would never have a chance to see what was inside. But if I didn't bring it to his attention, it might be overlooked. It might stay in the drawer, and eventually I might be able to get at it.

Now it seemed more important than ever.

When I turned onto Jana's street, the sky was a darkening gray. I pulled in under the oak and the branches swayed in the wind. Jana's front window floated in space, a black rectangle, a window into a void.

The police had put a seal on her door: CRIME SCENE, NO ENTRY. They seemed to have repaired the damage to the frame as well. They hadn't changed the lock and I still had my key, and it would be easy to tear through the seal. But maybe there was another way.

I walked around to the back, hoping I might find an open window. There was no second floor, so I had no chance of getting in with the ladder the way I'd done at Tolliver's house.

The windows were all locked. There was no seal on the back door, but it didn't do me any good. The door took a different key; mine wouldn't fit.

I went around front again to the landlady's side of the duplex. Her car was in the driveway, a big Mercury sedan alongside Jana's Plymouth. I knocked on her door. No answer. I could see lights behind the curtains of her front window. I knocked again and the lights went out.

I waited, listening for movement behind the door. I thought I heard footsteps.

"I'll just keep knocking," I said.

No answer. I knocked again, to show her I was serious.

The lights came back on. I heard a dead bolt turn and the door opened a few inches, until a chain-lock stopped it. The landlady's face appeared in the opening, scarf around her hair, eyes a bottomless black.

She spoke with a thick accent, like the loyal retainer in a vampire's castle.

"I don't like you, young man," she said.

I took it in stride. "Roger doesn't either. Hardly anybody does."

"Go avay," she said, "or I call the police."

"I wish you wouldn't."

"I vill."

"I don't like the police."

"Who can blame you?" she said. "They are idiots." She snorted to demonstrate her disapproval. "Who is Roger?"

"He's a dog," I said. "Or a lawyer. But the dog's the one that doesn't like me."

Her eyes narrowed. "This is a joke? I don't like jokes."

"It's not much of a joke."

"It is not a time for jokes. The girl is dead."

The breath went out of me. All at once I felt very tired.

"You're right," I said. "No jokes. I need to get into her apartment."

"You can't get in."

"I know it's sealed."

"No one gets in. That is what they tell me."

"There's no seal on the back door. If you could loan me your key—"

"What for?"

"It's personal," I said. "There are things in there I need."

"There is nothing in there anymore, nothing anybody needs."

"It won't take long. The police will never know."

She scowled, and somehow, for a moment, the scowl made her ancient face look young.

"Don't talk to me about the police," she said. "The police are fools. Are you a killer?"

The question came from left field, and when I didn't answer at once, she got impatient.

"Did you kill the girl?" she said.

"No."

"Good. Then stay away from the police. Stay away from this house. You have a family?"

"Not around here."

"Doesn't matter. Go to them. Knock on their door. Leave me alone."

She didn't wait for me to answer. She closed the door and I didn't try to stop her. I heard the dead bolt slide into place and stood for a moment on her steps, listening to the wind.

A path of paving stones led from her steps to the driveway. I walked down it, climbed into my truck, and sat looking at Jana's front door with its police seal: just a piece of paper, NO ENTRY, nothing really. I could walk up and use my key and tear the paper and I'd be inside, and what good would it do me? The old woman was right. There was nothing in there anymore.

She was full of good advice. *Stay away from the police.* Take away the accent and it was the same message I'd heard from Roger Tolliver. Maybe I should listen to them. And if I wanted to stay away from the police, the first step was not breaking the seal on Jana's door.

I sat in the truck and started the engine, but I didn't leave. I looked at Jana's door and the black rectangle of her front window and watched the wind sway the branches of the oak, and the police came to me.

It was a black sedan, a Chevrolet, a stereotypical detective's car. It pulled into the driveway and I watched its lights go dark in my rear-view mirror. Frank Moretti got out of it unhurriedly. He wore a gray suit like the one he'd worn the night before, this one a shade lighter. He crossed behind my truck, opened the passenger door, and climbed in.

"What are you doing here?" he said.

He looked different. Less tired than last night—that was part of it. But also smaller. In the room with the white-tile walls he had seemed like a large man, but now I could see he was no more than five nine.

"I can't answer you," I said.

"Can't or won't?"

"I spoke to a lawyer today," I said. "He warned me not to talk to the police."

"He should have told you not to return to the scene of the crime. What did Agnes have to say?"

"Agnes?"

Moretti nodded toward the old woman's door. "Agnes Lanik. What did you two talk about?"

I looked at his car in the rearview and wondered where he'd come from and how long he'd been watching.

"Have you been following me?"

"Yeah, I've been following you," he said dryly. "I've had a whole team of guys busting their asses following you, earning overtime. You're just that important."

I thought of another possibility. "You've got someone watching Jana's apartment."

"You're getting warmer. Are you going to tell me what Agnes said to you?"

"She told me to go away."

"Doesn't surprise me. So why are you still here?"

I thought about the green file folder in Jana's desk. I could tell Moretti about it now and he would go in and collect it, and I would never get a chance to look at it. Or maybe I was wrong, maybe he'd be grateful. Maybe we'd sit in the cab of the truck and go through the file together. Maybe Agnes Lanik would bring us cookies. . . .

I decided not to mention the file.

"What do you know about Gary Dean Pruett?" I asked Moretti.

He took his time answering. I tried to read his expression, but all

I could see was annoyance. Eventually he said, "I know he killed his wife."

"Some people think he might be innocent."

"What people are those?"

"Jana Fletcher was one."

He let out an irritated sigh. "Where's this coming from?"

"The lawyer I talked to—he was one of Jana's law professors. Roger Tolliver."

I gave Moretti a thumbnail sketch of what I'd learned: about Tolliver's Innocence Project and Jana's part in it. About Napoleon Washburn, who told Jana he lied about Pruett's confession.

"Napoleon Washburn," Moretti said when I'd finished.

I nodded. "Apparently, people call him Poe."

"I'm supposed to believe he killed Jana Fletcher?"

"Maybe not him. Maybe someone else who wasn't happy he was talking to Jana."

"And I'm supposed to go chasing after this shadowy figure?"

"I'm not telling you what to do."

Moretti gave me a slow-burning look. "No, you're not," he said. "You might keep that in mind." I started to respond and he stopped me with a raised hand. "Listen to me," he said. "I want you to leave here and go home. I want you to stop talking to people about this case. I want you to realize how lucky you are. I could go to a prosecutor right now with the information I've got about your relationship with Jana Fletcher and your nonexistent, I-was-out-driving alibi, and I'll wager I could get him to bring an indictment. I haven't done that, because I'm willing to dig deeper, to look past the obvious. And every word out of your mouth tends to make me regret that decision."

He opened the door beside him, started to climb out.

"Wait," I said.

He glared at me. "You've dodged a bullet. Stop trying to get back in front of it."

When I got home that night Sophie was asleep. I found leftover Chinese carryout in the refrigerator. I took the food onto the balcony, along with a bottle of beer, and sat out there as the night grew chill.

At some point I went in and found a candle, because candles made me think of Jana. I put it on the balcony railing and watched the flame. At another point I went into my office and brought back the phone book, because I wanted to know where Napoleon Washburn lived. Apparently, I liked dodging bullets.

There were four Washburns in the phone book, but only one with the initial N. The address was on Lynch Street. A rough neighborhood. Suitable for a thief.

By eleven o'clock the food was long gone, the bottle was empty. I hadn't made up my mind about Washburn. Eleven was too late to visit civilized people, but maybe not too late to visit Poe.

Moretti had given me a lot to think about. I remembered his glare as he climbed down from the truck, but that wasn't the end of our conversation. He was too keyed up. He had more to say to me.

He stepped up into the truck again, slammed the door. "I'm giving you a gift," he said. "You don't deserve it, but I'm giving it to you anyway. You think we've been watching Jana's apartment? Wrong. We've been watching the old woman's. There's an unmarked car across the street. Don't bother to look. We're watching for the grandson, Simon Lanik."

He paused before continuing. "Simon hasn't been seen since Jana died. There's a warrant out for his arrest in Massachusetts, for something that happened years ago. He assaulted his girlfriend outside a bar in Boston."

"That's not quite the same," I said. "Jana wasn't—"

"Shut up. Listen. Agnes Lanik owns seven other houses in this neighborhood. Simon collects the rent for all of them. We've spoken to the tenants. Most of them are young women. They told us how he operates. If Simon comes around for the rent and you don't have it, he suggests there might be another way you can pay. The suggestion's not very subtle. Sometimes he makes it even if you've got the cash. Sometimes he cops a feel on the way out, just because he can."

Moretti looked at Jana's door, then back to me. "So what do you think is more likely?" he said. "That Jana died because she talked to Washburn—or that Simon Lanik came to hassle her about the rent and things got out of control? Say Lanik propositions her. Maybe he gets grabby. She tells him to back off, says she'll file a complaint. That's the last thing he wants. He puts his hands on her throat, just to shut her up. It goes from there."

I could imagine it: Simon Lanik with his greased hair and silk shirt and leather pants. His arrogance. Jana, thinking she could handle him. Threatening to go to the police, because the law would be on her side. Was that the way it happened, on the spur of the moment, with no premeditation on Lanik's part? It didn't seem quite right.

"What about the popsicle stick?" I asked Moretti.

He shook his head as if I'd disappointed him. "What about it?"

"If Lanik didn't plan to kill her, if it just happened, how does that fit with the idea that someone was watching her from the woods?"

"We don't know that anyone was watching her."

"We don't know that Lanik killed her either. Was he violent with any of the other tenants?"

Moretti gave me the slow burn again and his voice went quiet. "I'm through discussing this with you. Go home." He reached for the door handle, opened it.

"Did you even look for the popsicle stick?" I said.

He held the door open and breathed the night air. "Yes," he said after a while. "I found it. I sent it to the county lab. One of these days, they'll get around to testing it. And they won't find anything on it, because it's been lying on the ground for who knows how long. Or maybe they'll find a fingerprint, and maybe they'll match it to Poe Washburn or someone he knows, someone involved in an elaborate plot to cover up the truth about who murdered Gary Pruett's wife."

Moretti climbed out of the truck, turned back to me, and said, "I can tell you right now it won't happen, because it doesn't happen. What happens is that women like Jana Fletcher are killed by men they know, men like Simon Lanik. And the reasons, when you discover them, turn out to be small and ordinary and stupid."

No anger in his tone, just resignation. He closed the door; he didn't slam it. I watched him in the rearview mirror, the same unhurried walk to his car. Engine. Lights. He backed out onto the street and drove away.

And at eleven o'clock I sat on my balcony, staring at a candle, thinking about Simon Lanik and Poe Washburn. One or the other could be involved in Jana's death. I didn't know where to look for Lanik, but I had an address for Washburn. Eleven o'clock. Not too late to go calling. The flame of the candle guttered. I made up my mind.

13

K found himself missing Jolene.

She had died easy. He felt glad of that. Oh, let's be candid, she had died hard at first: twisting, struggling, clawing at the arm he held around her throat. Luckily he'd been wearing long sleeves; otherwise she would have left marks.

She tried to step on his feet too. Tried everything. Pushing back against him. Kicking. The kicking accomplished nothing, apart from launching one of her shoes into the canal. And in the end, she went easy. All the flailing stopped and her limbs went slack, and there was only the gentle weight of her as he settled her down to the ground. Like putting a sleeping child to bed.

K thought of leaving her like that, lying by the side of the trail. He folded her hands over her stomach, crossed one slim ankle over the other. Used a handkerchief to touch her, because there was always a chance of leaving fingerprints, even on someone else's body.

He tried to close her eyes, but they wouldn't stay. He covered them with her hair instead, ribbons of bottle blond to make a blindfold.

The sunlight fell on the stone of her amethyst ring.

She looked peaceful, he thought, standing over her. Maybe even beautiful.

Sentimental K.

Putting her in the water would be better. He knew that. If her body held any trace of him, even a single hair, the water could wash it away.

He looked again at the ring on her finger and wondered who had given it to her. Someone who loved her, he thought. The idea filled him with something verging on regret.

He thought about taking the ring as a souvenir. Decided he'd better not.

After one last look he dug the toe of his shoe under her back, lifted her up, and rolled her over the edge into the canal.

Jolene had been good practice. In a way, she had saved him, because when he paid his visit to Jana Fletcher that night, he was ready.

He wore steel-toed boots, for one thing. And gloves, black leather. A commonsense precaution.

He wore a long-sleeved shirt again, of course. And a jacket over it, for extra padding. The padding made a difference when Jana came at him with the two-by-four.

That was unexpected.

She seized it from the fireplace mantel, candles and all, and swung it like a club. Fire and hot wax coming at him. He might have been burned if not for the jacket.

But she couldn't hurt him. He was too strong for her. He wrenched the board from her hands and got her down on the floor, and then it was a matter of time and pressure. Her legs kicked, her feet stomped. Her nails would have dug into him if not for the gloves and the long sleeves. She went out hard, and then easy, just like Jolene.

Afterward he felt no tenderness toward her. He gave no thought to closing her eyes or folding her hands peacefully. He kicked her in the ribs once with a steel-toed boot. Tore her blouse open, yanked her pants down from her hips. A nice, lurid scene for someone to discover. Let them interpret it any way they wanted.

K had nothing to connect him to Jana Fletcher. He had disposed of the clothes he wore when he killed her—bagged them and dropped them in a dumpster. The jacket too, and the gloves. Easier than trying to wash out the melted wax.

He had nothing from Jolene either—except for her red Solo cup. It was the first thing he had noticed when he reached his car, after the hike back along the trail beside the canal: the red cup lying empty in the footwell on the passenger side.

It was still there tonight. K leaned over and picked it up. He could see a trace of her lipstick inside. Jolene. He really did miss her. She had helped him. No denying it.

But she couldn't help him anymore. Not with Napoleon Washburn, for instance.

Washburn spent two hours in a roadhouse bar called Casey's. K waited outside for him all that time. He didn't mind waiting. When he got bored, after the first half hour, he opened his glove compartment and took out a popsicle stick and sat turning it over and over in his fingers.

After a while he put it back. He thought about Jolene. Thought about her legs. Remembered the strength draining out of her body. He took her red Solo cup and held it on his knee. He wished he could keep it, but he knew it had her fingerprints on it. Probably DNA too. He twisted around for a box of tissues in the backseat, tugged some out, used them to wipe the outside of the cup. He opened the car door and dropped the cup on the ground.

Add littering to the list of his crimes.

T he roadhouse had country music playing inside, on a sound system with too much bass. K could hear it thumping through the parking lot. People came and went, driving pickups and SUVs. They wore boots and jeans and flannel shirts. That was one of the secrets of upstate New York: it was full of rednecks.

Napoleon Washburn was a redneck. He lived in a rat-trap house on an unpaved street. Lived alone, as far as K could tell. K had watched the house from down the street. Washburn had come out around nine o'clock, stumbling down his front steps with a cigarette between his lips. He wore a black T-shirt and jeans and shit-kicking boots. Good luck strangling *him*. He was over six feet tall, much taller than he had a right to be with a name like Napoleon. K knew he wouldn't go down easy.

Washburn had a truck that looked a little like David Malone's, but with a lot more rust and a lot less muffler. He drove three miles to the roadhouse spewing exhaust, making as much noise as a tank division. K had no trouble following him.

And now K waited for him in the parking lot. He didn't go inside, because he didn't want to be linked in any way to Napoleon Washburn.

Around eleven the main door of the roadhouse opened and Washburn staggered out, grinning. K suspected that he had started the night out drunk, and now he would be two hours drunker. He had a cigarette in one hand and his arm around a woman in knee-high boots and jeans and a long tight sweater. She had teased-out hair and was a little too heavy to look good in the sweater.

The two of them walked hip to hip along a row of cars in the lot. They stopped by Washburn's truck and he ditched his cigarette. They shared a drunken kiss. The kiss turned into a make-out session—Washburn grinding against the woman until she broke away from him with a laugh.

He got into his truck and drove out of the lot, and she followed in her own car. K trailed behind them, three miles in the smell of Washburn's exhaust, to the unpaved street and the rat-trap house.

The woman went inside with Washburn and stayed for twelve minutes. K timed it.

Figure three minutes to get down to business, five for the meaningless sex, and another four to get dressed and realize there was nothing more and say an awkward good-bye. The woman came out alone, no last kiss at the door. She held her chin up and took a slow, steady walk to her car, a sign of either dignity or resignation.

When she was gone, K watched the house for any sign of movement. It seemed likely that Washburn would now stay put for the night. Which gave K a perfect opportunity. All he needed was a plan.

No movement behind the curtains of the front windows. Washburn was drunk. He could be asleep in there. He hadn't accompanied the woman to the door. The door could be unlocked. K could walk right in.

K watched the house. Imagined Washburn inside, sprawled on a bed or a sofa. If he wasn't asleep, K could make him go to sleep. All he had to do was think about it. Picture him with his head back, his mouth open, snoring. Easy.

K got out of the car and crossed the street. He took a pair of gloves from the pockets of his jacket and put them on. New gloves, new jacket. His clothes were becoming disposable. Washburn's front steps were made of cinder blocks laid dry. They led up to a sagging porch. A broom stood beside Washburn's door, broken in two pieces: straw bristles, thick wooden handle. As if it had been left there for K on purpose.

The knob turned when K tried it, and the door opened. K entered clutching the broom handle. The front room stood empty. Peeling wallpaper. Garish furniture upholstered in flower patterns. The place reeked of cigarette smoke. An overflowing ashtray sat atop a white milk crate that served as a coffee table.

K moved through the house with exaggerated care, one slow step at a time, holding the broom handle in front of him like a talisman. He checked the kitchen and the utility room on the ground floor. No Washburn. He climbed the stairs. Saw the open door of a bathroom. Saw Washburn's boots kicked off and abandoned in the hall.

Two bedrooms. The one at the back of the house was full of boxes and old clothes. K moved to the one at the front, eased the door open. Napoleon Washburn lay snoring on a mattress on the floor, just the way K had pictured him.

The room had a single window with long curtains. There was a lamp with a weak bulb on the floor between the mattress and the window. The lamplight fell on a scattering of girlie magazines. Beside the magazines lay a heap of tissues and a used condom—the remains of Washburn's tryst with the woman in the tight sweater. Washburn had gotten dressed again after, in the same T-shirt and jeans he'd gone out in. He hadn't bothered to zip up or to buckle his belt.

A cigarette still smoldered in a ceramic ashtray beneath the lamp. K watched the smoke rise, a strand of gray thread. He stood over Washburn with the broom handle held like a spear. He aimed the broken point of it at Washburn's heart.

Washburn stirred in his sleep, rolled onto his side.

K listened to Washburn's breathing, watched the thread of smoke. He got an idea. He crouched down by slow degrees, an inch at a time, until he was on one knee beside the mattress. He laid the broom handle on the floor without a sound. He reached for the smoldering cigarette with his gloved hand, then thought better of it because the black leather would be too clumsy. He stripped off the glove and dug his handkerchief from his pocket.

With the handkerchief he picked up the cigarette, leaving the ash in the tray. He brought the tip of the cigarette into contact with one of the tissues on the floor. He held it there patiently and nothing happened, and he waited, and at last the tissue began to smolder.

He bent down over it, let his breath fall on the charred black edge until he saw an orange glow, and then a flame.

He placed the cigarette on the floor, returned the handkerchief to his pocket. He picked up his discarded glove and used it to nudge the burning tissue into another. The second tissue caught fire.

K put the glove back on and opened one of the girlie magazines—last October's issue. He folded out the centerfold until one corner of the page touched the burning tissues.

The flames spread. They consumed Miss October.

He opened another magazine. Miss July. A blonde. July, like Jolene. She made an excellent bridge between Miss October and the curtains.

The curtains must have been made of some kind of synthetic. They burned greedily and gave off a plastic smell.

K picked up the broom handle and rose to his feet. Washburn was still snoring on the mattress. K looked at the ceiling. No smoke detector. He didn't remember seeing one in the hall either. He closed the bedroom door on his way out.

Down the stairs, out through the front room. He turned the lock in the knob and pulled the door shut after him. He left the broom handle propped on the porch where he'd found it.

Calmly he crossed the street. No need to hurry. He dropped his gloves on the passenger seat, started the car. This worked out well, he thought. Better than stabbing Washburn or beating him with the broom handle. That would have been a mess. And K knew that Washburn could be connected to Jana Fletcher. Both of them dying in the space of two days—better that one should look like an accident. Napoleon Washburn goes out to a bar, comes home drunk, falls asleep smoking.

K watched the upstairs window. The curtains had burned away; the flames would have moved on now to the walls. In the weak lamplight he could see smoke building along the ceiling, working its way down. Time to leave.

As he drove along the unpaved street he saw something that made him touch his brakes and curse out loud. He wanted to stop, but he kept going. What he saw was David Malone's pickup truck.

When I found Poe Washburn's house, it was on fire.

I didn't realize it at first. I was looking for the address, and the numbers were hard to see in the night. I parked the truck on the street in front of one of Washburn's neighbors, went up onto the neighbor's porch, and turned around when I realized my mistake.

But there it was, one house over. When I approached the steps I heard a burst of glass. The heat of the fire had shattered an upstairs window. Shards of glass slid down the roof of the porch and rained down into a flower bed beside me.

I looked up at the broken window and saw smoke. Called 911 on my cell phone. The woman who answered was all business. Nature of the emergency. Name and address. Is there anyone in the house? I told her I didn't know.

"Firefighters are on their way," she said. "Don't go back in the house."

"I was never in there to start with," I told her.

"Don't go in."

I closed the phone. In the gravel driveway alongside the porch was a rusted pickup, just the sort of thing Washburn might drive. He could be in the house.

It would be stupid to go in.

I went up the cinder-block steps and tried the door. Locked. I threw my shoulder into it halfheartedly, which did about as much good as you'd expect. Then I went back to the steps and hefted one of the cinder blocks.

One blow from the block and the door crashed open. The front room was empty of life and eerily calm. I could smell smoke but I couldn't see any, not here. I dropped the block on the porch and went in.

I found the stairs and stood at the bottom looking up at a mass of gray smoke. It was gathering there, getting ready to come down.

"Washburn?" I yelled. "Poe? Anybody there?"

No answer.

It would be really stupid to go up the stairs.

I dashed through the front room to the kitchen, ran water in the sink. Couldn't find a towel. Rifled through drawers until I had one.

Soaked it in water. Held it over my nose and mouth and breathed, just to see how it would work.

When I turned back to the front room I heard coughing. Washburn must have crawled down the stairs headfirst. He struggled to his feet at the bottom, tall and lanky, eyes blinking, a mess of dark hair. His left hand held a pair of boots; his right hand hitched up his pants, tried unsuccessfully to buckle his belt.

Suddenly he noticed me. I tossed the towel away and said, "Poe?"

His face twisted and his eyes blinked, and he took two steps toward me and threw a kick that sent a white milk crate flying in my direction. There was an ashtray on the crate and it spun through the air and broke against the wall in a litter of spent cigarettes. I batted the crate away but Washburn came in behind it, leading with his right shoulder, sending me sprawling on the kitchen floor.

He landed on top of me and scrambled to his knees, straddling me. He still had a boot in his left hand. He drew it back and slammed it into the side of my head.

"What the fuck are you doin' in my house?"

I watched his face go in and out of focus. The world spun slowly.

"I'm trying to help you," I said.

Washburn coughed and spat on the floor and shifted the boot to his right hand. His left hand gripped the collar of my shirt.

"Yeah, you're a big fuckin' help," he said, pushing his fist into my neck. "You want to help? Here's how you can help. Are you payin' attention?"

I started to say yes and he hit me again with the boot.

"Now you're payin' attention," he said. "Tell him I got it. I got the message. Tell him he doesn't have to worry about me."

"Tell who?"

A whiff of booze as his face moved closer to mine.

"Tell him he didn't have to burn my fuckin' house down. I'm not gonna talk. I never wanted to talk in the first place. That's what you tell him. You got that?"

I nodded because it seemed the thing to do. His fist bore down on my neck and the world spun and part of the world was his hand with the boot in it. I saw a halo of light and for some reason the light smelled like smoke, and the boot swung down and crashed into my temple.

14

For the next little while I was awake and asleep. When I was awake I saw faces above me. The faces had lips and the lips moved, but nothing they said made any sense. Sometimes I saw hands and the hands held pinpoints of light. And somehow the pinpoints got to be as big as suns. And all the suns smelled like smoke.

Once I felt someone holding my hand. I saw a face above me, the face of a bald man with bristly eyebrows. His lips moved and what came out was like someone practicing birdcalls through a long cardboard tube. A light passed in front of my eyes—not a sun but a very bright star. It flicked out and the sky went dark.

When I finally woke up for real it was in the room with the white-tile walls. But without the chairs and the table, without Moretti. Without the tiles either.

I woke in a white room with someone holding my hand. The walls were curtains. The bald doctor was there with his bristly eyebrows. He held a light in his fist. He asked me my name.

My lips felt dry. I tried to wet them with my tongue, but my tongue was dry too. I didn't tell the doctor my name. Instead I let him in on a secret.

"Normally I wouldn't hold hands with you like this."

His right hand clicked off the light. His left hand came into my field of vision and made a peace sign. "How many fingers am I holding up?" he asked.

"How many hands do you *have*?" I countered.

His eyebrows went up and he looked to his left. Someone moved there and another face came toward me. Hair brushed my cheek. It smelled sweet. Not at all like smoke.

"It's my hand you're holding, jackass," Sophie Emerson said.

I woke up again to find the bald doctor gone and Sophie reading in a chair by my bed.

"What time is it?" I asked her.

She closed her book. "Almost five."

"In the morning?"

"Yes, in the morning. Don't get any ideas. You're not going anywhere."

When I sat up I thought she would try to stop me. She helped instead. She fiddled with the controls on the bed, then held a cup of water so I could drink. Pretty soon I was holding it on my own.

"My name is Dave," I said.

She smiled. "Yeah, you're brilliant. You're still not going anywhere. You've had a concussion."

"Like drums?"

"That's percussion," she said. "A concussion is a traumatic brain injury. A percussion is what you call a concussion when you've had a concussion. How do you feel?"

"Like someone used my head as a drum."

She tapped her own temple. "You opened that cut up again. I told you to stop letting people shove you into walls."

I reached up, felt a bandage. "He used a boot," I said. "Did they catch him? Poe Washburn?"

Sophie shook her head. "You were the only one they found in the house."

"He must have slipped away."

She shrugged. "Maybe you could ask the police about him. One of them came to visit you while you were sleeping. A Detective Moretti."

"Oh."

"He's an interesting man," she said. "When he couldn't talk to you, he asked to talk to me."

"About what?"

"About where I was the other night."

The other night. She meant the night Jana died.

"I was here at the hospital," Sophie said. "We had a motorcyclist come in. Bad accident. Had to take out his spleen. There are about a dozen people who can vouch for me, in case you were wondering."

"I wasn't."

"Detective Moretti seemed satisfied. He said he never really suspected me, but he had to rule me out."

"I think that's true," I said. "He has another suspect."

"Not you, I hope."

"Not me. A man named Simon Lanik. Jana's landlady's grandson."

"That's good then," Sophie said. "But you should watch out for Moretti. He's not happy about last night. The fire. I think he wants to charge you with arson."

"He doesn't appreciate me."

"Fortunately it's not his call. I gather the police have an arson specialist, and the specialist thinks the fire was an accident. Someone smoking in bed."

It wasn't an accident, I thought. The timing was too convenient. Poe Washburn believed someone had set the fire to send him a message. I could imagine another possibility: someone had tried to kill him before I could talk to him. (A grandiose thought. I heard Moretti's voice in my head: *Yeah, you're just that important.*) But either way, it was no accident.

I kept these thoughts to myself. I asked Sophie, "When can I leave here?"

She sat on the edge of the bed. "If you insisted, they'd probably discharge you now. But I'm holding out for a CT scan."

I left the hospital five hours later, after a CT scan and a lot of paperwork and a wretched breakfast. I walked out into bright daylight, at ten o'clock in the morning.

Sophie drove me home. The scan showed no bleeding in my brain, so my concussion was just a concussion. The prescription was rest and Tylenol. I napped for a while, got up, wandered as far as the sofa, clicked on the television. Sophie appeared and covered me with a blanket. She made me soup. I asked if she would take me to get my truck. "That wouldn't be resting," she said.

I read the paper when it came in the afternoon. The *Rome Sentinel*. It had a front-page story about the fire. Neighbors had seen Washburn leaving the house, slipping into his boots on the porch, driving away just as the fire trucks arrived. The police wanted to talk to him.

The story mentioned me by name and said that I'd been injured. Roger Tolliver saw it and called to see if I was all right and if I needed anything. I told him I'd let him know if I did.

There was no mention in the paper of any connection between Poe Washburn and Jana Fletcher. A separate story on Jana's murder said that the police were still following leads. It noted that they were looking for Simon Lanik. They wouldn't come out and say he was a suspect, but that was the clear implication.

Frank Moretti stopped by the apartment twice that afternoon. The first time, Sophie told him I was sleeping. The second time, she told him that if he wanted to talk to me he could work it out with my lawyer. She gave him Roger Tolliver's phone number and sent him away.

Tolliver spoke to him and agreed that we could meet the next day—not at the police station but at Tolliver's office at the law school.

The law school at Bellamy University occupies a fine old build-ing with a broad front lawn shaded by willow trees. Tolliver had an office on the second floor: lots of bookcases and two casement windows and a sleek modern desk with a glass top.

When Moretti arrived, he had cooled down a little: he had dropped the idea of charging me with arson. But I wasn't in the clear.

"Obstructing a murder investigation—how does that sound?" he said to me. "I specifically told you not to talk to Poe Washburn." Which wasn't quite true: he'd told me in general not to talk to anyone about Jana's murder.

I didn't say that. I didn't say anything. Roger Tolliver was already mounting my defense.

"In the first place, Detective," he said, "merely talking to some-one doesn't qualify as obstruction. In the second place, Mr. Malone's encounter with Mr. Washburn was less a conversation than a physical altercation—one that Mr. Malone did nothing to provoke. And their discussion, such as it was, did not touch upon the murder of Miss Fletcher.

"In the third place," Tolliver said, "if I'm to believe the reports in the news, your investigation has been focusing on Simon Lanik. If Mr. Lanik killed Miss Fletcher, then it would seem Napoleon Washburn had nothing to do with her death. And therefore my client's dealings with Mr. Washburn could not reasonably be viewed as an obstruction of your investigation."

There was a fourth place, which had to do with my status as a citizen of the United States of America and my God-given right under the First Amendment to talk to anyone I pleased, but by then Moretti had begun to give me one of his slow-burning looks.

He asked a few questions about what had happened in Washburn's house and then stood up to take his leave. Tolliver asked him if he had any information on where Washburn might have gone. "Nothing I can share," Moretti said.

"But you do intend to arrest him for assaulting Mr. Malone."

"It's right at the top of my list," Moretti said.

After our meeting, Tolliver drove me out to Poe Washburn's house. The firefighters had done their best, but the place was a wreck. The second floor had been gutted and most of the roof had fallen in. The whole thing would need to be torn down and rebuilt from the ground.

Tolliver looked at it and said, "Maybe you should leave all this alone."

I knew he wasn't talking about the house.

I thanked him for the ride. Promised to let him know if Moretti contacted me again. My truck was where I'd left it. I climbed in and watched Tolliver drive away.

I didn't go looking for Poe Washburn. I went home.

That night Sophie cooked a stir-fry: peppers and broccoli and tofu served over brown rice. After dinner I went into the bedroom to lie down. Her shift at the hospital started at ten, but before she left she came in to see me.

"Does your head hurt?" she asked, kneeling by the bed.

"It's not bad," I told her.

"If it hurts, take something."

"All right."

"You're still supposed to be resting," she said. "A few more days."

She was telling me something, and asking me something too. I took her hand and she leaned in suddenly and kissed me hard on the lips.

Afterward she touched her forehead to mine and whispered, "Stop getting dragged out of burning buildings."

That was Saturday. I rested that night and all day Sunday. But on Monday I couldn't rest. On Monday they buried Jana Fletcher.

15

The funeral was held in Geneva, New York, the town where Jana grew up. Roger Tolliver told me when and where; he offered to let me ride with him. I drove myself instead, ninety-five miles, most of it on the Thruway. It rained for part of the drive but cleared at the end, and as I drove south on the town's main street I could see blue sky over the water of Seneca Lake.

I was early, so I parked the truck and walked to the lake. There were students riding bicycles on a path along the shore. Geneva is home to two colleges that share a single campus—Hobart and William Smith. The campus takes up nearly two hundred acres and the parts of it I saw were pretty: lush and green, with old buildings faced in weathered stone. Jana's mother worked as a cook in one of the dining halls; her name was Lydia—and those were the only two things Jana ever told me about her mother.

Lydia Fletcher had arranged for a service to be held for her daughter in a chapel called St. John's off the main quad. It started a few minutes after ten. The priest had a strong, deep voice that brought to mind monks chanting in Latin. I sat in the last row and let the rhythm of his voice carry me along, and time passed slowly, the way it always had for me in church as a child. I looked up at the vaulted ceiling, or at the tall thin windows behind the altar, and once in a while I tried to focus on the words. They were dark: *A thousand years in your sight, Lord, are like a day that has just gone by, or like a watch in the night. Yet you sweep people away in the sleep of death—they are like the new grass in the morning: In the morning it springs up new, but by evening it is dry and withered.*

There must have been fifty or sixty people there, most of them older—friends of Jana's mother, I thought. I spotted Roger Tolliver sitting by himself a few rows up, and we nodded to each other. I walked out before the service ended, while the rest of them were singing "Amazing Grace."

At the cemetery I hung back at the edge of the crowd. I wanted to talk to Lydia Fletcher and I dreaded it at the same time. I had picked her out in the chapel. It wasn't difficult; her resemblance to Jana was strong. She stood by the grave in the company of a young couple—among the few people I had seen who were Jana's age. The couple seemed to be husband and wife. The wife had a plump face and straight dark hair that reached her shoulders. She was pregnant—seven or eight months, if I had to guess.

The husband's hair was longer than the wife's. He wore it tied in a ponytail. He was on the heavy side, but he looked as if he had once been even heavier. His black suit was a size too large—as if he had lost weight but hadn't gotten around to buying a new wardrobe. He hovered around Lydia Fletcher the way a son might; sometimes they stood arm in arm. But I knew Jana didn't have a brother.

His name turned out to be Warren Finn. The priest introduced him to the gathered mourners as a friend of Jana's who had known her since elementary school. Then the priest stepped back and Warren stood by Jana's casket and read a passage from the Old Testament. Ecclesiastes. *For everything there is a season, and a time for every purpose under heaven.* He struggled to get through it, like someone who wasn't used to speaking in public. He hit the important lines—*a time to weep, and a time to laugh; a time to mourn, and a time to dance*—but he skipped over some others, like the one about throwing away stones and gathering stones together. I didn't mind. That part never made much sense to me.

Afterward the three of them lingered longest at the graveside: Lydia Fletcher and Warren Finn and his wife. Roger Tolliver spoke to them briefly, then drifted away to his car. Other people did the same. I took a walk along a row of headstones, and when I reached the cemetery fence I followed it around, one corner to another, until I came back to the place where I started. By then Lydia Fletcher was leaving, with Warren Finn on one side of her and his wife on the other. Warren looked back at me once over his shoulder, as if he wanted me to know he'd been keeping track of me. That wasn't the last I saw of him.

After the three of them drove away I spent a few minutes alone at Jana's grave, but it was hard to know what to say to her. I tried telling her I loved her, but it sounded empty. I'd never said it while she was alive. There hadn't been enough time.

Somewhere a lawn mower started up. A robin took off into the air. I became aware of distant voices: cemetery people, workmen who were waiting to fill in the grave. Now would be the time for some final gesture: a rose tossed onto the casket. I didn't have a rose. Too late to get one now.

I said a silent good-bye, then turned away and left the grave behind. It was a ten-minute walk to the place where I'd parked, and when I reached the truck it was warm from sitting in the sun. I started it up and drove around the edge of the lake. I came to the long, straight road that would take me away from Geneva and back to the Thruway. I watched fields pass by on either side. They moved slow, and I realized I was rolling along at thirty miles an hour. I pushed it to forty, to fifty, and it still didn't feel fast enough. Got it to seventy and that seemed better. I thought I'd try eighty. *Eighty miles an hour in your sight, Lord, is like a pleasant stroll along the beach.*

When the needle hit eighty-five I lifted my foot off the gas and glided along. Watched the needle fall. I waited for the truck to stop on its own, but it wouldn't. The engine's idle carried it along. I pulled over to the shoulder and made a wide U-turn and headed back.

Lydia Fletcher's address was off County Road 6 on the western edge of Geneva. I'd looked it up before I left home. The houses on her street were all the same: one level, ranch-style, attached garage. I searched for a shady spot to park and found one far down at the end of the street.

The Fletcher house had a front door painted green. It had flower boxes in the windows and bird feeders hanging from the trees in front. I stood on the sidewalk wondering what it had been like for Jana to grow up here, what I would say to her mother, whether I should say anything at all. Just when I had decided to walk to the door and knock, I heard a voice.

"I don't know if she wants visitors."

Warren Finn. He wore the suit he'd worn at the cemetery, minus the jacket and tie. He stood in the driveway of the house next door, the garage door open behind him.

I went over and introduced myself. "David Malone. I knew Jana in Rome."

He had to think about shaking my hand. Decided in favor. Showed me how strong a grip he had.

"Figured you were," he said. "We've had word of you here."

I thought Roger Tolliver must have mentioned me, but I was wrong.

"A detective paid us a visit—Moretti," Warren said. "He asked if Jana ever talked about you. If she told us you hit her. I couldn't help him. She never mentioned you to me."

"I never hit her."

He shrugged. "That's what her mother thought, but not from anything Jana ever said. Lydia never had patience for abusive men. She figured Jana knew better than to stay with anyone who raised a hand against her."

He had retreated into his garage, as if he felt more comfortable there. There was one car inside, and the rest of the space was devoted to a woodworking shop. He had a table saw, a drill press, a collection of hand tools. He seemed to be in the middle of a project: a dresser or a cabinet—I couldn't tell. There was a piece of wood clamped in a vise, something he'd been sanding. He ran his thumb over the smooth edge.

"I'll tell you something funny," he said, tripping over the word "funny" as if he knew it wasn't right. He hesitated, and now that I was close to him I noticed two things I hadn't before: One was the way his eyes wandered, not quite wanting to look at me. The other was a vertical white line that ran through his upper lip to his nose: a scar from a long time ago.

He started again. "I'll tell you something. When we were kids, Jana and me, we used to wish for something exciting to happen in this town. A kidnapping or an alien invasion. A murder. Anything that would break up the boredom. I'm not sure what the appeal was supposed to be—maybe having a mystery to solve. I'd like to have that boredom back."

He loosened the vise, turned the board over, tightened it again. "I don't know why anyone would want to kill her," he said, looking up at me suddenly, fixing his eyes on mine. "Moretti seemed to think it was someone she knew."

It was a quiet provocation. I didn't take the bait. If he wanted to accuse me of murder, he would have to come out and say it.

He stayed silent for a while and when he spoke again he seemed to have read my mind. "If I thought you killed her," he said, "I wouldn't let you out of here alive. So maybe it's better that I don't know."

I couldn't think of any way to answer that. I watched him open a drawer in his workbench and take out a metal file. He didn't stab me with it. He went to work on the board in the vise, rounding off a corner.

A moment later he looked up, as if he expected me to be gone. He waved the file toward Lydia Fletcher's house. "You can try to talk to her if you want," he said. "But don't stay long. I know she's tired."

16

"Warren's a sweet boy," said Lydia Fletcher.

"He seems a little..." I searched for a word. "...intense."

I'd knocked on her door with an apology on my lips: I didn't want to bother her; I could come back another time. But she had welcomed me in and insisted on brewing coffee. She had poured some for each of us, in fine china cups.

"Well, he's had a hard life," she said, "because of..." She twirled her finger in a circle, pointing to her own mouth. I thought of Warren's scar.

"Harelip," she said softly. "He was born with it and the doctors did what they could to fix it up. But the other children always teased him. Not Jana. She was devoted to him, even though she could have had...other friends." She had started to say "better friends" but caught herself.

We were sitting across from each other in a long, narrow living room. At the funeral Lydia Fletcher had worn a black sweater and a skirt; she had kept the sweater and traded the skirt for a pair of jeans. She had the same brown eyes as Jana and the same curly hair, though hers was streaked with gray. She must have been around fifty.

I could tell she'd been crying, but she had composed herself and now she seemed at ease. Or at least as much at ease as you could be in that house. Because there was something off about it, something out of sync. The furniture was old. There was no doily draped over the back of my chair, but I thought a doily would have felt right at home. The walls were papered, and the ones that weren't papered were covered in cheap wood paneling and hung with antique mirrors and paintings—oil paintings of cottages and lighthouses.

There were some photographs of Jana on a side table—school portraits—but nothing else to suggest that a child had ever lived here. Even the cups we drank from were misplaced in time: they were fragile and dainty, decorated with intricate geometric patterns like the windows of a Gothic cathedral. They were the cups of a seventy-year-old lady.

I tasted my coffee, added more sugar. Gestured at the room and said, "This is where Jana grew up?"

Lydia Fletcher nodded. "I could show you her bedroom, but there's nothing to see. She took everything with her when she went away. What she didn't take, she threw out. But I have pictures." She rose abruptly and disappeared down a hall, came back a minute later with a thick photo album.

She opened it on the coffee table and patted the sofa cushion beside her, inviting me to come around. I brought my coffee with me.

"That's me with Jana's father," she said. The photograph showed a pretty girl in tie-dyed clothes with braided hair, and beside her a tall, slender black man with a big smile. Jana's father wore a tweed jacket and glasses with round metal frames.

He had taught at the college here in town, Lydia told me. He'd been a visiting lecturer from Sudan, and she had been one of his students. Back then, she had wanted to teach history.

"All that went away when I got pregnant," she said.

Jana's father left the country before Jana was born. His visa had always been temporary. He meant to come back, but he died a year later in a protest in the streets of Khartoum, a victim of the riot police.

Lydia Fletcher had dropped out of college and moved back in with her mother, a stern-looking woman with beehive hair—the old lady whose house we were sitting in now.

"That's not a good picture of her," Lydia said to me. "She really did smile sometimes. She saved me from a lot of misery, letting me stay here. And she took good care of Jana."

Jana looked well cared for. In the pictures she was always beaming. Here she was, a tomboy in high-top sneakers, perched in a tree. And on a bike with patches on the knees of her jeans. Here she was on Halloween, Princess Leia with a lightsaber, and a chubby Warren Finn beside her, dressed as Luke Skywalker.

There were stories to go with the pictures, and Lydia Fletcher told them. Details poured out of her, about birthday parties and who attended and what presents they brought. Visits to the zoo in Rochester. A school field trip to Montreal.

In high school Jana started acting in plays. I knew she'd been in *As You Like It*, but there were others too: *Our Town*, *Guys and Dolls*, *The Importance of Being Earnest*, *Cyrano de Bergerac*. Jana played Roxane, ethereal in a white gown, with flowers in her hair.

After high school Jana attended college in Geneva. "She got accepted by other colleges," Lydia Fletcher told me, "and she could've gone, but she stayed to help me. My mother was ill. Kidney disease. Someone had to take her to dialysis three times a week."

So Jana took care of her grandmother, but she managed to thrive in college too. She majored in psychology. She had always been a good student. And there were more plays. I saw the pictures: she was Miranda in *The Tempest*, Beatrice in *Much Ado About Nothing*, Raina in *Arms and the Man*.

We came to the end of college—Jana posing on the front lawn in her cap and gown—and our coffee had long ago grown cold. Lydia took our cups away and came back with a bottle and two tumblers filled with ice.

"Do you drink Scotch, David?" she asked.

I told her no.

"Would you care to start?"

She needed the Scotch because things got rough when Jana finished college. She had applied to law schools, with her mother's blessing—and to theater programs, without telling anyone.

"I wanted her to study law at Cornell or the University of Pennsylvania," Lydia said. "She had her heart set on the drama program at NYU. We couldn't afford any of them, but with financial aid and loans, she could have gotten by. And if she studied law, she could have some hope of repaying the loans. I wanted her to be practical."

Jana bowed to her mother's wishes and accepted admission to Cornell Law School. But she never went. Her grandmother took a turn for the worse.

"Dementia," Lydia Fletcher said over the rim of her glass, in the same soft voice she had used for "harelip." "Looking back, I can tell you it had been coming on for a long time. But that summer after Jana graduated college, Mother went downhill fast. It got so you couldn't leave her alone. You couldn't predict what she'd do. She might wander into the street and start taking off her clothes."

So Jana gave up law school for her grandmother's sake. The

woman lasted almost another year, and toward the end she couldn't do anything for herself. She had to be bathed and changed and fed.

"She died at the end of May, two years ago," said Lydia Fletcher. "It was a mercy, for her and for Jana too. I saw what it did to her, and she never complained. But with Mother gone I thought Jana could finally live her own life. She could go to Cornell—they had agreed to defer her admission for a year—and she'd be happy."

I watched Lydia top off her Scotch. "She didn't go to Cornell," I said.

"No," she said. "She'd had a year to think about it, about what she wanted. A year of helping my mother out of her bed in the morning and helping her back into it at night—and everything in between. She needed to get out of Geneva, but she didn't want to go to law school. She wanted to act."

When Jana made up her mind, it happened fast. "I wanted her to take her time, to plan," Lydia said. "She would need to apply to drama schools all over again, and it was too late to apply for the fall. But Jana was tired of waiting. She had a car, an old Buick LeSabre my mother had signed over to her. One day in June I came home to find her packing.

"She told me she was going to New York City. She would find a job waiting tables and she would go on auditions. Maybe she would take classes. I told her she was being reckless. She didn't know anyone there. She didn't have a place to stay. Her life there would be hard—she had no idea. 'Harder than the last year?' she said to me."

Lydia leaned back on the sofa with her glass. "I was afraid for her, and we argued, and she wouldn't listen. She left that night, which was crazy. She could have at least waited till morning. But she was mad at me. She never called me from New York, not once, and I had no way to call her. She sent some postcards to let me know she was all right—I remember one from the Museum of Modern Art and another with a picture of the Statue of Liberty. I wanted to go and look for her, I wanted to call the police and make them find her. But of course they wouldn't have done anything, and if they did, she would've hated me for it.

"And in the end I was right: it was too hard. She came back three months later, just showed up here one day in September. The auditions never panned out and she couldn't make enough money waitressing. She had to sell my mother's car to pay the rent. She came home on a Greyhound bus."

Lydia held the glass in her lap. It was just a prop now; she wasn't drinking from it. She said, "Jana wouldn't stay here, in this house. I think she had the idea that I didn't believe in her, and having to come back only made it worse. She stayed next door, with Warren. It worried me, because there was something going on between them—and that was new. They'd never been a couple before. Warren's parents gave him that house when they retired. They live in Arizona now. Warren has a job at the college, working in the bookstore. I was afraid Jana would end up marrying him and they'd have babies and she'd be stuck in this town forever. But by the end of the following spring she had moved back in with me, and she was talking about law school again. At Bellamy University this time, because of a professor she'd heard about."

"Roger Tolliver," I said.

"That's him. I was relieved. Her life seemed to be on track. And now I wish she had stayed with Warren. I wish she had done anything but go to Bellamy."

Lydia turned toward a window and I followed her gaze. She had a view of Warren Finn's house.

"He's with someone else now," I said.

She nodded. "Rose. They were dating when Jana came back from New York. Warren broke up with her when Jana moved in with him. And when Jana left him, he got back together with Rose. Now they're married." She looked away from me, but not before I spotted tears. "I keep thinking it could be Jana over there, with a baby on the way. Would that be so terrible? But she did what I wanted her to do. She went away to law school. And now I've lost her."

The tears rolled down her cheeks and she sat up and wiped them with the back of her hand. She held her glass out and I took it, and she found a box of tissues and used one to dry her eyes. I put the glass on the coffee table.

She sat with her head bowed, holding the balled-up tissue. "Don't think too poorly of me," she said. "My daughter's gone and here I am crying for myself."

"I don't think—"

"I didn't mean to do this," she said. "It was nice of you to come here, and there's something I'd like to ask you. You can tell me the truth."

"Ask me anything you want."

"It's just that I never visited her there in Rome. I don't know what her life was like." She reached out to me, squeezed my hand. "There's only one thing that's important now. Maybe you can tell me. Do you think she was happy?"

17

got home that night after dark. It would have been sooner, but Lydia Fletcher wanted to fix me something to eat and I didn't want to refuse, and I thought it might be wise to give the Scotch some time to work its way through my system.

She made bacon and eggs and pancakes. Breakfast for dinner, she said—something Jana had always loved as a child. The eggs scrambled, the pancakes loaded with blueberries. Lydia cooked more than we needed and I ate more than I should have, and when she packed the leftovers in Tupperware and offered them to me, I took them.

I took a photo with me too—a portrait of Jana from her college yearbook. Lydia wanted me to have it and I was glad. As I slipped it into my wallet I realized it was the only picture I had of Jana. I'd never taken one; those were the days before everyone walked around with a camera in their cell phone.

At home I found Sophie asleep in our bed. I joined her. When I woke sometime later, she was gone. Intern's hours. I couldn't get back to sleep, so I went into the kitchen for a glass of water. She had left me a note on the table: *Missed you. Hope it went okay.*

I took my water onto the balcony. It was a cool, still night and the stars were out. I thought about Sophie's message: two lines and so much to read between them. *Missed you—because even though we're living in the same place, we're not connecting. We keep missing each other.* Or it could mean: *You were gone today and it made me sad. I missed you. Because I still care about you. Did you miss me?*

Hope it went okay—the funeral of that other woman you were sleeping with.

Hope it went okay, but now it's over and we have to move on. Don't we?

A good question. I drank some water and thought about the answer. It was time to decide: Keep obsessing over the woman you barely knew, the one who's gone; or hold tight to the living, breathing woman who's trying to stay with you, the one who misses you? What would a sensible man do?

The answer was obvious: I was not a sensible man. I needed to obsess, at least for a little longer.

I dug out my cell phone and called Roger Tolliver. It took four rings for him to answer.

I said, "Was she happy?"

Tolliver cleared his throat. "Was who—"

"Jana's mother asked me if she was happy," I said. "What was I supposed to say?"

"What time—It's after midnight."

"I knew her for ten days," I said. "She seemed happy. But how would I know?"

"David—"

"And what does it mean to be happy? It's different things to different people. Some philosophers would say you're only happy if you're leading a good life, a life of virtue."

"Philosophers?"

"Greek philosophers. Was Jana leading a good life? She was trying to do the right thing, trying to help Gary Dean Pruett, because she thought he was innocent. That's virtuous, isn't it?"

Tolliver sighed. "David, are you drunk?"

"No. This is what I'm like when I'm sober. I need to know more about Jana's life. Otherwise—"

"Hold on," Tolliver said. "Did you talk to Jana's mother like this?"

"Like what?"

"Like spouting nonsense about Greek philosophers when she asked you a simple question."

I got up and went to the balcony rail. "No," I said. "I did what I was supposed to do. I told her Jana was happy."

"Good."

"But it's not a simple question. That's the point. I saw one small corner of Jana's life. It's not enough."

"Not enough for what?"

"It's not enough. I need more. Who did she talk to?"

"What do you mean?"

"About Gary Pruett. She talked to Poe Washburn. Were there others?"

A quiet moment on the line. Then Tolliver said, "I'm sure she spoke to Pruett's lawyer. And maybe his family. I think he has a brother—"

"I want to talk to them," I said. "Can you get me names?"

"I suppose. But what do you hope to learn?"

"I want to know why she died."

A longer quiet this time. I could hear Tolliver moving around, maybe sitting up in bed. "Is that what this is about?" he asked me. "You think you can find her killer?"

"I want to know the truth about Gary Pruett," I said. "If she died because of him, and if he's guilty, then her death meant nothing. If he's innocent, then somebody should do something about it."

Tolliver's voice turned solemn. "You don't really care about Pruett."

"I care about Jana."

"But there's nothing you can do for her now."

I looked up at the stars. "I can find out if Pruett's innocent," I said. "Maybe get him a new trial. That's what she wanted."

"And you think that'll make a difference?" Tolliver said. "To her?"

"It will to me."

G ary Dean Pruett had been a high school algebra teacher before he went to prison for killing his wife.

If I had lived in a different neighborhood, he might have been one of my teachers. But he taught at East Rome High School, and I went to Rome Free Academy in the center of the city. My algebra teacher was a distant cousin on my father's side of the family, a strange little man with a buzz cut and horn-rimmed glasses, like a NASA scientist from the Apollo program. My father never liked him, but he never liked schoolteachers in general. He found them aloof. He noticed that they tended to socialize with one another and marry other teachers, and he concluded that they thought they were better than everyone else.

I don't know if Gary Pruett was aloof, but in one way he had conformed to my father's stereotype: he had married a fellow teacher. Cathy Pruett had taught history and geography before she died.

Gary had a brother, another teacher at the same high school. Neil Pruett. Chemistry and physics. I went looking for him the next day, around four-thirty in the afternoon. I didn't find him. I found his wife.

She was in her late thirties and very thin, with a long neck and a sharp chin and nose. She carried herself in a way my father would have called snooty: squared shoulders, rigid posture. I was unsurprised to learn her occupation. She taught English at a middle school.

Megan Pruett was leery of letting me into her house. She came out onto the porch to talk to me instead. When I mentioned Jana Fletcher she was sympathetic.

"It's tragic what happened to her," she said. "She was so young. She came here, of course, to talk about Gary and whether he'd gotten a fair trial. She had some story about a false confession."

"You didn't believe it?" I said.

Megan Pruett shook her head. "Maybe I'm biased—Cathy was my best friend. But as far as I'm concerned, Gary is guilty as sin."

Megan had known Cathy Pruett since their college days. "SUNY Albany," she said. "We were roommates freshman year. She was Cathy Dorn then, and I was Megan Linney. After we graduated, we found our first teaching jobs together, in Poughkeepsie. Then we moved here."

Cathy Dorn had met Gary Pruett at East Rome High. They had gotten engaged. She had introduced Megan to Gary's brother, Neil.

"So you were close," I said, "all four of you."

Megan Pruett stood by the railing of the porch, looking out at the street. "About as close as you can get," she said.

"And what did you think of Gary and Cathy as a couple? Were there warning signs? Was he ever violent?"

"No," Megan said. "She would have told me. The trouble with Gary was much subtler. He was a liar. You know about his affair?"

She didn't wait for an answer. She was eager to fill me in.

"After they were married a few years, Cathy started to feel like they were drifting apart. But if she tried to talk to him, Gary would say everything was fine. He tried to spin it into something positive. They were two different people, they should have their own interests. But that was really just a pretense for him to get out of the house. They taught at the same school, so he couldn't take advantage of the usual excuses. He couldn't say he had to work late. So he signed up for night classes: poetry and photography. Only she never saw much in the way of poems or pictures. Or he would claim to go to movies by himself. Sci-fi and horror, stuff she had no interest in seeing. Anything that would give him an excuse to be out at night.

"Cathy wasn't stupid. She thought there must be something going on. But when she asked him, he called her paranoid. She told me about it, because we talked about everything. And I decided to follow him."

Megan had been watching cars pass on the street. Now she turned to me. "You have to understand, we were like sisters," she said. "We used to watch out for each other in college. If I got drunk at a party, she'd make sure I got home. If she thought her boyfriend was cheating, I'd make it my job to find out for sure. We had each other's back.

"When I followed Gary, it was crystal clear that he hadn't been going to the movies, unless they were the kind of movies you could see in your room at a cheap motel. I waited there in the motel parking lot, after he went inside. I wanted to see who would meet him. I was afraid it might be someone we knew, someone Cathy worked with at the high school. But the woman who showed up didn't look familiar.

"I got a better look at her afterward, when they came out of the room together. And I realized she was young. I found out later that she was a girl named Angela Reese. She had just graduated from high school—this was in the summer. She was eighteen. She's twenty now.

"I dreaded telling Cathy, but I knew I had to. And when she confronted Gary he denied it. He said I must have mistaken him for someone else. But eventually he realized that lying wouldn't work. Cathy trusted me more than she trusted him. So he admitted it. But he swore it had only happened a few times. And yes, the girl had been his student, but he had never touched her until after she graduated. He wasn't some pervert."

Megan Pruett frowned, remembering. "I told Cathy she should divorce him, but she came from a religious family and she had always been the good daughter. She rarely drank anything stronger than wine, never smoked, never experimented with drugs, not even a joint—and as for her marriage, she took it very seriously. She wanted to fix it. Gary played along. He said he loved her and he was sorry. He put it all down to a midlife crisis. He'd gone a little crazy, but it was over now. He would prove to her that he could be a better man."

She looked out at the street again. "That went on for a few weeks, and he really did seem to change. He would take Cathy out. Buy her flowers. Leave her sweet little notes. Then one night after dinner he said he felt like going to a movie—would that be all right? Like he was asking her permission. She said she'd go with him. He told her he wanted to see some big action movie, not her kind of thing, she'd only be bored. That's when she realized nothing had changed.

"At that point I raised the idea of divorce again. I told Cathy if I were in her position I wouldn't think twice. It would be the easiest decision I ever made. She got angry with me. I wasn't in her position, she said. And maybe she wouldn't be either if I hadn't followed her husband around and caught him—which she had never asked me to do. She was lashing out. I couldn't blame her. She was heartbroken."

Megan Pruett turned her back on the street, and for the first time her rigid posture wavered. She slouched against the wooden railing. "I think she would have divorced him eventually," she said, "but she wanted to make one last effort: marriage counseling. Gary wasn't interested. I know they argued about it. I don't know exactly what happened next, but a few days after she brought up counseling, she disappeared. That was near the end of July. They found her body in mid-August."

"And you have no doubt Gary was the one who killed her?"

Megan tipped her head to the side. "She asked me the same thing—your friend Jana Fletcher. The answer's no. No doubts. Gary claimed that Cathy just left one afternoon without saying anything to him. But when she didn't come back that night, or the next, he didn't report her missing. He didn't do anything until I called their house—because I hadn't heard from her in days.

"When the police talked to him, he said he assumed she had left him. He thought she must be staying with me and Neil. But if that's what he believed, why didn't he call us to make sure?"

"If he killed her," I said, "what was his motive? You don't murder your wife just because you don't want to go into counseling."

"You might if she threatened to divorce you," said Megan Pruett. "Some men do. I wouldn't have thought Gary was one of them, but I never suspected he'd cheat on Cathy with an eighteen-year-old either."

It seemed weak, as a motive. But when I started to say so, she interrupted me.

"You have to remember Gary was a liar. He claimed his affair with Angela Reese started after she graduated. I didn't necessarily believe him. I'm not sure Cathy did either. If it started earlier, he was on dangerous ground. Sleeping with a student can cost you your job, even if she's over the age of consent. What if Cathy threatened to report him? I'm not saying she did, but she could have—in the heat of the moment, if they were arguing. And that might've been enough to make Gary snap."

It sounded plausible, I thought. But it was still guesswork.

"Doesn't it bother you," I said, "not being sure about the motive?"

She trailed a finger along the railing. "I suppose it would, if Gary hadn't treated Cathy so badly. But honestly, what's the alternative? Some stranger came along and killed her?"

"But don't you wish the case against Gary had been stronger?" I asked. "Doesn't it bother you that it relied on a confession that might never have happened?"

She answered after a thoughtful pause. "She asked me that too, your friend Jana. 'What would Cathy think of all this?' she said. And she really wanted to know. It was important to her. What if there was no confession? What if Gary turned out to be innocent? Cathy wouldn't want him to suffer, would she? And of course that's true. She hated the way he had betrayed her, but she wouldn't have wanted him to spend his life in prison for something he didn't do."

Megan Pruett stood up tall and straight again. "But that's all hypothetical. He killed her. I sat through the trial, every day of it. I was convinced—even without the confession."

18

When I left Megan Pruett I drove about a mile to the house Cathy and Gary Pruett had shared. It was a two-story place painted pale blue, taller than it was wide. It had a strip of grass on either side and hedges to separate it from the other houses. More grass in front, unmowed, sprinkled with dandelions.

I thought seeing the house might give me a sense of the couple who had lived here. It didn't. But I had another reason for coming. Megan Pruett had told me her husband was staying here. They had separated after the trial.

"It was just too hard," she'd said, "staying together."

When I rang Neil Pruett's doorbell, he answered right away. He'd been expecting me; his wife had called to let him know I was coming. He led me through to the back of the house and sat me down in the kitchen. The place looked a little rough—dishes piled in the sink, crumbs on the counter.

"I apologize for the mess," he said.

"It's not too bad."

"Megan doesn't think I'll last, living on my own. She thinks I'll wind up dressing in rags and eating off the floor."

Maybe he would, eventually. He wasn't there yet. He was dressed well enough, in a white oxford shirt, khaki pants, and loafers—the wardrobe of a high school science teacher. He had taken off his tie: navy blue with yellow stripes. I could see it dangling over the back of a chair. He was around forty, with sandy-blond hair cut short and a round, plain face.

"You talked to her," he said. "What's your impression?"

I realized he meant his wife. "She has strong opinions," I said. "About Gary."

He laughed. "Strong opinions. That's true. That's why she's there and I'm here. When you think your brother's innocent and your wife is sure he's guilty, it tends to put a strain on the marriage."

He let the subject go with a shrug, and we talked for a few minutes about Jana. Pruett confirmed that she had come around to see him. He told me he was sorry for my loss—she seemed like a nice young woman—and asked if the police were making any progress. I told him what little I knew and he sat quietly, taking it in. But after a while he steered the conversation around to his brother's case. He knew Jana had been working with Roger Tolliver on Tolliver's Innocence Project. He assumed I was too.

"Do you have news for me?" he asked.

I told him I didn't and he took it well. I didn't mention that I wasn't a lawyer or even a law student.

"Well, it's still early days," Neil Pruett said. "Gary's lawyer warned me not to get my hopes up. She's pessimistic about winning an appeal."

"Does she believe that Gary's innocent?" I asked.

"It's hard to know. If she didn't, I don't think she'd say it. She has a sort of mercenary attitude, if you ask me. She certainly charges enough." Pruett made a sour face. "Gary borrowed from his retirement account to pay for his defense. He took out a second mortgage on this house. He owes more on it now than it's worth. We could have let it go into foreclosure, but I decided to keep up the payments. I figured its value would go up eventually, and in the meantime we could rent it out. I never thought I'd be living here."

We talked a little about his brother's trial. I wanted to know what he thought about Napoleon Washburn, about the alleged jailhouse confession.

"It made no sense to me," Pruett said. "Even if Gary was guilty, why would he tell a stranger? Washburn was a criminal. He was lying in order to get his own sentence reduced. I assumed the jury would see through him."

"Why do you think they didn't?"

Neil Pruett scratched the side of his sandy-blond head. "Probably because Gary never testified. He never had a chance to deny the confession. His lawyer convinced him not to take the stand."

"You think that was a mistake?"

"I don't know. It was the strategy they went with. It could've worked. There were a lot of holes in the prosecution's case. They couldn't pinpoint when Cathy died. She was stabbed, but no matter how much they searched they could find no evidence that it had happened in this house. They never found the knife. They found Cathy's body in a field, and they couldn't say for sure how long it had been there. And there was nothing to prove that Gary had put it there."

I remembered something Tolliver had said.

"They found strands of her hair in the trunk of his car."

"That's true," said Pruett. "But the hair could've been from a blanket she'd used. And if her body had been in the trunk they should have found blood. They didn't. Gary's lawyer thought she could make a case for reasonable doubt, as long as Gary didn't testify. If he testified, he could be opened up to cross-examination—on all kinds of subjects."

"Like the affair," I said. "Angela Reese."

"Right. The local news people had already picked up on it, and I'm sure the jurors were aware of it. But if the prosecutor had been able to pick over every detail in court, it would've made Gary look horrible."

"What did you think when you found out about the affair?"

Neil Pruett's mouth twisted in distaste. "I thought it was incredibly stupid," he said, "and it marked Gary as a lousy husband, and maybe a rotten human being. But that doesn't make him a murderer—in spite of what my wife might say." He spread his hands. "She and I have gone round and round about this. I still hope she might change her mind, or at least admit the possibility that Gary could be innocent."

"What about you?" I said. "Are you willing to admit he could be guilty?"

"I've thought about it. It's tempting to give in to the idea—if only to make peace with Megan." He let out a soft breath. "If he did it, I can't believe he meant to. It must have been a mistake."

"You think he stabbed Cathy accidentally?"

"I don't think he stabbed her at all. I'm just saying that things happen, sometimes in an instant, and you can't take them back. When we were kids—"

He stopped suddenly. Looked uncertain.

"What happened when you were kids?" I asked.

He thought it over, searching my eyes. I don't know what he found, but he decided he could tell me the story.

"One summer, when Gary was fifteen and I was ten, he wanted a hunting bow. Our parents wouldn't let him have one, so he saved his money and bought one without letting them know. He couldn't afford a good bow; the one he got was made of plastic. But it wasn't a toy. The arrows were real, with metal tips. One afternoon when our parents weren't home, he took the bow into the backyard to try it out.

"He shot at trees for a while, but when that got old he waited for a dove. Our mother grew sunflowers, and doves would come around to eat the seeds. Gary took aim at one of them, and I don't think he expected to hit it, but the arrow went through one wing and into the body. I was watching. Both of us froze. The bird lay in the grass with one wing flapping. After a while it stopped.

"I knew Gary would be in trouble if our parents found out. They'd be angry. And I was ten and he was my big brother. So naturally I threatened to tell them. He had one last arrow left. He fitted it to the bow, aimed it at me, and told me I'd better not. He didn't have the string pulled back all the way, didn't really mean any harm, but his fingers slipped and the arrow whizzed past my neck. The metal tip grazed my skin as it went by."

Neil Pruett touched the collar of his shirt on the right side. "We buried the dove and gathered the arrows," he said, "and Gary never shot that bow again. We both knew how close he had come to something he could never take back."

His voice dropped almost to a whisper. "I don't believe he killed Cathy, but if he did, it must have been something like that. Maybe they argued and she felt afraid of him. So she picked up a knife to feel safe. Maybe he tried to take it away from her and they struggled. And the knife slipped, like his fingers on the bow. And then it was too late. That's the only way I can imagine it."

19

On Friday the ninth of May, three days after my conversation with Neil Pruett, I drove two hundred miles to the town of Dannemora to visit his brother, Gary, in prison.

Several things happened in between.

On Wednesday the police fished a body out of a section of the old Erie Canal. It had been discovered by a pair of teenage boys playing hooky from school. The local TV stations covered the story heavily, cutting away from the usual soap operas and talk shows.

By the time I tuned in late in the afternoon, they had identified the body as that of a woman named Jolene Halliwell. The six o'clock news showed a photograph: a blond party girl in a low-cut blouse with a drink in her hand. She'd been caught laughing and pointing at the camera.

A reporter did some legwork and found the woman's mother, who closed her door in his face, and some of the woman's friends, who were willing to talk. There were three of them, sketchy types in their late twenties. Two men with shaggy hair and goatees, a woman with a pierced eyebrow. They told the reporter they hadn't seen Jolene in a few days. When he tried to pin them down, they decided she had definitely come by last Tuesday night. "For beer and tequila," one of the men said.

"How long did she stay?" the reporter asked.

"Until the next morning," said the woman with the pierced eyebrow. "I remember she took a shower before she left. Used all the hot water."

"And that would have been?"

"A real downer," the woman said. "When I got in the shower I practically froze."

"I meant, what time would it have been," the reporter said, "when she left?"

"Oh. Maybe noon?"

The reporter had some other questions, like whether Jolene Halliwell would have gone walking by herself along the Erie Canal. "She liked nature," one of the men volunteered.

Was she cautious? the reporter asked. Was it possible she had gone off with someone she didn't know very well? The three friends exchanged glances. "Oh, sure," they said, almost in unison.

The interview took place in front of an apartment building, and when it ended the reporter stood alone for a moment with his microphone, summing up. The camera pulled back a little, to take in the wider scene. And I recognized the location: Reed Terrace, the apartment complex right across the street from Jana's duplex.

I tried to go out to the spot where they found Jolene Halliwell's body. Seifert Road, on the western edge of the city. I got there at twilight, after the television crews had packed up. The police were there in force, and they had set up a barricade to keep the gawkers out. They were checking IDs, only letting local people through. I got close enough to see the police cars lined up by the roadside—no sign of Frank Moretti's Chevrolet—and then a uniformed cop stopped me and made me turn the truck around.

I drove northeast and made my way to Jana's street. A few lonely porch lights illuminated the apartments of Reed Terrace. I saw a handful of cops going door-to-door, trying to coax people out to talk.

I found Moretti's black Chevrolet in the lot and parked next to it. Got out of the truck and walked along the perimeter, looking for spots where there were gaps between the trees—spots with a view of Jana's front door on the other side of the street. I found more than one.

I went back to the truck and waited. Frank Moretti came out of one of the apartments, tried the next door, got snubbed. The door after that opened for him. I watched him hold up a photograph and get a head shake in return. The door closed again. Moretti turned around and spotted my truck. He wandered over at his unhurried cop pace.

"You want to tell me this has nothing to do with Jana's death?" I said, climbing down to meet him.

His eyes narrowed. "I don't want to tell you anything."

"According to the news, Jolene Halliwell was here last Wednesday morning," I said. "The day Jana died. Do you still think Simon Lanik killed Jana—after an argument about the rent?"

"I don't answer to you."

"Because it doesn't make sense. The timing. Jolene left her friends' apartment around noon. Jana died between six and seven in the evening—you told me that. Are we supposed to believe Jolene Halliwell stuck around here all that time?"

"There's no 'we,' Mr. Malone."

"What's the theory? Jolene sees Lanik leaving Jana's apartment. And he sees her. So he has to kill her, because she's a witness? And he drives her out to the canal and dumps her?"

Moretti rubbed the back of his neck wearily. "I suppose you have a better idea."

I crossed my arms and leaned against the truck. "I do. Someone was watching Jana's apartment that day, from a parked car in this lot. Not Simon Lanik, someone else. The same person who had watched Jana before from the woods. Jolene Halliwell saw him here, and he worried that she would remember him. So he killed her."

Moretti nodded along with everything I said—an automatic nod that had nothing to do with agreement. He held up a hand when I finished, as though he feared I might start up again.

"I don't know yet what happened to Jolene Halliwell," he told me, "and neither do you. It's my job to find out. Not yours. So why don't you go on. You don't belong here."

I went home where I belonged, but the day had one more bit of drama in store for me. Sophie cooked us a late dinner and I washed up after. She camped out on the sofa, because she was scrubbing in on a surgery in the morning and needed to go over her notes on the procedure. I took care of some business in my office.

Around ten-thirty I came out, heated some milk on the stove and made hot chocolate. I gave a mug to Sophie and took mine onto the balcony. A cool night under a half-moon.

I barely had time to sit down before I heard it: the click of something small hitting the glass of the sliding door. A few seconds later it happened again. This time I saw a pebble bounce off the glass and skip along the floor of the balcony.

I went to the rail and saw him down below. A long white coat over a shirt and tie. Brad Gavin, surgical intern. The one who owned a house and always shot the best game of pool. Brad of the Condom Wrapper.

He tossed another pebble up, drunkenly. He wasn't holding a bottle, but he might as well have been. There'd been a bottle in his recent past. When he saw me, he waved me off. He was at a concert and I was the opening act he didn't want to see. He was impatient for the main event.

"Sophie!" he called, in a drunk's approximation of a whisper.

"Sophie," I said over my shoulder. She heard me through the screen and came out.

"Brad," she said. "For god's sake."

"Sophie," he said, louder now. "I need you."

"No. You don't."

He pointed up at her and then back at himself. "There's something here," he said.

"No. There isn't."

"It's real, I can feel it. We owe it to ourselves . . ." He stumbled a little, over what they owed themselves. Then he recovered. "We have to see," he said. "We have to try to make this work."

"We're not doing that," Sophie said. "I already told you."

"It's not fair," he said. "You've been avoiding me."

"Well, that part's true," Sophie said to me quietly.

"I can't accept that," Gavin said. "You're too important to me."

He had a long speech ready to let her know how important she was. I missed most of it. I went in from the balcony, took my mug of hot chocolate with me. Slipped my shoes on before I went out the door of our apartment. Down the stairs to the ground floor, out through the main doors.

There was Brad Gavin, a few yards away on the lawn. He made a passable romantic lead—five feet, ten inches of young-doctor handsome, pouring out his soul to Sophie on the balcony above. She saw me and I heard her say, "Dave, don't." I must have looked grim, though I wasn't aware of it. When Gavin saw me he said, "Really? Seriously?" And then: "What, are we gonna fight?"

I sipped hot chocolate and ambled toward him. Unhurriedly, like Frank Moretti.

Gavin started shrugging out of his long white coat. "Do you think I'm afraid of you?" he said. "I've studied karate since I was eight."

I'd never studied karate, but I had one advantage over him. I knew we were going to fight, and I knew we weren't going to talk about it first.

When I got close enough I tossed the hot chocolate in his face.

It wasn't hot enough to burn him, but it was hot enough to make him worry that it would. He had both arms free of the white coat, and now, blindly, instinctively, he brought it up with two hands to his eyes.

I dropped the mug and kept moving, took hold of his shoulders to pull him forward, drove my knee into his stomach. He groaned and bent forward and I stepped to the side and pushed him down to the ground. I got down there too, sat on him, pulled his right arm around to the small of his back.

"Let me ask you something, Brad," I said in a low voice. "Would they let you operate with a broken thumb?"

He tried to make a fist, but I got a grip on his thumb and bent it a little, experimentally.

I'll give him credit: he didn't scream. He cursed less than he might have. He said, "Don't do that. Please."

By then Sophie had come down. I heard her say, "Dave, let him up."

I eased off on his thumb, but I didn't let him up. "Call him a cab," I said.

"I don't need a cab," he said. "I've got my car."

I patted his shoulder in a friendly way. "You're too drunk to drive, and I wouldn't want anything to happen to you."

Sophie was still there, hands on her hips.

"Call a cab," I told her, "and I'll let him up."

I must have seemed calm, because she went upstairs to make the call. She wasn't worried I would damage him. While she was gone, I put some pressure on his thumb again. I leaned close to his ear and borrowed a line from Moretti.

"You don't belong here," I said. "I don't want to see you again. If you come back, I'll break both your thumbs, and all your fingers. We'll see what that does for your career. Maybe you can hold a scalpel with your toes. How does that sound?"

He didn't answer, which was just as well. We passed a minute or two in silence until Sophie came back down, and then I got up and went inside, stopping only to pick up my mug.

She stayed with him until the cab arrived, and when she came back into the apartment I was lying on the sofa, one arm dangling to the floor.

She stood over me, close enough to touch. There was music playing, a John Coltrane CD—what she'd been listening to as she went over her notes.

She said, "I asked him to stay away from here."

"So did I."

"I'm not sure how I feel," she said, "about what just happened."

I knew how I felt, and it was a dark feeling, a primitive one—the feeling of a caveman when another caveman tries to steal his mate. I looked at Sophie with her pinned-up hair and those glasses. Her blouse a wisp of nothing, capri pants, bare feet. Only a few buttons between me and her naked body. I wanted to reclaim her.

I think she felt the same way. I can't be sure. What I know is that she was within reach, and I reached for her, traced the swell of her calf. I saw her hands moving, slowly, as she looked down at me, her fingers working a button of her blouse. She would have done each of them like that, taking her time. I didn't want to wait.

The blouse got torn. My shirt too. There was a lot of tearing.

The first time was as primitive as you like, there on the living room floor. Hands and knees, hard and fast. Sprawled on the carpet after, eyes shut, breathing deep.

Sophie got up to run a bath. The second time was slippery wet, steam and bubbles, her legs wrapped around me, her cheek against my neck, her nails digging into my back.

Then towels and bed. Cool sheets. The third time almost didn't happen. I was drifting on the edge of sleep. I felt the skin of her thigh sliding along mine. Her hand coaxing. She was patient about it and I watched her in the light from the other room. Looming over me, her glasses off, her hair down around her face. Then a sweet gasp as she took me in, and I felt her moving, and I surrendered, closed my eyes.

She followed a rhythm of her own, quick and slow, advance and retreat. I opened my eyes to watch her, laid a palm against her stomach, told her to put her hands on top of her head, to arch her back.

"That thing you do," I murmured.

A small break in her rhythm, less than the click of a pebble on glass. Almost undetectable. Then she arched her back and sent me over, and followed me a moment later.

But we both knew. That wasn't a thing she did. Not Sophie.

We fell asleep together and the next morning I woke up late. She was gone, and so were her clothes from the night before. Mine were still strewn around the living room. I left them and went through to the kitchen. Found a note on the table. A single line.

Maybe one of us should think about moving out.

20

drove north to see Gary Pruett on Friday, a four-hour trip through the Adirondacks—pretty country, lots of lakes. I left early and by eleven-thirty I had reached my destination: the Clinton Correctional Facility in Dannemora, New York. The main street of the town was lined with businesses on the south side: restaurants and hotels, a post office. On the north side was the prison wall, gray concrete, sixty feet high.

I found the visitor center and checked in. I had arranged the visit through Pruett's lawyer. I got a laminated badge and went through a metal detector and wound up in a crowded room with a counter running down the middle. I took a seat across from Gary Pruett, and after we introduced ourselves he said, "I like to get it out of the way up front—the main question."

"What question?" I asked.

"Whether I murdered my wife. The answer's no."

I nodded but didn't say anything.

"I hope you believe me," he said.

I didn't have an opinion yet, but as I looked across the counter at Gary Pruett, one thing was clear: his appearance worked against him. His eyes were a cold, remote blue, his hair a darker blond than his brother's. He had very straight teeth and a dimple in his chin. He had the build of a former boxer—a middleweight, not a heavyweight. And though he was in his mid-forties, I could see that he would have stacked up well against the other high school math teachers. Eighteen-year-old girls might have had daydreams about him in class. And he would have liked it, you could see that too; you could read it in his face, in the corners of his mouth, in that dimple.

He looked like a man who might well have murdered his wife.

"I know it's a cliché, coming from a convict," Pruett said, "but I don't belong here. That girl, Jana Fletcher—she believed me. My lawyer told me you knew her."

"That's right," I said. "When did you speak to Jana?"

He closed his eyes to remember. There were people talking on either side of us, other inmates and their visitors, but he acted as if we were alone.

"The middle of March," he said. "She came here. She was a god-send. I'm sorry she's gone. It's a gift, when you're in a place like this: having someone who believes you."

"Did she talk to you about Napoleon Washburn?" I said.

Pruett nodded. "She gave me hope—that he would finally tell the truth."

"Have you thought about why he would have lied at your trial?"

"I've thought about all of it. Every minute of the trial, everything that happened beforehand at the county jail. I talked to him a few times there—Washburn. He was in the cell next to mine, and I would also see him in the rec room or the yard. The first time he spoke to me, he asked what I was in for, and I told him I'd been charged with killing my wife. That's the only time we talked about the subject. He brought it up a few times later, but it was nothing I wanted to discuss. In retrospect I should have known—"

"He was trying to draw something out of you," I said.

"It seems obvious now," said Pruett. "Once he found out who I was, he would've seen the potential. If he could get me to confess, he could get what he wanted—a shorter sentence for himself. When I didn't give him a confession, he invented one. That's the simplest explanation. I generally like to leave it at that."

"'Generally'?"

Pruett hesitated, picking at a thread on the sleeve of his gray prison uniform. "It's easy to overthink things in here. You can drive yourself mad. Sometimes I wonder if Washburn already knew who I was, the first time we met. If someone sent him to talk to me."

"Who?"

"The police, of course." He lifted his shoulders and let them fall again. "I know, it sounds paranoid. Even to me. But if you think about it long enough, it makes sense. They had a weak case against me. Why not try to shore it up with a confession?"

I would have liked to dismiss the possibility out of hand. I couldn't quite do it. Pruett was watching me. He must have read something in my face.

"See?" he said. "You've only been thinking about it for a few seconds. Try it for a whole day in a cell. Or a week. That's just one way I have of torturing myself."

"There are others?"

"Sure. There's the big one, the obvious one. I didn't kill my wife. So who did?"

"And how have you done with that one?"

"I've spent more than a week on it, I'll tell you that," said Gary

Pruett, quiet and wistful in his prison gray, his palms resting on the counter between us. "I've got an answer, for all the good it's going to do me. Two answers. Luke and Eli Daw."

The names meant nothing to me. "Who are they?" I said.

He rubbed a knuckle over the dimple in his chin, leaned closer to me. "A pair of cousins," he said, "former students at East Rome High School, though they'd be in their twenties now. As far as I know, neither of them ever had a class with Cathy, but they would've seen her there, they would've known who she was. And they were troublemakers, bullies. They got into fights, always with kids who were weaker. They spent a lot of time in detention."

"Does that make them killers?"

"There's more. They were strange kids. Brought up by their grandfather out in the boondocks. Lived in a trailer. You'd hear stories—about how they killed stray dogs, stuff like that. And worse. There was an incident at the school, in the boiler room in the basement. The two of them were caught down there with another student, a girl, fifteen years old. She had Down syndrome. There were never any charges, because it was never clear what happened."

He paused, waiting to see if I would go along with him.

"What else?" I said.

"Two things," he told me. "First, when Cathy went missing, three weeks passed before her body was found. During that time, the police organized searches. They were convinced I killed her, and that meant I must have disposed of the body somewhere. They called for volunteers to help search through parks and woods and fields. They kept a list of the volunteers, and my lawyer had access to it. Luke and Eli Daw were on the list. I wouldn't have thought they were the volunteering type."

"Did anyone question them?" I asked. "Where are they now?"

"That's the second thing," Gary Pruett said. "A few weeks after the police found Cathy's body, Eli Daw was shot dead in his trailer. Shot with a thirty-eight revolver owned by Luke Daw. Luke disappeared the same night. He hasn't been seen since."

"You think he shot his cousin."

No reply at first. Just Pruett tugging at the loose thread on his sleeve again. Then he said, "There's nothing but time here, time to work things out. Those two had a reputation at the high school. Luke was the dominant one. Smarter, tougher. Eli was the follower. I'm almost certain they killed Cathy. Maybe they took her somewhere first, the way they took that girl to the boiler room. Maybe Eli didn't want to kill her, but Luke made him go along. Suppose Eli felt guilty afterward. Luke might have decided he couldn't trust him to keep quiet. So he shot him."

Pruett spread his hands on the counter between us—an invitation for me to comment on his story. I'd thought his eyes were remote, but I realized that was an illusion. He was watching me intently; he needed to know if I believed him. I recalled what his sister-in-law had told me about him. Megan Pruett. *You have to remember Gary's a liar.*

He could be lying now, inventing killers to take the blame for his wife's murder. Killers who conveniently weren't around anymore.

But if he was telling the truth . . .

"Did you talk to Jana about this?" I asked him.

"Of course," he said. "It was one of the first things I told her."

I thought about the implications. Eli was dead, but Luke was out there somewhere. And someone had killed Jana.

"Do you think she might have gone looking for him—for Luke Daw?" I said.

The question sat Pruett back in his chair. He seemed genuinely puzzled. "That would be dangerous, wouldn't it? And even if she wanted to—I don't know. Where would you start?"

I had no idea. But I had questions about Luke Daw, and Jana would have had questions too. Even if she hadn't looked for him, she would have wanted to find out more about him.

"Do you know what her plans were?" I asked Pruett. "After her visit with you, do you know who she intended to talk to?"

He thought for a moment. "She asked me if anyone ever took the Daws seriously as suspects in Cathy's murder, and I couldn't really say. I told her she should ask my lawyer—and the police."

I knew she had talked to his lawyer.

"Do you know if she ever talked to the police?" I asked Pruett.

"I imagine she did. I know she meant to—she already had the lead detective's name."

He said it casually, but it made me frown. It was something I should have wondered about before. Nothing changed in the room, not really, but I felt a nagging sensation, like a tickle at the back of my neck. The noise around us seemed to fall down to a hush.

"What was the detective's name?" I asked, knowing what the answer would be.

"Frank Moretti," he said.

21

I t was early in the afternoon when I left Gary Pruett. The air felt crisp there up north, the second week of May. I had lunch at an Italian restaurant across the street from the prison, at a table with a view of the high gray wall.

I got back to Rome after six o'clock. I called Pruett's lawyer—a woman named Emily Beal—and asked if we could meet for a drink around eight. We agreed on a place, and I hung up and drove to Jana Fletcher's apartment.

I used my key and went in. No seal on the door now—the police had removed it. They had gathered all the evidence they needed. The apartment was mine for at least a month; I'd made a deal with Agnes Lanik.

I went to see her Thursday morning, not long after I read Sophie's note. *Maybe one of us should think about moving out.* I knew which one of us she meant. Agnes answered promptly to my knock; she seemed resigned to seeing me. I told her what I wanted and she agreed. I offered to pay whatever Jana had been paying—and to make up whatever Jana owed her as well. She scowled, as if I had offended her. "The girl owes me nothing," she said.

I took a long shower to wash away the hours I'd spent on the road. Stood toweling off before the steamed-over mirror and thought I heard something move outside the bathroom door. I went over and opened it slow on the rusty hinges. No one out there in the living room. No one in the bedroom, or the kitchen. Just me and my nerves and my imagination.

I'd feared it might be worse. Thought I might not be able to sleep here. But the first night reassured me; the bedroom seemed like home. Agnes had paid someone to clean the apartment, but Jana's possessions remained in place.

I felt strange walking over the spot in the living room where I'd found Jana's body, but I figured that made sense. I was bound to get spooked once in a while, until I got used to being here alone.

At eight o'clock I parked downtown and walked half a block to a restaurant called The Savoy. I gave the hostess my name and she led me to a table tucked away in a far corner. Emily Beal was there with a section of the *New York Times* folded in a neat rectangle on the white linen tablecloth. She'd been filling in the crossword puzzle.

She rose from her seat to shake my hand. Her voice on the phone had led me to place her in her thirties or forties, but she looked older, fifty at least, judging by the lines on her face. She had pale blond hair that was fading into white. She was drinking a cappuccino and asked if I would have one. I said I would.

"What do you think of Gary Pruett?" she asked after I settled in.

"It's hard to say. A lot depends on whether he's telling the truth."

"It always does. He told you his theory, I suppose. About the cousins."

I nodded. "Luke and Eli Daw."

"The real killers," Emily Beal said. "His own version of the one-armed man."

"You don't think they killed his wife?"

She sipped her cappuccino. "I think you'd have a hard time arguing it in court," she said. "That's what Gary wanted me to do, of course."

"But you didn't."

"There was no way to connect them to the crime. They went to the high school where Cathy Pruett taught, but that doesn't mean anything. They took part in the search for her body, but so did a lot of other people. If they'd been the ones to *find* the body, then maybe you could make an argument. You could claim they knew where she was all along, because they put her there. But they didn't find her."

"Who did?"

"A woman from Schenectady, driving into town to visit her family. She had her dog with her and she pulled over by the side of the road to let him out—to keep him from peeing in the car. He ran into a field and started barking, wouldn't come back. She went to get him and found him standing vigil over Cathy Pruett."

Emily Beal let a few seconds pass. Then a wan smile turned up the corners of her mouth. "If I could've pinned the murder on the woman with the dog, I would've. But the police checked her out. She had no connection to the Pruetts and no criminal record."

"Did the police ever question Luke and Eli Daw about Cathy Pruett?" I asked.

"No. Gary only began to suspect the Daws after Eli Daw turned up dead. He shared his suspicions with me, and I shared them with the detective assigned to Cathy's case—"

"Frank Moretti."

"Right. Moretti couldn't talk to Luke Daw, because Luke ran off

the night Eli died. As far as I know, they're still looking for him. By
that point Cathy's body had been found and Gary had been charged
with her murder. So I didn't expect Moretti to switch gears and try to
prove that the Daws killed her. But I expected him to consider the
possibility, the way any honest cop would."

"Did he?"

Emily Beal looked for the answer in her coffee cup. "Who knows?
The case against Gary went forward, that's the bottom line. But I'm
not sure how much stock I'd put in Gary's theory: that the Daws
killed Cathy and then Luke Daw killed Eli to keep him from talking.
I did some checking on my own. The Daws both had criminal
records. Minor drug offenses. Possession. That probably means they
were involved in something bigger but the prosecutor wasn't sure he
could make a case, so he offered them a plea bargain."

"You think they were drug dealers."

"Right. And if they were in business together—that kind of
business—then it doesn't take much imagination to explain why
Luke Daw might have shot his cousin. Criminals kill each other over
money all the time. You don't need to look for other reasons."

She drank from her cappuccino. By then the waitress had delivered one for me, so I did the same. I tried to decide which was more
likely: that Eli Daw died because of Cathy Pruett or that he died
because of drug money. I didn't reach any conclusion.

"Let's talk about Moretti," I said.

Emily Beal nodded. "Sure."

"You said you expected him to act like an honest cop. Is that what
he is?"

She pushed her coffee cup aside. "As far as I know."

"Do you trust him?"

"Within reason. As much as I trust any detective."

"Do you believe he could've tried to frame Gary Pruett? Do you believe he could've used Napoleon Washburn—encouraged him to make up a story about a confession?"

"I considered that," she said with a shrug. "But I had a hard time finding anything to back up the idea. I looked for a pattern—other cases of Moretti's that relied on jailhouse informants. I didn't find any."

"That just means he didn't do it before," I said. "Maybe this was the first time."

"All right. Suppose that's true. Then you have to ask how Moretti convinced Washburn to help him. Did he pay him a visit at the jail?"

"Why not?" I said.

"It never happened. The county jail keeps records of visitors. There's no record of Washburn being visited by Moretti—or by any other police officer. I checked."

"Maybe someone altered the records."

Emily Beal kept her expression neutral. "In that case, you're into conspiracy territory," she said. "Good luck. But if you ask me, it's not likely. Gary Pruett isn't worth conspiring over."

I traced a circle with my finger on the linen tablecloth. "I get the sense you don't like him very much."

"I try not to think in those terms," she said. "When you defend these people, it's best not to make personal judgments about them. You don't want to ask yourself if they deserve defending. But to be honest, no, I don't like him. Never mind whether he killed his wife. Think about Angela Reese, the girl he had an affair with. She was only eighteen. He was her teacher. You can say it wasn't illegal. Fine. But it was out-of-bounds. I have a daughter her age. I pray to God she stays away from men like Gary Pruett."

Her neutral expression had gone away, replaced by contempt. It occurred to me that a lot of people would feel that way about Pruett. Especially parents.

"Does Frank Moretti have a daughter?" I asked.

Emily Beal reached for the pen she'd been using on the crossword. "I believe he has an ex-wife, and a son in college somewhere down south. But no daughter." She tapped the pen idly on her newspaper. "You shouldn't get too hung up on Moretti," she said. "His reputation's solid. I looked for dirt on him and couldn't find any: no drug addiction, no gambling problem, no violent temper. The worst I heard is that perhaps he gets too close to certain crime victims."

"What does that mean? Which victims?"

"The female ones, especially if they're attractive," she said. "If a man gets killed and leaves a pretty widow behind, Moretti might take it on himself to comfort her. And by 'comfort her' I mean exactly what you think I mean."

"I see."

"So there's that," she said, waving the hand that held the pen. "Detective Moretti has his faults, but they don't seem to involve framing people or suborning perjury."

That night I fell asleep in Jana Fletcher's bed with the window open. I woke in the cold, with the clock reading 3:58. The numbers green in the dark.

I got up to close the window and remembered the green folder. Jana's folder, her notes on the Cathy Pruett case. I went to her desk and turned on the lamp. Opened the file drawer and found the folder—right where I'd seen it last. It had been thick with papers then; now it was empty.

I sat at the desk with a pencil and a legal pad and wrote a list of possibilities:

Moretti took Jana's notes because he thought they might help him discover who killed her. Or Moretti took the notes to cover up what Jana knew.

Gary Pruett killed his wife, Cathy. Or Luke and Eli Daw killed her. Or someone else.

Napoleon Washburn told the truth about Pruett's confession. Or he lied.

He lied on his own initiative. Or Frank Moretti put him up to it.

Moretti knew Pruett was innocent. Or knew he was guilty. Or wasn't sure.

Moretti framed an innocent man. Or he framed a guilty man, to ensure he'd go to prison.

Moretti's intentions were bad. Or they were good.

Too many possibilities. I dropped the pencil on the desk and drifted over to the fireplace. The mantel looked barren without the wooden board that Jana had used as a candleholder. The police had taken it away as evidence. Nothing on the mantel now but the clay bowl and the coin. Jana's quarter. I picked it up, touched my thumb to the edge where it was worn down to a point. I had never asked her how it got that way.

One more thing I didn't know.

I returned the coin to the bowl, switched off the lamp, and went back to bed.

On Saturday I could have gone to see Frank Moretti. I could have confronted him with wild accusations, just to see how he'd respond.

I paid a visit to Angela Reese instead.

She lived in an apartment on the margins of Bellamy University, a third-floor walk-up she shared with two other women—a place with character, if character meant cramped rooms with low ceilings, floors of scarred linoleum, appliances from the 1960s.

Her roommates were enrolled at the university, but Angela didn't believe in formal education. "Too much structure," she told me. "Sometimes I sit in on classes, but I don't need the rest of it. Assignments and grades. That's not the way I learn."

She was an artist, a painter. She showed me where she worked, in the apartment's largest bedroom, which wasn't saying much. It had good light, though, from two north-facing windows. She had a narrow bed pushed up against one wall and an easel set up where it would catch the light.

There were samples of her work here and there around the room, small canvases, eleven by fourteen. They were done in acrylics and they followed a pattern: a black line running vertically down the center, with a solid block of color on either side. Yellow and blue. Red and orange. Violet and gray.

"They're about duality," Angela told me.

"I can see that," I said.

"Because we're all more than one thing. None of us are just one way."

She went on for a while about duality, about how we start as one thing and turn into another, about how we carry the seeds of change within us. It got to be a little New Agey, which was not what I'd expected. I thought I'd find someone less self-possessed, someone damaged by her time with Gary Pruett. But Angela Reese seemed whole.

I could guess why Pruett might have pursued her. She had a kind of wholesome beauty, fair-skinned and brown-haired. She reminded me of girls I'd grown up with. She would never be a fashion model, but if you saw her on the street you wouldn't look away.

I wasn't so sure about her future as a painter. She was, after all, basically filling in rectangles. I might have let my skepticism show in my face.

"You think they're all the same," she said.

"No, no," I said.

"It's okay. Everybody says that. Sandy and Ginny make fun of me. I don't care. I'm doing what I want, and the paintings sell."

"They do?"

She laughed. "Don't look so surprised. There's a place downtown that sells them. I don't make a fortune, but I get by." She found a business card and gave it to me: THE WOODMERE GALLERY.

"But you didn't come to look at paintings," she said. "You want to talk about Gary."

That was true, as far as it went. I was also here because Jana had been here once—something I'd learned earlier, when I called Angela to ask if she would meet with me.

"I saw Gary yesterday at Dannemora," I said. "Have you ever been there?"

"No. I made a break with him. I was naïve when we were together, but not blind. When he got arrested for killing his wife, I figured the universe was sending me a message. Time to try something else."

She led me to a painting on the wall between the windows. "It's all right there," she told me. "All you need to know." The canvas was painted in two shades of red. On the left side of the black line, the red was muted and muddy; on the right, it was rich and vibrant.

"This represents Gary?" I said.

"It represents my life with him, and my life after. After has been better."

"How did things start between you, if you don't mind my asking?"

Angela lingered by one of the windows, sunlight falling on the fair skin of her face. Motes of white dust floated in the light.

"It's like you're twins," she said.

A strange remark. It floated in the air with the dust.

"Who? Me and Gary?"

"God, no," she said, laughing. "You and Jana. She stood right where you're standing and asked me the same thing, in the same delicate way. Like I might break if I had to talk about it—my miserable childhood and my father's abuse and how it drove me into a relationship with a man more than twice my age."

"I'm sorry."

"Oh god, relax. None of that happened. My father drank, but he never touched me. He died in a car wreck when I was twelve. Which, I know, probably had something to do with me getting involved with Gary. Looking for a father figure. I'm not an idiot. I've seen a therapist. But with me and Gary, it was nothing creepy. He didn't make me wear my hair in pigtails or put on a cheerleader uniform or anything. It started in the most ordinary way, one day after school when it was raining. He offered me a ride home."

"So it started before you graduated?"

"Near the end of senior year. But if you want to get technical, the physical part didn't start until after graduation. Gary wanted to wait. Of course, he only had to wait a few weeks. If he'd had to wait longer, he might not have been so virtuous."

"Did he ever talk to you about his wife?" I asked.

"He told me they weren't happy together," Angela said. "But I sort of knew that already, or else what would he be doing with me?"

"He never talked about leaving her?"

"No, and it's not like he would have left her for me. We knew we weren't serious. We were just having fun." She stepped away from the window toward the easel, which held a canvas. She'd drawn a black line down the middle, but the rest was white.

"I know it was wrong," she said. "I think I knew it then. I think Gary knew. When Jana came here, she asked me if he was a good person. I told her he was. Good and bad both. We're all more than one thing. He never made me do anything I didn't want to do. He was kind to me. He told me I was beautiful, and talented. Maybe he only did that so he could get what he wanted from me. But I didn't think so at the time, and I still don't."

She shifted the canvas a little on the easel. "And then there's the other Gary, the one who cheated on his wife. Lied to her. That's true too. I can't deny it."

"Do you think he killed her?" I asked.

"I don't know. The funny thing is, I've never talked to him about it. He sent me a note once, through his lawyer. It said he wanted me to know he was innocent. But really, what else would he say? I never answered him. Early on, I worried about it. I thought I needed to know, one way or the other. But Gary Pruett's not my problem. I have my own life. I'm not responsible for him, whether he's innocent or guilty. Maybe that sounds harsh."

"It sounds about right to me."

She left the easel and sat at the foot of the bed. "What about you? Do you think he's innocent?"

I perched on the ledge of one of the windows. "That's a big question. He's still claiming he is. He thinks he knows who really did it, but I can't decide whether to believe him. He says it was a couple of cousins named Luke and Eli Daw."

I watched her expression darken.

"Do you know them?" I asked.

"I know enough," she said. "We overlapped for a year in high school. They were seniors when I was a freshman."

"I understand they had a reputation. Something happened with a girl in a boiler room."

Angela nodded. "I heard about that. And other things too. I remember being warned about them—about Luke especially."

"Warned?"

"I was told to stay away from him. Luke liked to bring a girl to a football game on a Friday night and sneak away with her under the bleachers. And if you went with him—well, he considered that consent."

"Sounds charming."

Her eyes met mine. "I never went with him under the bleachers. Thank God. But I was in a class with him—an art class."

"Really?"

"And strangely enough I found him charming. He was friendly. He would compliment your work if he liked it."

I raised an eyebrow. "Was he any good, as an artist?"

"He could draw, in pencil or charcoal," she said. "I was never impressed with his painting—I don't think he had a sense of color. I remember he used to make models, though."

"What kind of models?"

"Buildings, like the Parthenon or Monticello. He made them out of balsa wood. They were really detailed. He could have been an architect. He tried to do the Coliseum once."

"Huh."

She shook her head suddenly. "Not balsa wood. What am I thinking of? He made them out of popsicle sticks."

22

Interlude:
June 1996

Jana Fletcher drove east on the New York Thruway in her grandmother's Buick LeSabre. She had an air freshener hanging from the rearview mirror, a little tree that was supposed to make the car smell like a pine forest, but she could still make out the smell of her grandmother underneath: stale cigarettes and old-lady perfume.

So far she had gone less than twenty miles, but she felt better already, more alive. She'd left Geneva at nine in the evening with three suitcases and a few hundred dollars. She had a map she hadn't looked at yet and the address of a youth hostel in Brooklyn. She guessed the trip would take six hours, which would put her there around three in the morning. So maybe not the smartest planning ever, but still. She was on her way.

She cracked the window beside her to let in the night air. Drew a deep breath. She could still smell the cigarettes and perfume, but she didn't mind. There were worse things. She'd spent a year dealing with her grandmother's smells, helping her bathe herself, helping her to the bathroom. And in the last weeks of her grandmother's life, when the woman could no longer rise from her bed, when she couldn't feed herself, Jana had done everything for her, everything you can do for another person.

So she could take the smell of cigarettes and perfume.

J ana pulled off the Thruway at the Port Byron service plaza, because the LeSabre's tank was low and she needed coffee. Inside, she wove through a motley crowd—young families, bikers in leather, retirees, a troop of Cub Scouts—and stood in line for McDonald's. The girl behind the counter looked half asleep. She passed Jana her coffee and mumbled the total. One twenty-four. Jana had a single ready. She pulled a quarter from her pocket, but just before she dropped it in the girl's palm she drew it back. She dug through her purse for another single instead.

The quarter had come from her mother. Jana had never told her what she meant to do until today, even though she'd been thinking about it ever since her grandmother's funeral. But today she'd been sure: she wouldn't go to Cornell Law School in the fall. She would go to New York, right now. No more waiting. She wanted to be an actress.

The news had sent Lydia Fletcher through the five stages of grief: Denial (*This is a whim. You'll get halfway there and come back*). Anger (*You're throwing your future away*). Bargaining (*Try Cornell for a year. If you don't like it, you can do something else*). Depression (*I give up. You never listen to me*). Acceptance (*Fine. If you're going, at least let me help you. I'll give you some money*).

The last one wasn't really acceptance—maybe grudging acceptance. Jana could have taken the money; it would have made her mother happy. But she was angry too, angry at having to play the good daughter for such a long time.

So she refused. But just before she left, her mother slipped a quarter into her hand.

"So you'll remember to call me," Lydia Fletcher said.

A token gesture. You couldn't call anyone for a quarter, not long-distance. Yet it was a peace offering too, and Jana should have thanked her for it. Instead, she stuffed it in her jacket pocket and drove away.

Now she moved it to a back pocket of her jeans so she wouldn't spend it accidentally. She took her coffee to a table and got her road map from her purse. Chaos reigned around her: bearded bikers laughing, a toddler crying, a Cub Scout chasing a rubber ball he'd bought from a vending machine. Across the room, a guy in an orange T-shirt was using his table as a drum, tapping away at it with a pair of real drumsticks. Jana didn't know the tune, but it sounded familiar, like something a marching band would play at halftime. A second guy in a second T-shirt sat across from him, shaking his head in mock disapproval.

Jana spread the map over her table, drank her coffee, tried to figure out her route. If she followed the Thruway it would take her to New York City eventually, but she would have to go all the way to Albany first. It seemed like a waste. She thought she could get there more directly if she left the Thruway at Syracuse and got onto I-81. Follow that south to Scranton, Pennsylvania, switch over to 380, then 80, then 280—a whole lot of eighties—and that would take her to New York.

As she refolded the map she heard a voice say, "Where you headed?"

She looked up to see the drummer in the orange T-shirt. He'd brought his food tray to the trash, left his drumsticks behind. He was tall and lean, with tousled black hair and an easy smile.

"Syracuse," she said. "Then south from there."

"We are too," said the guy in the orange T-shirt. "We've got a gig tomorrow night in Binghamton. Me and my idiot friend."

He pointed across the room at his companion, who had picked up the drumsticks and was trying to tap something out on the table. It sounded like hail on a roof.

"You're in a band?" Jana said.

"Yup. We're meeting up with the others tomorrow. If you're in Binghamton, you should come."

"Thanks, but I won't be."

"After that, we're in Newark," he said, with more of that easy smile. "Then a club in Boston next weekend. Stop me if you're going to be in any of these places."

She smiled back at him. He was cute. And Binghamton was on her way. She started to think she could afford to spend a day there. Why not?

Across the room, the idiot friend left off drumming and tried to spin one of the sticks around his finger. The stick went flying.

The guy in the orange T-shirt sighed theatrically. "You can't go by that," he said. "I swear he plays a hell of a bass."

"What's the band called?" Jana asked.

T-shirt guy's eyes twinkled. "Take a guess."

She waited a beat. "My Idiot Friend?"

He laughed. "Where were you when we were looking for names?"

She could definitely spend a day in Binghamton.

"What is it really?" she said.

"The Orangemen," he told her, pointing at his shirt.

She wrinkled her nose.

"I know," he said. "We're awful with band names. Don't let it stop you from coming."

"We'll see," she said.

"Cool. And now I'll leave you alone. 'Cause, you know, I don't want to be the weird guy at the rest stop. But something about you made me want to introduce myself."

He held out a hand.

"I'm Luke," he said.

23

Eli Daw died on the night of September 6, 1996. The *Rome Sentinel* covered the story on the front page, but the *Sentinel*'s archives weren't online yet. I wound up spending part of my Sunday afternoon in the basement of the public library, looking through old issues on microfilm.

The initial report contained the bare facts. Eli was shot once in the heart at approximately eleven fifty-five p.m. It happened at his home, a trailer on Humaston Road. No weapon recovered at the scene. Subsequent stories reported that Luke Daw's car had been found the next day, abandoned in a drugstore parking lot near the bus station downtown. A handgun had been recovered from a storm drain nearby. Luke was being sought for questioning.

The *Sentinel* ran pictures of both cousins. Eli Daw looked like an amiable goof, with ruddy cheeks and wavy hair and ears that stuck out from his head. Luke Daw was something else. You could have cast him as the bad boy in a soap opera. He had an intense expression and piercing eyes.

Two things from the coverage jumped out at me. One of them I expected: the lead detective on the case was Frank Moretti. The other surprised me: Eli Daw had a wife.

I asked the woman at the circulation desk for a phone book and found a number for Wendy Daw. I entered it into my cell phone and walked out into the sunshine on the library's front lawn. I let my thumb hover over the green call button, tried to imagine what I would say.

I think your late husband was a murderer. And his cousin Luke might still be running around killing people. Do you have time to talk?

I decided to fib. I punched the button and when she answered I said, "Hi, my name is David Malone. I'm writing a book about unsolved murder cases, and I'd like to talk with you about your late husband."

"Eli?" she said. "I don't think he's worth a book."

"Well, he'll be one chapter out of many. Could we meet? I can come to you."

"I can't. It's Sunday. I'm cooking dinner."

"What about tomorrow?"

"I work tomorrow."

"I could buy you lunch."

"I don't think so. I'm sorry."

I started to ask her to reconsider and realized she'd hung up on me.

I found her number under RECENT CALLS and punched the green button again. Waited as it rang. Four times, five, six. No answering machine. No voice mail. Seven, eight, nine. I punched the red button to end the call. Strolled on the library lawn. After a minute I tried again. Wendy Daw picked up on the fifth ring.

"You're persistent," she said.

"It's important," I told her.

"The thing is, I don't see any point in talking about Eli."

"I understand it could be painful—"

"It's not painful. It's just something better left in the past. I don't think I'd want to be quoted in a book."

"That's all right," I said. "We can talk on background."

"Background?"

"Just for research. I won't quote you."

"I don't know. I'd rather not."

"We can make it deep background," I said.

"What does that mean?"

"It means once we talk, you'll never hear from me again. If I pass you on the street, I'll pretend I don't know you."

She laughed. Not much of a laugh, but enough.

"All right," she said. "Tomorrow."

I met Wendy Daw at an outdoor café across from the IRS Regional Examination Center on Arsenal Street—a building of gray brick and few windows and undistinguished architecture. A suitable home for accountants who spent their days reviewing tax returns. Wendy worked there as a secretary.

"You wouldn't believe what goes on in there," she told me. "The drudgery."

"I think I can imagine," I said.

"You really, really can't."

She ordered a salad for lunch, said she was trying to lose weight. She had always carried an extra ten or fifteen pounds, she told me, and always right around her middle. She had fine, brittle hair that she wore parted in the center, and dots of acne on her cheeks. She was dressed very professionally, in a skirt and heels and a navy blue blazer. She was twenty-four years old, the same age Eli Daw would have been if he had lived.

I asked her how they met.

"We went to high school together," she said, "but he never said a word to me there. I ran into him a couple years after graduation, at a party at Mohawk Valley Community College. I was working on an associate's degree. Business and information sciences. Not much use, but it'll get you a job answering phones for the IRS."

"Was Eli a student there?"

"No. He played bass in a band, with Luke and a couple of others. Cover songs. He came over to talk to me between sets. Five months later he asked me to marry him, and I said yes. I had a good feeling about him. I thought he was going places."

She delivered the last line evenly, with no hint of irony. When I didn't respond, she said, "You're too polite to be writing a book. Either that, or you haven't done much research yet."

"I haven't," I said.

"Well, take this down then," she said, gesturing at the notebook I'd brought along for the sake of appearances. "Eli Daw dressed like a farmer and drove a beat-up white van. He wasn't going anywhere. The only reason he graduated from high school is that he kept showing up for four years and they wanted him to move on."

"Why did you agree to marry him?"

"I took a look in a mirror and asked myself how many proposals I thought I had coming my way."

"You shouldn't be so hard on yourself," I said.

She rolled her eyes. "Now you tell me. We got married in the spring of '95. He got shot a year and a half later. In the meantime we lived in a trailer. I finished my degree and worked temp jobs. He had the band."

"Did the band make any money?"

"The band played gigs that paid a hundred dollars a night, split four ways. The band didn't last."

She went quiet for a moment, picking at her salad. I ate a bite of the sandwich I'd ordered. The sun came out from behind a cloud.

"I've heard that Eli and Luke might've had other ways of making money," I said. "Maybe illegal ways."

Wendy Daw smiled. She had a gap between her front teeth that might have been sexy, if only it had been a bit smaller.

"Is that your way of asking me if they sold drugs?" she said.

"Did they?"

"We're on deep background?"

"The deepest."

"Then yes. Mostly pot, but other things too. Coke. Pills. Meth, if they could get it. Truth is, the band was mostly an excuse to sell pot to college kids. Professors too, from what Eli said."

"Professors?"

"You think professors at a community college don't smoke pot? How else would they make it through the day?"

"Do you think that's what got Eli killed—dealing?" I asked.

She moved the salad around on her plate. "I don't know."

"What happened that night?"

I waited for her answer. She stared off into the distance, recalling the details.

"I went to bed early," she said. "Eli stayed up with a beer watching television. I woke when I heard the shot. Only, when you wake up to a gunshot, you don't realize it was a gunshot. I sat up in bed, knowing something was wrong, not knowing what. I could hear the TV in the other room. I called out to Eli and when he didn't answer I got up and went out there. Found him bleeding on the floor. The door of the trailer stood open. I heard a car driving off, fast."

"But you didn't get a look at the car?" I asked.

"I was looking at Eli," she said, "and trying to cover the hole in his chest."

"Do you think Luke was the one who shot him?"

She shrugged. "That's what the police thought. If he was, I think he came there meaning to do it. I think he shot him as soon as he opened the door."

"Did the two of them ever argue?"

"They grew up together, with just their grandfather to raise them. They argued all their lives. Had fights too—knock-down, bloody-knuckle fights, from what I heard. Not as much when they got older."

"What happened to their parents?"

I watched her do the long-distance stare again, as if she were trying to decide how much to tell, and how to tell it.

"Their fathers were never in the picture," she said. "They were one-night stands who didn't stick around. Their mothers were young—Holly and Maggie Daw—sixteen and eighteen. They got pregnant around the same time. Luke was born first, Eli two months later. Eli's mother—the sixteen-year-old—died in childbirth, so Luke's mother took care of both boys for a while. But when they were old enough for kindergarten, she took off. They'd get a card from her now and then—Christmas and birthdays—but she never came back. Their grandfather took charge of them from then on."

"What was he like?" I asked.

"I never met him," Wendy said. "Eli called him a farmer, but what he really did was manage someone else's farm—a dairy farm out on Humaston Road. Luke and Eli worked for him every summer, as soon as they were old enough. And if they screwed up, Grandpa would knock them around—take them out behind the toolshed or lock them in the root cellar or whatever people do out in the country."

"Is he still alive?"

"He died a few years ago. Ran the farm into the ground first. The owner couldn't afford to pay the taxes. I think the state owns the land now. Grandpa Daw moved himself and his grandsons out of the farmhouse, which was falling down anyway, and into a trailer. He didn't own the patch of ground where he put the trailer, but no one cared enough about it to chase him off. He spent his last years drinking and collecting Social Security."

"Is that the trailer where you and Eli lived?"

She looked across the table at me with a faint smile. "No. Luke kept that one. Eli got another one, about a mile down the road. I told him we had to have a place of our own, if he wanted me to marry him." The smile turned bitter. "I didn't sell myself cheap."

I felt bad then—for deceiving her, for tricking her into talking about things best left in the past. But I didn't stop.

"If I wanted to find Luke Daw," I said, "how would I go about it?"

"What would you want him for?"

I stuck with my lie. "For the book."

"He's on the run from the police," she said. "You think he'd talk to you?"

"It's worth a try. Who would he go to for help? Would he try to get in touch with his mother?"

"I don't even know if she's still alive."

"What about friends—maybe the other guys in the band?"

She shook her head. "One of them OD'd. The other moved out west. Luke wasn't all that close to either one."

She finished her salad, glanced at the gray building across the street as if she might be thinking about heading back.

"Do you remember a teacher named Cathy Pruett?" I asked her. "She taught at your high school."

"Sure. She died—she was murdered."

"Did Luke or Eli ever talk about her?"

I watched Wendy Daw tip her head to the side, puzzled.

"No. Why would they?" she said.

"I just wondered. She was killed a few weeks before Eli."

We sat in silence while the waitress came with the bill and went away again. I could see Wendy thinking, putting things together.

"Wait—do you think Luke killed her?"

Luke and Eli both, I thought. But I didn't say it. I didn't want to speak ill of her dead husband.

"I'm wondering if there might be a connection," I told her. "Two unsolved murders in the same city around the same time . . ."

"But Cathy Pruett's murder was solved. Her husband did it."

"He was convicted," I said. "Some people think he's innocent. One of them was a woman I knew, Jana Fletcher. I think she might have believed that Luke killed Cathy Pruett. Did Jana ever try to contact you?"

"No. But her name's familiar. She was murdered too."

"Yes."

Wendy Daw stared at me with narrowed eyes. "You're not really writing a book, are you?"

I decided to resort to the truth.

"No. I'm trying to find out who killed Jana." I pulled my wallet from my pocket and found the photograph of Jana that her mother had given me. "Jana spoke to a lot of people about the Pruett case," I said, showing the photo to Wendy Daw. "Are you sure she never tried to talk to you?"

I didn't really expect her to recognize the photo, and after she looked at it she said, "I'm sure. I never saw her."

She might have studied the photo a little too long. It seems that way to me now, though it could be a detail I'm inventing. At the time, she seemed natural enough.

Not long after, she thanked me for lunch and crossed the street, steady in her high heels. I watched her slip inside the gray brick building.

I never suspected she was lying.

24

Interlude:
September 1996

Jana Fletcher heard the calls of owls—a whole chorus of them in the dark. *Hooo, hooo, hooo, hooo, hooo.*

She walked in starlight along the shoulder of the road. The air felt clean and cool. The road made a gentle arc through the woods, and up ahead she saw a single lighted window.

She looked back the way she'd come. She could barely make out the shape of the car she'd left behind.

Hooo, hooo, hooo.

She turned again to face the window, and the deer came out of nowhere.

Three of them—one larger than the others. They bounded up into the road in a clatter of hooves, the big one leading. Jana watched them cross the center line coming toward her, and the big one passed in front of her, an arm's length away. A dark eye taking her in as it went by, cantering down from the road and into the deep of the woods.

The second one followed without looking at her, leapt down and thrashed through the brush. A flash of white tail, and then nothing.

The third one stopped.

The clip of hooves turning a quarter circle. Then quiet. Even the night chorus seemed to fade back: *Hooo, hooo.* The deer's sober eyes fixed on Jana's. The animal gave off a wet, earthy smell. Its brown ears shifted; its nostrils breathed.

Jana focused on the deer's eyes, took a gentle step toward it. The creature ducked its head down and brought it up again. Jana lifted a hand to touch its shoulder. Felt it tense and then relax.

"Beautiful," she whispered.

She felt the fur beneath her fingers, spread her fingers wide apart. The deer ducked its head again and turned away. Her hand trailed along its back as it moved. She watched it climb down from the road and trot off into the woods.

J ana reached the window, but she couldn't see in through the curtains. She could hear muffled voices inside. She stood on a patch of grass in her bare feet. A few drops of rain began to fall.

She mounted two steps and knocked on the door. Felt a raindrop on her cheek. She knocked again, louder, with the side of her fist. Started counting, one two three, in time with the beating of her heart. When she got to twenty, she pounded on the door again. Pounded until her hand began to ache.

The door opened.

He filled the doorway, wearing jeans hastily put on, no shirt. She watched his face. Annoyance. Then shock. Then disbelief.

He sputtered out her name: "Jana."

Stupid girl, she thought. You're not even ready. She reached behind her and pulled the gun from her back pocket and shot Eli Daw in the heart.

There was more noise than she expected. The gunshot, of course, a whip-crack sound that she felt through her hand, her arm, her whole body. Plus the television: the source of the muffled voices. Not so muffled now, with the door open.

Also the screaming.

Not from Eli Daw. He had fallen back obligingly and lay now on the floor with blood bubbling out of him. A big dumb animal with wide eyes, his mouth moving, making empty words. No screaming from him.

It came from farther back in the trailer. A woman's voice. "Oh my god! Eli! Who's there? What happened?"

On and on like that, with minor variations. Jana stepped over Eli Daw and went to find the voice, holding the gun out in front of her. She glanced at the television. An interrogation scene on a cop show, the hotheaded detective railing at the suspect. Jana moved through the trailer and came to a half-open door.

A bedroom. A naked woman.

Jana brought her arm up instinctively to cover her face—her mouth and nose at least. Like a hold-up man in a Western, wearing a bandanna to rob the stagecoach.

"Who are you?" the woman screamed. "What did you do?"

Her legs kicked against the mattress. Her arms strained against handcuffs, two sets of them, locking her to the cast-iron spindles of the headboard. There was a folding knife open on a bedside table, and a small cut trickling blood on the woman's left breast.

Jana went to the bed and took hold of a corner of a sheet with her gun hand. She drew it up to cover the woman's body.

That brought more screaming. "What are you doing?"

"Hush now," Jana said. She gestured at the handcuffs with the gun. "Do you know where the key is?"

"Who the hell *are* you?"

Jana tucked the gun into her pocket and found the key on her own, in the drawer of the bedside table. She held it up and said, "I'll unlock you. I can take you away from here if you want. I have a car."

She spoke softly and it seemed to help. The woman grew calmer.

"What happened to Eli?" the woman asked. "Is he dead?"

"I hope so," Jana told her.

"Oh my god. Oh my god."

Jana slipped the key into the nearest handcuff, heard it click open. One down, one to go.

"It's all right," she said. "I can drop you off somewhere. All I ask is that you forget about me. Nothing happened here. You never saw me."

"Nothing happened?" the woman said. "Nothing happened? You shot Eli."

Jana nodded. "That's the part I'm asking you to forget."

"But he's my husband."

No screaming now, just a quiet lament. But to Jana it was more jarring than a scream.

"He chained you," she said.

The woman lowered her eyes. "It's something he likes."

"He cut you," Jana said, pointing at the woman's left breast, where blood spotted the sheet.

"He didn't mean to. Sometimes he goes too far."

Jana wrapped her fingers around the key. She felt the pulse of her own blood pumping through her hand. She still had her left arm blocking her face. She still had the gun in her pocket. For a fraction of a second, she was tempted to draw it out.

She dropped the handcuff key onto the bed. "My offer stands, if you want to leave."

The woman's fingers found the key, but her eyes came up to meet Jana's and never left them.

"I should stay," she said.

Jana turned and crossed to the doorway. She stood for a moment looking out—at Eli Daw's body. No movement there.

"Go," the woman said. "I never saw you."

25

I drove out to Humaston Road on Monday afternoon, looking for the trailer that had once belonged to Wendy and Eli Daw. I found an empty patch of gravel and tall grass. Someone had used the spot to throw away an old electric stove; it lay on its side in the weeds. Not too far away I saw a rusted mailbox, fallen over on its wooden post. The name was still on the box. Most of it anyway: D W.

A mile down the road I found Luke Daw's trailer, the one where he had lived with Eli and their grandfather—until the grandfather died and Eli moved out. It had a screen door gaping open, attached by a single hinge. When I climbed the steps and went in, the air felt warm and dense. I'd brought a flashlight from the truck and I aimed it into the murky corners. The place had been picked over, stripped of furniture and fixtures.

At some point someone had built a fire in a steel washbasin on the kitchen floor. There were charred popsicle sticks in the basin. Probably the remnants of one of Luke Daw's models.

There were clothes strewn over the floor, and broken dishes.

Cereal boxes, empty soup cans. A plastic pill bottle with no pills. According to the label, it had once held Ambien. The prescription was in Luke's name.

Pocketing the bottle, I made my way toward the back of the trailer. I came to a small bathroom, foul-smelling, with something scurrying inside. I pulled the door shut and moved on.

In one of the two bedrooms, I found another model: the shattered hulk of the Parthenon. Then, on a closet shelf, a small hollow cube glued together out of popsicle sticks, curiously intact.

The bedroom had a tiny window, the glass broken long ago. I heard a flutter of wings and a black bird came to perch in the window frame. A crow. We stared at each other for a while. I was the first to back down.

I left the trailer, taking the wooden cube as a souvenir. I put it in my truck and waded out into Luke Daw's overgrown backyard. Milkweed and butterflies and Queen Anne's lace. A rutted lane led through a stand of birch trees, and the trees gave way to a broad field—the pasture of the ruined dairy farm that the Daws' grandfather had once managed. On the north side of the lane was a pond as wide as a football field, the surface a scum of green algae. A thicket of cattails swayed in the wind along the far shore.

The lane ended west of the pond, and the ground sloped up to a long red barn. The barn doors stood open at either end, and a wide aisle ran down the center of the building, with cattle stalls on either side.

I walked along the aisle under a bright afternoon sky, because most of the barn's roof was gone. A framework of posts and beams remained, but the rest had fallen away. I could see the debris piled in some of the stalls: wood and tar paper and shingles.

The farmhouse was in worse shape than the barn. It had been a square building, one story, on a foundation made of field stones. One corner of the structure still stood—where the north side and the east came together. They formed a high point from which the rest of the building sloped away, a cascade of slate roof tiles and rotting timber.

I wondered if Cathy Pruett had ever been here. I recalled something her husband had said up in Dannemora—Gary Dean Pruett, who claimed the Daws had murdered his wife. *Maybe they took her somewhere first,* he said. The police had found her body in a field on the other side of town, but they never found the spot where she died. Could the Daws have brought her out here?

I walked around the perimeter of the house and I didn't see anything that looked like a killing ground. I picked my way through a collection of junk: old milk cans and coils of barbed wire, a rusted bicycle, broken bottles, a wheelbarrow, a plastic kiddie pool filled with rainwater and wet leaves.

Near the southwest corner of the house was a toolshed with a hasp on the door but no padlock. I drew the door open to look inside. Nothing there but a scattering of nails and wood screws on the floor.

When I came around again to the front of the farmhouse, I saw something I hadn't noticed before: an old wagon wheel half-buried in the ground. I only noticed it now because there was a crow perched on the rim of the wheel, a twin of the one I'd seen in the trailer. Maybe the same bird. It opened its wings and folded them again. Stared at me as I went by.

I walked back along the rutted lane with the eerie feeling that the crow was keeping watch on me. I thought if I turned around I might find it hopping along in my wake. I held things together until I reached the pond, then looked back. The crow wasn't following me, but the rim of the wagon wheel was empty.

Spooky.

I kept walking, and that's when I heard the sound of a car's engine and something else, maybe tires on gravel, coming from the direction of the trailer. I hurried along the lane, with the pond on my left. The birch trees obscured my view of the trailer. When I came through at last to the other side of the trees, there was no car. Just my truck and the trailer. I approached the truck expecting to find damage—a broken windshield, punctured tires. A warning. But everything looked fine. I checked the cab, thinking that Luke Daw's wooden cube would be gone. It was on the seat where I'd left it.

Crows and mysterious visitors, I thought. You're letting yourself get carried away.

Probably someone had pulled in here to turn around. Nothing more.

R eckless.

K let up on the gas pedal, felt the car slow, watched the needle drop down to forty-five. No sense risking a ticket. He checked his rearview mirror for David Malone's pickup truck. Saw nothing but empty road.

A dumb move, driving by the trailer. There was no reason for it. Why had he done it? For the thrill? For the sense of comfort it gave him? He didn't know.

And why had he stopped? He should have sped by as soon as he saw the truck. But he had pulled over. He had even gone into the trailer.

Reckless.

K drove into Rome at the limit and lost himself in city traffic. He didn't like the thought of Malone poking around the trailer or the farm. It worried him. But something else worried him more. He had gone into the trailer without knowing if he would find Malone inside. With no plan. What would he have done if Malone had been in there? Would he have tried to kill Malone with his bare hands?

The idea appealed to him, and that was part of the problem. K worried that he was starting to lose control.

He turned onto a side street and parked. He needed to think. Jana Fletcher was dead—mark that down as a win. Her landlady's grandson, Simon Lanik, seemed to be the prime suspect. Not something K had planned, but he liked the way it had fallen into place. Another win.

The fire at Napoleon Washburn's house had been a disappointment. Washburn had survived. Still, he seemed to have skipped town. Call it a draw.

Which left Jolene. Her body had been discovered, and that was a loss. No way around it. K knew he should have hidden her better, weighted her with chains or stones. Then she would have sunk to the bottom of the canal and stayed there.

There was nothing he could do about it now. He needed to put her out of his mind. But that was part of the problem too. He kept thinking about her at odd moments. He had killed four women in his life, but Jolene was the only one he regretted. Part of him wished she was still alive, because she was an innocent girl who had died because she'd been in the wrong place at the wrong time. And part of him wished she was still alive so he could kill her again.

Sentimental K.

He smiled to himself and shook his head. This was not the time to think about Jolene. He needed to focus on David Malone. He would take things slow and think them through. No more recklessness.

That night I had a visitor.

I was eating a late dinner at the desk in Jana's apartment: Chinese takeout, shrimp lo mein. I had candles burning on the shelf above the fireplace, four tea lights lined up on a piece of two-by-four.

It was my own poor counterfeit of Jana's candleholder—something I had put together over the weekend. I picked up the lumber from a home-improvement store, where a middle-aged man in a blue apron cut it to the length I wanted. I made the holes for the candles with a power drill and a one-and-a-half-inch bit—standing on the board to keep it steady. A drill press would have done a neater job, but I didn't have one.

The candles were supposed to smell like vanilla. It would have been hard to tell. The apartment smelled like boiled cabbage. Agnes Lanik had been cooking next door—a recipe from the old country, I assumed.

The knock on my door came around ten-thirty. It was Sophie.

She looked weary yet wide-awake, and I thought she had probably just come off a long shift at the hospital. She must have stopped at home, though, because the clothes she had on were nothing she would have worn at work: a blouse with a low neck and a skirt that ended well above her knees.

"Is this a bad time?" she said.

"No. Come in."

"I don't want to intrude."

"You're not intruding."

She came in and dropped her handbag on the kitchen table. Moved into the candlelit living room and looked around, taking things in.

"I didn't really believe it," she said.

"Believe what?"

"When you moved out, and you told me you were going to live in the dead girl's house. I thought you were just being cruel."

"Sophie—"

She waved the idea away. "Sorry. I shouldn't have said that." She stood looking at the wall adjacent to the fireplace, where I had pinned up a map of the city—with an *X* to mark the spot where Cathy Pruett's body was found and another to mark Luke Daw's trailer and the abandoned farm. I had other things pinned to the wall as well: newspaper stories I'd printed out at the library, down in the microfilm room. Stories about Cathy Pruett's death and her husband's trial. About the shooting of Eli Daw.

"What's all this?" Sophie asked.

"Do you really want to know?"

"Yes."

I told her a little about what I'd been doing, the people I'd been talking to. It was difficult to know if she was listening—her eyes were on the papers on the wall—but when I finished she cut through to the heart of things.

"So you think if you find out what happened to this woman, Cathy Pruett, that'll tell you who killed Jana." It sounded a little unreal, hearing her say Jana's name.

"That's right," I said.

Sophie turned her attention to the shelf above the fireplace. The wooden cube was there, the one I'd found in the trailer. She took it down.

"What's this?" she said.

"A clue."

"A clue to what?"

"I don't know. I think Luke Daw made it."

She put it back on the shelf and took down the empty pill bottle.

"Ambien," she said. "Is this another clue?"

"It might be. It's a kind of sleeping pill, isn't it?"

She nodded. "A strong one. It can cause sleepwalking. Blackouts. Memory loss. It's nothing you want to mess around with."

The bottle went back on the shelf. There was something else up there, a canvas resting against the wall. One of Angela Reese's paintings. She had given it to me on Saturday after our talk about Gary Pruett and the Daws.

It was like all her other paintings: eleven by fourteen with a black line drawn vertically down the center. The left side of the line was painted a vivid blue; the right was purple, verging on black. Angela had taken it down from the wall as I was leaving. "You should have it," she had said. "I made it the day I found out Jana Fletcher died."

"Who painted that?" Sophie asked me.

"A woman I talked to."

"What does it mean?"

"It doesn't mean anything," I said. "It's abstract art."

"I think it's depressing."

"I think it's supposed to be."

"Do you like her?"

"Who?"

"The artist. The woman whose painting you bought."

"She gave it to me."

"Even better. Is she pretty?"

She turned to look at me expectantly, Sophie in her cat's-eye glasses, with her hair up in a clip.

"I don't know how to answer that question," I said.

"She's either pretty or she's not."

"She is."

"See? How hard was that?" Sophie laid a palm against my cheek, turned my head a little. The smell of Agnes Lanik's cooking lingered in the apartment, but I could still make out the strawberry scent of Sophie's shampoo.

"You haven't asked me why I'm here," she said.

I felt the warmth of her hand. I had a view of candlelight and shadow and her low-cut blouse.

"I'm getting the sense you're here to torture me," I said.

She laughed. "That's close." She touched my temple. "I came to take out your stitches."

T hey should have come out days ago," Sophie said.

I was sitting at the kitchen table. Sophie was making preparations: bringing out forceps and scissors from her handbag, washing her hands, sterilizing her instruments with alcohol.

She stood over me, bathed my cut with Betadine solution.

"This probably won't hurt," she said.

"'Probably'?"

"Well, you never know."

She lifted the knotted end of the thread with the forceps and snipped it with the scissors. Tugged the thread free from my skin, bit by bit. It didn't hurt.

She bathed the wound again and dried it. "The thing to remember," she said, "is that your skin is still healing. It'll take weeks to get all the way back to the way it was. You want to be careful not to injure it again."

She had three small adhesive bandages arranged on the table. She peeled the wrapping from one of them and placed it over the center of the cut.

"You still need to keep this clean and dry," she said. "You don't want it to get infected." She opened another bandage and put it in place. "People don't worry about infection as much as they should. I remember a kid who came into the emergency room one time, eight years old.

He'd fallen out of a tree. He had an open fracture of the tibia—that's the bone in your shin. 'Open' means the bone had broken through the skin.

"A hundred years ago, people died routinely from open fractures—because they get infected so easily. But now we've got antibiotics. Powerful ones like cephalexin, which is what we gave to that eight-year-old. Then we got him into the operating room and debrided the wound, and irrigated it. We reduced the fracture and stabilized the bone with steel pins. We closed the wound and sent him to recovery, and after a couple days they sent him home."

The third bandage was in place now, and Sophie stood behind me with her hands on my shoulders. "Less than a week later, his parents brought him back in," she said. "He was lethargic and confused. He had a fever and a rash. Classic symptoms of sepsis. Sepsis is what happens sometimes when your body is trying to fight off an infection. The chemicals in your blood that are supposed to fight the infection cause inflammation, and the inflammation winds up reducing the flow of blood to your limbs and organs. Which is what happened to this kid."

She paused, and in the quiet I heard the clock ticking on the kitchen wall.

"He wasn't a surgical patient anymore," she said, "but I followed his case anyway. Brad Gavin did too. Because both of us had been there when he came in the first time, with his broken leg. This time they admitted him to the ICU and put him on IV fluids. The cephalexin hadn't worked, so they tried other antibiotics to knock out his infection. Brad and I checked on him every day."

She paused again. Maybe she expected me to bristle at the mention of Brad Gavin. I didn't. After a moment she went on.

"Sepsis doesn't always kill you, but when it does, it kills you by shutting down your organs. Sometimes it takes weeks. With this kid it was a matter of days. When his lungs started to fail they put him on oxygen, and when his kidneys failed they tried dialysis. His parents were hopeful to the end. His mother was with him constantly, except when she stole an hour or two of sleep in a lounge down the hall. That's where she was when he died. His blood pressure crashed and his heart stopped, and they couldn't revive him. I saw it happening. I went to find his mother and bring her back, but it was over."

Sophie's voice sounded calm, but I thought she was crying. If I turned around I would see. I didn't turn around. I didn't think she wanted me to.

Her right hand came off my shoulder. Maybe she was wiping tears.

I reached for her other hand. "You never told me about that," I said.

"I should have," she said. "I wonder if it would have made a difference."

"What do you mean?"

"If you still would have left me. The day that kid died was the day I slept with Brad Gavin." She came around from behind me and gathered her forceps and scissors. Dropped them in her bag. "Not the best excuse for infidelity," she said, "but maybe not the worst either—mourning the death of an eight-year-old whose only mistake was climbing a tree."

All business now. She picked up her bag, headed for the door. I rose to follow her.

"Sophie, I'm sorry. I wish you had told me."

She turned back to me, her eyes dry.

"Dave," she said. "You never asked."

26

The smell of boiled cabbage carried all the way to K's hiding place in the woods.

He sat on the fallen tree trunk with a pair of binoculars. They were big and clunky—army surplus. He was using them to watch David Malone and his woman. With the lights on in the kitchen, he could see them plainly through the window of the back door.

Finding Malone had been relatively easy. The first place he looked was the second-floor apartment, the one with the balcony where he had first seen Malone with his lady doctor.

K had gone there earlier in the evening, but Malone's pickup truck wasn't there. He watched and waited for half an hour, until the lady doctor came out and got into her car. He followed her, almost on a whim, and she led him right to Jana Fletcher's duplex.

The curtains were drawn in the front window, so K had decided to go around to the back. He had left his car on the street by Cypress Park and made his way through the woods by the light of the moon.

He had no trouble, even when he had to cross the narrow footbridge over the ravine.

Now he watched Malone and the woman. He didn't know at first what they were doing, because the woman had her back to the window, but then he got a glimpse of the wound on Malone's temple. He realized the woman was tending to it.

Then they talked. About nothing very cheery, apparently. And finally Malone got up and both of them moved out of view. When Malone came back into the kitchen, he was by himself.

Disappointing. K would have liked to see more of the woman.

He lowered the binoculars and set them on the tree trunk beside him. He would have hung them around his neck, but they were old and worn-out. The strap was broken.

He could see Malone without them—through the window of the back door and the window of the bedroom. Malone wandered around the apartment with his head bowed. He seemed sad, preoccupied. K had no way to guess what he might be thinking about. It would have been useful to know. But what K really needed to determine was how much of a threat Malone posed. That was the reason he had come here.

Malone seemed bent on learning the truth about what had happened to Jana Fletcher. But how much did he know? Too much, clearly. He shouldn't know about the farm on Humaston Road. That made him dangerous.

On the other hand, though Malone had visited the farm this afternoon, he must not have uncovered its secret. If he had, he would have gone to the police, and the police would have gone to the farm. The discovery would have made for a big story. But there'd been no mention of it on the news. K had wanted to be sure, so he had taken a chance and driven past the farm again around dusk. No police cars, no activity at all.

K stood now and stretched his legs. He looked up through the canopy of the trees at the night sky. Reluctantly, he came to a decision. Malone was a problem, but killing him would only draw more attention to Jana Fletcher's death. Better to let things lie. With any luck, the secret of the farm would remain hidden and people would begin to forget about Jana. Simon Lanik would take the blame for her death. Lanik wasn't guilty, but he looked guilty—as long as he stayed in hiding, as long as he was on the run.

So Malone would go on living. K raised the binoculars and caught sight of the man again through the bedroom window. He was still on his feet, moving through the apartment restlessly. He went out through the bedroom door and disappeared from view, and K shifted the binoculars to the back door and picked him up again when he moved into the kitchen. Who knew how long he might go on like this?

K started to lower the binoculars, but something made him raise them again. Maybe fate. He shifted them farther to the left and found another window—the window of the back door in the other half of the duplex. It gave him a view into the old woman's kitchen. He saw her in there—the landlady. Hard to tell what she was doing, because there were curtains in the window and the curtains were only open about six inches. She moved back and forth across the gap, and K realized she was carrying dishes from the table to the sink.

K yawned and decided it was time to leave—to head back through the woods. The old woman passed out of view. Then K saw something that banished all thought of leaving from his mind.

A fter Sophie left, I felt unsettled. I paced around, thinking about what she'd said.

I thought about the Night of the Condom Wrapper, when she

confessed to sleeping with Brad Gavin. I thought about what might have happened if I had asked her why.

I might never have left our apartment that night, might never have met Jana. She would be a stranger who died in the city where I lived. I wouldn't be here, with maps and papers pinned to the walls, candles burning on the mantel.

I could still have that life, if I wanted it. I could ask Sophie to take me back. I thought she would. I would have to ask for her forgiveness, because my transgression was worse than hers. She had slept with Gavin, but only once. She hadn't fallen in love with him. She hadn't left me for him.

I stopped pacing and stared at the wooden cube on the fireplace mantel. I reached up suddenly and swept it off onto the floor. It held together; only one of the popsicle sticks broke away.

You can do better than that, I thought. Put your fist through a wall and then go to her. She'll wrap it. She'll take care of you. She'll tell you to stop putting your fist through walls.

But you'll have to leave Jana behind.

I picked up the cube and looked through the gap left by the missing stick. There was nothing inside, only empty space.

It was supposed to be a clue. I had all kinds of clues. The pill bottle. Angela Reese's painting. The candleholder made from a two-by-four. The mangled quarter. Maybe they were all trying to tell me something. Maybe everything in the apartment was a clue.

I put the cube back on the mantel and breathed deep, taking in the smell of cabbage. Maybe that was a clue too. Why not?

After a while I lay down and tried to read one of Jana's books— *The Count of Monte Cristo*. But before Edmond Dantès' ship dropped its anchor in the harbor of Marseilles, I drifted off to sleep.

I came awake less than ten minutes later, sat up, and swung my feet off the bed.

The smell of cabbage—it really was a clue.

I rose and moved through the stillness of the house. In the kitchen I picked up a chair and carried it as quietly as I could through the back door onto the patio. I sat beside the forsythia bush and listened to the night sound of crickets. The moon provided a little light, and a little more leaked through Agnes Lanik's curtained windows next door.

Sometime later, I heard furtive noises on the other side of the forsythia: a bolt turning, a door creaking in the jamb, murmuring voices, a screen door yawning open and falling shut. Footsteps on patio bricks.

He started out across the lawn toward the woods, and I got up to follow him.

"Hello, Simon," I said.

Simon Lanik spun around to face me, his mouth twisted in surprise and anger. He wore his tan overcoat, his hands buried in the pockets. His left hand came up, still in the pocket, as if he had a gun concealed there.

I faded back a step and showed him my palms. "Take it easy," I said.

He recognized me and broke into a grin. "Jesus, *kámoš*, you scared me. Have you been waiting there? We thought you were asleep."

"I was. Then I realized your grandmother had company. What did she cook for you?"

The question relaxed him. His pocketed left hand moved down to his side.

"*Holubky,*" he said. "You know what those are?"

I nodded. They were cabbage rolls stuffed with beef and rice and covered with tomato sauce. Something my own grandmother used to make.

"You'd like them," Simon Lanik said. "But she only makes them on special occasions."

"What was the occasion tonight?" I asked him.

"What do you think? She gave me a little send-off. I might not be able to come back here for a while. The police have foolish ideas about me. This city—I can't stay here."

"I know about their ideas," I said.

He looked at me gravely. "Don't believe them, *kámoš*. I never touched that girl."

"I heard you're not above touching girls," I said, "especially when they're slow with the rent."

Lanik smiled the smile of a ladies' man—an expression belied by his pockmarked face and greasy hair. "That's different," he said. "Some of them—you just know. If you do them a favor, cut them some slack, they'll do a favor for you. Who am I to turn them down, if that's how they wanna pay?" His left hand stayed in his pocket, but his right came out so he could wag a finger at me. "Jana was different," he said. "I never tried that with her. And for sure I never killed her."

"I believe you," I said.

"But the police, they already made up their minds. They're looking for me. I think they're watching this house."

"They are."

"But they only watch the front. Fucking idiots." He started to back away from me. "Good-bye, *kámoš*. You won't see me again."

"Wait," I said, trailing after him. "Maybe there's another way." I thought of Roger Tolliver. "I know a lawyer. I could ask him to help you. You could turn yourself in. You didn't kill Jana. The police can't prove you did."

Lanik stood in the grass unmoving, staring at me. I couldn't tell what he was thinking. We listened to the chirping of the crickets.

"I'm sorry, *kámoš*," he said at last. "I don't trust lawyers. Or police." He lifted his left hand again, in the pocket of his tan coat—like a gangster in a movie. "I'm leaving. Don't try to stop me."

He backed away. I smiled. "Come on, Simon. Do you even have a gun? Or are you going to shoot me with your finger?"

He stopped and grinned at me. The crickets chirped in the far-away dark.

"I have a gun," he said. "A Makarov pistol, made by the Russians. My grandfather brought two of them with him when he came over from Czechoslovakia. He's dead now, but he used to tell me stories. He always said he was part of the resistance against the Soviets. But I don't know how much resisting he did. I think he was a criminal. I think he made his living in the black market."

Lanik's eyes held steady on mine. He wasn't grinning anymore.

"I'm not lying to you, *kámoš*," he said. "You try to follow me, you'll find out."

From his hiding place in the woods, K watched Simon Lanik talking with David Malone.

It bothered him that he had almost missed this. He had been on the verge of leaving when he spotted Simon Lanik in the old woman's kitchen. He had watched Lanik approach the back door and look out, then close the curtains tight.

It bothered him too that he couldn't hear what Lanik and Malone said to each other. He made out Malone's first words: "Hello, Simon." But the rest was indistinct. The distance was too great. One thing came across clearly, though: Lanik had a gun in his pocket, or was pretending he had one.

K lowered the binoculars. Lanik and Malone finished their conversation, and Lanik started walking toward the woods. K crouched down by the fallen tree trunk and kept still.

Lanik passed him in the dark. A rustling of footsteps. The crack of a twig.

Less than fifteen feet away.

K got up slowly. He looked for Lanik's tan coat among the moonlit trees. Caught a glimpse of it. Another choice to make.

He followed Lanik.

Funny how quickly things can change. K had made up his mind that he should do nothing. He had decided he would be fine as long as the police went on believing that Simon Lanik was responsible for Jana Fletcher's death. That would be easier for the police to believe if Lanik remained at large, a fugitive.

But what if Lanik got caught? After all, a fugitive who was foolish enough to visit his grandmother couldn't really be counted on to avoid capture indefinitely, could he?

It was something K needed to consider. If Lanik got caught, there was a fair chance he would be convicted, in spite of his innocence. But nothing was certain. He might find a good lawyer; he might establish an alibi. The whole case against him, such as it was, might fall apart. The police might go looking for another suspect.

It would be better for K if that never happened. It would be best of all if Simon Lanik disappeared for good.

Could he be counted on to disappear on his own—or did K need to help him along?

K stumbled over a stone. He caught himself against a sapling. The binoculars slipped from his hand and fell to the ground. He could see Lanik up ahead, the tan coat among the black trees. Lanik didn't stop. Didn't turn.

K picked up the binoculars and moved on. The ravine was up ahead, and the bridge. K thought of racing to catch up with Lanik. The bridge had no railing. One solid push would send Lanik over. The fall was twenty feet, enough to kill him if he landed just right.

But the body would end up at the bottom of the ravine. And it would stay there; K couldn't very well haul it out. And eventually someone would find it.

A fall would only work if it looked like an accident: Simon Lanik murders Jana Fletcher, then slips off a bridge accidentally.

No one would believe it.

Lanik needed to disappear. There could be no body left behind.

Up ahead, Lanik reached the bridge. The man made no effort to move quietly. K heard Lanik's boots clomping over the wooden planks.

He waited for the tan coat to get lost among the trees on the other side, then crossed the bridge one careful step at a time.

When K reached solid ground again, he started to pick up the pace. A light rain began to fall. He felt its touch against his cheek. He rounded a bend in the path. Looked around, trying to catch sight of Lanik. He saw nothing but trees and shadows.

Before long he would come to the end of the trail. It might be wise to break off the pursuit. He hadn't forgotten that Lanik might have a gun.

Still, he was reluctant to let Lanik go.

K's car was parked on Clinton Drive. He assumed that Lanik would have one too. Did it make sense to try to keep following the man?

Suppose they wound up on a lonely road somewhere. A road with sharp curves. That might be something K could work with, especially if the rain kept falling. Simon Lanik murders Jana Fletcher, then dies in a car wreck. Would that be plausible?

It might be worth trying. K jogged along the path. He felt a current of night wind. He had let Lanik get too far ahead. The path twisted among dead beech trees. K came to the trailhead by the ball field in Cypress Park. He stopped at the wood's edge. Saw his car in the distance. He spotted another—a sports coupe with a spoiler on the back—that could have belonged to Lanik. K couldn't tell if there was anyone inside.

He waited for the lights of the coupe to come on, for the vehicle to pull away. Nothing happened. Could Lanik have left on foot? There was no sign of him on the street. Was it possible that K had gotten ahead of him—had passed him in the woods without realizing it?

K listened to the rain. It was falling more steadily. He heard a subtle change in its sound. He turned very slowly, knowing what he would see—and there stood Simon Lanik in his tan coat. Lanik had his left arm extended and a gun in his fist, inches from K's face. The rain pattered his sleeve.

Lanik said, "You are not as quiet as you think, my friend."

K stared at the muzzle of the gun and felt afraid. "Oh god," he cried. "Don't shoot me."

He could hear the panic in his tone. It sounded quite authentic. But part of him felt calm; part of him was observing and calculating. He could get through this if he handled it right. The panicked voice was good, he thought. Let's have more of that.

"Please," he said. "I've got money in my wallet. Take it. Whatever you want."

Lanik stood impassive in the rain. "Who are you? Why were you following me?"

"Following? I wasn't, I swear." That's good, K thought. More. "I'm looking for my dog," he said, the lie coming easily. "My wife brings him to the park sometimes and lets him off the leash. She brought him today, and he ran off—"

"So you look for him now," said Lanik. "At night. In the rain."

"I swear."

"With binoculars."

K had his arms spread at his sides, to show that he was harmless. He had the binoculars in his right hand. He glanced at them as if he had forgotten them.

"I found these in the woods," he said. "Someone must have dropped them. Look, the strap is broken."

Simon Lanik held his gun steady. "I don't think you found them. I think maybe you were spying on me."

K dialed up the panic in his voice. "Spying? Why would I? I don't even know you."

"Maybe you spy on other people too. Maybe you are *zvrhlík*. A pervert. You look at girls through their windows at night. Yes?"

"No. That's not true. My dog—"

Lanik inched forward. The muzzle of the gun hovered in front of K's forehead. "Maybe it is not enough to look," Lanik said. "Maybe you kill them too."

"Jesus, no—"

Lanik moved the muzzle down and pressed it against K's cheek. "Maybe you looked in Jana Fletcher's window. You know who I'm talking about. The girl who died."

K let the panic drain from his voice until there was nothing left but anguish. "No. I'm just trying to find my dog. I swear."

What happened next gave K hope. Lanik dragged the muzzle of the gun across his cheek, but he didn't pull the trigger. K watched

Lanik's face. He could almost see the man thinking. Lanik didn't believe the story about the dog. That was plain. It was also plain to K that Lanik wanted to shoot him—but was afraid to do it, because someone might hear. There were houses across the street from the park. So Lanik wouldn't shoot. But he wouldn't let K go either.

Lanik made a decision: he moved the gun away from K's cheek. Time slowed and K knew what would come next. Lanik would take his finger off the trigger and adjust his grip on the pistol. He would draw it back and use the butt to hit K hard on the temple, to knock him out. After that, if he wanted, he would be able to finish K off quietly.

K was unafraid. Once Lanik took his finger off the trigger, the gun would be nothing but a blunt instrument. And K had a blunt instrument of his own.

It was happening. K saw it all with an unnatural clarity. Rain on the sleeve of Lanik's coat, and the man's finger moving outside the trigger guard, his arm drawing back. K tightened his hold on the binoculars and swung them up under Lanik's chin.

They found their mark and Lanik's head snapped back. He groaned. His finger fumbled for the trigger of the pistol but he was too slow. K slammed the binoculars against his wrist and the gun dropped to the ground. Lanik took a step backward, but before he had a chance to recover, K charged in and swept the binoculars across his face. The blow connected with the side of Lanik's nose, and K heard the sound of cartilage cracking.

From there something primal took over. Lanik stumbled—K remembered that. He remembered the rain going silent and the dark wood turning to inky black. The blackness went on for a long time. When it passed, K was kneeling on the ground. His muscles ached. His fingers were tangled in Lanik's greasy hair. He was pushing the man's face into a pile of wet leaves.

The rain had soaked through the back of K's shirt. He let go of Lanik's hair. Lanik didn't move. The binoculars lay on the ground nearby. K picked them up and realized they were slick with blood.

He got to his feet and turned in a dazed circle. Saw Lanik's gun lying at the base of a tree. He reached for it. It felt solid in his hand, and light. He slipped it into his pocket.

He stood over Lanik's body and thought: You shouldn't leave him here. You should take him away. Hide him.

He stepped to the edge of the woods and looked out. At the lights glowing in the windows of the houses across the street. How many people were still awake? How many potential witnesses? There was his car, on the other side of the park. If he wanted to take Lanik's body, he would have to drag it all the way across the ball field. Without anyone seeing.

He knew better than to try.

He checked Lanik's pulse before he left. The man was dead. Call it a win, K thought. He spent a minute going through Lanik's pockets. Nothing of any value except a wallet. K took it.

A cold wind followed him across the field to his car. He tossed the binoculars on the passenger seat, started the engine. He switched on the wipers and sat with his hands on the steering wheel. A shiver ran through him. He thought about the rain. He could make it stop, if he really wanted to. All he had to do was concentrate.

He turned the car's heater on as he pulled away—heading south, toward home. He let the rain fall.

27

After my talk with Simon Lanik, as I watched him disappear into the woods, I thought about dialing 911. He was a murder suspect, after all. A solid citizen would have made the call. But I think it would have felt like a betrayal. Not because I cared so much about Simon, but because I thought I owed something to his grandmother, who had given me a place to live.

So I left my phone in my pocket. I stayed outside, looking up at the clouds and the moon behind them. Even after I felt the first of the rain, I didn't go in. I was listening to the crickets and thinking about Jana.

My clothes were wet through by the time I went inside. I got out of them and took a warm shower and went to bed.

The next morning, when I heard about Lanik's death, I wondered what might have happened if I'd done things differently—if I'd made that call to the police. I wondered if it could have saved him.

———————

It was a jogger who discovered Lanik's body, a man who lived on Clinton Drive and regularly ran through the woods next to Cypress Park. He found Simon around seven a.m., long after the weather had cleared.

The local news outlets got wind of the story shortly after the police were called to the scene. I heard about it first on the radio Jana kept in the kitchen, and that sent me looking for the spare TV I'd brought over from the old apartment. I found it and set it up on the kitchen counter, and soon I was watching reports shot from the basketball court in the park—which was as close as the TV crews were able to get to the body.

By ten a.m. there was a news van on the street outside and I was looking at live video of the duplex—as a backdrop for a correspondent with a microphone. The news people knocked on Agnes Lanik's door and she ignored them, and they came over and knocked on mine and I did the same.

Frank Moretti turned up around eleven, and the correspondent shouted a question at him as he went by. He didn't say anything. Agnes let him in and he spent an hour with her, and when he left he went by the back way and came onto my patio. I saw him through the window in the back door. He waved.

"That woman makes me tired," he said as I let him in.

"Have a seat then," I said. "Do you want coffee? It's already brewed."

He nodded and I poured him a cup and refreshed my own. He didn't sit down right away. He went over and looked at my boots by the front door.

I put out cream and sugar and switched off the TV. Both of us settled in at the table.

"I know she speaks English," Moretti said. "But if she doesn't like the question, she'll pretend to be confused. She'll rattle on in Czech. I got her to admit that her grandson visited her last night. But I still don't know where he was staying for the last week and a half, or who might have been helping him. We found his car on Clinton Drive near the park. For all I know, he's been leaving it there every night and coming here to sleep. Do you have any insight on that?"

I stirred my coffee. "I'm afraid not."

He frowned. "Are you going to start talking Czech to me?"

I thought it over and said, "I saw Simon last night as he was leaving—around eleven-thirty. We talked. He might have come here other times, but I don't know."

"What did you talk about?"

"He told me he didn't kill Jana Fletcher."

"Naturally."

"I tried to persuade him to turn himself in. Sort things out."

"That was good of you," Moretti said dryly. "To try persuasion."

"There wasn't much else I could do," I said. "He had a gun."

"Really?"

"He claimed he did. I didn't see it. Did you find a gun on his body?"

Moretti tasted his coffee without taking his eyes off me. "Maybe you could let me ask another question," he said, "before we get to yours. Did you go into the woods last night?"

"No," I said. "But you already knew that. You've inspected my boots."

Moretti shrugged. "You might've worn a different pair."

"Do I need to call my lawyer?"

"If you do, I might start to think you're guilty." He took a moment to rub his eyes. "As it happens, Agnes backs you up. She watched you talking to her grandson last night, and she says you stayed out on the lawn afterward. You didn't follow him into the woods. That was the one useful piece of information I got from her. She says you were out there for ten or fifteen minutes after Simon left. You stayed out even after the rain started. She thought it was odd."

"It probably was," I said.

"Why did you do it?"

"I guess the rain felt good."

Moretti turned quiet for a moment. Then he asked, "How convinced are you that Lanik had a gun?"

"I can't be sure," I said. "But I think he did. He said it was Russian. A Makarov. Ask Agnes. Maybe she can tell you."

"I don't expect her to tell me anything," he said, tapping a finger against his coffee cup. "We didn't find a gun. And if he had one, you have to wonder why he didn't use it to defend himself."

"Maybe he never got a chance."

"Maybe. It's also possible there was no gun." Moretti hesitated, then decided to share something with me. "All we really know so far is that someone beat him to death—using a fairly heavy object. Whatever it was, the attacker took it away with him. He took Lanik's wallet too. So it could've been a robbery that went too far."

"A robbery?"

"Sure. There've been a dozen robberies and assaults in or around Cypress Park over the past year. And those are only the ones that got reported. It's not a place you want to hang around at night."

I studied Moretti's face, trying to tell if he was serious. "You don't really believe that, do you? That Simon Lanik ran into a robber in the woods?"

"What's your alternative?" he asked. "What should I believe?"

"What if someone was looking for him," I said, "waiting in the woods, watching his grandmother's house?"

"And who would that be?"

"Whoever killed Jana Fletcher."

Moretti let out an impatient breath. "You know my view about that—Simon Lanik killed Jana Fletcher."

"I know that's your theory. I think you need to reconsider it."

He planted his elbows on the table. "You need to give me a reason. You want me to believe that some unknown person killed Jana, and the same person was hiding in the woods last night, hoping for a chance to kill Simon Lanik. What's his motive?"

"He's been watching the news," I said. "He knows Lanik is your suspect. If Lanik's dead, you're less likely to keep working on Jana's case. The real killer can stop worrying."

"If that's what he wanted, he could've done nothing. I would've gone on suspecting Lanik, and he would be in the clear."

"Maybe he's impatient. Maybe he doesn't have much self-control."

"You're making up a story about him," Moretti said. "That's fine, but I can't just make things up. I need evidence."

He was right. "What about footprints?" I said. "If someone was watching the house, he would have seen Lanik here and then followed him through the woods. There'd be a trail."

Moretti nodded. "There would be. Ideally. I'll tell you about the footprints we found. There are three recent sets of prints crossing the baseball field in the park. They show up clearest in the dirt of the infield. There's one set leading toward the woods that belongs to Simon Lanik. Another set belongs to the jogger who found the body. The third probably belongs to the killer. His prints lead toward the woods and then away from them again."

He paused to sip his coffee. "Once you get into the woods, things are different. The ground there is covered in layers of old leaves. It's just about impossible to make out distinct footprints. I doubt if we'll be able to tell for sure if someone was following Lanik."

Another pause. Moretti let out a long breath. "To be honest," he said, "if I thought someone followed Lanik, I'd be inclined to think it was you. But Agnes gives you an alibi. It should have taken Lanik about ten minutes to walk through the woods, and you were in the backyard all that time. Apart from that, I've got the third set of footprints in the baseball field. I know they're not yours—they're not the right size. So you didn't kill him."

"No, I didn't."

"Which means I need to find another explanation," Moretti said. "And it seems to me the likeliest one might be the one I've been suggesting: Lanik ran into someone who was lurking around the park— someone who tried to rob him and wound up killing him."

I shook my head. "I don't believe it."

"You don't have to. But it fits the evidence I have right now."

"I don't believe that Simon Lanik killed Jana either."

Moretti showed me his palms. "We could argue about that as much as you like," he said. "But the fact remains that Lanik knew Jana, and he had a history of preying on women. I can't reject him as a suspect in her murder just because you have a different theory."

He looked sincere, I thought. A careworn cop in a dark gray suit. Those tired eyes, steady on mine. But I couldn't be sure of him. And after all, that was the question: whether Frank Moretti was sincere.

"It's more than a theory," I said. "It's a fact that Jana was trying to exonerate Gary Dean Pruett—trying to prove he didn't kill his wife. Which means that whoever did kill her would have a reason to want to silence Jana. You know all about the Pruett case. You were the lead detective."

I half expected a denial. I didn't get one.

"Yes, I was," Moretti said.

"You never told me that," I said. "I had to find out from Gary Pruett."

He looked unfazed. "I think we've been over this, Mr. Malone. I don't answer to you."

"Pruett told me something else. He said Jana intended to talk to you about the case. Did she?"

"Yes, she did. I talked to her back in March."

"So you knew from the start that there could be a connection between Jana's murder and Cathy Pruett's."

"The only way there's a connection is if Cathy Pruett's murderer is running around free," Moretti said patiently. "I happen to know he's in a cell in Dannemora."

"What if he's not? What if Gary Pruett is innocent?"

"He's guilty. That's what I told Jana Fletcher, and that's what I'm telling you."

"And if you're wrong?"

"I'm not wrong. But why don't you go ahead and tell me who you think I should be looking for."

I traced the rim of my coffee cup. "Let me ask you something first. Jana had a file of notes on the Pruett case. I saw it in her desk before she died, but now it's gone. Did you take it?"

"No, I didn't take any files."

"Then her killer must've taken it."

"I can think of other possibilities," Moretti said. "She moved it. She threw it away."

"Let me ask you something else. When you talked to her in March, did she mention Luke and Eli Daw?"

He showed me an indulgent smile, as if he'd been waiting for me to bring up the Daws. "Yes," he said. "Jana thought they might have killed Cathy Pruett. She got the idea from Gary Pruett."

"And what did you tell her?"

"I told her Gary Pruett is bound to try to sell that idea to anyone who'll listen. He tried to sell it to his lawyer, who tried to sell it to me. I didn't buy it."

"Why not?"

"Because there's nothing to connect the Daws to Cathy Pruett, other than the fact that they were once students at her high school. Forget about the Daws."

"I can't," I said. "I think Luke Daw killed Jana. You asked me who you should be looking for. That's my answer."

"Well, unfortunately, he's long gone."

"Maybe not," I said. "Maybe he was in the woods last night."

Moretti pushed his chair back from the table and stood. I did the same. I watched him rub his brow as if it ached. Heard him sigh.

"Luke Daw hasn't been seen for a year and a half, not since he shot his cousin Eli," he said. "But you want me to believe that he killed Jana Fletcher, and Jolene Halliwell, and Simon Lanik. Why should I?"

I thought of the wooden cube on the fireplace mantel. "Popsicle sticks," I said.

"Oh, for god's sake," said Moretti. "Don't start in again about popsicle sticks."

"When Luke shot his cousin and disappeared—that was your case too. You investigated. So you must've gone into Luke's trailer. You must've seen his models. So when I told you I found a popsicle stick in the woods, you must've thought of Luke Daw."

"No, I didn't."

"Not even for a moment?"

"Maybe for a moment," Moretti said. "And then it occurred to me that there might've been a child in the woods with a popsicle. Look, you need to think about whether you're taking this too far. You're living in a dead girl's apartment, and apparently you've been talking to convicts and snooping around trailers and who knows what else. Maybe I can't stop you, but I don't have to follow your lead. You're not going to convince me that Luke Daw was involved in Jana Fletcher's death, because there's no reason to think he was anywhere near her on the day she died. Never mind killing her—there's no reason to think he ever heard of her."

28

Jana Fletcher and Luke Daw lay naked under the stars.

Jana tried to take in everything: the texture of the woolen blanket underneath them, the heat coming off Luke's body, the clean smell of the night air. Other smells too: the old timber of the barn, her own sweat, Luke's sweat. And something lingering, a memory of the smell of cows—inoffensive, because the cows had been gone for a very long time.

There were other animals here, though: birds in the high rafters. Jana could hear them up there, hopping along the wooden beams. The bare beams were all that was left of the barn's roof. A pair of birds took wing and Jana watched them fly away. Watched their silhouettes against the background of the stars.

"What kind of birds are those?" she asked Luke.

"*Corvus brachyrhynchos,*" he said.

"In English."

"Crows," he said. "There are swallows up there too, but the swallows are way smaller."

Jana focused on a star that looked brighter than the ones around it.

"They're bad omens," she said.

"Swallows?"

"Crows, genius."

"That's a myth," Luke said. "I read somewhere that they're kind. They'll feed their parents, when their parents get old and weak."

"They remember who their parents are?"

"Sure. They're smart. They're supposed to be able to remember human faces. They can recognize someone they've met before."

Something passed over the empty framework of the roof—maybe one of the crows, maybe a different bird altogether. Jana lost track of the bright star, then found it again.

She pointed at it. "Is that anything?"

"Which one?" said Luke.

"The bright one."

He tipped his head against her shoulder, looked up along the length of her arm. "It might be part of Sagittarius."

"You think so?"

"Do you see a teapot?" he said. "Sagittarius is supposed to look like a teapot."

"I thought it was supposed to be an archer."

"It's a centaur with a bow, but the middle part is like a teapot."

Jana tried to see a teapot, or a centaur, or a bow.

"I don't think that's Sagittarius," she said.

She brought her arm down, and Luke's hand found hers. A breeze passed through the barn, cool on her skin.

Luke squeezed her hand. "See?" he said. "This is good."

She closed her eyes. "It is."

"We could be happy like this, couldn't we?"

"We could."

He shifted beside her, getting comfortable. "You were wrong about me. You didn't like me at first."

She remembered the night they met, at the rest stop on the Thruway. "I liked you a lot at first," she said. "I didn't like you at second."

He laughed. A low, gentle sound. It trailed off and he breathed deep, let the breath out in a yawn. Jana opened her eyes and gazed at the stars. Not at one in particular, but at the whole field of them. She saw a red dot pass among them, blinking. A plane flying high.

Luke's breath fell into a steady rhythm. Jana listened to it, and the plane flew out of sight. She slipped her hand free of his, sat up slowly on the blanket, got to her feet.

She stepped around him and found her clothes piled on the ground, bra and underwear on top. She put them on, then put on her shirt and jeans. Luke's clothes made their own pile—topped off with something metal and black in the starlight. A thirty-eight revolver.

As she buttoned her jeans she realized that Luke was lying on his side, watching her.

"What are you doing?" he said.

She smiled at him in the dark. "Thought I might go for a walk."

"What if I don't want you to go?"

"Then I'll stay here."

He pushed himself up, sat cross-legged on the blanket. "Where would you go, if you went for a walk?"

"Timbuktu."

"That's a long way."

"Down to the pond then, for a start."

He leaned back, bracing his weight on his arms. "You're very smooth."

"Smooth?"

"Calm."

"That's me," she said. "Smooth and calm."

"Are you pretending you don't see it?"

"See what?"

He nodded toward his clothes and the revolver. "The gun," he said.

"I see the gun, Luke."

"You're not going to pick it up?"

"Do you want me to pick it up?"

"I want you to do what a person would do."

Jana bent down and picked up the gun. "Will you come with me to the pond?" she said.

"Forget about the pond," said Luke. "The pond's not what you want."

"What do I want?"

"I don't know. Do you want my car keys? They're in my pants."

"Are you giving me your car keys?"

"You can take them," he said. "You've got the gun."

She aimed the gun at him. "Is that what I should do, take your keys?"

"That would be the sensible thing."

"And then what? Shoot you?"

"I'd say shoot first, then take the keys."

She pulled back the hammer of the revolver. "Is that what you think of me? Don't you know me at all?"

"I have a pretty good idea," he said.

"Apparently, you don't."

She turned the gun up suddenly and held it under her chin, the steel cold against her neck. She pulled the trigger and heard the click of the hammer falling on an empty chamber.

"Jana—"

She worked the hammer with her thumb again, and the trigger with her finger. Five more times, with Luke saying "Stop it!" all the while. When she had gone through every chamber, she dropped the gun on the ground between them.

He was on his feet now, pulling on his clothes.

"That was dumb," he said, his voice heated. "You should never do that. You should always assume a gun is loaded."

She turned her back on him. "Stop screwing around," she told him. "If you don't trust me by now, you might as well shoot me in the head."

He was quiet behind her, but she imagined him buttoning his shirt, picking up the revolver. She heard mechanical sounds that might have been the cylinder opening and then closing again. He might have put a round in the chamber. She waited for him to press the muzzle against the back of her skull.

He didn't. He came up behind her and put an arm around her waist, the other around her chest. "I'm sorry," he said.

June 7, 1996

Jana left the service plaza smiling, thinking about Luke the drummer with his orange T-shirt, and his idiot friend who played a mean bass. She motored east on the Thruway in her grandmother's LeSabre—stale smoke and perfume—and when she reached Syracuse she headed south on I-81.

She had the name of a bar in Binghamton scribbled in the margin of her road map: Dino's on Conklin Street. Luke and his band would be there tomorrow night. She had seventy-five miles between Syracuse and Binghamton to make up her mind. The band might be awful and Luke might be boring, and then she would have wasted a day. Or the band might be brilliant and Luke might be irresistible, and she might get tangled up with a drummer and never make it to New York City.

She reached Binghamton and kept on driving, with a small twinge of regret. There would be other musicians in New York.

She crossed the border into Pennsylvania, moved into the left lane to pass a line of semi trucks. The wind whipped through the window beside her. She had a Melissa Etheridge album cranked up loud in the LeSabre's cassette deck.

A short time after midnight she decided to take a break. She got off the interstate at a town called Harford and pulled into an Exxon station. The lone attendant was missing one of his front teeth and most of his hair. He was listening to a rock station on a boom box radio.

The ladies' room was hidden in a far corner, behind stacked cases of soda and racks of potato chips. Jana found it surprisingly clean, though there were no paper towels.

She came out drying her hands on her jeans. The attendant didn't see her; he had his nose in a hunting magazine. A Tom Petty song played on the radio: "You and I Will Meet Again."

When she walked out the front door, she saw a white panel van parked next to the LeSabre. She went around the front of the van with her keys out and there was Luke Daw leaning against her car, wearing his easy smile.

"I know this seems weird," he said, "but I can explain."

And then there were two Janas: one who agreed that this seemed weird; he shouldn't be here; he should be back in Binghamton; maybe his gig got canceled. And another, half a step behind, who thought: He followed you. He's a crazy guy with a van.

Jana backed away. She should have screamed. The attendant would have heard her. He would have been a witness. She meant to scream, but she backed into something solid and a hand went over her mouth. Not Luke's hand—the idiot friend's. He had come up behind her.

Later on, she would remember the sensation of trying to twist away from him, trying to stab her keys into his thigh. She would remember the sound of the gas station radio—a fresh Tom Petty song, "Kings Highway."

Music for an abduction.

She watched Luke slide open the side door of the van. The two of them forced her in. The door slammed shut. No more music, just the weight of Luke Daw on top of her and his voice saying, "Don't worry. This won't be as bad as you think."

Ninety-two days—from June seventh to September sixth—that's how long she spent with the Daws. She passed the first few hours lying in the back of the van, her ankles bound together, hands cuffed behind her, a rag stuffed in her mouth and tied in place with a bandanna.

They drove north to Binghamton, retracing her route in reverse. Then they left I-81 and followed Route 12 for a hundred miles, all the way to the city of Rome. Not that Jana knew that at the time. She didn't know the destination or how long it took to get there. It seemed to take forever.

She was alone with Luke in the van. The idiot friend had gone off with her keys. She assumed he must be following them in her grandmother's car.

Luke drove in silence at first, then switched on the radio and flipped through the stations. Jana tried to get his attention, but the rag in her mouth turned everything she said into gibberish. She tried faking an attack—breathing hard and shaking as if she were having a seizure. Luke glanced back at her through the space between the seats, then returned his eyes to the road. "Knock it off," he said.

She kept it up, but only for a little while. She was afraid she might start to hyperventilate for real. She lay with her cheek pressed against the carpeted floor of the van and focused on breathing calmly through her nose. Luke gave up on the radio and started to hum. He seemed full of nervous energy. He retrieved a drumstick from the dash and tapped out a complex rhythm on the seat beside him.

By the end of the trip he had tossed the stick aside and seemed to have retreated into himself. He didn't say anything when he pulled the van off the road and killed the engine. He came around and opened the side door and showed Jana a knife and a revolver. He used the knife to cut the cord that bound her ankles, then folded it and put it away. The handcuffs stayed in place. He dragged her out and stood her up against the side of the van.

She saw trees and a night sky and an overgrown lane running off into the dark. Luke had parked the van behind a trailer, but the road was there on the other side, not so far away. No sign of the idiot friend.

She lifted her chin defiantly. Said, "Take off the gag." It came out muffled, but he got the gist. He tucked the gun away behind his back, turned her around, picked at the knot in the bandanna until it came free. He turned her again and pulled the rag from her mouth.

She spat out the taste of it. "I have asthma," she said. "You put that in again, you could kill me."

Luke shot her a skeptical look, opened the van's passenger door, and took out her handbag. He dumped the contents on the ground and nudged them with the toe of his shoe.

"I don't see an inhaler," he said, laying a hand on her throat and pushing her back against the van. "You don't have asthma. If you lie to me, we're not going to get along."

"You want the truth?" Jana said. "I don't like rags in my mouth."

"All right, we'll leave it out. But if you scream, I'll have to shoot you."

"That sounds fair," she said, and drove her knee up into his groin.

It didn't put him on the ground as she had hoped, but it knocked him back. It gave her a chance to break free and rush along the rear wall of the trailer, around the corner, toward the road. She saw headlights and ran out to meet them, yelling "Help me!" at the top of her voice. The headlights slowed, the car swerved to avoid her. She recognized it too late: her grandmother's LeSabre, with the idiot friend at the wheel.

She turned to run and Luke Daw caught her and dragged her out of the road. He hauled her back to the van and the idiot friend brought the LeSabre around and joined them. Luke stuffed the rag in her mouth again, tied the bandanna in place. They bound her legs and picked her up. Carried her along the lane that led away from the trailer and the road and any help she might hope to find.

A half-moon shone low in the sky. They passed the edge of a pond to the sound of bullfrogs croaking. The ground sloped up. Jana twisted her head from side to side. She saw a barn looming in the distance. She saw a farmhouse that had fallen in on itself.

She thought they would take her to the barn, but she was wrong. They took her underground.

29

July 1996

Y ou could bring me a puppy," Jana said.

"What kind?" said Luke Daw.

"A golden retriever. I always wanted one."

"That's a hunting dog."

"I wouldn't have to take it hunting," she said.

His dark eyes were studying her. Sometimes they seemed full of intelligence; sometimes they seemed empty. Right now she couldn't tell.

"A dog like that needs to be outdoors," Luke said. "I don't know if I'd want to keep one down here. It seems cruel."

"I wouldn't want you to do anything against your conscience."

"Let me think about it," he said. "What else?"

"Coffee," she told him.

"No coffee."

"Mocha with whipped cream."

"You're lively enough without coffee."

"Caramel macchiato."

"I could bring you ice cream."

"I'll take ice cream," she said, "but I still want coffee."

There were no chairs in her prison underground, so they were sitting on the floor—Jana in the middle of the room, Luke with his back against the door. He had brought a light with him: a battery-powered lantern that rested on the floor beside him.

Jana thought it must be nighttime, but she wasn't sure. She tended to lose track. Luke came down on his own schedule; she never knew when the door would open. Sometimes—like now—he came down just to talk, and they pretended they were civilized people, rather than a lunatic and his captive. They were a couple negotiating the terms of their living arrangement.

"I'd like Syrian food," she said.

"That's Middle Eastern."

"It's a kind of Middle Eastern."

"Shish kebobs?" he said. "Like that?"

"Something like that."

"I'll see what I can do."

"Or Ethiopian."

"That's, what, African?"

"Northern African."

"Aren't they always starving, the Ethiopians?"

"Not all of them," Jana said. "Some of them come here and open restaurants."

"What do they serve?"

"Chicken and lamb," she said. "Lentils. And a spongy kind of bread called *injera*."

"We don't have that around here. Sorry."

"Too bad," she said. "It's my favorite." It wasn't really. She'd had it once, in Montreal. You couldn't get it in Geneva.

"What else?" Luke said.

"Italian."

"I've given you Italian."

"You've given me cold pizza."

He sat there turning a popsicle stick over and over in the fingers of his right hand. Jana thought about what it would be like to break the stick in half and jam both halves into his eyes.

"Maybe you need to lower your expectations," he said.

"How low do you think they go?"

I t was the fifteenth of July—at least that's what Luke Daw told her when she asked. She had to accept his word; she hadn't seen the sky since the day they locked her underground.

The place where they kept her was a wooden box: twelve by twelve, with an eight-foot ceiling. Not quite a perfect cube. The walls were made of hundreds of pieces of two-by-four, each piece four feet long. The boards ran horizontally. They were screwed into studs behind the walls, or so she assumed. Two screws in each board. The floor and ceiling were made the same way.

There was a single door in the middle of one wall. It looked like it had been salvaged from an old building, maybe from the farmhouse she had seen the night they brought her here. She couldn't reach the door, because there was a chain around her ankle that limited her movement. The chain passed through the wall opposite the door, and the end of it must have been bolted to something on the other side.

They gave her blankets and a thin mattress to sleep on. They left her hands free most of the time. Not out of mercy, she was sure. Out of practicality. They wanted her to be able to feed herself and use the bathroom. The bathroom was a plastic bucket with a lid.

If it was the fifteenth, then Jana had been here for more than five weeks. She tried to decide if that felt right. She was reluctant to trust her own perception of time, because she spent so much of it alone in the dark. And because they were drugging her.

It started early on. The first time Luke Daw raped her, she fought back; she managed to land an elbow in his face and split his lip. It didn't matter. He still took what he wanted. But after that, they started putting something in her food. She felt groggy after she ate; she slept more than she thought she should; and even when she was awake, her mind didn't feel clear.

When she realized what they were doing, she went on a hunger strike. And when the grogginess continued, she decided they must be drugging the water they gave her. So she stopped drinking. They retaliated by taking away her clothes, her mattress, her blankets, the plastic bucket. They left her with nothing but the chain around her ankle.

She still didn't give in. Until Luke came down one day and held something up for her to see: her driver's license. "Will you eat?" he said. "Or should I go to this address and kill whoever I find there?"

I had a dog once," Luke Daw said.

Jana had let her mind wander, but now she focused on him: Luke and his popsicle stick.

"What kind?" she asked.

"Just a stray we took in. A mutt. He knew how to fetch, though. I didn't teach him. He already knew when he came to us. I miss him."

"What happened to him?"

Luke put the popsicle stick between his teeth. Took it out again. "He got old. Went blind. Got so he couldn't walk. We had to shoot him."

"That's terrible."

"I did it myself. My grandfather made me. I'd like to say he thought he was teaching me a lesson about personal responsibility. But mostly Grandpa was a prick."

Luke chewed on the popsicle stick for a while and added, "He used to lock me down here if I did something bad. Not actually in here," he said, waving the stick at the room. "I built this myself, after he died."

He had told her that before, as if he wanted to impress her. She would have liked to tell him what she thought of his creation, but she kept it inside. She wanted him to keep talking to her.

She discovered early on that he would bring her things if she asked. Soap and warm water to bathe with, towels, fresh clothes— her own clothes, from her grandmother's LeSabre. He took away her dirty clothes too, and brought them back clean.

She wondered what had happened to the car. He told her he had gotten rid of it. "No one's going to find it," he said.

He told her other things as well, bits and pieces about himself. His mother had left when he was young; his grandfather had raised him. His idiot friend was named Eli and was actually his cousin. The band was real, but it had broken up; there was never any gig in Binghamton. The white van belonged to Eli; Luke drove a Mustang.

"It's got a sunroof," he told her. "You'd like it."

"One of these days," she said, "you should take me for a ride."

"I wish."

If you wanted the essence of Luke Daw, it was right there, in that deadpan-earnest *I wish*. Full of regret. As if they were both victims of circumstance.

"What are you thinking?" Luke asked her.

A dangerous question, one she never answered truthfully.

"I'm thinking about coffee," she said.

"You're always thinking about coffee. You're obsessed."

"I wouldn't be if you brought me some."

He laid the popsicle stick on his knee and picked up a plastic bottle of water from beside the lantern. He'd brought one for her too— had set it down in front of her as soon as he came in.

She watched him take a long drink.

"Spring water," he said. "Much better for you than coffee."

He put the bottle down and took a card from his shirt pocket. "Before I forget," he said. "It's time to write home again, don't you think?"

He flipped the card through the air so it landed within her reach. A picture postcard with an image of the Statue of Liberty.

"Vague and upbeat," he said, tossing her a pen. "We don't want Mom to worry."

Jana wrote out the address first, then the message: *Everything's great here. Don't worry about me. I love you.* Vague and upbeat. No tricks or hidden meanings. The first time Luke made her write a postcard, she had tried to write something out-of-character. *Dear Mother*, she wrote, because she was never that formal. But Luke caught on to her right away. "I don't think so," he said, tearing up the card. "Let's go with 'Dear Mom.'"

So now, no tricks. She signed her name and tossed the pen back to him. Then the card. He read it and slipped it in his pocket.

He gathered up his water bottle and the popsicle stick and got to his feet. "I should go," he said. "I might come back to see you a little later, but maybe not. It's been a rough day. Eli's been nervous."

"Has he?"

"He never thought this would go on so long. He thinks maybe we should end it."

"Maybe that's not a bad idea."

"The ending he has in mind—you wouldn't like it."

"Oh."

Luke opened the door. "I told him it ends when it ends. We've never done this before. We're all feeling our way through this thing." He picked up the lantern. "He's not happy. But that's Eli. Skittish. Always needing to have his hand held. And I'm the one who has to hold it."

"That must be hard on you," Jana said.

No reaction in his face—his dark eyes didn't blink—but something happened. He dropped everything he was carrying—lantern, bottle, stick—and dove toward her. Pushed her over so the back of her head struck the floor hard. His hand squeezed her throat. She tried to breathe, heard the lantern rolling across the wooden boards, watched its light play crazily over the ceiling.

"Do you want to repeat what you just said?" he asked her. Mildly, softly.

She didn't try to speak, just shook her head no.

"Do you think I'm stupid?"

Another head shake.

"That's good. You're not smarter than me. I know what sarcasm is. All these little things you say, they're not going over my head. You should remember that."

She nodded. He removed his hand from her throat and helped her sit up. She looked away from him, trying to catch her breath. Felt her heart beating wildly. When she looked back, he was smiling.

"Oh my god," he said. "You should've seen your face. Were you really scared?"

She didn't trust her voice to answer.

"You were," he said, stroking her hair. "But you know I wouldn't really hurt you. When did I ever hurt you?"

He pressed his lips to her forehead and held them there, the way you might kiss a child. She shut her eyes and kept perfectly still until he drew away.

"We're okay, aren't we?" he said.

She whispered her reply. "Yes."

A fter he left, she sat in the dark unmoving, her back straight, trying to breathe slow and deep. She flashed back to the feeling of Luke Daw's fingers on her throat, and that set her off—a trembling in her shoulders that grew into a shudder that passed through her whole body. She cried with her face buried in her hands. She lay down on her side, her knees drawing up to her chest, the chain on her ankle skittering over the floorboards.

A long time later she retreated to the far wall, taking the water bottle he had given her. She twisted the cap to see if it would open hard or easy. If she had to break a seal, then he couldn't have tampered with it.

But she never had to break a seal; the bottles always opened easy. This one too. She drank a mouthful of water and it tasted fine, but there was never anything wrong with the taste. She replaced the cap and put the bottle aside, though she was still thirsty. She wanted to be awake if Luke returned.

She sat in the dark with the wall at her back and thought about the postcard. She wondered if he would really send it. To make it convincing, he would have to mail it from New York City; otherwise the postmark would be wrong.

She had never told him she was headed to New York, but he had her map with the route traced out. He wasn't stupid—that was true. He was shrewd. He figured things out. He knew her plan wasn't just to visit New York, because she had brought things along that a mere visitor wouldn't bring: her birth certificate, her Social Security card. So he knew that she had left home.

He knew about her mother too. His first threat had been a general one: to go to her address and kill whoever he found there. Since then, he had learned more: that Jana had been living with her mother, and that her mother would expect to hear from her. Hence the postcards.

When Luke first mentioned her mother, Jana assumed he had done some research. It would've been easy: there was a listing for Lydia Fletcher in the Geneva phone book with an address that matched the one on Jana's driver's license. But she learned that Luke had a different source of information.

"You told me about her," he said.

"No I didn't."

"Sure you did, the other night."

"What did I tell you?"

"Different things. Like how she wanted you to go to law school."

"I never told you that."

"Well, you were a little out of it," he said.

"'Out of it'?"

"You know, sleepy."

"Are you saying I talk in my sleep?"

"Not exactly. It happens when you're awake, but not all the way awake. Eli thinks you're having blackouts."

"Eli? Has it happened with him too?"

"Once or twice. He doesn't usually stick around for pillow talk. Not the way I do."

The idea of pillow talk with Luke Daw—or Eli—made Jana feel like she might throw up. She bowed her head, hoping the nausea would pass.

Luke misinterpreted the gesture. "Don't be embarrassed. It's not your fault. It has to be from the pills."

It was the first time he had acknowledged that they were drugging her. He wouldn't tell her any more—not about the pills or about what she might have said to him. The news that she was having blackouts devastated her, and yet it wasn't really news. The one thing she had known all along was that she couldn't remember everything that happened to her.

There were bruises on her body that she couldn't account for. There were times when she woke up alone in her prison, but knew that someone had been with her, someone had been inside her, and she didn't know who—didn't know which of them to blame, which to hate: Luke or Eli.

It was one more level of violation: not knowing.

Jana ran her fingers along the seam where the floor met the wall. She panicked when she didn't feel the thing she expected to feel, but a little farther on she found it: the quarter her mother had given her.

They had taken everything from her pockets when they brought her here, except for this one thing. Somehow they missed it. That first night, when they left her alone, she held on to it like a talisman and thought about her mother.

She never put it back in her pocket. She left it lying on the floor instead, out of the way, in the closest thing she had to a hiding place. Which turned out to be wise. Because not long after, Luke Daw took away the jeans she'd been wearing when they abducted her. He decided he liked her better in skirts. It made things easier for him.

Now, in the dark, Jana closed her hand around the coin. The one thing she had that they didn't know about.

She stood up and paced the room, as far as the chain would let her go. Not very far. The chain was wrapped around her ankle and secured with a heavy padlock that passed through two of the links. It was tight—not tight enough to cut off her circulation, but tight enough that she couldn't slip free. She had tried. She would have to find a way to break the lock, or the chain itself. Or she could go at it another way, from the other end.

The chain passed through the wall, between two boards. It had to be anchored to something on the other side. So she needed to break through the wall. Simple.

The place where the chain went through was low on the wall. Jana sat down in front of it and explored the surface with her fingertips. One board above the chain, one below. She focused on the one above. Found the two screws that secured it to the studs. Phillips-head screws. She needed a screwdriver. She had a quarter.

She fitted the quarter edgewise into the head of the screw. It wasn't a bad fit. It was a tantalizingly good fit, as a matter of fact. She tried turning it. Lefty loosey. She wasn't surprised when the screw didn't turn. She had tried it before.

There were hundreds of boards in the room, hundreds of screws. Luke Daw would have used a power tool to drive them all, a cordless screwdriver with a Phillips-head bit. What chance did Jana have with a quarter?

But she didn't need to take out every screw. She only needed two of them. Then she could remove one board and find out what was behind it. Maybe the chain was attached to a steel plate, and the plate was screwed to a wooden post back there. That would be, what, another four screws? Six screws, grand total. Could she remove that many, with a quarter?

One thing at a time. She fitted the quarter into the screwhead again, holding it with two thumbs and two fingers. When she turned it, the quarter slipped free. A good fit, but not good enough. The quarter had a rounded edge. A Phillips-head screwdriver came to a point.

Jana gathered the chain in her lap, singled out one of the links with her left hand. She used her right hand to rub the quarter against the link. The quarter was never going to be a screwdriver, but maybe she could put a point on it. It might take days, weeks, but what else did she have to do with her time?

Maybe it wouldn't work; maybe Luke would find the quarter. Maybe Jana would never be able to work the chain free of its anchor. Even if she did, she would still be in a prison. She didn't know how to get through the locked door. But she knew Luke Daw would keep coming through it. He would come to feed her and talk to her and use her. And if she could get the chain free, she would have surprise on her side, and a weapon.

One day she might wrap the chain around Luke Daw's neck.

30

ate Tuesday afternoon. The newspeople had come to the realization that Agnes Lanik wasn't likely to give them the tearful interview they wanted. They'd packed up and moved on. In their wake came a succession of elderly ladies, decked out in formal clothes and topped with hats or head scarves, who knocked on Agnes's door to drop off casseroles and offer their condolences for the death of her grandson.

I thought about sending Agnes flowers. Went as far as dialing a florist, but it seemed too impersonal. I got in the truck instead and drove to a garden center. Picked out a pot of begonias and another of impatiens. I brought them back and left them on her patio. I figured she could plant them in her garden if she wanted.

In the evening I set up my computer on Jana's desk. I had a business and I'd been neglecting it: canceling jobs, putting things off. I needed to get back to work. I started putting together a list of clients I needed to call, appointments I needed to reschedule.

At eleven o'clock I turned on the television and watched the opening of the local news—a long segment on Simon Lanik that included footage from a police press conference. Frank Moretti was there, but he stayed in the background. The chief of police took center stage—white-haired, stout, pleasant. He looked like someone's uncle.

A reporter asked him about the connection between Lanik and Jana Fletcher. The police had been seeking Lanik for questioning. Would it be fair to say that he had been their main suspect in Jana's murder? In light of his death, had the department changed its thinking? Was it possible that Jana's killer was still at large?

The police chief danced around the questions. The investigation of Jana's murder was ongoing. He couldn't comment on who was or wasn't a suspect. The department was still pursuing every possible avenue to uncover the identity of her killer. As for the Lanik investigation, it was in its very early stages. The chief was unwilling to prejudge the outcome. It remained to be seen whether, or in what way, the two cases might be connected. It might turn out that Lanik's death was unrelated to Jana's. There had been a series of assaults and property crimes in Cypress Park over the years. Lanik's murder might be part of that pattern.

It was Frank Moretti's theory: that Simon Lanik had been killed by someone trying to rob him. I wondered if Moretti really believed it. Maybe he wanted to believe it, because it would prevent him from having to question his assumptions about Jana's murder.

I switched off the TV and went back to my computer. Tried to focus on what I needed to do tomorrow. But the problem of Frank Moretti stayed on my mind. I got up and lit the tea-light candles on the mantel, four of them in a line. Cathy Pruett, Jana Fletcher, Jolene Halliwell, Simon Lanik. Luke Daw might have killed every one of them, or maybe I was chasing a phantom.

Cathy Pruett was the first to die. Frank Moretti insisted that her husband killed her. I tried to put aside the question of whether it was true, and asked myself instead if Moretti genuinely believed it. Suppose he did.

Suppose I'm Frank Moretti and I'm convinced that Gary Pruett killed his wife. The evidence in the case is weak, but maybe I can make it stronger. Pruett's in jail awaiting trial. I find another inmate—Napoleon Washburn—and convince him to make up a story. I get him to say that Pruett confessed.

Would Moretti do that? He had a reputation as an honest cop. Even Gary Pruett's lawyer couldn't find anything very bad to say about Frank Moretti. Just that he might get too close to certain crime victims.

If a man gets killed and leaves a pretty widow behind, Emily Beal had told me, *Moretti might take it on himself to comfort her.*

But in the Pruett case, the victim was a woman. There was no widow left behind. No pretty victim for Moretti to comfort.

Or was there?

Megan Pruett was left behind—Cathy's sister-in-law and best friend. What if Moretti tried to comfort her?

Megan Pruett never had any doubt about Gary Pruett's guilt. She would've wanted to see him sent to prison for life. Could she have persuaded Moretti to frame him?

I couldn't make myself believe it. She wasn't right for the role. Megan Pruett was a slightly snooty, late-thirties schoolteacher, not a temptress who could convince an honest cop to pin a false confession on a murder suspect.

I watched the four flames glowing on the mantel. Turned away from them and walked across the room. And remembered that there was another woman involved in the Pruett case—a victim of sorts: Gary Pruett's student, the eighteen-year-old girl he'd been seeing on the side.

Angela Reese.

Angela the artist. I had one of her paintings on the mantel. Everything on the mantel was a clue. She had given me a business card from the gallery that sold her work. The Woodmere Gallery. I found the card in my wallet.

The following afternoon, a few minutes after five, I parked my truck on the street behind the old courthouse downtown—the central station house for the Rome police, the place where Moretti had questioned me about Jana's death. I thought he must be inside; I could see his car in the lot.

I'd spent the morning on the phone talking to clients, mending fences. Setting up new appointments and rescheduling old ones. I had a home inspection scheduled for five-thirty, halfway across town. I should have been on my way already. Instead I was here.

Earlier in the afternoon I'd made a visit to the Woodmere Gallery, which occupied half a converted warehouse not far from the university. It had high, tin-plated ceilings and a lot of old ductwork and exposed brick. The owner was a bone-thin woman in her fifties, dressed in black, who might have given Megan Pruett a run for her money in the snootiness department. Her assistant was a slacker in his twenties who wore the same black but not as well. He had a sketchy goatee and smelled of cigarettes.

I talked to the owner first. She was happy to show me Angela Reese's paintings—she had seven on display and more in storage—but when I started asking questions, she shut down fast. She seemed to think the answers were none of my concern.

I left by the front entrance, drove around to the back, and waited. After thirty minutes or so, the slacker assistant came out for a cigarette break. I went over and told him what I wanted. He said he couldn't help me. I handed him twenty dollars. He still couldn't help me, but he said it with less conviction. I let him have another twenty and a ten, and he said he would give me his best effort but it was a delicate matter and he would need time. He promised to call me.

The call came at four forty-five. It lasted less than a minute. And now I was parked at the old courthouse, trying to decide if I should go in, wondering what I should say to Frank Moretti.

Before I could make up my mind, Moretti appeared at the back entrance of the courthouse. He walked to his car, the black Chevy sedan, moving at a fast clip, not his usual easy pace. I watched him get into the car and drive out of the lot.

He turned a corner out of sight and I had to make a decision. I followed him. I could have waited to see him another time, but I was curious about where he was going in such a hurry. He drove north, along the edge of Bellamy University, past the football stadium and a row of frat houses. College kids playing Frisbee on a lawn. He got onto Turin Road and followed it through residential neighborhoods, past the Knights of Columbus Hall. He drove by a 7-Eleven and a veterinary hospital, out toward Lake Delta.

We passed a bait shop and a canoe livery and suddenly I saw red and blue flashing lights in my rearview mirror. Heard the *whoop* of a patrol car's siren. I slowed. Up ahead, Moretti did the same. I turned off the road and into the horseshoe driveway of a day care center. The patrol car drew in behind me. I cut the truck's engine.

A young cop in uniform climbed out of the car, leaving the lights flashing. He took his sunglasses off as he walked up to my truck. I rolled down the window.

"License and registration," he said.

I had them ready.

"Do you know why I stopped you, sir?"

He didn't really expect an answer. I didn't say anything.

"You failed to signal your turn," he said.

"I've been on this road for miles," I said. "I haven't made any turns."

"You turned off just now."

"That was after I heard your siren."

"You should have signaled that turn, sir. Please step out of the vehicle."

Moretti's car pulled into the day care driveway.

"It doesn't have to go this way," I said. "If he wants to talk to me, I'm happy to talk."

"Step out of the vehicle. Now."

I stepped out of the vehicle. The young cop told me to place my hands on the hood of the truck. I did. He patted me down, cuffed my hands behind my back, walked me to the patrol car, put me in the backseat. Moretti watched it all from his black sedan.

The young cop went to talk to Moretti. I don't know what they had to talk about; I think they just wanted to let me stew. After a few minutes, Moretti came over and climbed into the patrol car beside me.

"It's insulting," he said.

He sat at ease in yet another gray suit, not looking at me, looking straight ahead, his palms resting on his thighs.

"It's bad enough you think you can follow me," he said. "But to do it in a red truck with your name plastered all over it—I find that insulting. It's as if you don't respect me."

"I respect you," I said. "I came to see you at the courthouse because I found something out today and I wanted to make sense of it. But I shouldn't have followed you."

"This thing you found out, does it have to do with Jana Fletcher?"

"Not directly."

"Am I going to like hearing about it?"

"Probably not."

"Well, that's fine," he said. "Let's have it."

"It's about the Pruett case."

"The Pruett case is over and done."

"It's about Angela Reese."

Moretti turned to me for the first time. Gave me a dead-eyed look.

"What about her?"

"She's an artist now," I said. "She does paintings. Some people might say they're not much to look at, but she sells them—through a gallery. She makes a little money, enough to get by. The first time I saw her work, I wondered who would want to buy it. But she gave me one of her canvases and it sort of grew on me. I can see the appeal."

"Make your point."

"Sorry. The point is, I got curious about who was buying Angela Reese's paintings. I found out the market's not very broad. Almost every painting she's sold has been bought by one person. An anonymous buyer. Who turns out to be you."

Moretti faced forward again, gazing into the distance. "That's why you wanted to see me?"

"Yes."

"To tell me I've been buying paintings?"

"To understand why."

"You think it has to mean something."

"Yes."

"Of course you do. So what do you think it means?"

"I don't know. But I have a theory."

"I don't doubt it," he said. "Even when you have nothing else, you have theories. Why don't you lay it out for me."

I tried to relax. Hard to do, with the handcuffs. "All right," I said. "You met Angela Reese when you were investigating Cathy Pruett's murder."

"That's true."

"Angela Reese has a certain quality. She's pretty, but it's more than that. She has a kind of wholesome beauty."

"That's a good word," Moretti said. "'Wholesome.'"

"And she's attracted to older men. She was having an affair with Gary Pruett."

"I think I see where this is leading."

"So you got involved with her," I said. "There's nothing wrong with it; she was eighteen. And she wanted to paint, so you decided to help her out."

"Like a sugar daddy."

"Like a patron of the arts."

"That sounds much better," Moretti said. "But let's hear the rest. You didn't follow me just to accuse me of having an affair with Angela Reese. There must be more."

"There is. But I'm not as sure of it."

"Don't let that stop you."

"All right. Napoleon Washburn—"

"Oh god," Moretti said in a defeated voice. "Please don't start with me about Napoleon Washburn."

"He lied about Gary Pruett's confession."

"So you claim."

"And I wondered if he lied on his own, or if someone put him up to it."

Moretti closed his eyes. I could see his shoulders tense. "You want to be very careful right now," he said.

"I *am* being careful. I didn't believe you would do something like that. But if you felt certain that Pruett killed his wife, you might be tempted to take a shortcut. And if you were sleeping with Angela Reese, you'd have a whole other motive. By sending Gary Pruett to prison, you'd be getting rid of a rival."

Silence in the car. Outside, the uniformed cop was strolling along the curve of the driveway with his hands on his hips. Frank Moretti tipped his head back and sighed.

"What do I have to do?"

He said it to himself first, in the voice of a man who had come to the end of his rope. Then he opened his eyes and sat straight in his seat and directed the question to me. "What do I have to do to get you to stop playing detective?"

"You could tell me the truth," I said.

"I've tried that. I've tried patience. I've given you more of my time than you deserve. So what will it take? Violence? Do I have to break something to get your attention?"

His tone was calm and his eyes had their usual tired look, but I caught a hint of something harder underneath, something he had to work to keep under control.

"You have my attention," I said.

"I wonder if I really do. If I'd run into you when I was younger, I might've punched you in the kidney. Have you ever been punched in the kidney?"

"Not yet."

"It hurts. Sometimes you piss blood. I haven't punched anyone in the kidney in years." He looked through the window at the uniformed cop. "These young guys—they'd probably faint away at the thought of it. This one, Officer Tyler, is one of the best of the lot, but if you put him in a situation he hasn't read about in a book, he gets nervous. I asked him to pull you over for a broken taillight."

"My taillights aren't broken."

"I meant that he should break one. But of course he didn't. What did he tell you?"

"He said I failed to signal a turn."

"Heaven help us all," Moretti said. "I'm going to tell him to keep you here for another five minutes and then cut you loose. I don't care where you go, but if I see you following me again I'll get angry. And if I'm as corrupt as you seem to think I am, then you don't want to cross me. If I framed Gary Pruett, I can frame you. I can make a case that you killed Jana Fletcher, and Simon Lanik too. Understand?"

"Yes."

He reached for the door handle but he didn't leave. He had one last message to deliver.

"You asked for the truth," he said. "The truth is that Angela Reese is a sweet girl who got used by a creep who wound up murdering his wife. If Angela wants to be an artist, then I want her to be an artist. I plan to keep buying her paintings, and that's no one's business but my own. She doesn't need to know. You can spread any lies you want about me, to anyone you think will listen, but if you tell Angela what I've been doing, we really will have a problem. Things will get broken and things will bleed. You'll end up in a worse place than the back of a squad car."

31

Wednesday was a restless night.

Roger Tolliver called my cell phone around eight. I didn't answer. He left a voice mail message: *I heard from Frank Moretti. He urged me to get my client under control. I think you and I need to talk.*

At nine it occurred to me I'd had nothing to eat since lunch. I found a box of spaghetti in a cupboard, and a jar of sauce—things Jana had left behind. I heated the sauce on the stove, got some water boiling, dropped the pasta in. I timed it for ten minutes. Strained it in a colander, fixed a plate, ladled on some sauce. It looked fine; it smelled good. And it was nothing I wanted to eat.

At ten I decided it couldn't hurt to go to bed early. At eleven I was still awake. I got up and took a shower, the water as hot as I could bear it. I walked into the living room, barefoot on the hardwood floor, toweling off.

I stepped on dried wax and it reminded me of the night Jana died. She had tried to use the two-by-four as a weapon against her killer.

The candleholder. Four tea-light candles had gone flying. One of them landed right side up; the others spilled their wax across the floor.

Another Wednesday night, two weeks ago.

I got on my knees and traced my fingers over the lines of wax. Someday someone would scrape them away, but it wouldn't be me.

I finished toweling off, got dressed, and went out onto the patio. The air was cool. I walked into the grass, looked back at Agnes Lanik's half of the duplex. She had the lights on in her kitchen. I could see the pots of flowers I'd left for her, still on her patio.

I walked toward the woods and saw a spark of pale red light in the distance. It hung glowing in the air for a second and flared out. Then another spark. Then two more, rising up like silent fireworks. I stood and watched the show, points of light appearing and disappearing. I heard a sound behind me: the clap of Agnes Lanik's screen door. She came out bundled in a shawl and picked her way through the grass like she was walking over a field of stones. She stopped a few feet from me and we watched the lights together.

"*Světlušky,*" she said.

Fireflies.

"I used to catch them in a jar when I was a boy," I told her.

"Simon too. Did you remember to punch holes in the lid?"

Her accent was especially thick. "Lid" sounded like "leed."

"Sure," I said.

"Sometimes Simon had to be reminded." She held the shawl close around her and shrugged her shoulders. A very European shrug.

"I'm sorry about what happened to him," I said.

Another shrug. This one meant that the world was a hard place. Agnes glanced back at her patio and added, as an afterthought, "The flowers are nice."

The lights slowed down and seemed to recede toward the woods. The day caught up to me and I felt tired. I yawned.

"Maybe you are thirsty," Agnes said, and I thought we had our signals crossed, as if a yawn meant something different where she came from.

She turned abruptly and began to walk back to the house.

"Come in if you want," she said. "Want" sounded like "vant."

Her kitchen was a mirror image of Jana's, with the same appliances and even the same table and chairs. The drink she offered me was a bitter liqueur called Becherovka. It tasted a little like cinnamon and a lot like mouthwash. She drank hers with ice and cut mine with a healthy dose of seltzer water.

She lit the oven as soon as we came in, and while I made peace with the Becherovka she filled a plate with some of the food her visitors had brought: roasted potatoes, pork goulash, sauerkraut, pierogi.

She warmed the plate in the oven and put it down in front of me. I picked at the food at first, then laid into it like a starving man, then made myself slow down again. Agnes tended to her kitchen, washing dishes, drying them, wiping off the counter. We didn't talk. I might have been playing a part: the traveler in a foreign land, lost on the road at night. She was the cottager who took me in and gave me a meal and sent me on my way.

I don't know what she wanted; maybe just companionship, something to ease the loss she was feeling. I think she would have been content to carry on in silence, but there were things I needed to say.

"Frank Moretti talked to you yesterday."

She was scrubbing the stove top now. She nodded without turning around.

"Did he tell you his theory about how Simon died—that it could have been a robbery that went too far?"

"He told me."

"I don't believe it," I said. "Do you?"

"No."

"That night, I spoke to Simon."

"This I know."

"He said he had a gun, but I never saw it. I wondered if he really had one."

She finished wiping the stove, dropped the rag in the sink. I watched her shuffle through the doorway to the living room and out of sight. She returned a minute later with a small black pistol, a semi-automatic. She put it on the table beside my empty plate.

"Viktor, my husband—this was his. And another just the same. Simon had the other."

I reached for the gun. Stopped myself. "Is it loaded?"

Agnes was sitting now, perched like a bird on the edge of her chair. She took a sip from her Becherovka, put the glass down carefully. Picked up the gun and thumbed a lever on the side to eject the clip. Her hands—skin and tendon and bone—moved with a slow grace. She put the clip aside, aimed the pistol at the floor, and pulled back the slide. A little round-headed bullet jumped from the chamber and skipped across the floor. She passed the gun to me.

I looked at the side of the barrel and saw some Cyrillic characters there, along with the more familiar Latin letters spelling out the name: MAKAROV. Just as Simon had claimed.

I remembered something else. "Simon told me his grandfather was involved in the black market, back in Czechoslovakia." I held up the gun. "Is this what he sold?"

She took another drink of Becherovka, shook her head. "You hear about the black market, you think of guns. Or drugs. But this was after the war. This was under the Communists. My Viktor sold food, clothes, transistor radios. That was the black market. Those were the things men hid in the shadows to sell each other. The things they killed each other for." She scowled and turned her withered face away from me.

"Simon didn't have his gun when they found him," I said. "Moretti's not convinced he ever had one—"

She cut me off with a wave of her hand. "Moretti is a policeman. He believes what he wants to believe."

She was half right, I thought. Moretti wanted to believe that Simon's death was a random crime. But he couldn't really believe it, I thought. He was too intelligent and too honest. It was frustrating, trying to understand him. I found myself telling Agnes Lanik about how I had followed him, about our conversation in the back of the patrol car. "I practically accused him of framing an innocent man," I told her. "But that's not what bothered him. He was worried that I might tell Angela Reese he'd been buying her paintings. And he was angry that I followed him. So that raises a question."

"What question?" she asked.

"Where was he going today? What's he hiding?"

The lines on Agnes Lanik's ancient face arranged themselves into a look of disapproval. She levered herself up from her chair and took her glass to the sink. She bent at the waist like a crooked tree falling slow and picked up the stray bullet from the floor. She brought it back to the table, eased herself into her seat again, and held her hand out for the gun. I gave it to her.

"You are a child," she said. "Simon was a child too. He believed in fantasies." She held the gun up between us. "My Viktor used to brag about his Makarov pistols. He said he took them from two Russian soldiers he killed in the war. Simon believed him. After his grandfather died, I told him the truth. My Viktor never killed any

Russians. He bought his pistols from a *zastavárna*. You would say a pawn store."

"A pawnshop."

"Yes. And they are not real Makarovs. They are false. Like false money. Counterfeit. Made in East Germany. I tell Simon this. He does not believe me. He would rather believe the fantasy. Like a child."

Agnes laid the gun down. "You are very foolish," she said. "This policeman, Moretti, he threatens you. He says he will make you bleed."

"That's true."

"But you want to know where he goes. So you will follow him again."

"I might."

"To learn his secret."

"Yes."

The lines of her disapproval deepened. "What secret do you think he has?"

"I don't know."

"Can he work magic, your Moretti? Can he bring back the dead?"

"No."

"Then what good are his secrets to you and me?"

32

Becherovka stays with you.

You drink it with a lot of rich Eastern European food, and it stays down, everything stays down, and it sends a thick fog through your brain and you drag yourself through the fog to your bed. But the next day, when you wake up around one in the afternoon, the Becherovka is still there, and it's not the way you remember it from the night before, soft and foggy. It's there pounding on your bedroom door, asking to see your papers, demanding to know what business you have in the Czech Republic. And when you finally throw off the covers and get up on your feet, it smiles a crooked smile and cracks you in the skull with the butt of its rifle.

Aspirin doesn't help. A shower doesn't help. Coffee doesn't help. More Becherovka might help, but I couldn't say for sure. I didn't have any more and I never wanted any more again. I wanted to bar the door and climb back into bed and sweat it out of my system.

Instead I made myself eat a bowl of cereal and checked my calendar. I had three home inspections listed for today. The first one I'd already slept through; the other two I could still make. But the prospect of crawling through attics and walking on rooftops in my current state was unappealing. I checked my bank balance and did some math and figured I was okay for now. I could afford to reschedule. I spent the next twenty minutes on the phone, making apologies.

My Becherovka headache hung on long into the afternoon. It followed me wherever I went in the apartment, so I decided to give it the slip. I went out driving.

I drove to the abandoned farm on Humaston Road, but I didn't stop there. I kept going and lost myself in a labyrinth of back roads. I didn't care where they were leading. I didn't care about the scenery. I tried to ignore the regiment of Czech soldiers marching through my head. I tried to let my mind wander, but it kept returning to one subject: Frank Moretti.

When I'd spoken to him the day before, I had more or less accused him of using Napoleon Washburn to frame Gary Pruett. His response had been enigmatic: neither an admission nor a denial. *You want to be very careful right now,* he'd said. A subtle warning, which had been followed by a more explicit one: that I should stop playing detective.

The more I thought about his reaction, the more I believed I must have hit a nerve.

Still, I had some doubt. Two things bothered me about the idea that Moretti had used Washburn to frame Pruett, one practical and one moral. The practical issue was something Pruett's lawyer had brought up when I talked to her. Moretti would have needed a way to contact Washburn, and there was no record of Moretti visiting Washburn in the county jail.

But how difficult would it have been to get around a little jailhouse record-keeping? Just yesterday Moretti had enlisted a young patrolman to pull me over for no reason. Wouldn't he have been able to persuade a guard at the jail to pass a message to an inmate? Or if he really wanted a face-to-face meeting, off the record, couldn't he have arranged one?

The moral issue was more complicated. I'd told Moretti yesterday that I respected him. It was true. So I had trouble accepting that he would ask Washburn to lie.

But maybe it wasn't so black and white.

As I drove in loops and circles along those back roads, I began to see how it could have gone. Moretti arrested Gary Pruett for murdering his wife. Suppose he believed Pruett was guilty but realized the evidence left something to be desired. So he reached out to Napoleon Washburn. He could have chosen some other inmate at the jail, but Washburn was being held in the cell next to Pruett's. More important, Washburn had been convicted of stealing a car and was about to be sentenced; he would have every reason to cooperate if it meant serving less time. These were things Moretti could have learned easily, assuming he had connections at the jail.

So he found a way to contact Poe Washburn. But did he ask Washburn to lie? Not necessarily. Maybe all Moretti wanted was for Washburn to try to get close to Gary Pruett, to get him talking about his wife, to see if he would confess. Maybe Washburn tried it that way; maybe he got nowhere. So he pretended. He made up a story about Pruett confessing.

By the time I worked all this out, I had doubled back to Humaston Road. I figured I'd done the best I could, if I wanted to go on respecting Frank Moretti. On some level the scenario I'd come up with made it easier to understand what I believed he had done. But I knew it didn't let him off the hook. If it was true, then he had never directly asked Washburn to lie—but he must have understood that he was giving Washburn a strong incentive to lie. There would be no reward for Washburn unless he said that Pruett confessed. Moretti knew that, and he must not have cared. Which meant he had a reason for not caring. I didn't know what the reason was. Not yet.

I drove by the farm again and then headed back into Rome, making my way to the south side of the city, to an unpaved street—to Poe Washburn's house with its cinder-block steps and shattered windows and burnt-out second floor. I had plenty of guesses, but I wanted to find Poe and get at the truth. This seemed like the place to start.

Someone had nailed a NO TRESPASSING sign to the front door. I walked around to the back, through a small yard bordered by scraggly hedges. At the rear of the house there were more cinder-block steps and a whitewashed door. Another NO TRESPASSING sign. The door was locked, but it was a simple spring lock, not a dead bolt. You could have opened it with a credit card. I used one of the blades of my Swiss Army knife.

When I swung the door inward and stepped inside, the smell hit me hard.

There's nothing like the smell of a house after a fire: it's not a clean, campfire smell; it's a chemical smell that worms its way deep into your lungs. I was in the kitchen where the fire never reached, but the smell was here, and a dampness too. The firemen had pumped water through the windows of the second floor, and the water had come through the ceiling. The drywall hung in shreds, and the wooden bones of the house showed through.

I stood in the spot where Poe Washburn had tackled me. He had come down the stairs through a cloud of gray smoke, he had seen me, and he had made a natural assumption: that someone had sent me to burn down his house.

Tell him I got the message, Washburn had said to me. *Tell him he doesn't have to worry. I'm not gonna talk.*

Tell who? I'd said. Because I didn't know at the time. But I thought I knew now: Frank Moretti.

I couldn't quite make myself believe that Moretti had been responsible for the fire. But I could see how Washburn might have thought so.

I moved from the kitchen to the living room, as far as the bottom of the stairs. The burnt-chemical smell was stronger there. I didn't try to go up.

I went down instead. I found a door off the kitchen that opened on a set of wooden steps leading to a basement. The air was cooler there and the smell fainter. A space had been cleared in the middle of the concrete floor, and someone had laid down cushions and spread a bedroll on top of them. There was a pillow on the bedroll and clothes hanging on a rack nearby.

Next to the rack was a wooden chair with three items on the seat: an open carton of cigarettes, an ashtray, and a flashlight. Beside the chair I saw a Styrofoam cooler. No ice inside, just two longneck bottles of beer and a few inches of tepid water.

All this could have been left behind by a squatter, an opportunist who found a way in, just as I had. But I didn't believe that for a minute. I thought it had to be Poe.

Cigarettes and beer and a place to sleep. All the comforts of home.

I left the basement and went out to my truck. Turned on the radio for company. The police were supposed to be looking for Poe Washburn, because he had assaulted me on the night of the fire. He seemed to have found a good hiding place—one where they wouldn't think to look for him.

I didn't care about the assault. I just wanted to talk to him. Maybe all I needed to do was wait. It looked as if he would be back. Otherwise, why would he have left anything behind?

I knew I could stay here and watch the house, but if he saw me parked out front, it might scare him off. More likely, he wouldn't approach the house from the front at all. If he was clever, he would park around the block and cut through the backyard. I might never see him.

The only way to be sure I didn't miss him would be to park my truck somewhere else and come back on foot. I would need to wait for him down in the basement. I might have to wait a long time, and there was no guarantee he would show. If he did, he'd be angry to find me in his house; I thought I could count on that.

There had to be a better approach. He wouldn't talk if he was angry, and I needed him to talk. I turned off the radio and sat in the truck under a sky of washed-out gray, and an idea occurred to me. It seemed like a long shot. I thought it might work, and then I thought it couldn't possibly work, and then my cell phone rang.

It was Roger Tolliver.

"You didn't return my call last night," he said.

I thought I heard an edge in his voice, but I could have been wrong.

"I meant to," I said.

"Detective Moretti told me you've been following him around."

"That was just one time."

"You probably shouldn't do that."

"I'm not following anyone right now," I said.

"That's good," said Tolliver. "Why don't you come see me. We can talk about all the things you probably shouldn't do."

"When?" I asked.

"The sooner the better."

"All right. I need to take care of something first. It won't take long."

"Is it dangerous?"

"No."

"Is it illegal?"

"I guess, if you want to be a stickler about it."

"If it's illegal, don't do it."

I reached for a pen lying on the truck's passenger seat.

"It's nothing," I said. "I just want to leave Poe Washburn a note."

33

"You left him a note," Roger Tolliver said, "on his pillow."

"I wanted to be sure he'd find it," I said.

We were sitting on Tolliver's deck with less than an hour to go until sunset. I'd given him an outline of everything I'd been doing: my dealings with Moretti and the other people I'd been talking to. People I probably should have left alone: Megan and Neil Pruett; Gary Pruett in Dannemora; Pruett's lawyer; Angela Reese; Wendy Daw. I saved Poe Washburn for last.

"What did the note say?" Tolliver asked.

"Just that I need to talk to him about Frank Moretti and Gary Pruett. I kept it short. I wrote it on the back of a business card."

Tolliver took a drink from a bottle of beer. He had offered me one and I had turned him down. The memory of Becherovka made me wary of anything alcoholic. The beer didn't seem to be doing Tolliver any good. He seemed uncomfortable. Anxious.

"You've ticked off Moretti," he said, "and now it seems like you're asking for trouble from Poe Washburn. Do you really think he'll call you?"

"He might. Or he might come to see me. I wrote my address on the card."

Tolliver frowned. "Why?"

"It's part of the message I'm sending him. We're two civilized people. I'm not chasing him; I'm asking him to come to me. I'm showing him respect."

Tolliver looked doubtful. He leaned forward in his chair, put his beer on the deck. His dog's leash was lying at his feet. Roger the dog had been running wild in the fenced-in dog run when I arrived. He was still there, but he had settled down. Now he lay gnawing on a rawhide bone.

I watched Tolliver pick up the leash—a long chain with a clip on one end and a loop of leather on the other. He slipped his fingers through the loop and wound some of the chain around his hand. The rest of it trailed over the wooden deck. My headache had mostly gone away, but the clink and rattle of the chain threatened to bring it back.

"Stop doing that," I said.

He glanced at me sharply, then started to unwind the leash.

"What's wrong with you?" I asked him.

"Nothing," he said, dropping the chain in a heap.

"You're restless. You don't look good."

He didn't. He had a sheen of sweat on his forehead. His clothes looked like he might have slept in them. I wondered if he'd been drinking more than the beer.

"I'm fine," he said.

"You're not."

"Okay, I'm worried," Tolliver said. "If you're right about Moretti, he could be dangerous. I'm not sure you've thought it through."

"I've thought it through."

"You think he framed Gary Pruett," Tolliver said. "Maybe Jana suspected the same thing. If Moretti knew that, he would've had a motive to kill her."

"It's possible. But I have a hard time seeing it."

"And if Moretti was afraid that Poe Washburn might tell the truth about Pruett, then he could've set the fire at Washburn's house."

"I don't know if that's his style," I said. "He could've found other ways to handle Poe. He could've threatened to punch him in the kidney."

Tolliver sat with his elbows braced on his thighs. He picked at a patch of dry skin on the palm of his left hand.

"You should stay away from Frank Moretti," he said. "You're not going to follow him again, are you?"

I looked at my watch. "It's too late in the day now."

"You're not taking this seriously."

"Yes I am. That's why I'm thinking about following him again. He warned me not to do it, Roger. Then he called you and told you to get me under control. I think he's afraid I'll learn something he doesn't want me to know."

"Just leave him alone," Tolliver said.

"I don't know if I can. I thought you'd be more sympathetic. I hoped you might lend me your car."

"Why?"

"Because I'm driving a truck with my name on it. I need something less conspicuous."

Tolliver stood up suddenly, shaking his head. "Absolutely not. If you're determined to play with fire, I can't stop you. But I won't help you. Someone has to act like a grown-up here. I should have done it a long time ago."

He went to the edge of the deck and looked out at the yard. Inside the chain-link fence, Roger the dog was on his feet now too.

"What do you mean?" I asked.

Tolliver turned back to me. "I mean if I had done the right thing, we wouldn't be in this situation. Jana should never have been working with me. She was only a first-year law student. But she was eager, so I made an exception. If I hadn't, she never would've taken that call from Poe Washburn; she never would've heard of the Pruett case. But she did, and she got caught up in it. I should have made her drop it. Then she might still be alive."

"Is that what this is about?" I said. "You're not responsible for what happened to her."

Tolliver came away from the edge of the deck and sat down again across from me. "I'm more responsible than you are," he said. "But look what you're doing. You're trying to fix what happened, even though you know it can't be fixed. And you're going to keep pushing until you get yourself killed. I'd like to prevent that."

He bowed his head and ran his hands over his curly hair. When he spoke again, there was a plea in his voice. "Look, I know what you're feeling. Jana was precious. She didn't deserve what happened to her. You think there ought to be something you can do for her, even now. But it's too late. She's gone."

He wouldn't meet my eyes. He picked up his beer bottle but he didn't drink. I thought he might be crying.

"Do you need a minute, Roger?" I said.

"No."

"Do you want to take a break, go wash your face?"

"No, I'm fine." His voice cracked. Definitely crying.

"How much longer then?" I said.

"What?"

"I just want to know if we're getting close."

"Close?"

"To the thing you want to tell me."

He wiped his face on his sleeve, looked up at me, cleared his throat.

"You don't want to hear it," he said.

"That's where you're wrong, Roger. There's nothing else I want to hear from you. But you need to clue me in. How big is it? You didn't kill her."

The idea stung him. "You know I didn't."

"All right. How bad could it be? You made a pass at her."

He sat back slowly in his chair. Held the bottle in his lap.

"How long have you known?" he asked.

"I didn't know until just now, when you told me how precious she was. But I've suspected for a long time, ever since you tried to blame her bruise on the dog."

He glanced at the dog run. We both did. Roger the dog was pawing the dirt at the base of the chain-link fence.

"He does play rough," Tolliver said.

"I know he does."

"And Jana played with him that day. Sunday, a week before she died."

It was ten days. I knew that as well as I knew anything at all. I let it pass.

"She had him playing fetch in the house," Tolliver said. "And he barreled into her once, knocked her down. But he didn't give her that bruise. Didn't hurt her. She just laughed and got up again. She had come here to discuss Gary Pruett and Napoleon Washburn, but we talked about other things too. About my kids. I've got a daughter and a son, seven and nine. They live with their mother in St. Louis. I only get to see them in the summer or on holidays. Jana wanted to hear all about them. I liked talking to her. I forgot who we were. Forgot she was my student."

He was looking down at his lap, telling his story to the bottle. "Time passed and Jana got up to leave," he said. "But she lingered and we kept talking, standing in the living room, the dog lying quiet on the floor. And Jana—you know how beautiful she was. And I kissed her.

"I had my hands on her, to pull her close to me, and it felt smooth, but it was probably clumsy as hell. It frightened her. I didn't expect that. She didn't just push me away; she ran. I think I had hold of her blouse; that's how she lost her buttons. And suddenly the dog was up and barking, and Jana running for the door. I followed her. I wanted to apologize. And there's a dead bolt on the door, and it was locked. But she didn't realize. She was struggling with the knob and it wouldn't open. It made her panic.

"I came up behind her, trying to tell her how sorry I was, and that made it worse. She was pulling on the door and I reached to turn the dead bolt to let her out, and the door jerked open, and the edge of it hit her cheek."

Tolliver paused to take a breath. "She was better once she got outside, but she wouldn't stay. I could've given her something. An ice pack. She hurried to her car and drove out of here fast. I thought of going after her, but it seemed wrong. Because it felt awful, to have her be so scared of me."

His head came up and his eyes fixed on mine. "I've gone over it again and again," he said. "And I don't know, maybe this is self-serving, but it seems like there was something else going on that night. Like it wasn't me, or my clumsy pass. For those few moments she was someplace else. And not a good place—not a place I'd like to think about."

Interlude: July 27, 1996

Jana Fletcher had cruel dreams.

She dreamed of her life before the Daws. Dreamed of waking up in her mother's house, safe in her own bed. Sometimes her grandmother was still alive, sometimes not. Sometimes she knew it was the day she would leave for New York. But every time, when she opened her eyes, she saw sunlight streaming through her bedroom window.

There were other dreams too, but they followed the same pattern. On the twenty-seventh of July, Jana dreamed she was back in college, playing Beatrice in *Much Ado About Nothing*. There was a shy boy who auditioned to play Benedick, but he was hopeless; he didn't get the part. He stayed on to build sets, to work on lighting and props, and on the night of the last performance he got up the courage to ask her out for a drink. In the dream she woke the next day in his bed, his palm resting on her hip. The curtains were drawn in his dorm room, but she could see the light of morning filtering through. She slipped out of bed, went to the window, swept the curtains open wide—

And woke up in the black dark. Always a hazy time before she remembered where she was—before she remembered that the part that should have been a nightmare was real. She rolled onto her back, heard the familiar rattle of the chain. Her body ached. She felt the thin mattress underneath her. A blanket thrown over her, scratchy on her bare skin. She sat up and flung it away. Now a search for her clothes. Underwear down around one ankle, skirt pushed up around her waist. Blouse and bra within reach—she found them by touch.

No memory of who had been with her. But someone, obviously. Eli, if she had to guess. She had a sense that Eli tended to take what he wanted and leave. Luke was more likely to stay around and try to put her back together. Which may have been worse, if you really thought about it.

A question for another time: which of them was the worse rapist. For now, Jana wanted a bath. A real bath in a tub with hot water. She wouldn't get one, but she could think about it. The sound of the water running. The sensation of floating with just her face above the surface, the rest of her submerged. Gleaming white tiles. Candles burning on the edge of the tub. The window open to the summer air, a vase of flowers on the sill.

She gave herself a minute to surrender to the image, then felt around until she touched a plastic bottle lying on its side. She uncapped it, poured water into her hand, bathed her face and neck. She recapped the bottle and put it aside. Got dressed. Made her way to the back wall of her prison and searched along the seam between the wall and the floor until she found her mother's quarter.

Her thumb traced the round edge and found the point she'd been making. It was a slow, mechanical task, rubbing the coin against a link of the chain. Trying to turn a quarter into a screwdriver. Jana set her back against the wall, gathered the chain, and went to work.

No sound but the scrape of metal on metal, but she had her own voice in her head for company. Sometimes she ran lines from plays. Miranda in *The Tempest*: *O, wonder! How many goodly creatures are there here! How beauteous mankind is! O brave new world, that has such people in it!* Or *Cyrano de Bergerac*. She had played Roxane, but Cyrano had better lines: *To sing, to laugh, to dream, to walk in my own way and be alone, free, with an eye to see things as they are . . . To travel any road under the sun, under the stars . . .*

Other times—like now—she got a piece of music stuck in her head. This time it was a song by Sheryl Crow: "All I Wanna Do." Peppy and relentless. Jana tried to resist it at first, then surrendered.

Eventually her hand grew tired from gripping the coin. She took a break and the scraping stopped. But it didn't stop. She thought she heard a sound on the other side of the room.

Scraping. Scratching.

The Sheryl Crow song faded from her head. Jana put the coin down, stood up slowly. Listened.

Now she heard nothing.

No telling how long she stood there in the dark, her back against the wall, a chill along the nape of her neck. There couldn't be anyone else in the room with her. Luke Daw always brought a light with him. He wouldn't stand silent in the dark. She would be able to hear his breathing.

Scratching. She heard it again.

An animal, she thought. Maybe a mouse. Her prison was well built, the boards set close against each other, but there had to be gaps. There was air coming through. If there weren't, she would have suffocated a long time ago. She had never felt a gap big enough for a mouse to crawl through, but she hadn't explored every corner of the room. The chain prevented it. There were parts she couldn't reach.

Jana stepped away from the wall, stopped again, and listened. Scratching. Definitely. The sound a claw would make. Or a fingernail.

"Luke?" she said.

"Not funny," she said. Her voice higher than she wanted. She could hear a tremor in it.

"Eli?" she said.

She took another step, her hands held out in front of her, groping at empty space. Another step and her arms sweeping through the air, and the fear growing that she would touch something solid.

She came to the end of the chain.

"Luke!" she screamed.

The room swallowed up the sound. She froze with her arms outstretched.

She was alone. She had to be.

Scratching. Straight ahead.

Jana crouched down and pried her fingers underneath the chain around her ankle. She tried to force it down over her heel. But there was no way. She knew. She sat down and wrapped both hands around the chain and strained to tug it free from its anchor. She moved back toward the wall and braced a foot on either side of the place where the chain went through, and pulled with all her strength, over and over, until she was sweating and couldn't keep her grip on the metal.

She fell back in the dark with her breath coming in gasps.

Minutes crept by. She used them to get her breathing under control and to convince herself that the scratching had to be a mouse. She wasn't afraid of a mouse. She found the water bottle, took a sip. Got up and walked toward the door until the chain stopped her. From there she knelt, then lay on her stomach. If she stretched out an arm, she could touch the bottom of the door with her fingertips.

Scratching. She heard it clearly. She shifted the water bottle from one hand to the other, rapped it once against the door. Heard a mouse scuttling away on the other side.

Jana let go of the bottle, surrendered to relief. Her breath sighed out of her and she laid her cheek against the floor. The bottle rolled away. She closed her eyes and let herself feel her lungs filling up, emptying out. The bottle stopped rolling. When she opened her eyes some time later, it wasn't because the mouse came back and the scratching started again; it was because she realized there was something different about the air on this side of the room.

It might have been a subtle difference in smell—although a subtle difference might have been hard to detect. The wood that made up her prison had its own smell, and there were layers underneath it: earthy, musty, primal. And other smells too—inevitable when your toilet is a plastic bucket, even if the bucket has a lid, even if it gets switched out every day or two and replaced with a clean one. So maybe it wasn't a difference in smell that distinguished this side of the room from the other, but it was something. A feeling in the air. A heaviness. A presence.

The mouse scratched at the door and Jana got to her hands and knees. She lifted her right hand from the floor and extended it as far as she could, exploring the space to the right of the door. She went as far as the chain would let her go, her fingertips straining, but she couldn't reach into the corner of the room.

She crawled back the other way, raised her left hand this time. Fingers spread, searching high in the air, and then lower. Urgently. She shifted farther left, the chain scraping the floor. She reached out blindly in the dark.

And jerked her hand back, and scrambled away with a scream caught in her throat. She hit the far wall, lost her balance, fell sideways, and huddled there, rocking, her knees drawn up, her hands clutched between them. Her body rocked, rocked, and finally the scream tore out of her. Because she knew she had touched someone's face.

34

drove away from Roger Tolliver's house just before sunset, thinking about his story and what it meant. He'd been trying to tell me more than one thing.

He wanted me to know how Jana got the bruise on her cheek. It was the bruise that first brought us together, Tolliver and me; it was the reason I had broken into his house, the day after Jana died. He had lied to me about the bruise then, and now he had told the truth.

He'd been trying to tell me something about himself too: that he felt guilty; he regretted the way he had treated Jana. Maybe he wanted me to forgive him, or maybe he wanted me to agree that he was a wretched man. I didn't feel inclined to do either.

The third thing he'd been trying to tell me had to do with Jana's reaction, the way she panicked when he tried to kiss her. It seemed strange, but I didn't know what it meant. I wondered if Tolliver had exaggerated it, if the incident had grown in his mind after Jana's death, so that an awkward situation and a meaningless accident became something more significant.

I didn't realize that Jana's reaction was the most important part of the story. It troubled me, but not as much as it should have. It was a hint, a clue. It was trying to tell me that I had no inkling yet of what had really happened to Jana Fletcher.

I drove east on Quaker Hill Road, past the spot where I'd first seen Jana on the Night of the Doe. I went on and came into Rome and found Jana's street. Though the sun had gone down, the sky was still light. It was all familiar, rolling down her street, seeing her car in the driveway. The blue Plymouth.

It wasn't mine, but I had the key in the apartment. I looked for it when I went inside, found it on the kitchen counter, on a ring of its own. I thought that tomorrow I might try to follow Moretti again. I wondered if I should use the Plymouth, but it didn't seem right. Moretti might recognize it—that was one reason. But there was another. Following Moretti would be stupid. I could say I was doing it for Jana's sake, but she had no choice in the matter, so it didn't seem fair to draw her into it.

I poured myself a glass of orange juice, took it with me to the bedroom. Jana's possessions were all around me: her sheets on the bed, her clothes in the closet, her copy of *The Count of Monte Cristo* on the night table. None of these things were mine.

I had her mother's number in my wallet. I punched it into my cell phone and hit the call button. Three rings and a voice said, "Hello." A man's voice.

"Sorry," I said. "I might have the wrong number. I'm trying to reach Lydia Fletcher."

"No, you've got it right," the voice said. "Who's this?"

"David Malone."

"Of course. I thought we might hear from you again."

He spoke with a casual arrogance—the tone of an insider talking to an outsider. I recognized him now: Jana's friend, the one who had read from the Bible at her funeral. *For everything there is a season . . .*

"Hello, Warren," I said. "Can you let me talk to Lydia?"

"I don't think so. She had a bad day. She's resting."

"What's the matter?"

Quiet on the line. He was deciding if I deserved to know.

"She'll be all right," he said at last. "The detective came to visit her. Moretti. He wanted to give her an update. You've heard about this guy who died, Sam Lanik?"

"Simon Lanik."

"Right. Well, Moretti wanted Lydia to know that he thinks Lanik was the one who killed Jana. He said it may not be possible to prove it, but that's what he believes."

"He told me the same thing."

"It sounded sketchy to me," Warren Finn said. "Do you believe him?"

I didn't, but my own theory would sound just as sketchy.

"I haven't made up my mind," I said.

"Moretti said the case would stay open, but he hoped Lydia might take some comfort in knowing that Lanik was dead."

"How did she react?"

"She went to bed as soon as Moretti left. I've been checking in on her. I think she'll be better tomorrow."

"I don't want to bother her, then," I said. "The reason I called—I've been living in Jana's old apartment. Her car is here, and her clothes and books and other things. I thought her mother would want them."

"I'm sure she will."

"I could load everything in the car and bring it there, or someone could come and pick it up. There's no rush. I don't want her to worry about it."

Warren took his time responding. The arrogance had been fading from his voice, and when he spoke there was no trace of it left.

"I don't either," he said. "I'll take care of it. How about tomorrow night? Will you be home?"

"Sure."

"I'll get a friend to drive me out there. It might be a little late, nine or ten."

"That's fine."

"Good. I'll see you tomorrow."

We ended the call. I opened the bedroom window to let in some air. Drank some more orange juice. I knew I should start packing Jana's things, but it was a job I didn't want to face. I told myself I could do it tomorrow. I knew I should eat something too. Agnes Lanik had given me provisions: a bowl of goulash and a loaf of home-made bread. I put the goulash in a pan on the stove and let it simmer while I sliced the bread. The crust was thick as tree bark.

I set a place at the table and fixed a plate and made myself eat, but it wasn't what I wanted. I wanted to get out of the apartment, away from everything. I came close to leaving but then I pictured Poe Washburn finding the message I'd left for him. It was an invitation. I needed to be here in case he decided to come by.

I finished up and washed the dishes and tried to imagine how my hypothetical meeting with Washburn would play out. It might not go well. Roger Tolliver had said I was asking for trouble. I thought I should be ready.

Around nine-thirty I went next door and asked Agnes for a favor. When I came back, I had her Makarov pistol. Just in case.

I settled in for the evening. Me and my gun and Jana's copy of *The Count of Monte Cristo*. I stayed up reading till midnight and discovered I really liked Edmond Dantès.

Washburn never showed.

The next morning I behaved like a responsible adult. I had two inspections scheduled: an old Victorian house on a hill overlooking a golf course, and a Craftsman-style bungalow on the east side of the city. The work kept me busy until one in the afternoon. Then I drove to Poe Washburn's house and let myself in again. He wasn't there, but the note I'd left on his pillow was gone.

Back home, I gathered empty boxes and packed some of Jana's things. It went okay at first. I started in the kitchen and moved on to her desk. I boxed up her files and papers, her books. I saved the bedroom for last. The closet was hardest: taking the clothes from the hangers and folding them and piling them on the bed. After a while I had to stop. Because it was too sad—and not an overpowering kind of sad, not the kind that breaks you down and leaves you sobbing on the floor. It was a small, detached, empty kind of sad.

I left the clothes on the bed and went out. I locked the door of the apartment behind me and climbed into my truck. And drove.

The first place I went was the hospital. I circled it three times before turning into the lot. Sophie's car was there. I could have left a note on her windshield. It would have started with *I'm sorry*. I don't know what it would have said after that.

I went to the old apartment next and sat looking up at the balcony. There was a potted plant on the railing, something viney with dark green leaves. That's new, I thought. That's Sophie's plant. It could be yours but you don't live there anymore.

I still had my keys. I could go up there and let myself in. Sophie would come home and find me lounging on the balcony, and she might be angry or she might be happy, I didn't know. But I knew she'd be wearing her cat's-eye glasses and I knew how her hair would smell and I knew what her voice would sound like when she called me Dave.

I didn't go up. I headed over to the university campus and the law school. It was Friday afternoon and the sun was out, at least for the moment. The students were walking around in shorts and tank tops, baring their pale arms and legs. Springtime in upstate New York.

From there I kept moving. I drove past familiar places: the apartment where Angela Reese painted her canvases, the gray-brick IRS building where Wendy Daw worked. I wound up on Bloomfield Street, the neighborhood where Gary Dean Pruett had lived with his wife, Cathy.

A quiet neighborhood, nothing flashy. The houses looked alike, but not *too* alike, not mass-produced. The people who owned them made a comfortable living. A lot of them were probably schoolteachers like the Pruetts. If they had children, they had one or two at the most.

The people who lived here had fences or hedges to separate them from their neighbors. Some of them had small detached garages tucked out of sight, but others parked their cars on the street. The cars were like the houses, nothing flashy. They were midsize sedans in dull colors: blue and black and gray. They didn't stand out.

I drove by the Pruett house—tall and narrow, painted pale blue— then came back around again and parked across the street. I looked at the front lawn. The last time I was here—talking to Neil Pruett— the grass had been long and spotted with dandelions.

It looked better now: Pruett had gotten around to mowing it. Of course he had. In a neighborhood like this, there were informal rules that everyone understood. You kept your lawn mowed and your hedges trimmed. You never turned your music up too loud. You cleaned up after your dog. You went easy on the decorations at Halloween and Christmastime.

One of Neil Pruett's neighbors came out onto her porch to get her mail. An older woman, gray-haired and slump-shouldered. She looked around and saw me parked on her street in my red pickup truck. She stared at me. I had the driver's window down. I gave her a smile, a wave. I tried to look harmless. I succeeded. She went back inside.

I thought about Cathy Pruett, living on this street in the final weeks and days of her life. On the outs with her husband, Gary. Gary had been cheating. Cathy had suspected it. She had talked about it with her best friend, her sister-in-law, Megan Pruett, and Megan had followed Gary to a hotel and caught him with an eighteen-year-old, Angela Reese. So Cathy's suspicions were confirmed. She had tried to work it out with Gary, but in the last days of her life she believed that Gary had gone back to his old ways. She would have been preoccupied, distracted. What were those days like?

If Gary Pruett was innocent, then someone else had killed his wife. Maybe Luke and Eli Daw. The Daws could have known Cathy Pruett because they were students at the high school where she taught, but when Cathy Pruett died they were in their early twenties; it had been years since they were in high school.

Why did they choose Cathy Pruett?

And once they chose her, what then? How did it work? Gary Pruett claimed that his wife had left the house one Saturday afternoon and never returned. She had taken her car. Where had she been headed? He didn't know.

Where did she cross paths with Luke and Eli Daw?

Maybe right here, on this street.

When you decide to abduct a schoolteacher, what's the first step? Maybe you've got a place to take her—an abandoned farm out on Humaston Road. But that's the end point. The starting point is your victim: you need to observe her, learn what she does, where she goes. So you start right here, at her house.

In the last days of her life, when Cathy Pruett was preoccupied with her failing marriage, her husband's infidelity, were the Daws watching her?

Did the Daws spend time here, parked on her street?

Eli drove a white van.

How did I know that? From a news story? No. I'd heard it from Wendy Daw.

A van: the vehicle of choice for abducting schoolteachers.

I tried to imagine the two of them, Luke and Eli, parked on this street in a white van. The van would have stood out among all these dull sedans. Luke and Eli would have attracted attention. They would have been noticed by gray-haired ladies collecting their mail, by people walking their dogs.

When Cathy Pruett went missing, the police would have questioned the neighbors; they would have asked about unfamiliar vehicles parked on the street. Wouldn't they? Frank Moretti led the investigation. Did he take it seriously or did he go through the motions? Did he keep an open mind or did he assume from the start that Gary Pruett was guilty?

Was Frank Moretti a good cop or a bad cop? I kept coming back to that question.

I needed to make a decision about whether to try following him again. If I was going to do it, I couldn't use my truck; it would be an insult to his intelligence. I looked at all the dull sedans parked along the street. I needed one of those. Something plain, something invisible.

It should be easy to get one. I could go to Enterprise or Avis, and they would be happy to rent me a dull sedan.

I checked my watch. It was almost five o'clock. I'd lost track of the time. On Wednesday, Moretti had left the station house a few minutes after five. He might do the same today. By the time I drove to a car rental place and filled out the paperwork, it might be too late to catch him.

As I debated whether to try it anyway, I saw a car approaching from down the street. A dark blue sedan, nice and plain. It pulled up in front of the Pruett house.

Neil Pruett climbed out of it. He started toward the house, then glanced my way and did a double take. Confusion showed on his round face. I waved and got out of the truck. He waited for me on his side of the street.

There were things I wanted to ask him about his sister-in-law. I wanted to know what she was like in the last days of her life and if she ever mentioned having the feeling that she was being watched. But that could wait.

I stepped up onto the curb beside him and said, "Is there any way I could borrow your car?"

35

There were stairs on the other side of the door. This Jana knew from the night they brought her down. She heard footsteps now descending, a heavy tread. She sat up and faced the sound.

A key turned in the lock and the door opened. Lantern light filled the doorway, harsh and glaring. Jana raised a hand, palm outward, to block out the worst of it. She heard the thump of the door closing. A figure approached, set something down, and retreated again. Jana's eyes adjusted to the light. It was Eli holding the lantern, standing with his back against the door.

"Coffee," he said. Just a word, detached from anything, until she realized he had put a mug on the floor, within her reach.

"It's instant," Eli said. "With milk and sugar. It's not very hot."

More words. Jana wasn't listening. She was staring at the body on the floor. Not so far away from her, not as far as it seemed in the dark. A small, slender woman, maybe forty, with golden-blond hair. She was laid across a corner of the room, her head closest to the door. A pale blue blouse and denim capris. A swath of red across the front of the blouse.

"The coffee was Luke's idea," Eli said. "He thought it would help."

"Help?"

"Didn't make a lot of sense to me either."

"Where is he?"

Eli shifted his weight from one foot to the other. "He's thinking. That boy does a lot of thinking. He's the clever one, and I'm delivering coffee. He wanted me to give you the news. I told him you'd probably work it out on your own—that there's a dead woman in your room."

He stumbled over the words: *a dead woman.* He didn't look at the body.

"Who is she?" Jana asked. "What's her name?"

"Her name's not important."

"What happened to her?"

"You don't want to know," Eli said. "Try the coffee."

Jana picked up the mug. It smelled gorgeous, instant or not. She didn't taste it.

"The coffee's supposed to smooth things over," Eli said. "That's genius, isn't it? That's Luke. He's the big thinker. I'm the dumb one." He looked around the room—everywhere but at the body. Then he looked back at Jana. "You can drink it. It's not gonna kill you."

No guile in his face, none that she could see, but his face wasn't built for guile; it was the face of an overgrown child. One thing she knew: she wouldn't drink the coffee. She raised the mug to her lips and tipped it up, pretending.

Eli went on talking. "I'd like to know what he's thinking, I'll tell you that. I'd like to know what we're supposed to do now. Just a complication, he says. Nothing we can't handle. That's the trouble with him. Thinks he can handle anything."

There was more. Jana listened and pretended to drink from the mug. After a while Eli trailed off into silence. He set his eyes on her—grown-up eyes in his child's face. She brought the mug to her lips again, self-consciously.

Four strides brought him across the room. He eased himself down on one knee, rested the lantern on the floor. He held a hand out for the mug, and when she didn't offer it, he took it—but gently. He glanced down into it and chuckled at what he saw. He brought the mug to his mouth without hesitation, swallowed a big gulp, and handed it back to her.

"You can drink it," he said. "It's not poison. I wouldn't do that to you." He leaned closer and reached out to touch her. She stiffened, but there was nowhere to go; she had the wall at her back. He took hold of a lock of her hair, rubbing it between his fingers.

He spoke to her in a hushed voice. "I won't lie to you. We both know there's only one way this can end. But when the time comes, it won't be bad. I promise. I'll smother you in your sleep, or put a bullet in the back of your head." Eli's fingers moved from her hair to her cheek, a slow caress, feather-soft. "It won't hurt. I'll make sure. It'll be me, not him. Better for you that way, trust me. Did he tell you about the time he had to shoot the dog?"

She turned her face away and didn't answer. His hand withdrew. He got back on his feet, picked up the lantern.

"I know he told you," Eli said. "He likes to tell that story, how Grandpa made him do it. It makes people feel sorry for him. Poor Luke. He leaves out the worst part. He shot the dog all right. Killed him, eventually. But it took him three tries."

Early August 1996

A half-moon in the deep of an August night. A candle burning atop a wooden milk crate. The smell of tall grass.

Jana Fletcher was floating.

Legs together, arms spread wide. Cool water.

Luke Daw had asked her if she wanted a real bath. He had opened the padlock that held the chain around her ankle and had brought her up into the clean air, to a spot beside the fallen farmhouse. To a real bath in a shallow plastic pool, a kiddie pool, six feet wide.

Jana's cast-off clothes lay in the grass. She had stripped down to her bra and panties, no further. An absurd kind of modesty under the circumstances, but it seemed right.

She lifted her head from the water, looked at the moon and the stars and the barn looming in the distance. She could hear bullfrogs croaking down by the pond. And another sound, faint and far-off: a car passing on the road.

Like the wind running over the grass.

The road made her think of escape. If she could make it to the road, she could wave down a car. If there were no cars, she could look for a house. There had to be houses, and people.

"What are you thinking about?" Luke Daw asked.

She tipped her head back to let the water cool her brow. "I'm not thinking," she said.

Luke was sitting beside the pool, on a second milk crate resting upside down on the ground. He had his revolver. Jana hadn't seen it since the night he and Eli took her, but he had it now, ready in his hand.

The road called to her. Sooner or later, Luke would make her get out of the pool. He would want to take her back to her prison. What if she didn't go? She could do something crazy. Throw water in his face and run, head for the road, in her underwear with no shoes. Luke could shoot her in the back. But what if he did? That would be another kind of escape.

Or he could chase her. He would catch her before she reached the road. He would take her underground and never let her out again.

Jana floated. She focused on the cool of the water against her cheeks. She could pull her face beneath the surface and breathe it in. One more way to escape. She wondered if she had the willpower to do it, or if instinct would take over and send her sputtering back up into the air.

Luke was watching her. "What are you thinking about now?" he asked.

In the grass beside her clothes there were two towels, a big one and a small one. She sat up and twisted round to grab the small one, then lay back again and rested her head against the side of the pool with the towel as a pillow.

She decided to tell him the truth. "I'm thinking about drowning."

"I wouldn't let you drown."

"No, I guess you wouldn't."

The pool held about a foot of water. Jana wondered where it had come from. There didn't seem to be a hose or a spigot nearby, though she might have missed them in the dark. She could see two plastic jugs, a gallon each, lying in the grass. Luke might have used them to haul the water out here from the trailer, a little at a time.

It was a lot of water if you thought about it that way. In another sense, it wasn't much at all. Not enough to do what he wanted it to do. It was supposed to wash away a week spent living with a corpse. With flies buzzing in the dark and mice clawing at the door to get in.

Jana thought it had been a week; she couldn't be sure. They'd been drugging her more than usual. She felt sluggish even now.

Tonight, when she struggled out of a thick sleep, she found the woman gone. She found the bright light of the lantern and Luke bearing coffee. Not instant this time, but real coffee in a takeout cup, still warm. And after the coffee—the bath.

Luke pulled his milk crate closer to the pool.

"Are you really worried about drowning?" he asked her.

"I wouldn't say worried."

"You shouldn't think about it—about dying."

"That's a funny thing for you to say."

"Why?"

"You're holding a gun."

"I don't see the connection."

"I know."

She wanted to ask him about the dead woman. She had tried before, the day after the woman appeared, when Luke came down with a sheet of plastic to roll the body in, with blankets to cover it up, as if that could make a difference. But Luke would tell Jana nothing— not the woman's name or where she'd come from or how she had died.

Still, Jana thought she knew what must have happened. An abduction gone wrong. They must have dragged the woman into the white van, at a rest stop or a gas station, the same way they had taken Jana. They must have brought her to the farm, and she must have fought back—just as Jana had. Only it had gone much further.

"Which one of you killed her?" Jana had asked Luke.

"It doesn't matter," he'd said.

"I'd like to know."

"It was Eli."

A tossed-off answer. She didn't believe it. As far as she could tell, the woman had been stabbed—and Luke carried a folding knife. Jana remembered it; he had used it the night they took her, to cut the cord that bound her ankles.

She had other questions, ones she would rather not think about and didn't dare ask: Was Luke growing tired of her? Is that why he and Eli had taken the woman with the golden hair? And if the woman had lived, what then? Would they have kept Jana around, or would she have been expendable?

She tried to put the questions out of her mind, but she couldn't. Because the answers were easy to guess, if you were honest. And if you followed them to their logical conclusion, they could mean only one thing: that Jana owed a debt to the woman with the golden hair. The woman had fought a battle, and she had lost, but she had done something else without knowing it: she had spared Jana's life, at least for a while.

Even now, as Jana watched the half-moon riding low over the trees, the woman was still in her thoughts.

"What was her name?" she said aloud.

No lead-in, but Luke didn't need one. He understood.

"You're obsessed," he said.

"Why can't you tell me?"

"I could tell you," he said. "It wouldn't change anything."

"It would change one thing. I'd stop asking."

"Fine. Her name was Maggie."

"Was it really?"

"You said you'd stop asking."

"I'll stop when you tell me the truth."

Luke waved the revolver carelessly through the air. "Maggie, Sheila, Holly," he said. "Call her whatever you want. A name is just a word."

"She was a real person. She deserves her own name."

He slouched on the crate. The flame of the candle made a yellow mask of his face.

"It was Cathy," he said. "Cathy Pruett." He gestured with the gun. "You see? It doesn't change anything."

But it did, for Jana. *Cathy Pruett.* It sounded right. It fit the woman with the golden hair. *Cathy Pruett saved my life.* Jana spoke the words in the privacy of her mind, but they made her throat tighten, made her eyes well with tears.

Luke was watching. The corners of his mouth turned down. "Now you're upset," he said. "This is not what I wanted." He tucked the gun away behind his back, picked up the big towel from the grass. "You should dry off. I'll take you back."

"No," she said. "Not yet."

He draped the towel over his knee. "A few more minutes. Then we have to go."

"Why?"

"We have to. You know how this works."

The tears rolled down her cheeks. She wiped them with wet hands and sat up in the pool. "I know," she said. "I can see it. One day I'll be the body in the corner. And there'll be another woman down there, terrified. Maybe she'll wonder what *my* name was."

"That's not—"

"Yes it is. That's the future. You could at least be honest. Eli is. He told me he's going to kill me."

Luke looked away, shaking his head. "He shouldn't have."

"Why not? We all know that's how it goes. I die in the end." Jana's wet hair clung to her face. She brushed it back angrily. "But I don't want to die. So we need to work out a different ending."

It was a random idea, tossed out in a moment of frustration. Jana never expected Luke to take it seriously. In the real world, nothing would have come of it, but Luke Daw didn't live in the real world. In the place where he lived, he wasn't an aggressor, she wasn't his victim. They were collaborators. *We've never done this before,* he'd said to her once. *We're all feeling our way through this thing.*

He sat in the candlelight and drew a popsicle stick from the pocket of his shirt. Started turning it over and over with his fingers.

He said, "What happens—in this different ending?"

It took her a long moment to process the question, and a shorter one to find an answer.

"You let me leave here," she said.

"And?"

"And that's all. I just walk away."

The popsicle stick turning, like a gear in an elaborate machine.

"You don't go to the police?"

"No. I never tell anyone what happened here."

Still water around her. The chill of the air on her skin. She waited.

The stick turned slower, came to a stop.

Luke said, "You'd go to the police."

Of course I would, Jana thought. First thing.

"I wouldn't," she said.

"You say that now. But how can I trust you?"

You can't, she thought.

"That's the hard part," she said. "You have to take a chance."

She watched a pair of lights flickering in his dark eyes—reflections of the candle flame. He touched the popsicle stick to his lower lip.

"No," he said. "It wouldn't work. I couldn't trust you."

He flipped the wooden stick into the grass and the light in his eyes faded. Jana's hope left her. She had led him to the brink of something, but he had stepped back.

"It's not your fault," Luke said. "It's just the way things worked out. It might be different if we could go back and start over. Do you remember what it was like, the night we met?"

She answered him reflexively. "I remember."

"We had something. A spark. We talked about meeting up in Binghamton. Remember?"

"Yes."

"And when we followed you in the van, me and Eli, I told him, 'Jana's cool. You wait and see. She'll stop. Dino's Bar on Conklin Street. She'll meet us there.' Eli didn't think so. But I believed. We followed you down I-81 and we came to the exits for Binghamton, and I was sure you'd get off—"

"I almost did."

"I wish you had. Everything would've been different. We would've met up at Dino's. And I know I told you we were playing there, the band, and that was a lie. But it wouldn't have mattered. I would've said it was a mix-up. We would've laughed about it. And you and I would've hit it off. I know. We had a spark. But you didn't stop. You kept driving. And now it's too late."

There was longing in Luke's voice. Jana almost missed it. She was thinking of last stands, of desperate measures. She wondered if she should run for the road, even though she would never make it. Or if she should try to attack Luke and wrestle his gun away. Mostly she was thinking about death and how it would find her, and whether she should wait for it or hurry it along.

But part of her mind was listening to Luke—and that part realized he was telling her what he wanted. It was something he could never have, not in the real world. But Luke didn't live in the real world.

"Maybe it's not too late," she said. "To start over."

Luke looked wistful. He shook his head. "We can't go back there."

"We don't have to. I can stay here."

He wanted to believe they were in this thing together. She would let him believe it. She would use the time Cathy Pruett had bought her, and buy herself some more.

"I can stay," she said again. "But things have to change."

He put the towel aside and stood up. Alert. Wary. "What things?"

Jana got to her feet as well. "First, no more Eli," she said. "It has to be just you and me. You need to keep him away. Can you do that?"

"I can handle Eli. What else?"

"No more drugs," she said. "I sleep when I want to sleep, and wake up when I want to wake up."

He hesitated. Then said, "All right. I guess we could try that."

"And I don't want to be down there all the time in the dark. I want light. And I want to come out here, every day."

She saw at once that she had pushed too far. Luke set his hands on his hips. "I can't have you out here in the day," he said. "It's too much of a risk."

"Every night then. I need to see the sky."

His dark eyes were on her. Searching. "How do I know you won't try to run?"

She could have lied, but he was shrewd. He would have seen through it.

"You don't," she said. "But if I try to run, you can kill me."

He nodded and let his arms relax at his sides. He looked up at the stars and then at her body in the candlelight. He had one last thing to say.

"If you get all that, what do I get in return?"

Jana stood in the pool and smoothed her wet hair away from her forehead. She reached behind her back and unclipped her bra. Shrugged it off, cast it away.

"I stay here," she said. "Willingly. For as long as you want. And we can see if we still have a spark."

36

Neil Pruett let me borrow his car.

He took some convincing. We stood together on the lawn in front of his brother's house and I explained to him that I thought Frank Moretti had a secret. If I could follow him and find out what it was, it might help me prove that he had framed Gary. It might bring us one step closer to getting Gary released from prison. The problem was that Moretti would recognize my truck. I needed something that would blend into traffic.

Neil looked a little bewildered, but he let me have his keys. I left him the keys to the truck, thinking it would reassure him. He didn't really know me. He might have been wondering, in the back of his mind, if he would ever see me or his car again.

I made it to the police station in the old courthouse downtown at ten minutes after five. The fountain was running in the plaza at the bottom of the courthouse steps. I drove to the parking lot in back. Frank Moretti's black Chevy was nowhere to be seen.

I circled the block and thought about what to do. Moretti might have left just a few minutes ago. Then again, he might not have been here at all. He was a detective; he didn't spend his life behind a desk or knock off at five every day. He could be out talking to a witness right now, or at a crime scene. He could be anywhere.

I began to see the limits of my plan.

I came to the parking lot again as a cop in a patrol car was pulling out. He gave me a steely look as he rolled by. I could find a place to wait or I could keep circling. Maybe Moretti would show up here. Maybe no one would notice that I was staking out the police station.

I made one more trip around the block and then drove north, following the route Moretti had taken two days ago. The streets were full of commuters heading home. I left downtown behind and found Turin Road. I saw familiar markers: the Knights of Columbus Hall, the veterinary hospital, the canoe livery, the day care center where the young cop had pulled me over.

I used the day care's horseshoe drive to turn around. I went back half a mile and picked out a spot in the parking lot of the veterinary hospital where I could watch the road. It seemed like the best option I had. Moretti had come this way once, at about this time of day. Maybe he would come this way again.

I turned on the radio and settled in to wait. The station that came on was NPR, a natural choice for a schoolteacher like Neil Pruett. Snooty radio, my father would have said. I listened to *All Things Considered* and heard about unrest in Indonesia. After that, there was a report about an economic summit in England, then a retrospective on Frank Sinatra, who had passed away earlier in the week. Then a piece on bears—hibernating bears in Alaska. They were waking up early because of a mild spring.

Bears can sleep for almost half the year, the correspondent said, and yet their muscles don't waste away the way ours would.

It seemed impossible. Maybe there was a scientific explanation, but I don't remember. I tuned out when I saw Frank Moretti drive by in his black Chevy.

I didn't have to follow him far, maybe four miles. He stayed on Turin Road at first—a public park and a cemetery floating by on our left. I kept him in sight, but there was always at least one car between us.

We came to Stokes Road and he turned west. Blue water stretched out on either side of us. A reservoir. Then houses and a church and a fire station. Then a low stone wall with evergreens growing behind it. Moretti slowed and turned onto a side road that passed through a gap in the wall. To the right of the gap stood a sign that read SUMMER-BROOK MANOR.

I didn't follow him. I drove another half mile and then looped back. When I came again to the gap in the wall I thought I might find Moretti waiting for me, but he wasn't there. I made the turn and followed the side road up a gentle slope past the evergreen trees. The trees gave way to a broad swath of lawn. There were buildings, but none of them looked like a manor. They were long and narrow, single-story, institutional. There were three of them, arranged like three sides of a square, with a courtyard in the middle.

I parked at a distance from the buildings, as far away from Moretti's car as I could. Which gave me a nice short walk to the courtyard with a breeze at my back and the air smelling of pine needles. On one side of the courtyard an old woman sat in a wheelchair with a blanket over her lap. On the other side a guy with a linebacker's build and a shaved head leaned against a wall drinking a Coke. He wore jeans and a faded green smock that might have been the top of an orderly's uniform.

I gave him a friendly nod and asked, "Is this a nursing home?"

He held the Coke can under his chin and looked me over. "That's not what they call it," he said. "They call it a continuing care facility."

"Is that anything like a nursing home?"

"You'd have a hard time telling the difference."

He spoke in a soft voice, as if he didn't want the old woman to overhear us.

"I might want to look around," I said. "We're trying to find a place for my grandmother."

I waited for him to call me out on the lie, but he didn't blink.

"There's a lady you can talk to. She handles intakes."

"I'd rather look at the grounds first on my own," I said. "If that's allowed."

He shrugged. "I won't stop you," he said. "But don't wander too far."

I didn't need to. I left the courtyard and made my way around the building on the west side of the square. There were picnic tables and a garden, and beyond the garden the lawn ran down to a winding stream—the brook of Summerbrook Manor. There was a paved path that led down there, wide enough to accommodate two wheelchairs, and at the bottom of the path lay a wooden platform that overlooked the stream. A place where you could sit and take in the view.

Three people on the platform. One of them was Frank Moretti. Another was an African-American woman wearing the same pale green as the linebacker with the shaved head.

The third was a woman in a wheelchair. Not an old woman, not what I would have expected. She had pale skin and dark brown hair.

Because of the distance I couldn't be sure of her age, but I would have guessed young. College-student young. About as young as Angela Reese.

I watched them from the top of the path: Moretti chatting with the woman in green, then crouching beside the wheelchair to talk to the brown-haired girl. The girl had a stuffed bear, and Moretti picked it up from her lap, waggled it in the air, and made it talk—the way you would to entertain a child.

After a while the woman in green left them and started up the path. She was on the heavy side and she took it slow. Moretti continued his business with the bear, and when that got old he rolled the girl's wheelchair a little closer to the stream. He pointed out something in the water. He pointed to the clouds in the sky. To a hawk gliding overhead.

When the woman in green reached the top of the path, she was breathing hard. She passed me without a word and went to sit at one of the picnic tables. I gave her a minute to herself, then walked over.

"Nice day," I said.

She looked up, more at the weather than at me. "Supposed to be a storm later."

"Really?"

"It's what I heard."

I moved a step closer. "Mind if I sit?"

She looked up again, took me in this time. Her expression told me she would tolerate my company, even if she didn't welcome it. I sat down.

"I might move my grandmother here," I said.

"It's a good place."

"Seems nice. I've been looking around."

"You go to the office, they'll give you a tour."

"Maybe I will."

We spent a quiet moment together. I thought she might leave; she had recovered from her walk up the path. But she stayed and watched me with her hands folded on the table. She had beautiful hands, the nails shaped and painted. A lot of care had gone into those hands. And into her hair as well: it was done up in tightly woven braids. Her face looked as heavy as the rest of her, but there were strong bones underneath. I could see intelligence in her eyes, along with caution and reserve.

"We have a mutual acquaintance," I said. "Frank Moretti."

"Is that right?"

"Have you known him long?"

"He's a regular."

"I was surprised to see him today. I didn't know he came here. That girl he's visiting, she's young."

"She surely is."

"Is she his daughter? I didn't know he had a daughter."

The woman in green didn't answer. Her eyes were steady, her mouth a long neutral line.

"I'd ask him myself, but it might be awkward," I said. "I don't want to give him the impression that I'm prying into his private life."

"That *would* be awkward," she said, "to give him that *impression*."

"Right."

"Of course, you could just not pry at all."

"That's true."

"Leave everybody with a better *impression*."

She had smile lines around her eyes, but by then it was clear that she wouldn't be smiling for me. It didn't matter. She didn't have to like me. I brought my wallet out.

"I need to know about the girl," I said. "Maybe we could help each other."

I got a smile after all. A weak one. "What's your name?" she said.

"Napoleon Washburn."

"That's a hell of a name."

"Some people call me Poe."

"What are you offering me, Poe?"

I opened my wallet. Laid two twenties and a ten on the table.

The smile went away. Her expression turned stony.

"That's not so much. You know who that man is—Mr. Moretti?"

"I know," I said, adding another twenty to the pile.

She made no move to take the money. "You ever gamble, Poe?"

"Sure."

"You know what gamblers do?"

"Tell me."

"When they're serious, they go all in. You willing to go all in?"

I pulled the rest of the bills from my wallet, showed her there was nothing left.

"All in," I said.

She unfolded her beautiful hands and stacked the bills in front of her. She didn't count them. She didn't put them away.

"What do you want to know?" she said.

"What's the girl's name? How old is she?"

"Her name is Erin. She's twenty-one." She took a bill from the top of the stack, tore it in half. "Ask me something else."

I watched her toss the pieces over her shoulder. They landed in the grass. No change in her stony expression.

We were playing a different game now, not the one I'd counted on. But I needed to see how it ended.

"Is she his daughter?" I said.

"I never saw her birth certificate," said the woman in green. "I know she calls him Daddy. I know he comes here almost every day. I know she draws him pictures. The pictures are in crayon. They look like the work of a talented three-year-old. Because that's what she is now."

She tore another bill and tossed it in the grass. "Ask me something else."

"What happened to her?"

"Car accident. She was seventeen. Happened after midnight on the highway. Car she was riding in crossed over the median, hit a big truck just about head-on. She was in the passenger seat. She was paralyzed from the waist down, suffered a brain injury. Two weeks in a coma." She tore another bill. "Ask me who was driving."

"Who was driving?"

"One of her teachers. Ask me why he was cruising around after midnight with a seventeen-year-old girl."

Her voice had been carefully controlled all along, but now I could hear the anger in it.

"I don't need to," I said.

"I guess not," she said. "He died instantly. She's the way she is. She doesn't remember him, most days. She always remembers Mr. Moretti. She misses him when he's not here. Cries every time he leaves."

"Where's her mother?"

The woman in green gathered the rest of the bills. "She used to come here too, the first year or so. Then it sank in that her daughter wouldn't get any better. Girl was three and would always be three. That's hard. Too hard for Erin's mother. She ran herself a bath and opened up her wrists."

The woman tore through the bills once, twice. The pieces went over her shoulder and littered the grass.

She said, "Does that answer your questions, Mr. Malone?"

No emphasis on my name. She used it casually.

"Yes, it does," I said.

"Good. Because that's as much as Mr. Moretti wants you to know. Anything more, you'd have to ask him yourself. And I know he doesn't want to talk to you. You're not his friend."

"No."

She looked around at the garden. Nothing blooming yet but a few crocuses. "I believe I'm his friend," she said. "He treats me that way." She looked back at me and her voice fell—a way to make me pay attention. "He's the gentlest man I've ever met, but I don't like to think what might happen if you came here again, if you tried to approach Erin or speak to her."

"I won't," I said.

"Or if you did anything at all that might disturb her life here, or expose her to unwanted attention."

"I understand."

"Good. You can go now."

She glanced over my shoulder and beckoned to someone there. I turned to see the guy with the shaved head walking toward us. The linebacker.

"This is Karl," said the woman in green. "Karl, this is David Malone. His visit is over. He's leaving."

She didn't rise. A breeze came up and drifted the torn bills over the lawn. Down on the platform by the stream, Frank Moretti was reprising his routine with the toy bear. I went with Karl. He had four inches on me and about thirty pounds. He didn't take me by the arm, but I knew he was there.

He kept silent until we reached the edge of the parking lot. Then he said, "I owe you an apology."

"What for?"

"If I'd known who you were, I could've warned you to take off. Saved us all some trouble. But I believed what you said, about your grandmother."

"Sorry."

He ambled along beside me. "My grandmothers are gone. Both of them."

"One of mine is still around," I said. "In her seventies. Not ready yet for a place like this."

"It's kind of shitty then. Lying about her."

He had a point.

"Yeah," I said.

We reached my borrowed car. Karl lingered, rubbing a palm over his bare scalp.

"You need to go and stay gone," he said. "Do I have to tell you?"

"I've been told."

I got the keys out of my pocket and turned away from him to unlock the door. A mistake. Karl put a hand on my shoulder and pushed me against the car. Then he hit me fast, one time, off center in the small of the back below the rib cage. A kidney punch.

I've never been gored by a bull, but it can't be much different. My lungs emptied and my knees gave way. I slid down the side of the car. Ended up on my hands and knees on the ground. I thought I would throw up, waited for it to happen, drool trailing out of my open mouth. It didn't happen.

I raised my head and the movement made me dizzy. I sat on the ground. Saw Karl standing over me, shaking his right hand, flexing the fingers.

"That wasn't so bad," he said. "I went easy on that one."

He got a grip on my arm and tried to haul me up. I swatted at him. He bent his knees and lifted, tried to brace me against the car. The small of my back touched the side mirror and I groaned and almost went down again, but he held me up.

"You're okay," he said. "Just breathe."

I tried to push him away and stand on my own. Too soon. I would have fallen, but he didn't let me.

"Take it slow," he said. "You'll be fine. I had to make sure you listened. There's being told, and then there's listening. You get that, right?"

I nodded once to let him know I got it. After a while he helped me into the car.

37

A strange thing had begun to happen to K. He wasn't sure what it meant. He had started seeing Jolene in different spots around the city.

Not the real Jolene, of course, but copies, clones, Jolene *types*.

Blond, athletic, good legs—those were the basics. But it was more than a physical type. There were swarms of leggy blondes roaming the quads of Bellamy University, but they didn't remind K of Jolene. They lacked a certain quality. Some people would have called it damage; K thought of it as vulnerability.

A woman selling sunglasses at a kiosk at the mall, bored to death. A shy girl with a pockmarked face working the cash register at the place where K got his hair cut. A woman stranded on a roadside at night, anxious, waiting for a tow truck. K saw Jolene in all of them.

He saw her again, late Friday afternoon. A crumbling street in south Rome—definitely Jolene territory. A hardware store next to a liquor store next to a laundromat. K walked out of the hardware store and saw her in an empty lot across the street. A near-perfect match, down to the short skirt and the tight top. She was even holding a red Solo cup.

K stopped to watch her. She lit a cigarette and sat on a graffitied concrete wall. The wall separated the lot from a train yard. West of the lot stood an abandoned building that had once been a skating rink. All the entrances were boarded over.

As K watched, a tall, skinny kid with a patchy beard walked along the front of the skating rink. Ripped jeans, black T-shirt, late twenties. If he had been cleaner and more prosperous, you could have described him as bohemian.

He joined the girl in the lot—the near-Jolene. They sat together on the wall. He bummed a cigarette. K got the impression they knew each other, but not well. After a minute or two the skinny kid reached into his pocket. Something passed from his hand to the girl's. They got up from the wall and went off together, disappearing behind the skating rink.

Time to leave, K thought. The girl was a distraction. He didn't need distractions. He needed to stay in control. He knew that.

But he didn't leave. He walked into the liquor store, bought a cold six-pack of beer, made the clerk put it in a paper bag. He took it across the street and found a spot to sit on the concrete wall, a few yards down from the spot where he'd seen the girl. He twisted the cap from a beer and took a drink. Put the bag on the wall and hid the bottle behind the bag so no one would see it from the street.

Before long, near-Jolene and the skinny kid reappeared from behind the skating rink. The skinny kid went on his way—head down, fast clip—and near-Jolene walked to the wall. A tiny hitch in her step when she saw K, an unfriendly glance, and then she lit another cigarette. She still had her red Solo cup.

K drank his beer. He finished a bottle, pulled another from the bag. He checked in on near-Jolene now and then, but he didn't stare at her. He stared at the laundromat across the street or at the weeds growing through a crack in the pavement at his feet. He thought she might come over when she ran out of whatever she had in the red cup. He was right.

"Hey, Steve," she said.

She stood before him, one bare leg in front of the other, putting herself on display. Medium smile. Teeth ever so slightly crooked.

He said, "How'd you know my name was Steve?"

"I didn't," she said. "I like to guess. It's fun. You try me."

He tilted his head, pretending he had to think about it.

"Jolene."

"Jesus, Steve. It's like you're psychic."

K reached into the bag and brought out another beer. Twisted the cap and started to pour it into her red Solo cup.

"I can drink from the bottle, Steve."

He kept pouring.

"Or whatever," she said.

He moved the bag off the wall and out of the way. She sat beside him.

"What are you up for, Steve?"

"It's hard to say."

She flicked her used-up cigarette onto the pavement.

"You can tell me," she said, toasting him with the cup. "We're buddies."

"I want to spend some time with you."

"You're reading my mind again, Steve."

"Let's go somewhere."

She nodded in the direction of the skating rink. "There's a place nearby we can go, if you want it quick. Or I know a hotel. If we go to the hotel, it's more. But you get more. Know what I mean?"

K felt himself frowning. "Maybe we could slow down."

"Slow. Absolutely. We'll go as slow as you want."

"I don't like the way you make it sound—like it's cheap."

"Oh, it won't be cheap, Steve."

"I want to talk first."

"Absolutely," she said, digging in her purse for a fresh cigarette. "We're talking now, aren't we?"

"I mean about real things. Important things. Like what you wanted to do, before you started doing this."

She tapped the unlit cigarette against her thigh. "Oh god," she said. "Are you one of those?"

"One of what?"

"Are you gonna try to rescue me? Save my soul?"

K laughed. "No, no."

"'Cause that's not my thing."

"It's not mine either, Jolene," K said. "I just want to go for a drive."

Her body language changed. She'd been leaning toward him, intimate, but now she leaned away. She lit her cigarette and dropped the lighter in her purse.

"I don't go for drives," she said. "I don't get in anybody's car, unless it's a friend."

"But you said we were friends, Jolene."

"I said we were buddies."

"I want to go for a drive," K said. "And then get out and take a walk."

"Sounds like we want different things."

"It'll be nice. A walk along the water. What do you say?"

"I say I'll have to pass."

She started to get up, but K took hold of her left wrist.

He felt her muscles tense. She glared at him. "That's not cool, Steve."

"We're going for a drive."

She tried to pull away. He knew he shouldn't try to stop her. Someone might see. He should get himself under control. But he felt his grip on her wrist tightening.

"You can finish your beer," he heard himself say. "Then we'll go."

"You're hurting me, Steve."

"Don't try to fight me, Jolene. I have a gun. Finish your beer."

Her beer was sitting on the wall. She didn't reach for it. She took a hit from her cigarette and let the smoke run out between her lips. In a soft voice she said, "My name's not Jolene." Then she twisted around suddenly and jabbed the tip of the cigarette into the back of his hand.

A pure shock of pain and the sound of his own flesh sizzling. K jerked his hand away and his whole body jerked with it, throwing him off-balance. The girl followed through with a solid shove—the heel of her palm against his sternum—and the force of it sent him backward over the wall.

Dirt and weeds on the other side. K landed hard on his shoulder and rolled. Sprawled on his back for a moment—everything hurting, nothing broken—then scrambled to his knees. He stood up with the Makarov pistol in his hand, the one he'd taken from Simon Lanik. Not sure how it got there, because he'd been carrying it around on his ankle. He didn't have a holster; the gun had been stuffed in one of his socks and held in place with a couple of thick rubber bands. Now he had it out, his finger on the trigger.

You could call it good reflexes—except that he was facing the wrong way, his back to the wall. He whirled around, brought the gun up, found the girl. She was walking fast, not running, but she was already at the street. He aimed the pistol at her back.

Daylight. Witnesses. A woman loading laundry into her hatchback. Two young kids passing on bikes. The girl who wasn't Jolene yanked open the door of the laundromat and went inside. K came to his senses and moved his finger off the trigger. He sank down behind the wall. Returned the pistol to his sock.

Reckless, he thought.

After a few minutes he got up and looked around. There were people on the street, but none of them paid any attention to him. He climbed over the wall, picked up his bag of beer, and left the lot.

The water calmed him.

He had gone for a short drive, and then for a walk—just as he had planned, only without the girl. Now he squatted on the bank of the Mohawk River, not far from the neighborhood where he grew up. He listened to the water gurgling over a fallen tree; he watched a family of ducks floating downstream. He held his right hand under the water. The cold felt good.

The cigarette burn was a small red circle. K studied it on the drive home. In time, it would leave a scar, he thought.

He flexed his hand on the steering wheel, just so he could feel the pain again. The burn was a punishment for his recklessness. He would need to be more careful. He had been wrong to go after the girl in the lot. He had crossed a line. It was hubris. Like Icarus with his wax wings, flying too close to the sun. You shouldn't overreach. That was the lesson.

Or was it? There could be another way to look at it, K thought. The girl in the lot was a prostitute. She was nothing. So when he tried to take her, he wasn't overreaching. He wasn't aiming too high; he was aiming too low. Aiming too low was a waste. A sin. What if that was the real lesson?

The more K considered it, the more he thought he was onto something.

He would need to remember. He had the red mark on his hand to remind him.

Next time he would aim higher.

K made the turn onto his street. He saw one of his neighbors picking up her newspaper from the sidewalk. He saw his house in the distance. Saw someone sitting on the front steps. Saw the man rise to his feet, haltingly, as if he might be in pain.

David Malone.

For a split second, K forgot himself. He had an urge to hide his face, to keep driving. The urge passed. He eased on the brakes and parked at the curb. Cut the engine of Malone's pickup truck.

He took the bag with him—his beer—and crossed the street. He called out a greeting. He touched his own car as he walked past it. And traded keys with David Malone.

38

Neil Pruett was a chatterbox.

He apologized for using my truck. He'd had some errands to run. He hoped it was okay. I told him it was.

He wanted to know about Moretti—if I'd been able to follow him, and where he had gone, and if I'd learned anything useful. I didn't feel like talking. There was a storm coming. The woman at Summerbrook Manor had warned me. The sky was still light, but I could see the clouds gathering. They looked unnatural, like clouds on an alien planet.

I still had that gored-by-a-bull feeling. It hurt to stand and it hurt to walk. I felt unsteady on my feet—and more than that: I felt like the world was an unsteady place. So those alien clouds made sense; they were the right clouds for the world I was living in.

I told Neil Pruett I was sick and we would have to talk another time. I left him standing on his lawn with his grocery bag and climbed into the truck and drove out of there. I drove slow, the way you would if you were traveling along the edge of a cliff.

Halfway home I felt nauseous. That's not true: I felt nauseous the whole trip, but it peaked when I was halfway home. I pulled into the lot of a fast-food joint and stood by the side of the truck with my hands on my knees and didn't throw up. Then I went inside, into the men's room, and bent over a sink and didn't throw up again. After a while I went into a stall and unzipped and peed for a very long time. It came out a vivid yellow, maybe too vivid, like the color of the sun on that alien planet. But not pink or red. Not bloody.

I got back on the road and the world seemed steadier. The ground stayed solid and no chasms opened underneath me. I reached Jana's apartment and pulled into the driveway. The wind blew through the leaves of the oak as I stumbled to the front door. The storm was coming. I turned my key in the lock and went in and found Napoleon Washburn sitting in my kitchen.

A haze of cigarette smoke hovered in the air. I saw that Washburn had taken the clay bowl down from the mantel—the one that held Jana's quarter. He was using it as an ashtray. He sat with one elbow resting on the table, his long, lanky frame sprawled in his chair. He wore jeans and a gray fleece shirt, the sleeves pushed up to his elbows. His dark hair was unruly.

He had his feet up on a second chair. His work boots were worn and stained. I recognized them. I'd seen one of them up close.

"Come on in," Poe Washburn said. "Shut the door. Sit down."

He was mellower than I remembered—but the last time I'd seen him, his house had been on fire. I heard confidence in his voice, along with a trace of menace. He gestured at the chair across from him with the hand that held his cigarette.

I could have gotten angry, but I didn't have the energy. I sat.

"I'm glad you're here," I said.

He drew on the cigarette, let out a plume of smoke. "I bet."

"How'd you get in?"

"Back door. I broke the window and reached through."

I looked back there and saw the remnants of the glass in the frame. I had to lean sideways in the chair to do it. The effort made the room sway a little. I felt sweat breaking out on my forehead.

"You didn't have to do that," I said.

"Tell you the truth, I kinda wanted to." He tapped ash into the clay bowl. "I came here thinking I would bust some things up, maybe kick your ass. I thought it would make me feel better. But now that I see you, I don't know. You look like you're barely holding it together. What happened to you?"

"I've had a rough day."

"It shows." He brought the cigarette up. Inhaled. Exhaled from the side of his mouth.

He said, "Do you have any money?"

"Why?"

"I could use some."

I thought of all the bills from my wallet, torn in pieces, lost in the grass of Summerbrook Manor.

"I don't have any."

"That's what I figured," Poe Washburn said. "I was looking around before. You've got a thirteen-inch TV that might get me ten bucks at a flea market. You've got a computer, but it's not a laptop. It's a desktop and it's probably four or five years old—"

"Six."

"—which means maybe I could donate it to the Salvation Army. They'd be happy to have it. No one else would. You've got a clock radio and an electric toothbrush. You've got jack shit. Some people keep a roll of cash in a coffee can or in a baggie in the freezer, but not you. How long have you been living here?"

"Not very long."

"It's kind of a dump. You know that, don't you?"

I didn't answer him.

He shrugged. "I grew up living in dumps. So I'm not judging." He tapped the cigarette out in the clay bowl. "I did find one good thing," he said, "in your nightstand." He reached below the table and pulled out Agnes Lanik's pistol. It had been resting on his lap, out of sight.

"It's got a foreign name," he said. "Markov."

"Makarov," I told him.

He leveled it at me across the table. "I've never seen one like it."

"Funny story about that gun—"

"Yeah?"

"I borrowed it from a woman I know, after I left that note at your house. I figured I should have it in case you came here with the wrong attitude."

"That *is* funny."

"You can put it away," I said. "You don't need it. We're not enemies."

"We sure as hell aren't friends."

"I didn't set the fire at your house."

"Somebody set it. I don't believe it was an accident."

"Neither do I."

Washburn brought his feet down off the chair, kept the gun trained on me.

"Doesn't matter," he said. "Let me have your wallet."

He didn't say I should reach for it slowly, but it was implied. I brought it out and pushed it across the table. Every little movement hurt.

He opened the wallet with his left hand and looked inside.

"You don't have any money."

"I already told you."

"You don't have *any*."

"Funny story about that—"

"Save it," Washburn said. He snapped the wallet shut and slammed it on the table, but it was too small a gesture. It didn't soothe him. He aimed the gun at the ceiling and I thought he might fire off a round. He rocked it back and forth instead. A bobblehead motion. Letting off steam.

"I don't want to hear stories," he said. "I don't ask for much. Honestly, I don't. All I'm looking for is some traveling money."

The words might have been for me or for the world at large. He delivered them with downcast eyes.

"Where are you headed?" I asked him.

He looked up sharply. "Away from here."

"How much do you need?"

He scowled the way you might if a homeless person offered you a loan. But I could tell he was thinking about it. I watched the gun rocking back and forth.

"Five hundred," he said.

"I have questions about Gary Pruett."

"I know."

"If you answer them I can give you five hundred."

"So says the man with the empty wallet."

"It won't be cash," I said. "I'll write you a check."

He sneered and shook his head. "I don't take checks."

"I heard you used to steal bicycles."

"So?"

"So what's harder, fencing a bike or cashing a check?"

"A check could bounce."

"This one won't."

"Or you could stop payment."

"That won't happen either. You'll get the five hundred."

The gun stopped moving. "Just for talking to you?" Poe Washburn said. "Because I'm not talking to anyone else, and I'll never testify to anything."

"Just you and me."

I watched him thinking and then I watched him open my wallet again and fish out my ATM card. He pointed the gun at me and said, "If you've got five hundred in your checking account, then I could take you to an ATM right now and make you withdraw it."

"You could."

"And I wouldn't have to answer any questions."

"That's true."

"So why don't we do it that way?"

I didn't relish the idea of going for a ride with him. Out there with the storm growing and the ground threatening to give way.

"We could," I said, "if I were afraid of that gun."

Washburn's eyes narrowed. "You're not afraid of guns?"

"Not that one."

"I know it's loaded. I checked."

"If it were a real Makarov I'd be worried," I said. "But it's a cheap East German knockoff. It's been sitting in a drawer for thirty years. If you pull the trigger, maybe it'll fire. Or maybe nothing'll happen. Or maybe it'll blow up in your hand. If I were you, I wouldn't be too eager to find out."

He turned the gun sideways, examined it, aimed it back at me. "You're bluffing," he said. "If you don't think it'll fire, why did you keep it in your nightstand?"

"I wanted it around, for show. I'd never be crazy enough to use it."
I stared past the muzzle of the pistol and focused on Washburn's face.
"Maybe you should think about why you're trying so hard to steal
the money that I'm offering to give you voluntarily. I'm going to get
up now and go to the desk and bring back my checkbook. You can
keep that thing pointed at me if it makes you happy."

I got up without waiting for him to respond. The floor stayed
level. He didn't try to shoot me. I dug my checkbook out of a drawer
and came back and wrote a check to Napoleon Washburn in the
amount of five hundred dollars. I tore it out and started to pass it
across the table to him, but at the last moment I held it back.

"The gun's not mine," I said.

"So?"

"So you'll have to leave it. That's part of the deal."

Washburn chuckled. "Do you think I'm dumb enough to hand
you this gun?"

"You don't have to hand it to me. You just can't take it with you."

We passed a moment in silence while he decided I wasn't trying to
trick him. Then he aimed the gun toward the living room and
popped the clip. He ejected the remaining round from the chamber
and laid the gun on the table. For good measure he used his thumb to
flick each bullet from the clip until they were scattered like marbles
over the floor. He tossed the empty clip after them.

I gave him the check and he looked it over and slipped it in his
pocket.

"Gary Pruett never confessed to me," he said.

"I know," I told him. "Frank Moretti convinced himself that Pruett was guilty. He had his reasons. I understand that. He wanted to
make sure Pruett was convicted. But he needed help. I've wondered
how he contacted you in jail. Did he talk to you in person?"

"He sent a message through a guard."

"Okay. So he asked you to get a confession from Pruett. And you gave him what he wanted. He didn't want the truth, because in his mind he already knew the truth."

Outside, the wind picked up. A branch of the oak scraped the front window. I continued: "I want to know about what happened after, when you made the decision to come clean and tell the real story—when you decided to contact Roger Tolliver and his Innocence Project. Why did you do that?"

Washburn was shaking his head. "I didn't. That's not what happened."

"Sure it is. You called Tolliver, and Jana Fletcher was the one who answered the phone."

He waved a hand dismissively. "You've got it wrong. I'm not the one who called. It was never my idea. Jana Fletcher called me."

39

oe Washburn left twenty minutes later. I stood in the doorway and watched him cross the street to the parking lot of Reed Terrace, where he had left his truck.

We'd spent those twenty minutes talking. I'd asked him more questions, and the answers he gave me left me feeling even more like the world had turned unsteady. I shut the door and looked around and everything seemed to lean a little sideways. It needed to be set right.

I started with the clay bowl that Washburn had been using as an ashtray. I fished out Jana's quarter with its strange, sharp point. I dumped the cigarettes and ashes in the trash. Rinsed the bowl and the quarter and dried them. I'd grown used to having them around. I wondered if I could justify keeping them. I slipped the quarter in my pocket and returned the bowl to its place on the mantel.

I gathered the clip and the bullets from the kitchen floor and reloaded the Makarov pistol. I put that on the mantel too.

I swept up the glass from the broken window in the back door and used duct tape to secure a piece of cardboard over the opening. I began to feel better, to move easier. The bull that had gored me was still following me around; he nudged a horn into my back now and then. But he was a smaller, weaker bull. I wasn't so afraid of him.

I knew my next move. There was someone I needed to see.

I thought about Warren Finn, who was supposed to have a friend drop him off here tonight so he could pick up Jana's things and drive her car back to Geneva. I wrote a note for him and taped it to the front door on my way out: *Back soon. Come in. The door's unlocked.*

I'd never been to Wendy Daw's apartment; I had to look up the address. She lived in the basement of a house on Dominick Street, a few blocks from the IRS building where she worked. She had her own entrance, at the bottom of a set of concrete steps.

She answered the door in sweatpants and a flannel shirt. Her brittle hair was parted down the middle. The wind blew strands of it across her face.

I had Jana's picture out, the one I'd been carrying in my wallet. I held it up and said, "I think you knew her."

Wendy Daw backed away from the picture and I took the opportunity to step inside. She had her television on, the sound muted, an old black-and-white movie on the screen. I saw a bowl of popcorn sitting on her sofa.

"I don't want you in here," she said.

"I'm already in."

"This isn't fair. I never wanted to talk to you about Eli. You told me if I did, I'd never see you again."

I waved the picture. "You said you didn't recognize her. You lied to me."

I hadn't been sure before, but now I knew I was on the right track. The picture made Wendy uncomfortable. Afraid.

"I want you to go," she said. "I don't have anything to say about her."

She held the door open for me, as if it might be that easy. I pushed it shut.

"Sit down," I told her. "You don't have to say anything yet. Just listen. I'll tell you about Jana. She was a law student, working with one of her professors on an Innocence Project, trying to exonerate people who were wrongly imprisoned. She got caught up in a case—that's what her professor told me. Cathy Pruett's murder. You know about Cathy Pruett. Her husband went away for killing her. The crucial testimony against him at his trial came from a thief named Napoleon Washburn. Washburn claimed that Gary Pruett confessed to him in jail."

Wendy had stayed on her feet. She backed away from me toward the television.

"Washburn's story was a lie," I said, "and eventually he decided to set the record straight, so he got in touch with the Innocence Project. At least, that's what Jana told her professor. I found out today it wasn't true. Washburn didn't call Jana. She called him."

I stepped closer to Wendy Daw.

"That's not the way it's supposed to work," I said. "Jana's professor, Roger Tolliver, told me he gets requests for help from convicts and their families constantly. He has to turn most of them away. He never has to go looking for cases to get involved in. But that's what Jana did.

"She called Washburn in February. When he wouldn't talk to her on the phone she went to his house. She told him she knew he had lied about Gary Pruett's confession. Washburn stuck to his story and sent her away, but she wouldn't give up. She kept coming back. Finally she wore him down. He admitted that Pruett never confessed.

"He still didn't want to get involved. Jana wanted him to sign a statement, to testify again, this time on Pruett's behalf. But Washburn couldn't see the point. Gary Pruett didn't confess, but so what? It didn't mean he wasn't guilty. Wasn't the husband usually guilty? Somebody murdered Cathy Pruett. If it wasn't Gary, then who?"

The wind gusted outside. It pummeled the basement's small, high windows.

"Washburn posed that question to Jana," I told Wendy Daw. "And he remembered her answer. I heard it from him tonight. 'What if it was a stranger?' she said to him. 'It could have been anyone. What if Cathy Pruett ran into the wrong people? What if she got kidnapped by a couple of crazy farm-boys in a white van?'"

Wendy closed her eyes and stood with her back against the television.

"Washburn thought Jana was just offering him a wild example," I said. "*What if?* But we know better, don't we? 'A couple of crazy farm-boys in a white van'—that's Luke and Eli. They killed Cathy Pruett. And somehow Jana knew."

She knew in February—before she talked to Gary Pruett or anyone else about the case. That was the most important thing I'd learned from Poe Washburn.

"That's why Jana couldn't let the Pruett case go," I said to Wendy. "She knew Luke and Eli and what they'd done. I don't know how she could have met them. That's what you need to tell me."

Wendy's eyes came open. "I can't," she said. "I don't know."

I held up the photograph of Jana—the only weapon I had. "Stop lying to me. You recognized her the first time I showed you her picture. You knew her. You saw her—"

Wendy shook her head. "I saw her one time. I don't know how she knew Eli or Luke. I don't know how they met. I only know one thing about her."

"Tell me."

"I don't think it's what you want to hear."

"If it's about Jana, I want to hear it. Tell me."

The screen of the television went blank and the lights flickered around us but stayed on. I watched Wendy Daw's face. She looked away from me and looked back again. And then she told me the one thing she knew.

The rain held off for a long time. Well after nine o'clock, when I drove away from Wendy Daw's apartment, the storm was still only wind. I watched it bend the trees as I drove along, but the windows of the truck were rolled up tight. The wind never touched me.

The neighborhoods I passed through all had power—until I got to Jana's street. There the lights were out. The Reed Terrace Apartments had gone dark as a void. When I walked to Jana's door, my note was still there. *Back soon. Come in. The door's unlocked.* I slipped inside as quickly as I could and shut the door behind me.

There was light in the apartment: four candle flames burning atop the two-by-four on the mantel. Warren Finn was in the living room, sitting in Jana's desk chair. He leaned forward, elbows on his knees, staring at something. Something not there, something far away.

He held the Makarov pistol loosely in his right hand.

He looked up and saw me standing in the archway of the kitchen. He had a habit of not looking people in the eye; I'd noticed it the first time I met him. His eyes found me and slid past me and found me again.

"The power went out," he said softly.

"The wind must have knocked down a line," I told him.

"It's getting pretty bad. Maybe I shouldn't have come tonight."

"I'm glad you're here." The same thing I'd said to Poe Washburn.

I picked up a kitchen chair and carried it into the living room. I put it down in front of the bedroom door, turned it around, and sat with my arms folded over the back.

"Where's your friend?" I asked Warren.

He looked blank at first, then realized who I meant: the friend who had driven him here.

"I told him he could take off. He's got a wife and kid waiting. He wanted to get home before the worst of the weather hit."

"I hope he does."

"I've got a wife waiting too. It's funny to say that. And a kid—I'll have a kid before long." Warren paused, trying out the idea, marveling at it. "But I'm still here."

I didn't say anything. Warren was calm. Both of us were. It didn't bother me too much that he was holding the gun. He didn't look like he wanted to use it. He looked sad and a little lost. He wore a white dress shirt and a pair of black trousers, and they were too big for him—just as the suit he'd worn at Jana's funeral had been too big.

He had a fleshy face. Pink cheeks. He had a high forehead and the same long hair I remembered, tied back in a ponytail. And he had that scar: a white line running through his upper lip.

"This is the first time I've seen this place," he said, in a lost voice to go with his lost look. "I never visited Jana here. But she lived here. She sat at this desk."

I nodded.

"And she died right here, didn't she? In this room."

"You don't want to think about that," I said.

"Show me where."

I pointed to the spot. It was midway between us. Nothing to see, just the hardwood floor. Bits of dried candle wax. Warren didn't move from his chair.

"I loved her," he said.

"I know."

The words fell flat. I didn't have any right to say them. Warren frowned, but he didn't overreact. He didn't shoot me.

"You don't know," he said. "I grew up next door to her. I saw her every day of my life. We walked to school together every morning. She was the most beautiful girl I knew, and I was a fat kid named Warren with a harelip. So don't pretend you know how I loved her."

He had more to tell me, about how he loved her. I would have listened even if he hadn't been holding the gun. I wanted to hear.

"When I was a kid, I had a stutter," he said. "It made the other kids laugh, but not Jana. I couldn't talk to anyone, but I could talk to her. My parents spent a fortune on speech therapy, and it never did any good. But one summer Jana bought a secondhand guitar and taught herself a few chords. She had this ridiculous songbook—John Denver's greatest hits—and we sat out on a blanket on the lawn and she made me sing every one of those songs with her. 'You Fill Up My Senses.' 'Rocky Mountain High.' 'Sunshine on My Shoulders.' Over and over, day after day. And somehow at the end of that summer I didn't have a stutter anymore."

He paused for a moment, and the wind swelled up to fill the silence.

"When we were fourteen she had her first boyfriend," he said. "A football player. It didn't amount to much. They went to a school dance, a few movies, a party at someone's house. It was over in a month. He broke it off. It hit her hard, the way it does when you're fourteen. It made her cry. I felt awful—and wonderful too. Because when she cried she let me put my arms around her."

He wanted to tell her how he felt, but he couldn't, because if she didn't feel the same way, it would ruin everything they had. "And what we had was a lot," he said. "Jana had started acting in plays by then, and plays were a foreign world to me—as foreign as school dances and parties. I was too shy to ever stand on a stage. But when she had to learn a part, I was the one who helped her. We read all her scenes together."

When they were sixteen, Jana played Roxane in *Cyrano de Bergerac*.

"Do you know what it's about?" Warren asked me.

I said I did, but he went on as if he hadn't heard.

"It's about an ugly man who's in love with a beautiful woman. The only way he can tell her he loves her is if she can't see him, if she thinks he's someone else. When he's standing under her balcony in the dark, then he can tell her. But he can never come out of that dark, because then she would see him. We read that balcony scene, Jana and me, when we were sixteen. I spoke those lines to her: '*I love you beyond breath, beyond reason. Your name is like a golden bell hung in my heart; and when I think of you, I tremble, and the bell swings and rings.*'"

I watched his hand come up—the one with the gun in it. It touched his heart and then went down again.

"But I was hiding in the dark," he said. "I wasn't brave enough to tell her the truth in my own voice. I never told her—not till later, after her grandmother died, when I found out she was leaving for New York City. And then I had to. It wasn't bravery; it was desperation. I thought I might never see her again. So I told her I loved her and I wanted to go with her. But she . . . she didn't . . ."

His voice faded and he didn't finish the thought. But this was a part of the story I knew. I'd heard it from Jana's mother. Jana had gone to New York on her own, because she wanted to be an actress and she couldn't wait any longer. She lasted in New York for three months—three months without a phone call to her mother, with nothing but a few postcards.

"Did she ever call you from New York?" I asked Warren.

He was staring at the hardwood floor. "No."

"You never got a letter or a card?"

"No. I didn't hear from her until she got back."

"Her mother told me Jana had a hard time in New York," I said.

"That's right."

"And when she came back, she stayed with you."

His chin came up. His eyes fixed on me. They didn't wander.

"All through the fall and winter," he said. "All the way through the next spring."

"Tell me what she was like."

"What do you mean?"

"Anything you remember. I need to know. When she left for New York, she drove her grandmother's car, but when she came back—"

"She came by bus. She had to sell the car. She called me from the bus station and I picked her up."

"How did she look?"

"Exhausted. Like she'd been riding a bus for hours and hours."

"What did she have with her?"

He pursed his lips, remembering.

"She had a big duffel bag."

"Nothing else? No suitcases?"

"No."

"But she must have taken suitcases when she left," I said.

Warren nodded. "She took a whole carload of stuff when she left."

"And came back with one bag. What happened to the rest?"

I watched him knit his eyebrows together. Irritated. Because I was asking him about trivia.

"She never told me," he said. "She never wanted to talk about what happened in New York."

"You must've wondered."

"It was a bad experience for her. I think she fell in with some shady people. Maybe her roommates stole things from her. Maybe she met someone there and he turned out not to be what she expected. Maybe she had to get away from him, fast, and that's why she left some things behind."

"Did she tell you that—that she'd met someone?"

He seemed to hesitate, but just for a second. "No."

"She never mentioned anyone named Luke Daw? Or Eli Daw?"

"No. Who are they?"

"It's a long story," I said. "You mentioned roommates. Did she ever tell you their names, or the address of the place where she stayed?"

"No. No address. I always imagined a place with roaches, and gang symbols painted in the hallways. And I know she waited tables, but I don't think the restaurant was a good one. And she went on auditions, but they never led anywhere. She didn't want to talk about any of it. I think she was ashamed."

The details were familiar: waiting tables and going on auditions. I'd heard them before, from Jana's mother. Familiar and vague. I wondered what would happen if I asked Warren to name a single part that Jana had auditioned for. I had the feeling he wouldn't be able to answer.

I didn't ask. I said, "When Jana came back, what did she do? How did she spend her time?"

"She took it easy," he said. "That's what I wanted her to do. She spent time outdoors. She cooked. I never ate better than I did for those few months when she lived with me. And she took baths. Long, hot baths with a book, and music playing. Candles burning."

He turned to look at the two-by-four on the mantel. "She made that to hold the candles on the edge of the tub. Only that one's different—"

"I made that one," I said. "It's a copy. The police took the original. You're saying she made it herself?"

He nodded. "A couple days after she came home. It didn't take much. I showed her how to use the drill press in my garage."

"Where'd the wood come from?"

"I don't know. It looked like it was salvaged. She might've brought it with her, in the duffel bag."

The flames glowed on the mantel, four of them in a row. Tea-light candles on a chunk of wood. But it meant something, the wood. Jana had crafted it herself. *Everything's a clue.* I didn't know what it meant. Not yet.

Warren Finn was staring at the floor again, the Makarov pistol forgotten in his hand. I had more to ask him, and we were coming up on delicate territory. Jana's mother had talked to me about what happened when Jana came back home, but she had only given me the bare outline. I knew that Warren had been seeing someone else at the time: Rose, the woman who was now his wife. I knew they had broken up when Jana reappeared. It wasn't hard to understand. Warren had given up on Jana when she left Geneva. But everything changed when she came back and moved into his house.

"I'd like to know the rest," I said to him.

He looked up, confused. "The rest?"

"Jana took baths and she cooked for you and she lived with you for months. And you loved her. And you don't want to tell me the rest. It's private. I understand. But it might help me to know."

Confusion gave way to other reactions. Suspicion. A hint of anger. I watched his grip tighten on the gun.

"How could it help you?" he said.

"I've been trying to figure out who killed Jana. I think her death might have had something to do with her trip to New York City. It's hard to explain. Look, you don't have to answer my questions. But right now I'm making assumptions, and it would be better if I knew. So here's what I think happened. I think when she got back she slept in a separate room at first. Maybe not for long. Then one night she wanted to sleep with you, in your bed, but she didn't want you to touch her. And you went along with that. You would've gone along with anything, because you loved her. And I don't know how long it took, but at some point she changed her mind. She wanted you to touch her, just to hold her. And finally she wanted you to do more than just hold her."

Warren endured my little speech with a quiet dignity, and when it ended I thought he would tell me to go to hell. But he let his grip loosen on the pistol and said quietly, "That's all true."

"She stayed with you," I said, "through the fall and the winter and the spring. And then she ended it. It must have been hard for you, at the ending. Hard for her too. She felt guilty. It wasn't fair, the way she used you."

I could see from his reaction that I'd come close to the mark. He held himself still, reliving a memory of old pain.

"Did she tell you that?" he asked.

"No. Jana never said a word to me about her time in New York, or what happened after. She kept secrets. I've been a little slow to figure that out. She kept secrets, and she lied."

The idea offended him. "What did she lie about?"

"I'll get to that. But you need to tell me one more thing. You said she never talked about the people she met in New York. But you thought she had a boyfriend there."

"I didn't say that."

"You implied it. *'Maybe she met someone there and he turned out not to be what she expected.'* What made you say that?"

He shrugged. "It doesn't matter."

"Yes, it does."

The wind ran wild outside, making the oak tree claw at the window. We listened to it for a while, and Warren ran his thumb along the barrel of the Makarov. Eventually he sighed and said, "The week after Jana came home, she asked me to drive her to Syracuse. She had an appointment. It was tricky for me to get time off work, so I suggested that she ask her mom. It's hard to describe her reaction. She looked like she hated me or she wanted to cry, or both. All she said was, 'She can't know. It has to be you.' So I drove her to Syracuse. To a clinic. And I waited for her, and I drove her home. And we never talked about the procedure—the one her mother couldn't know about."

He turned the pistol over and ran his thumb along the other side. "She never told me her reasons, or who the father was. But I assumed it was someone she met in New York."

I got up and walked to the fireplace. The wooden cube was on the mantel, intact except for the one popsicle stick that had fallen away. I picked up the stray stick and bent it until it broke.

Warren stood up too. "Do you know who he was—the father?"

"No," I said.

"But you think he's important."

"I don't know what's important."

Warren narrowed his eyes. "Don't do that. I've told you every-thing you wanted. You've given me nothing. You said Jana lied. Start with that."

I dropped the two halves of the stick onto the mantel.

"All right," I said. "But put the gun down. You don't need it."

He looked down at his hand as if he'd forgotten what he was holding.

"Never mind about the gun."

"Put it down," I said. "I understand the appeal of the thing. You're a guy with a wife, and a kid on the way. They should be your top priority. But you can't stop thinking about a girl who died, a girl you loved. Some people would say that makes you a bad person. But you and I know that's not true. So you don't need the gun. You don't deserve to be punished."

Maybe I managed to hit upon some deep truth about his psychol-ogy, or maybe he got tired of listening to me. Either way, he opened the middle drawer of the desk and laid the gun inside. I was glad to see him do it. I had some things to tell him that would make him angry—maybe angry enough to shoot somebody. I didn't want it to be me.

I watched him close the drawer.

"Jana lied," he said, prompting me.

I moved away from the mantel, trying to decide where to begin.

"There was a schoolteacher named Cathy Pruett," I said. "Some-one killed her. It happened here in Rome the summer before last—the same summer Jana left home to go to New York City."

I went through the whole thing for him: the details of the case and Gary Pruett's conviction and Jana's desire to free him from prison. How she had contacted Napoleon Washburn to try to get him to recant his testimony. I repeated what she'd said to him: *What if Cathy*

Pruett ran into the wrong people? What if she got kidnapped by a cou-ple of crazy farm-boys in a white van? I talked about Luke and Eli Daw and why I believed that Jana's remark referred to them.

Warren's brow furrowed. "You mentioned them before—Luke and Eli."

"Yes, I did."

"You think they killed this woman, Cathy Pruett?"

"Yes."

"And you think Jana knew them? You think she met them in New York?"

We were coming to the terrible part. It was something I didn't want to think about. I hated it. And I didn't want to tell him, but I thought he deserved to know.

"The thing is, Warren, I think she lied about New York. What is there, really, to prove that she ever got there? No phone calls, no address. Think about how little she told you about her time there. And the things she did tell you—did they sound real, or could they have been made up?"

I waited while he considered the question. He was standing near the mantel, with the candles in the background behind him. His eyes were pools of gray shadow.

"Why would she lie?" he asked.

"I think she just didn't want you to know," I said. "I think she meant to go to New York, but she never made it. Because somewhere along the way, she met up with the Daws."

I sketched it out for him: the story I'd been working out in my mind ever since I drove away from Wendy Daw's apartment. I had nothing to work with but bits and pieces of information: the words Jana had used to describe Luke and Eli—*crazy farm-boys in a white van.* The fact that she had left home in her grandmother's car but returned without it. Her reaction when Roger Tolliver made a pass at her—the fear that came over her when she couldn't get away from him, because his front door was locked.

Bits and pieces. They meant nothing on their own. But when you put them together with Jana's lost summer—when no one heard from her apart from a few postcards—they started to seem more ominous. I kept coming back to Luke and Eli. What if no one heard from Jana because they took her? What if they brought her to the farm on Humaston Road? A hideaway, abandoned and remote. What if they kept her there?

I went over all this with Warren. He took it in. He didn't want to believe it.

"You're guessing," he said. "You don't know anything for certain."

"You're right," I told him. "But there's one last thing. Eli Daw died, just a few weeks after Cathy Pruett. Someone shot him. Everyone thought it was his cousin Luke, because the murder weapon belonged to Luke. But Luke didn't kill him. Tonight I talked to Eli's wife. She was there. She knows the truth. She told me Jana shot Eli Daw."

That was Wendy Daw's revelation—the one thing she knew about Jana. She had described the scene for me: that night in their trailer when Eli died. Once I convinced her to talk, Wendy didn't spare any of the details, so I knew that she'd been cuffed to the headboard of their bed, courtesy of Eli. There'd been a knock on the trailer door and he had gone to answer it. Then she heard the gunshot. She screamed. And the next thing she saw was Jana in the doorway of the bedroom.

Now I described the scene for Warren. I could see the tension growing in him as he listened. I was glad he had put away the Makarov pistol.

"She could be lying," he said. "If she knew who killed her husband, why didn't she tell anyone at the time?"

I had asked Wendy the same thing. Her response made sense to me. Her marriage to Eli had been nothing like what she signed on for. He had abused her. She had fantasized about killing him herself. She was horrified when Jana shot him, but once the horror passed, she realized that Jana had done her a favor.

"She's not lying," I told Warren. "The pieces fit together. I believe Luke and Eli took Jana and kept her at the farm. I believe that's where she encountered Cathy Pruett—that's how she knew that Luke and Eli killed Cathy. And somehow Jana escaped from them. It must have happened on the night of September sixth. That's when she shot Eli. Luke disappeared the same night. The police found his car abandoned here in town, not far from the bus station. When Jana came home to you, she came on a bus. Do you remember what day that was?"

He did. I could see it in his eyes before he spoke. Jana meant everything to him. Of course he remembered.

"She came home on a Saturday," he said. "September seventh."

He went silent and we stood there together for a while. I watched him thinking. The wind gusted against the house and tore over the roof above us. The four flames burned behind him on the mantel.

"If that's what happened," Warren said softly, "then I'm glad she shot him."

I nodded. I was glad too.

"What about the other one?" Warren asked. "Luke. What happened to him?"

"I don't know," I said. "But it's a question I need to answer."

40

A giant spaceship hovered over the White House.

"Watch," said Luke Daw. "This is the best part."

A beam of white light flashed down from the ship, and the building exploded into splinters of wood and stone and glass. An orange fireball engulfed the movie screen.

People cheered. Someone honked his horn. Jana sat with her bare feet up on the dash of Luke's Mustang. The sunroof was open to the night sky.

Luke was beside her, behind the wheel, grinning. Handsome in profile, a two-day stubble on his chin. He held her hand.

Up on the screen, people ran in the streets. Cars flipped end over end through the air. More explosions—the tinny sound of them came through a drive-in speaker clipped to Luke's window. Air Force One taxied down a runway with flames rolling in behind it, threatening to swallow it up. It broke free from the ground at the last possible moment and rose into the air.

A pair of teenage girls sat cross-legged on the hood of the next car over. They clapped their hands and laughed as they watched the plane take off. Jana heard herself laughing too.

"See?" Luke said. "I knew you'd like it."

The key to Jana Fletcher's release turned out to be missing her period.

On the morning of the sixth, she woke at twenty minutes after nine. She knew the time because she had a watch now, a cheap one on a plastic band. She had light too—a battery-powered lantern. She switched it on and let her eyes adjust.

She twisted the cap from a bottle of water, felt the seal break, drank half of it, and put it aside. She saw a plastic grocery bag in the middle of the room, something Luke had left for her the night before. She scooted over and opened it. Fresh supplies. More bottled water, granola bars, a box of tissues. A new tube of toothpaste. Tampons and pads.

She hadn't asked for those—though she'd been thinking about them for the past couple of days. She thought she was overdue. She tried to work it out. The last time had been after Cathy Pruett died but while her body was still in the room. When Jana counted back, it came out to thirty-two days at least, maybe thirty-four. Not good.

But there was nothing she could do. She drank some more water, then used a little to brush her teeth. She stretched and ate a granola bar and lay on the mattress with a pillow propped under her head and read by lantern light. She had a sack of paperbacks that Luke had brought her: slim mysteries with yellowed pages. Mickey Spillane and Rex Stout. Luke said they had belonged to his grandfather. Jana spent a couple of hours with *Some Buried Caesar*.

She heard footsteps on the stairs around noon. Felt a current of cool air when Luke opened the door. He came in and knelt and planted a kiss on her forehead.

"Jana's got her nose in a book again," he said.

She folded the page to mark her place and laid the paperback on the floor. Sat up and accepted the coffee that Luke offered her. He had orange juice for himself, and bagels with cream cheese.

"Sesame or blueberry?" he asked.

"Blueberries don't belong in a bagel."

"Sesame it is."

"What's new?"

"The Mets lost."

"I said what's *new*."

"Funny."

He passed her a copy of *USA Today*. She had asked him a month ago for a newspaper, and he had started bringing it three or four times a week. Always *USA Today*. Never a local paper. Never what she wanted.

She wanted news about Cathy Pruett. She knew Luke and Eli had dumped the body, and the police had found it. That was the limit of what Luke would tell her. If she asked him, he would say, "Don't worry. We're in the clear." And she would smile and pretend it was good news.

Maybe it was. Part of her hoped the police would find a link between Cathy Pruett and the Daws, and it would draw them here, to the farm, and they would find her. But part of her feared what might happen if the police caught up with Luke and Eli. If the two of them kept silent, no one would know to look for her. The door to her prison might never open again. The chain might never come off her ankle. She might be left behind, forgotten underground.

Jana tasted her coffee and wondered if Luke had slipped something in it. He hadn't drugged her since the night they made their bargain. He'd been true to his word. He had kept Eli away from her, and he had brought her out every night to see the sky. But she knew things could change. There could be something in the coffee now and she wouldn't taste it. She thought about it but kept the thought to herself. She couldn't afford to let Luke see it.

She never hesitated to eat or drink anything he gave her. That was part of the performance. Every move she made was part of the performance. The way she held her coffee and scanned the front page of *USA Today*, pretending to be engrossed in the lead story—a piece about a hurricane off the coast of the Carolinas. The way she reached casually for a plastic knife and used it to spread cream cheese on her bagel.

The performance was always evolving. Early on, she never reached for the knife; she left it to him to prepare the bagels. But over time she realized her mistake. She wanted to convey that she was harmless, that she could be trusted with a knife, and the way to do that was to take the knife without asking and toss it down again when she was through with it. Only a desperate person being held against her will would look at a plastic knife as a potential weapon.

Jana wasn't desperate—not in the scenes she played out with Luke Daw. She wasn't being held against her will. She was glad to see him, grateful for the things he brought her. When he took her out at night and let her bathe in a plastic pool, she was happy. And when he spread a blanket on the dirt floor of the barn, she lay down on it and wanted the same thing he wanted. Because the scene demanded it.

She was going to walk away from him. That was how the play ended. She only had to make it through to the end. So she drank her coffee and ate her bagel and talked to Luke about the hurricane that might make landfall on the coast of North Carolina. No script. They improvised their lines.

The scene wound down and he gathered the cups and the nap-kins and the plastic knife. Exit Luke with the leavings of breakfast. Jana watched him cross to the door, where he paused and threw out a line she wasn't expecting.

"Are you late?" he said.

Decisions. She could pretend she didn't know what he meant. She could lie. But he was smart; he knew the answer already. And she wasn't afraid of him—not in the play she wasn't.

She shrugged and said, "Maybe a day or two."

No strong reaction. He said, "Okay," and went out. The door closed.

Five hours later. Enter Luke with the key to the padlock that secured the chain around her ankle. Jana had finished one book and picked up another. Mickey Spillane, *I, the Jury*.

Luke worked the key in the lock and set her loose. He let her walk ahead of him up the stairs, and when she opened the trapdoor at the top she saw daylight for the first time in three months. The barn against a blue sky. The pond in the distance. A heron taking flight.

"Well, this is different," she said.

Luke Daw laughed and took her hand and they walked together down the slope of the hill, to the lane that ran past the pond. The lane cut through a grove of trees and she could see the trailer and the road and a car passing in the late afternoon. She didn't run for the road, because the Jana she was playing didn't need to get away. The Jana she was playing hadn't spent the last five hours worrying about what Luke would do if she was pregnant.

Luke took her into the trailer, and in the trailer there was takeout food laid out on a table: chicken shawarma, rice pilaf, pita bread and hummus, fattoush salad.

"It's Lebanese," Luke said.

"It looks good."

"Maybe you want a shower first."

She did want a shower. The bathroom was barely bigger than a phone booth, and the window was too small even to put her head out. She wouldn't have climbed out even if she could, because Luke Daw was no fool, and she wouldn't have been surprised if he had Eli out there somewhere, watching.

And the Jana she was playing didn't need to climb out a window. She belonged here.

She showered and washed her hair and dressed in clean clothes. Jeans and a T-shirt. And afterward she ate Lebanese food that Luke warmed for her in the oven.

A sweet scene after dinner. Luke Daw, bashful. He had a plastic bag from a drugstore. A small box inside, light as air. "I thought, you know . . ." he began. "We should find out for sure, don't you think?"

Into the bathroom again. She opened the box. Peed on the plastic stick. Came out to wait with him, both of them silent. Sitting on his lap with his arms around her waist. They looked at the result together, saw the plus sign.

Celebration. Luke on his feet, picking her up, twirling her around. Then his mouth on hers, eager. His hands undressing her. He carried her to his bedroom—narrow bed like a teenager's—and laid her down. This is right, Jana thought. This is what young lovers would do. She opened herself to Luke Daw and felt him inside her.

Fierce and gentle. She looked up into his eyes. He kept them open. Dark eyes. Sometimes they seemed empty, but not now. There was something in them that might have been love.

She closed her eyes and let herself surrender. As the part required. And when she cried out, he cried out a moment later, and she wrapped her legs around him and held him inside her. He'd been bracing himself up with his arms, but now she felt his weight settle onto her. She felt the heat of him, the brush of his lips against her temple. She felt the rhythm of his breathing. She heard him whisper, "This changes everything."

A t dusk they went for a drive. Fast in the Mustang around the bends of Humaston Road. Jana put one arm out through the passenger window and the other up through the sunroof and felt the wind on the palms of her hands. Eric Clapton playing on the radio. They flashed by a trailer on a gravel lot at the roadside.

"That's where Eli lives," Luke said.

They left Humaston and drove east. There were houses and a few businesses. Luke paid more attention to his speed. The road ran long and straight, lots of cars, a few semi trucks.

"Do you want ice cream?" Luke said. "There's a place up here— my grandfather used to take us."

The place was called the Frozen Cow. A tiny building with picnic tables in front. You walked up to a window under an awning to place your order. Luke parked and stepped out of the car. Jana got out too—barefoot on the warm asphalt. The *thunk, thunk* of the car doors shutting. The voices of a family at one of the picnic tables: mom and dad, daughter and son.

Luke paused to tuck something into his waistband and cover it with the tail of his shirt. The revolver. He'd pulled it from a drawer before they left the trailer. Because not everything had changed. Jana was tempted to ignore the gun, but that seemed wrong. She went around the front of the car, shaking her head, amused, indulgent. She slipped her arm through his and said, "Come on, killer."

They walked to the window and a woman came to take their order. She looked to be in her forties and wore a spotless white apron. She recognized Luke, called him Mr. Daw.

She worked the levers of the soft-serve machine, filling two cones. Jana got chocolate. Luke got a twist. The woman tapped the cones on the counter so the ice cream would settle in, then turned them upside down and dipped them in a pan of melted chocolate. She brought them out and righted them again and passed them through the window.

Luke paid with a twenty-dollar bill, and the woman made change. She winked at Jana before they left.

"How's this fella treating you?"

Jana smiled. "He's holding me against my will."

"Is he now?"

"But at least he feeds me."

Laughter all around. Jana felt Luke's hand resting easy on the small of her back.

The counter woman pretended to scold him. "Next time, you buy this girl a sundae."

"I will," he said.

They ate their ice cream in the Mustang with the sounds of traffic behind them and the sky growing darker. The family at the picnic table departed, and another came to take their place.

Cut to an image of Luke Daw with sticky fingers and chocolate on his face. Jana left the car and jogged to the counter for napkins and brought them back. An experiment. She wanted to see how far she could go.

Then they were on the road again, heading east. A Walmart store and a Fashion Bug. A Sears outlet. Then flickering pictures against the blue-black sky—on a movie screen a hundred feet wide. The marquee in front read WEST ROME DRIVE-IN. NOW PLAYING: INDEPENDENCE DAY.

Luke paid the admission and they passed through the gate. Three dozen cars inside and more coming in. Luke parked in the back row. The feature had just started.

Friday night at the drive-in: Teenagers shouting. Kids running between the rows of cars. The smell of popcorn. Jana and Luke tilted their seats back and held hands and watched the aliens blow things up.

Near the end, when Will Smith and Jeff Goldblum flew up to the aliens' mother ship, when they saved the planet with a laptop and a computer virus, Luke brought Jana's hand to his lips and kissed it.

"You can go if you want," he said.

She kept her eyes on the screen. "Hush," she said.

"I mean it. You can go. I won't stop you."

It could have been a trick, a way to test her. But it sounded true. And it tempted her. She could picture it: easing open the door of the Mustang and climbing out. A slow walk to the concession stand, where there would be a crowd of people. There would be phones. She could call her mother, and her mother would come and pick her up. It would be over.

I won't stop you.

It tempted her. Maybe Luke meant it, or maybe he only thought he meant it. Maybe he loved her. Or maybe his love would last only as long as she stayed. He still had the gun. It wasn't in his waistband now, but he had it within reach, in the space between his seat and his door. Maybe he would let her go. Or maybe he would change his mind as soon as she turned away from him. And if he did, there would be no long walk. No phone call. There would only be a bullet in the back.

Patience, Jana thought. It's not time yet for your exit.

She pushed Luke's shoulder playfully. "Hush. I'm trying to watch the movie."

L ater, when the credits rolled, Luke started the Mustang and joined the stream of cars flowing to the exit of the West Rome Drive-In. A right turn would take them back to Humaston Road, but Luke turned left instead, heading east on Erie Boulevard, deeper into the city of Rome.

A quick tour of Luke Daw's life: his grade school, his high school. St. Mary's Church, where he had received his first communion. Bars where he and Eli had played, when the band was still together.

He drove her around the campus of Bellamy University. Music blasting from frat houses, throngs of students in the streets. Banners welcoming the new freshman class. Luke took her away from the noise, to a building with a stone façade and hydrangeas growing up the walls. The School of Art.

He stopped the car, letting the engine idle.

"I always wanted to go there," he said.

"You should," said Jana.

"They'd never let me in."

"They might."

"It costs a ton."

"We'll figure something out."

He shook his head and fell silent, looking away from her. Staring at the building through his open window. Caught up in his own thoughts.

Right then, Jana believed that she could slip away from him. She could run back the way they'd come, back to the noise and the people. She wouldn't need to run far. He would be slow to react. He could chase her or he could shoot at her, but he couldn't do both at the same time. To run would be a risk, but sooner or later she would need to take a risk.

She made up her mind. And as she reached for the button of her seat belt, Luke turned to her and seized her hand.

"I'm sorry," he said, "sorry for everything I did to you."

It took all the control she could muster, not to snatch her hand away.

"It's all right," she said softly.

"No, it's terrible, the way I treated you. You don't even know."

She didn't get to hear how terrible it was. There was a flash of red light, and a siren sounded behind them. Close and loud. *Whoop, whoop.* Both of them froze, Luke staring in the rearview mirror. She felt him squeezing her fingers.

"What is this?" he murmured. "What did I do?"

The siren sounded again.

Jana looked over her shoulder at the patrol car.

"I think you're blocking the street," she said.

Luke released her hand and put the Mustang into gear. He waved an apology and drove off slowly. Found the boulevard and headed west toward home. The patrol car followed. They came to a red light and it drew up in the lane beside them. A heavyset cop with ginger hair tipped his hat to Jana Fletcher and smiled. When the light turned green, the cop pulled ahead of them and sped away.

Luke drove through the intersection, a long breath escaping him. Jana reached over and laid her palm against his chest, felt his heart racing.

She laughed. "Take it easy, killer."

They ended their night back at the farm on Humaston Road. Luke parked the Mustang by the trailer and they walked together along the lane in the light of the waning moon. They came to the pond and went out on a little dock half hidden in a jungle of reeds.

The planks of the dock felt rough under Jana's bare feet. Luke put an arm around her shoulder and she put an arm around his waist. She breathed the green smell of the water and touched the soft cotton of his untucked shirt. He didn't have the revolver; he had left it in the car.

"I think we should talk about names," he said.

"Do you?"

"For the baby."

"I figured for the baby."

"Unless you think it's too soon."

"No," Jana said. "We can talk about names."

The water looked black in the moonlight. She could see a popsicle stick floating in it. A few others lay forgotten on the dock. This was a place where Luke came to think.

"People use family names, don't they?" he said.

"Sometimes."

"My grandfather was Ben. Benjamin. But I wouldn't want to name a kid after him."

"We don't have to."

"I never knew my father. My mother said his name was Luke, but I don't even know if that's true."

"Luke's a good name."

"We can do better," he said. "What was your father's name?"

"Sadiq."

"That sounds foreign."

"He was from Sudan. But I never met him. He died when I was a baby."

"Sadiq Daw. It doesn't really work."

"No."

"What about Fletcher?"

"Sadiq Fletcher's no better."

Luke smiled. "I meant as a first name. Fletcher Daw."

Jana rested her head against his shoulder. "That's good."

"It is, isn't it?"

"There's only one problem."

"What?"

"Suppose it's a girl."

A long, quiet moment, broken only by a *plup* somewhere far out in the pond. Maybe a fish breaking the surface of the water.

"If it's a girl, that's easy," Luke said. "We can call her Margaret. Maggie. After my mother. If that's okay."

"Okay."

"Maybe Margaret Lydia, so your mother doesn't feel left out. Or Lydia Margaret—I guess we could do it that way."

"We've got time," Jana said, "to work out the order."

A longer quiet. Luke's left hand went into his pocket and came out with a popsicle stick. He held it with two fingers and a thumb. Spun it slowly once. Twice.

"My mother used to bring me here," he said, "in the mornings after breakfast. We'd watch the ducks, and sometimes we'd feed them. Scraps of bread. You're not supposed to; it's not good for them. But I don't think she knew. The day she left, we came here and fed them, and then she put me on the bus for school. When I got home, she was gone."

Jana looked up at him. His eyes were truly empty now. A lost boy. He dropped the popsicle stick into the water.

"I'm tired," he said. "Are you tired?"

"A little."

"Tired. And I don't think I'll be able to sleep. But we should head back."

They went down off the dock and when they came to the lane Jana looked to the left, the direction of the trailer and the road. She thought for sure they would go that way. But Luke turned right, leading her by the hand up the slope toward the barn and the fallen farmhouse. The roof of the barn was a bare frame against the dark sky. Jana could see the silhouette of a crow perched on the peak.

Luke brought her to the trapdoor. He meant to take her down.

She stopped him and they stood toe to toe. Her hands went to his collar and then to the sides of his face. She held him steady as if she could make him see her.

"You don't have to," she said. "I won't leave you."

He drew her in close to him, folded his arms around her. She felt his chin on the crown of her head. "I know you won't," he said. "It's just for tonight. I need some time on my own. I need to think. This is a big change. I need to figure out how it's going to work. And I want to talk to Eli—give him the news."

He stroked her hair. "Just one more night," he said. "That's all I ask. Then we'll move you into the trailer. I promise. One night. You'll give me that, won't you?"

Jana knew she could argue, she could plead. She could cry and try to persuade him. Those were choices, but they weren't the right ones for the scene. The Jana she was playing wouldn't resist. She would take him at his word and give him what he wanted.

"One night?" she asked.

"I promise."

"Okay."

She turned her face up to kiss him. A long kiss. Long as a night underground. When it ended, they broke apart. Luke opened the trapdoor. She went down first and waited at the bottom of the stairs. He joined her and brought out a key to unlock the door. They went in together and she switched on the lantern. She moved to the back of the room and stood over the coiled chain on the floor.

The chain glowed a dull gray in the lantern light. He looked down at it, then back at her.

"We don't have to use it," he said.

"Why not? It's just one more night."

"Are you sure?"

"Put it on. You'll feel better."

Jana stood passive with her hands in the pockets of her jeans. Luke knelt and wound the chain around her ankle. He slipped the padlock through the links. She heard it click.

He started to rise, laid a palm against the wall to steady himself— right at the spot where the chain passed through the wall. He touched the piece of two-by-four above the chain.

It shifted slightly.

He stayed down and looked more closely. There were two holes in the board where it had been screwed into the studs. The holes were empty. He touched them with a finger, one after the other.

"What's this?" he asked.

"What's what?"

He found the ends of the two-by-four and wiggled it free from the wall.

"What happened to the screws?" he asked.

"I took them out."

A tricky line to deliver. She thought she gave it just the right spin. Innocent. Disarming.

He looked at the board, and at the space in the wall.

"Why?" he asked.

"Just to see if I could," she said. "It's no big deal. You can put the screws back in. They're over in the corner."

He turned on cue and looked at the corner. She brought her hands out of her pockets, each one holding a four-inch woodscrew. She sank the screws into Luke Daw's neck, as far as they would go, one on either side. She held them in with the heels of her hands.

An ugly sound came out of him, part scream and part growl. The board he'd been holding dropped to the floor with a hollow clatter, and he reached to pry her hands from his neck. At the same time, he threw his weight back against her, knocking her off-balance.

She lost her grip on his throat and fell backward onto her mattress. Luke struggled to his feet and his fingers clawed at his neck. He took hold of one of the screws by the head and yanked it free. A jet of blood sprayed the wall.

Rage and pain twisted his face. He lunged at Jana and she rolled aside, sweeping her leg to pull the chain taut. The chain tripped him up, sent him sprawling. He landed badly, one arm beneath his body, and Jana heard a snap of bone, and a howl.

She stood up. The chain rattled. Luke Daw rolled onto his back and used his feet to push himself across the floor. Blood spurted from his neck. Jana picked up the length of two-by-four.

"Wait," Luke said. "Just wait."

She held the board like a baseball bat.

"I don't want to wait anymore."

He tried to rise, bracing himself against a side wall. One arm hung useless; he dragged himself up with the other. Jana stepped in and swung the board at his left knee—a good, square, solid hit that made him scream. A proper scream, high and frightened as a child's. He slid down the wall, and she tightened her grip on the board and took aim and brought it down hard on the other knee.

I n the end, Luke tried to crawl, tried to make it to the front of the room, to the door, where the chain would prevent her from reaching him. He tried to crawl with a broken arm and two wrecked knees. Jana caught him and dragged him back and used the board to break his ribs.

When he stopped struggling, she dug his keys from his pocket: the keys to his car and trailer on a ring, and the padlock key by itself. She opened the lock and set herself free from the chain.

She didn't leave him. She sat beside him on the floor and listened to him sob. He had his good hand pressed against his neck, but the blood pulsed through his fingers and ran down through the spaces between the floorboards. She thought she should talk to him. She couldn't think of any words, not her own words, not for him. But she spoke some lines that came into her mind.

"Farewell, my love, because today I die . . . No more shall my eyes drink the sight of you like wine . . . My heart cries out and keeps crying: Farewell, my dear, my dearest, my own heart's own, my own treasure . . .

"I am never away from you. Even now, I shall not leave you. In another world, I shall be still that one who loves you, loves you beyond measure, beyond—"

The life faded out of him and his hand fell away from his neck. Jana spent another minute on the floor and then got up slowly and looked around. She had his keys. What else did she need? Money. She found his wallet and took the cash. What else? Nothing. Or maybe one last thing. She picked up the two-by-four and carried it with her. Up the stairs and out into the world.

The moon still hung in the sky. The crow was missing from the roof of the barn. She glided down the slope of the hill—you couldn't call it walking—she felt too light. She found the lane and headed for the trailer. She knew she could find fresh clothes there. And the Mustang was waiting. And the revolver.

She passed the dock, hesitated, turned back. She dropped the two-by-four on the ground. The sound of wind in the reeds drew her, and she walked to the end of the dock and stretched out on her stomach on the planks. She saw her face looming dark in the water. She reached down and touched the surface with her fingertips. Reached with two hands and scooped water and bathed her face. She washed away tears and Luke Daw's blood.

She waited on the dock until the surface of the water turned smooth again. And then she wanted to stay longer, even though the planks were hard and rough beneath her. She wanted to stay with the girl in the water. The girl who couldn't stop laughing.

41

thought Warren Finn would drive back to Geneva, back to his wife, but he wanted to see the farm on Humaston Road. I told him I could show him the place another time. The storm was building outside. The rain had started: soft at first and then hard. He didn't care. He would have gone by himself. I decided to take him.

We left Jana's street and traveled south on Clinton Drive and all the houses were dark, but eventually we came to neighborhoods that still had power. We reached Erie Boulevard and turned west. The stoplights were working. Traffic was sparse. Most people had the wisdom to stay home.

I took it slow on the curves of Humaston Road. The rain fell long and white in the light of the high beams. The truck's wipers slapped out a fast rhythm. I pulled onto the soggy gravel beside Luke Daw's trailer. The screen door of the trailer had been held on by a single hinge, but now it was gone. The wind had taken it away.

Warren got out of the truck as soon as it rolled to a stop. I let him go. He ran to the trailer as if Jana might be waiting for him there. I put on my nylon jacket and walked around to the bed of the truck and found two flashlights. The rain drenched me, in spite of the jacket.

When I entered the trailer I found Warren in the kitchen. The steel basin was at his feet—the one that held the burnt remnants of one of Luke's models. Warren's face looked pale and blank. There was nothing to discover here, no trace of Jana.

They wouldn't have kept her here, I thought. Not for three months. They would have needed someplace more secure.

Warren drew his foot back and kicked over the basin, spilling popsicle sticks across the floor. The steel rang out, a bell in the rain.

I handed him a flashlight and said, "Come on. I have an idea."

The storm turned the lane into mud. We trudged through it, under the birch trees and along the edge of the pond. The beams of our flashlights swept the ground ahead of us. I tried hunching my shoulders, keeping my head down, but the rain found me anyway. Warren Finn strode along with his chin up, heedless, his ponytail plastered to the back of his neck.

We left the lane and started climbing the slope. I lifted my head and saw a bright light over the skeletal roof of the barn. The full moon, veiled by a cloud. Warren would have gone that way, toward the barn. But I tugged his arm and led him toward the heap of timber that had once been the farmhouse.

"Luke and Eli lived here with their grandfather," I said. "In the summers, they worked for him on the farm." Wendy Daw had told me that the first time I spoke to her. "And if they didn't behave, he'd lock them in the root cellar."

My flashlight beam passed over the ruins of the house. Rotting wood. Stones from the foundation. Slate tiles from the roof. The root cellar would be buried underneath, but there might still be a way in—an access point from outside the house. A door leading underground.

Where would it be? I remembered something I'd seen the last time I was here: a plastic kiddie pool. I walked to the west side of the house and found it, overflowing in the rain. Warren and I dragged the pool along the ground, water and wet leaves sloshing over the rim. But there was no door underneath.

The second place we looked was the toolshed near the house's southwest corner. A cheap metal structure with a rusted roof. We couldn't get purchase enough to slide it, so we tipped it over on its side. There was nothing underneath but a patch of bare ground.

I couldn't think of a third place to look. Warren and I split up to explore the perimeter of the house. I turned a corner and heard a strange sound over the heavy beat of the rain. A rush of wings. I remembered the crow I'd seen here before. I waved my flashlight, searching. There was no bird. The flashlight beam fell on a hoop of wood: the wagon wheel half-buried in the ground. I stood over it and scanned the weeds and wet grass. The light glinted on something metallic.

A ring of iron, the size of a bracelet.

I bent down and lifted it up. Heavy. The grass and weeds came up with it, revealing an opening three feet wide and five feet long. A door into the underworld.

Stairs leading down, and another door at the bottom. A more conventional one, standing open. I passed through it into a room that resembled a wooden cube. Like the one on the mantel in Jana's apartment. Not a perfect cube, but close enough: a dozen feet long and a dozen feet wide and maybe eight feet high.

I knew it had to be the work of Luke Daw. He had traded popsicle sticks for lengths of two-by-four. And I knew Jana had been here, because there was one two-by-four missing, one gap in the wall at the back of the room.

I knew what had become of Luke Daw. He was here. Pieces of him lay scattered on the floor. Skull and bones. He'd been gnawed on and picked apart, his clothes reduced to rags. He'd been eaten by mice and rats, bugs and worms. They'd had him for more than a year and a half. There was no flesh left. No scavengers either. They had moved on.

I found his wallet, and his driver's license gave me the confirmation I didn't need. I dropped it on the floor and moved to the back of the room. I saw a chain and a padlock—a makeshift shackle. The chain ran through the gap in the wall. I crouched down and shined my light through and saw a vertical beam, three feet away, out of reach. The chain was bolted to the beam. Beyond the beam there was nothing but the dirt wall of the root cellar.

I shifted the light to the piece of two-by-four above the gap. Two screws held it in place. Something made me reach into my pocket and dig out Jana's quarter. Maybe intuition. I slipped the pointed edge of the coin into the head of one of the screws. A snug fit. I tried to turn it. Got nowhere. I put the flashlight down and tried it with two hands. I struggled with it, sweat running over my skin. I held my breath and strained against it and managed to move it a quarter turn.

I sat with my back against the wall and clutched the quarter and breathed. My clothes clung to me. I heard the muffled sound of the rain up above. My flashlight's beam lit the padlock and the chain. There was a key in the lock. It made me think of Jana setting herself free. I felt a chill and then a flush of heat running through me, because I knew I'd only had the smallest glimpse of what it must have taken for her to turn that key.

I heard footsteps on the stairs, Warren Finn coming down. He stood in the doorway taking things in. His flashlight sliced through the dark. He came into the room and the circle of light found Luke Daw's license on the floor. The circle floated over a dirty mattress, a battered paperback. A grubby blanket. It found a plastic bucket. It moved here and there, seeking out Luke Daw's bones. It climbed the walls and found dark ribbons that looped and curled. The ribbons looked like blood.

The circle of light moved into a corner. Warren followed it. He nudged something with the toe of his shoe. I heard it roll over the floorboards. Luke Daw's skull. Warren worked it clear of the corner and gave it a sharp kick that sent it crashing into the far wall.

"I want to kill him."

I heard the words over the muted rain. But barely. Warren spoke them in a tight, low voice, carefully controlled. The kind of voice you use in lieu of screaming.

"I know," I said.

Warren kicked the skull again and the damn thing bounced off another wall and wouldn't break. He stomped it with his heel and I heard it crack. He stomped it again and it broke in three pieces, and he stomped each one of those. He broke the pieces into smaller pieces, and when they wouldn't go any smaller he went looking for more bones to break.

He wanted to kill Luke Daw. I wanted to do the same. Neither of us would get what we wanted, because Jana had already killed him. Which meant that I was wrong. Luke Daw wasn't the one who spied on Jana from the woods. He wasn't the one who broke through her door and put his hands around her throat and left her on the floor for me to find.

Luke Daw didn't light the fire at Poe Washburn's house. He didn't kill Jolene Halliwell or Simon Lanik.

I had believed all those things, and none of them were true. What was left? I still believed that the Daws killed Cathy Pruett, and that it happened here at the farm. I believed that Jana knew about it, which was why she'd been convinced that Gary Pruett was innocent.

I got up and leaned against the wall, felt the kidney-punch ache in the small of my back. I watched Warren Finn stalking the room in a quiet rage, grinding bits of Luke Daw's bones under his heels.

I was struck by the smallness of the space. Twelve by twelve. One thin, narrow mattress. One chain coming through the wall. It was a prison designed to hold one prisoner.

Luke and Eli Daw had Jana here, but they went out and abducted Cathy Pruett. They watched her from their white van and they took her. That's what I believed.

But why would they do that? Maybe they intended to replace one prisoner with another. But why Cathy Pruett? They started with Jana, a girl in her early twenties, a stranger to them. Why would they choose to replace her with Cathy, a woman in her late thirties— someone familiar to them, because she had taught at their high school?

What if I was wrong? I'd been assuming that the Daws abducted Cathy and brought her here—in part because that was what Jana seemed to have believed, based on what she'd said to Poe Washburn. But would Jana have been in a position to know, or had she made assumptions about how Cathy Pruett died?

What if there was a different explanation?

What if Cathy Pruett came to the farm on her own, and saw something the Daws didn't want her to see?

What would have drawn Cathy here?

Luke and Eli were drug dealers. Wendy Daw had told me they sold pot at the community college. They sold it to students—and professors too. So they probably wouldn't have hesitated to sell it to high school teachers.

But Cathy Pruett never experimented with drugs. I'd heard that from her sister-in-law, Megan. Cathy never even smoked a joint.

What about Gary Pruett? He cheated on his wife with an eighteen-year-old. He had a looser set of morals. Lighting up would not have been beyond him.

In the last days of her life, Cathy Pruett suspected that Gary had resumed his affair. Suppose she wanted to make sure. Suppose she followed him.

Picture Gary driving out here to Humaston Road to buy pot from Luke Daw. Gary would knock on the door of the trailer. That's where the deal would be made. Not here, not in this room underground.

Unless Luke was selling more than pot.

Picture Luke leading Gary up the lane on a day in late July. He's got something to sell. Not a drug. Something better. The two of them come to the wagon wheel and Luke finds the iron ring. He opens the door in the earth.

But Cathy has been following them. They see her. Luke can't afford to let her know his secret. He kills her.

A clever theory, but it didn't ring true. Because if it were, then why did Gary Pruett keep silent about what really happened? Why did he let himself be put on trial for his wife's murder and sent to prison in Dannemora? And who killed Jana? Not Luke or Eli Daw. Not Gary from his prison cell.

I put aside my speculations and from my spot against the wall I watched Warren Finn drive his heel down on a long bone—a femur, if I had to guess. It wouldn't break. He needed leverage. He picked it up and rested one end on the floor and the other against a wall. He kicked at the center point and the bone snapped. He took the two halves and propped them against the wall and went on with his vendetta against Luke Daw.

Irrational. But that was what happened when people were angry. They did irrational things. I decided I'd give Warren a few more minutes and then I'd lead him out of here, through the rain, to the truck. I'd take him back to Jana's apartment.

That's when I thought of Neil Pruett.

There were four Pruetts: Neil and Megan, Gary and Cathy. Megan and Cathy had been best friends before they married the Pruett brothers. The two women looked out for each other. When Cathy first suspected her husband was cheating, she confided in her friend. Megan decided to follow him, to find out the truth. But the truth made Cathy's marriage unravel.

Megan Pruett had laid it all out for me: Gary was a liar. He would never change. She told Cathy she should divorce him.

I told her if I were in her position I wouldn't think twice. She got angry with me. I wasn't in her position, she said. And maybe she wouldn't be either if I hadn't followed her husband around and caught him—which she had never asked me to do.

Cathy Pruett was angry. She blamed Megan for her misfortune. It wasn't fair: Megan was just the messenger. But anger makes people do irrational things.

Megan had followed Cathy's husband and uncovered his affair. What if Cathy decided to turn the tables?

Picture it: a day in late July. Cathy follows Megan's husband, Neil. She doesn't know what to expect, but maybe Neil is like his brother: maybe he has a girlfriend on the side. She trails him out to Humaston Road. He goes to see Luke Daw. Luke leads him up the lane. To the wagon wheel. To the door. Cathy follows. Luke catches her and kills her.

He keeps her body on the farm—maybe in this room—until he can figure out the best thing to do. Then he dumps it in a field across town.

Gary Pruett goes to prison for the murder. His brother, Neil, lets it happen. Neil can't tell the truth. He can't admit he was at the farm that day, or reveal his reason for being there.

Jana escapes. She knows about Cathy, but she thinks Cathy was a random victim of the Daws. She knows Gary Pruett is innocent, but she can't say how she knows. Because she has her own secrets. She killed Luke Daw in self-defense. But it didn't end there: she drove to Eli Daw's trailer and shot him. A justified killing, as far as I was concerned. But the law might take a different view.

Jana was a girl who spent years caring for her ailing grandmother. She needed to do the right thing. It was in her nature. So she found a way to help Gary Pruett: Roger Tolliver's Innocence Project. She started talking to people about Gary's case. Which brought her to Neil Pruett's doorstep.

Outside, a wave of thunder rolled over the farm. I felt it in the wall at my back. Warren Finn looked up, aiming his flashlight at the ceiling.

"Are you finished?" I asked him.

Warren turned his gaze down again and stepped on Luke Daw's jawbone. I heard it snap in two.

"I've been waiting for *you*," he said.

"I'm ready to go."

I watched him kick at Luke Daw's teeth.

"Are you going to share?" he asked.

I didn't answer. I crossed to the doorway and stood at the bottom of the stairs.

"Luke didn't kill Jana," Warren said. "But someone did. You've been quiet. Doing a lot of deep thinking. So I'm wondering if you're going to share."

I brought my cell phone out of my pocket.

"I have a thought," I said.

"Let's hear it."

"It's nothing I know for sure."

"I don't mind."

"If I tell you, I need to know I can rely on you. You have to stay calm."

"I *am* calm."

I looked at him soberly. "The guy I'm thinking of, he might be innocent. We can't just go and break his jaw, much as we might want to. What we really should do is call the police. Show them what we've found here. Let them deal with it."

He scuffed his shoe along the floor and one of Luke's teeth skipped across the room. The sound died away, lost in a rumble of thunder.

Warren said, "This is about Jana."

"What does that mean?"

"It means you don't want to call the police."

"Doesn't matter if I want to. I should."

"You haven't called them yet."

I glanced at my phone. "There's no signal down here."

"You think you'll get a signal up there?" Warren said. "Forget the police. Tell me who he is. We'll go talk to him together. I won't hurt him."

He had his flashlight turned up toward his face. He wanted me to see that he was serious. His eyes were steady. They didn't wander. They burned into me. They told me what he'd left unsaid. *I won't hurt him. Not until I'm sure he's guilty.*

A mirror is a dangerous thing—and right then Warren Finn was a mirror. He was urging me to do what I already wanted to do. I wanted to confront Neil Pruett, even though I had no real proof against him. I wanted to forget about the police, because I didn't know if I could count on Frank Moretti.

I thought of the house on Bloomfield Street, the one painted pale blue. I thought I would find Neil Pruett there. If Warren wanted to come, he could come. We would talk to Pruett. We wouldn't hurt him. Not until we were sure.

I could hear the rain pelting the ruined farmhouse above us. Warren joined me by the doorway.

"Who is he?" he said softly.

I turned and started up the stairs.

"Come on," I said. "I'll tell you on the way."

42

At the house on Bloomfield Street, Neil Pruett drew back the string of his brother's bow.

He heard a sound that annoyed him: a knock on the door.

Letting out a breath, he released the arrow. It sailed across the room and buried itself in the wall.

Another knock, slightly more insistent.

Neil ignored it. He paced across the room—sock feet on the smooth hardwood floor—and pulled the arrow from the wall. It left a neat round hole. One of many. Six of them ran in a vertical line. Four ran diagonally, up and to the right. Another four, down and to the right. Forming a letter *K*.

A third knock.

Neil took his time. There was a sofa in the room, and a love seat. They faced each other, a coffee table in between them. The table held five pillar candles—each one burning, each one a different height. Neil laid the bow and arrow on the sofa. He picked up a mirror in a mahogany frame. He had taken it down to clear a space on the wall. Now he put it back. It covered all the arrow holes.

A fourth knock. Neil opened the door to the sound of thunder and rain. And saw Megan.

"Were you asleep?" she said.

"No."

"You took a long time."

"Sorry."

"Maybe I shouldn't have come."

"Don't be silly," he said. "Come inside."

He took her coat and hung it in the closet. She slicked her wet hair back from her forehead. Brown hair bobbed short.

"The storm—" she began.

She didn't have to finish. He'd been married to her for nine years. Technically they were still married. He knew she didn't like to be alone during a storm, especially at night.

"I don't have power at home," she said.

He gestured at the candles. "I don't either."

"Maybe I should go."

"You should stay."

He told her to sit. Left her for a moment. Went to the kitchen and came back with a bottle of wine and a corkscrew and two glasses.

She sat sideways on the love seat with a pillow at her back, her long legs stretched out over the cushions. He opened the bottle and poured. Gave her a glass: medicine for dealing with the storm. She bent her knees to make a space for him to sit.

He had drawn all the curtains in the room, but the wind still rattled the glass behind them. Each new gust made Megan turn her head. Neil put a palm on her ankle to comfort her.

By the time he poured her a second glass, she seemed more at ease. She settled in. Rested her feet on his lap.

"Have you been eating popsicles?" she asked.

A bizarre question. He shook his head.

"I thought maybe things were melting in your freezer," she said. "So you figured you'd better eat them."

Bizarre. Until he looked down and saw a popsicle stick in his hand, spinning between his fingers like a baton. He hadn't been aware of it.

"It's not from a popsicle," he said. "I bought a box of them at a craft store."

"Why?"

"I like the way they feel." He spun the thing faster. "It's a habit I picked up a couple years ago."

"I never saw you do it."

"I never did it while you were around."

Megan smiled. "What else have you been keeping from me?"

"Nothing I want to tell you about."

"Neil with his secrets," she said indulgently. "What happened to your hand?"

He looked down at the red circle. The cigarette burn.

"I had an accident," he said. "I was frying bacon and the grease splattered."

"Neil the bachelor," she said. "You were never much for cooking." She reached to swipe a finger over the surface of the coffee table. It came away dusty. "Never much for housekeeping either. What would I find if I went into the kitchen? Probably crumbs all over the counter."

That had always been one of her stock complaints: crumbs on the counter. There were others: wet towels on the floor, laundry thrown in the wrong basket, unwashed windows, unraked leaves, mail left unsorted, dishwasher left unrun, thermostat set too high, thermostat set too low. It was a long list.

"Let's talk about something else," he said.

She sipped her wine. "All right. You've got a bow and arrow in your living room. Are you taking up archery?"

"They used to belong to Gary," he said. "I dug them out of the attic."

He watched her frown at the mention of Gary's name. She had sharp features and the frown didn't suit her. It made her look like a fairy-tale witch.

"I don't think I ever told you about the bow," Neil said. "It has sentimental value. Gary shot me with it once."

He got the reaction he wanted: shock and curiosity. The story had been on his mind. He had told it to David Malone. Now he told it to Megan. A story about fifteen-year-old Gary and ten-year-old Neil.

Gary wants a bow, but their parents won't let him have one. He saves up and buys one anyway. He tries it out on a summer day when he and Neil are home alone. He shoots at trees in the backyard. But trees are boring. So he shoots at a dove.

The arrow finds its target. Gary and Neil watch the bird die.

If their mom and dad find out, Gary will be in trouble. So Neil threatens to tell them. He's ten. That's what little brothers do.

Gary threatens him back. Like older brothers do. But he goes further than other brothers might. He fits an arrow to his bowstring and aims it at Neil.

And his fingers slip.

An accident.

That was one version of the story. The one Neil had told David Malone. But it wasn't the truth.

Now, in the candlelight, he told Megan the truth.

"Gary pulled the string back and let it loose. Everything seemed to move in slow motion. I saw the arrow coming toward me. I thought I was dead. But it passed over my shoulder. It grazed my neck as it went by."

Megan gasped.

"I guess that's what you'd call it—a graze," Neil said. "What it really did was slice open the side of my neck. If it had gone an inch or so to the right, I think it would've hit my carotid artery."

"Oh my god," said Megan. "What did you do?"

"I backed away from him, terrified. I tripped over my own feet and landed on my back in the grass. My hand went to my neck and felt the blood. I looked at my palm and it was shiny red. I screamed."

Gary had laid down the bow. A peculiar detail, one that Neil remembered after all these years. Gary didn't drop the bow or throw it aside. He knelt in the grass beside Neil and set the bow carefully on the ground.

"He looked down at me," Neil said to Megan. "I'd put my palm over the wound again. But he tugged my hand aside. He was curious. He wanted to see."

Neil remembered the look of fascination in Gary's eyes. He remembered screaming again. And Gary raising a finger to his lips—the kind of gesture you would use if you were asking someone to keep a secret. When Neil screamed the third time, Gary put a hand over his mouth—in the same careful way that he had laid the bow on the ground. The pressure was light at first, just enough to quiet him. But Neil struggled, and something changed. Whatever emotion had been in Gary's eyes faded out of them. And Gary's hand pushed down harder.

"It was a neighbor who saved me," Neil told Megan. "An old spinster we never liked, because she always complained when we rode our bikes across her lawn. My screaming drew her out of her house. We heard her coming, yelling, *'What have you boys done now?'* and Gary took his hand away from my mouth, and by the time she came around the hedge to our backyard he had me sitting up."

The neighbor had driven them both to the emergency room. Their parents showed up there an hour later. Gary told them a story—the same one he'd already told the neighbor and the ER doctors: He'd been shooting arrows at a tree and Neil had run by out of nowhere. It happened so fast he couldn't help it, and he was sorry. He laid it on thick, how sorry he was. He cried real tears. Their father got mad, but he didn't want to make a scene in the ER. Their mother cried along with Gary.

Neil never contradicted Gary's story. He was in shock, and the whole thing seemed unreal anyway, and in the back of his mind he was afraid—afraid of what Gary might do to him if he told the truth, and afraid that his parents might not believe him.

That September when he returned to school he had a scar. Whenever someone asked about it, he lied: He'd been running through the woods and a low-hanging branch scraped his neck. Over the years the scar faded. People rarely noticed it anymore. If they did, he told them he'd had minor surgery—a couple of moles that had to be removed.

That was what he had told Megan, the first time she noticed the scar. Now, as he finished telling her the true story, she sat up on the love seat beside him. She slipped her fingers inside the collar of his shirt and touched his neck.

"Neil, that's awful," she said. "You could have died."

Neil stared at the candles on the coffee table. "I guess I was lucky."

"You can say it was luck. I think maybe someone was watching over you."

The suggestion shouldn't have bothered him. He knew she was sincere. But he looked up from the candles and said, "Who was watching? God?"

Megan moved her hand away from his neck. "Or angels," she said.

"That's just another way of saying God. I don't remember God being there that day. He sure wasn't there for the dove. If he wanted to protect me, the arrow never should've touched me."

Neil took a drink of his wine, but it tasted bitter. He put the glass aside. "There's no God," he said. "And no justice as far as I can see. No one gets rewarded for being good or punished for being bad. That's the one thing I'm sure of. My own brother almost killed me when I was ten. And what for? Because I said I would tattle on him. Let's be serious. No one was watching over me. Nothing happened to Gary. He didn't get punished—"

"He's in prison now."

Neil shook his head impatiently. "He's in prison for killing Cathy. Something he didn't even do."

"I don't know how you're so sure," Megan said. "I never understood it. And now—after what I've heard tonight—I understand it even less."

"I'm sure," Neil said. "But let's let it go. I don't want to argue."

Megan touched his shoulder. "I don't either," she said. "But I'm worried about you. I don't like you being on your own. Not if this is what you get up to—going through Gary's things, dredging up bad memories. I think you should come home. We'll both be better off. I miss you."

"It wouldn't work," he said.

"We'll make it work. We won't talk about Gary. We'll agree to disagree. Everything else is trivia."

Neil closed the fingers of his right hand around the popsicle stick. Squeezed it. Felt the pain of the cigarette burn.

"That's what I'm afraid of," he said. "Trivia."

"What do you mean?"

"I don't want to spend my time arguing about little things."

"We won't."

"Arguing about whose turn it is to dust, or how long to let the grass grow. Or about crumbs on the counter."

Megan smiled. "We may need to negotiate about the crumbs."

Neil flexed his fingers and closed them again around the stick. The pain of the burn seared into him. He thought about what it would be like to go back to her. Part of him was tempted. The weak part, the part he didn't like.

"It won't work," he said.

She watched him over the rim of her wineglass. "It will if you try," she said. "If both of us try. Come home."

"It's no good."

"Why?"

"I can't explain it," he said. "I could show you."

"Show me, then."

"You'll think I'm weird."

Megan nudged him playfully. "Oh, Neil. I already think you're weird."

He slipped the popsicle stick into his shirt pocket and stood.

"All right," he said. "I'll show you."

He took her wineglass and set it on the table, then helped her to her feet. He led her to the wall with the mirror. "Stand over here," he said.

He stood behind her with his hands on her shoulders, guiding her. She watched him in the mirror, amused.

He released her and stepped back.

"Now take the mirror down," he said.

Puzzlement. "What am I supposed to do with it?"

"Doesn't matter. Put it on the floor."

She did. "What happened here?" she said. "Why is there a *K* on the wall?"

"Don't turn around," he told her. "And don't ask questions. Not yet."

Rain fell steadily against the windows. He picked up the bow from the sofa. Nocked the arrow to the string and pulled it back.

"Now you can turn around."

She turned. Confusion. Anger. "Neil, what are you doing? That's not funny."

He let the arrow fly. It whistled through the distance between them and pierced her heart.

Megan Pruett crumpled to her knees. She fell forward. Caught herself on one arm. Neil laid down the bow and went to her. He eased her over onto her back.

Blood on her blouse, but not as much as he expected. The arrow shivered with her heartbeat. She licked her lips. Whispered his name.

"Don't try to talk," he said.

He was sure she wouldn't last, but she brought her right hand up and wrapped her fingers around the shaft of the arrow. She tried to draw it out. He put his hand over hers and held it in place.

The corner of her mouth trembled. She whispered, "Why?"

He could feel her chest struggling to rise, her lungs trying to fill themselves with air.

"Megan," he said. "There's not just one reason."

She mustered all her strength and whispered again: "Why?"

Her eyelids fluttered. He leaned close so she could hear him.

"I've wasted too much time with you already," he said. "I'm not going to listen to you whine about crumbs for the rest of my life."

43

Interlude:
Spring and Summer 1996

When he got tangled up with Luke Daw, Neil Pruett was thirty-eight years old. He had a stable job, an affordable mortgage, a passable wife. He drank moderately, smoked marijuana on weekends, and kept a collection of *Playboy* magazines in an old file cabinet in his basement.

His parents were dead: his father from a heart attack, his mother from leukemia. His brother, Gary, had delivered eulogies at both funerals, and the eulogies had reduced Neil to tears. Gary's eloquence and kindness on both occasions convinced Neil of two things: that Gary had genuinely loved their parents and that he might genuinely love Neil as well.

His memory of what Gary had done on that summer day in the backyard when they were kids kept him from being certain on the second point.

Neil didn't believe that any one thing had made him the way he was. But he knew that the incident with the bow and arrow had left him with the sense that people were unfathomable and the world was treacherous and unpredictable. It was a sense that stayed with him all his life. Which was probably why he ended up as something of an underachiever, teaching basic physics and chemistry to bored high-school students, even though he had once dreamed of working in a lab or an observatory, discovering new planets or new kinds of sub-atomic particles.

As Neil grew older, he came to believe more and more that the universe was a hollow place, that there was no God, no morality. If the world had a secret, it was that you could do whatever you wanted, as long as you were smart enough to get away with it. Knowing the secret set you apart from other people. Gary knew it, or so Neil believed. Neil knew it himself, though he had never really acted on it. Not until he got involved with Luke Daw.

On a Saturday afternoon in March 1996, Neil told Megan he was running out to buy some sealant to patch a crack in the concrete of their patio. He drove instead to an apartment building in south Rome and climbed the stairs to the third floor. The woman who met him at the door of apartment 3B was a part-time substitute teacher named Sheila Cotton.

She invited him in and they sat together on a long red leather couch. He passed her some folded bills and she brought a shoe box out from under the couch and gave him a baggie that held an eighth of an ounce of pot.

She said what she always said when he came around: "I could sell you more."

He answered the way he always answered: "If I had more, I'd smoke more."

He borrowed a rolling paper, as he always did, and rolled a joint on the lid of the shoe box. They lounged on the couch, their thighs touching, and passed the joint back and forth. Sometimes they would talk. Never about anything serious. This time she had music playing: Blues Traveler.

Neil knew things about Sheila Cotton. He knew she'd been married and divorced twice even though she wasn't yet thirty. He knew if he told a joke she would laugh—a throaty laugh like a barfly's.

He knew the feeling of her thigh, because they always sat like this, close together. It was the reason he bought so little at any one time, so he could justify coming back more often.

She had thick thighs, not like Megan's. Megan was slim and angular, but Sheila had a lush, rounded body, an hourglass figure. She tended to wear tight sweaters and tight jeans. Neil would be able to picture her, even after he left. He would hold an image of her in his mind, and when he got home later he would sneak down to the basement and find a *Playboy* with a centerfold who looked the way he imagined Sheila must look naked. And he would spend a feverish few minutes fantasizing about her.

Sheila had just passed the joint back to Neil when they heard a rap on her door. A comic moment followed: Neil in a panic, guilty at being caught, pinching out the joint and looking for a place to hide it; Sheila laughing as she got up, patting him on the knee, telling him to relax.

Sheila turned down the stereo, went to the door, and let her visitor in. A young guy with messy black hair: Luke Daw. He wore a long coat and carried a padded envelope under his arm. He was chewing on a popsicle stick.

Neil recognized him, and wished at once that he hadn't. He'd never had Luke in class, but he knew him by reputation. One of those kids you stay away from. You wait for the day when they'll drop out and you'll never see them again.

Neil could guess what was in the envelope. If he'd been asked to predict Luke Daw's future, it would have been something like this: a small-time dealer selling to an even smaller-time dealer.

Sheila took Luke into her bedroom and shut the door. They emerged a few minutes later, their business complete. The envelope was nowhere in sight. At the door, Luke turned his dark eyes on Neil and smiled. Brought two fingers up to his brow and flicked them away: a mock salute.

After he had gone, Sheila returned to the couch. She used her lighter to get the joint burning again. When she tried to pass it to Neil he waved it away.

"How well do you know that guy?" he asked her.

"Luke? Well enough."

"And you're comfortable with him?"

"Comfortable?"

"You trust him?"

"As far as I need to."

"I'm not sure I would. Did he ask you about me?"

She slouched beside him, looking up at the smoky air.

"He asked if you were a friend or a customer," she said.

"What did you tell him?"

"I told him you're a friend. More than that he doesn't need to know."

"You didn't tell him my name?"

"No."

"I think he recognized me."

"So what if he did?"

"I don't like having a student know about my . . . habits."

"He's not a student anymore."

"He's young, though. Suppose he talks to one of my students. I have to think about my reputation."

Sheila laughed and offered him the joint again.

"Relax," she said. "Your reputation's safe. Luke's cool."

Neil left her a short time later. A parting hug at the door—a promise of something that would never be delivered. He trudged down the stairs and out into the afternoon. He found Luke Daw waiting on the sidewalk in front of the apartment building.

Neil tried to ignore him, but when he headed for the parking lot he heard Luke's footsteps behind him.

"I feel like I know you," Luke said.

Neil stopped at the edge of the lot and turned. "I don't think so."

"What's your name?"

Neil hesitated and said, "Kevin." His middle name.

Luke smiled. "That's not the name I remember."

They stood a few feet apart in the cold afternoon light. Bleak springtime. Puddles around them.

Luke still had the popsicle stick. He held it with two fingers like a cigarette.

"Are you happy, Kevin?" he asked.

An odd question. Neil's first instinct was to ask, *In what sense?* But that would have invited a longer conversation. Better to keep things brief.

"Sure," he said.

"Because if there's anything you need," Luke said, "you can tell me."

"I don't need anything."

Luke moved closer. "I've got more than Sheila's got. That's all I'm saying. Coke. X. Or pills—Vicodin, Oxy. Whatever you need."

"I'm all set."

"You don't look happy."

"I have to go," Neil said.

He turned away and headed for his car, but he soon realized he wouldn't be free of Luke so easily.

Neil had parked at the edge of the lot facing a steel fence. The spaces on either side of his car were empty, but there was a black Mustang parked behind it. There was no way he would be able to back out.

As Neil stood by the driver's door of his car, Luke walked up and said, "Is this your ride?"

"Yes, it's mine," Neil said.

"It's nice."

Luke leaned his back against the car. He started turning the popsicle stick end over end between his fingers. He glanced at the Mustang. "I guess I blocked you in," he said.

Luke had already known which car was his, Neil thought. Obviously. It wouldn't have been hard to guess. There was a parking decal on the windshield from the high school where he taught.

Neil nodded toward the Mustang. "I'd appreciate it if you'd move that," he said.

"Oh, sure," said Luke. "But we were talking, weren't we?"

"I have to go."

"I heard that the first time. But I was saying before that you don't look happy. I'd like to help you."

Neil felt the air turning heavy around him. "You don't have anything I want," he said.

"How do you know," said Luke, "if you won't talk to me?"

He stared at Neil but said nothing more. His eyes were empty of expression—except for a cold amusement.

Neil thought about walking away. He didn't want to play mind games with Luke Daw or, worse, get into a fight over nothing. But he had his pride. He stood his ground.

"Will you please move your car?" he said.

No answer.

"I'm not looking for trouble," he said.

Luke gave a quick smile that was really just a flash of teeth. "Who said anything about trouble?" He bent the popsicle stick with his thumb. "You're not afraid of me, are you?"

"No."

"Good. I'm just trying to get you what you want. Listen, do you have a hundred?"

"What?"

"A hundred dollars."

Neil frowned. "Come on."

"What does that mean, 'Come on'?"

"Knock it off," Neil said. "I really need to go."

"Why do you feel like you have to run off, Kev? I'm not trying to scare you."

"I'm not scared."

"That's good. So give me a hundred and I'll give you something you want."

"There's nothing—"

"Sure there is. And I'm telling you you can have it. The price is a hundred dollars."

Neil hesitated, then took out his wallet. He felt like a coward, but he'd had enough of Luke Daw. He found four twenties and two tens and held them out. Luke tossed his popsicle stick into a puddle. He took the money casually and it disappeared into his coat pocket.

"See?" he said. "That wasn't so hard."

He walked away and got into his Mustang. Neil stood by his car.

He wasn't sure what had just happened. Had he been robbed, or did Luke actually intend to give him something in return for his money? What would that be? Was he supposed to wait for it?

He got an answer quickly. Luke started up the Mustang, waved good-bye, and rolled out of the lot and into the street.

Over the next few days, Neil kept his eye out for Luke. He was afraid the kid might show up at his school—or his house. He didn't want Luke talking to Megan. She didn't know anything about Sheila Cotton, and she didn't need to know.

When a week passed with no sign of Luke, Neil laughed at himself for being paranoid. He considered staying away from Sheila and finding a new source to buy from, but decided he had no reason to. He waited the usual interval and drove to her apartment on another Saturday afternoon. It went the way it always did.

"I could sell you more."

"If I had more, I'd smoke more."

They shared a joint on the couch and when there was nothing left but the roach, something happened. Sheila sat up and bent close to him. Put her hand on his knee and said, "You don't have to leave, do you?"

Her eyes held a plain invitation. Hard to believe, but Neil let himself believe it. After a moment he kissed her shyly: a dry, awkward kiss. Then another with their mouths open, their breath tasting like smoke. His shyness passed. He was eager and she laughed her throaty laugh and told him to take his time. She straddled him and he got her sweater off, and her bra was red and silky—like nothing Megan would ever wear.

He reached for the button of her jeans and she got up and took him by the hand and led him to her bedroom. She swept the bedspread aside and fell back onto white sheets. He peeled her jeans off and discovered she had a thong to match the bra.

He kissed her stomach. Skin flawless, the color of cream. She lay with her arms spread, surrendering. Her dark hair fell over a pillow. The bra unhooked in the front and the thong came off, strings of silk skimming down over her thighs. He saw the lush body he had imagined. Soft and yielding. Not like Megan. A body you could sink into.

The first time was too intense. He couldn't last. But she let him have a second time, and the second time was good. It ended with her clutching at the sheets and wrapping those thighs around him. Her eyes closed, her mouth whispering *Yes*.

Afterward she got up to crack the bedroom window. She came back and they lay side by side on the sheets. Neil looked at the ceiling: swirls of white stucco. He felt the sweat evaporating from his skin.

"I didn't expect this," Sheila said.

"Neither did I," Neil told her.

"I'm glad it happened."

"Me too."

She turned onto her side to face him. "I don't want you to have the wrong idea."

"What's the wrong idea?"

"That I do this all the time, with every man who comes through here."

"Oh."

"Because I don't."

"Of course you don't."

"In fact, I thought it was a joke at first."

Neil felt a momentary tightness in his chest.

"A joke?" he said.

"When Luke suggested it. I thought he was messing with me."

Neil focused on the swirls in the ceiling. He should have been more alarmed to hear Luke's name. But part of him had known all along.

I'll give you something you want.

"It didn't add up," Sheila said, "that you would go through him. Not after what you told me, about how you didn't trust him. But he kept saying it was for real. And I guess it was. I mean, here we are. Right?"

"Right," Neil said.

"At first I was offended. But then I thought: It's sort of sweet. Because you were too shy to ask me yourself. And maybe it's better you didn't, because I probably would've slapped you in the face. And we would've missed out on this. And why should we miss out?"

"We shouldn't," Neil said.

"I know. And I like you anyway. I always did. But I'm happy to have the cash too. Because I really need it." She laid a palm against his ribs. "And it's not like I'm going to start sleeping with random men for money. This can be our thing. A special arrangement."

"That sounds fine," Neil said.

Sheila moved her palm over his stomach, snuggled closer. "There's just one problem," she said. "We can be honest with each other, can't we?"

"Sure."

"Well, honestly, the more I think about it, a hundred seems low. Would you mind if we went higher? Not this time. But from now on."

Neil couldn't see her face. He was still focused on the ceiling. But he could feel her body pressed against him. All that perfect flesh.

"How much higher?" he asked.

"What about two hundred?" she said.

He didn't react—at least, he didn't mean to. But she must have seen something.

"Or one fifty," she added quickly.

He sat up and turned to take in the sight of her. That body. And the face too. A brave face, but it was masking something. Doubt. Vulnerability. Insecurity.

He smiled gently. "One fifty seems fair."

When he left her apartment, he thought he would find Luke Daw waiting in the parking lot. He didn't. He drove home and Megan asked him where he'd been, and he made up a story about running into an old friend from college. And she believed him. It was easy.

The following Saturday he went to see Sheila again. Too soon for him to need more pot, but he bought some anyway. He started to roll a joint on the shoe box lid and she told him to leave it. She led him to the bedroom and pulled her sweater off over her head. Her bra was purple this time. Her thong too.

They smoked the joint after. Sheila had an old-fashioned claw-foot tub, with a rubber drain plug on a chain. She ran a bath and got in to soak. Neil, half dressed, sat on a straight-back chair by the tub and kept her company. He held the joint for her to keep it dry.

When the water started to cool, she hooked the chain between her toes and pulled the plug. She stood up—a naked goddess rising out of the sea—and he helped her towel off. The tub took a long time to drain.

He left her money on the bathroom sink. One fifty. She put a robe on and walked him out. Kissed him at the door.

That was their routine, week after week, through the spring and into the summer. It was a high point of Neil Pruett's life, but there were signs, even early on, of how it would end. Small things. Sheila started wanting more of his time. She wanted to talk—and not any kind of interesting talk. She wanted to share the mundane details of her life.

And she started to ask him for favors—little ones, here and there. Once as he was leaving she asked if he wouldn't mind carrying her trash down to the dumpster. Other times she wanted him to check the oil in her car, or fix a leaky faucet, or a faulty light switch.

One Saturday he showed up to find her half hysterical. There'd been a mouse in the living room, and she had put down a trap. Now she had a dead mouse with a broken neck—and could he please do something with it? She couldn't bring herself to touch it.

But those were minor drawbacks. Neil found ways to make up for them. A few days after the mouse, he turned up at her apartment in the middle of the week. A Wednesday afternoon. Sheila came to the door wearing a white T-shirt and sweatpants, her hair in a ponytail. He caught a glimpse of a bewildered look; she hadn't expected him. But she slipped easily into her usual manner: gave him a slow kiss, took him by the hand, led him toward the bedroom.

They never got there. He pinned her against a wall, peeled the T-shirt off her—and the plain white bra he found underneath. He tugged the sweatpants down over her hips and pushed her to the floor. She didn't resist. He heard her throaty laugh. "Different rules on Wednesday," she said.

She ran a bath afterward and he sat with her. They smoked a joint. Steam rose from the water and beaded on the bathroom tile. Sheila rested her arms on the sides of the tub and tipped her head back.

"That was wild," she said.

Neil said nothing.

"I think you gave me bruises," she said.

He passed her the nub of the joint. "Maybe I'll give you more."

He climbed into the tub with her, his feet slipping on the bottom so he had to catch himself. She shifted forward and he got around behind her and let her lie back against him. Water flowed over the rim of the tub and onto the floor. Sometime later she wriggled around and raised herself up and took him inside her.

Later still, she climbed out. Left him there to soak. When she returned she had her robe on; she had a towel for him. He dried off, and as he was dressing she said, "You're a sweet man."

It gave him pause. He hadn't intended to be sweet.

He left that afternoon without giving her any money. It was the beginning of a new pattern: from then on he saw her twice a week, on Wednesdays and Saturdays. On Saturdays he gave her the usual hundred and fifty. On Wednesdays he gave her nothing. He thought she would complain, but she never did.

He didn't think to wonder why. Later on, when he looked back on it, he realized it had been a warning sign—just like the moment when she called him a sweet man. She was giving him clues, and he missed them. If he had paid more attention, he might have recognized that she was starting to think of herself as his mistress.

If Neil paid less attention to Sheila Cotton than he should have, it might've been because he had something else on his mind. He didn't know what to make of Luke Daw.

He had hoped that Luke might leave him alone, but he wasn't so fortunate. Luke seemed to take an ongoing interest in his arrangement with Sheila. How much she might have told him wasn't clear, but at the very least Luke knew that Neil visited Sheila on Saturdays. Once in a while Luke would turn up in the parking lot on a Saturday afternoon.

The first time it happened was at the beginning of May. Neil came down to find Luke's Mustang parked near his own car. Luke lowered the window and called him over.

"Kevin! Good to see you."

Neil approached him, reluctantly. "What do you want?"

"I want to make sure you're happy," said Luke.

"I'd be happier if you left me alone."

"Don't be like that, Kev," Luke said. "I'm your friend. I was right, wasn't I?"

"About what?"

"About what you wanted," Luke said, looking up at Sheila's third-floor window. "But Jesus, that wasn't hard to work out. I mean, who wouldn't want that? Am I right?"

Neil stood perfectly still. The sun threw his shadow onto the door of the Mustang. Black on black. He didn't speak.

"Don't be rude, Kev," Luke said. "I like you. I'm trying to help. You let me know if you need anything else."

He put the Mustang into gear and drove away. Neil watched him go, hoped he might not see him again. But Luke Daw kept coming back, every two or three weeks, always with the same line of patter: *I'm your friend. You let me know what you need.* He never made any threats, never asked Neil for money. Never even called him by his real name. To Luke, Neil was always Kevin or Kev. Or sometimes K.

As time passed, the glow started to fade from Sheila Cotton. Neil began to withdraw from her. He still went to see her, but she was less real to him. His mind wandered when she talked. He found reasons to cut his visits short.

Sheila seemed not to notice. She acted as if they could go on forever. She talked to him about her future in a tone that took for granted that he cared about her future. She wanted to find a permanent teaching job. She wondered if she needed to go back to school for a master's degree. She wanted to move to a better apartment, or at least fix up the current one. It was too gloomy. The walls needed a fresh coat of paint.

That's what she was talking about on the first Saturday in July, the day Neil finally broke it off with her. Paint.

"I've thought about going with white," she said. "White walls, white trim. I got the idea from a magazine. But maybe that's too, you know—"

"White?" he suggested.

"Yeah. So now I think I want color, but I want it faded out. Like in here, I was thinking yellow. But a really pale yellow, so it looks almost—"

"White?"

"Exactly."

They were in the bathroom. Sheila had the tub to herself. Neil sat in the straight-back chair, keeping her company. They'd burned through a joint and the smoke still lingered in the air.

"What do you think?" she asked.

"White sounds fine," he said.

"But it won't be white, it'll be yellow."

"Right. Yellow."

"What about the kitchen?"

Neil stared at his reflection in the mirror over the sink. "You mean what color?"

"Yes."

"I thought you were going to use yellow all over."

"I can't paint every room the same."

"I don't know what to tell you."

"I'm thinking green for the kitchen."

"*Green* green or green that looks like white?"

"That's what we have to decide."

Neil-in-the-mirror made an unhappy face. "It's really your decision, isn't it?"

"It won't kill you to help," Sheila said. "You spend time here too."

"All right. Green seems fine."

She sat up in the tub. He heard the *swush* of the water.

"Maybe we could order pizza," she said. "You could stay, and we could look at samples."

"What for?"

"To pick the colors."

"We already picked yellow and green."

"There's different shades. I've got swatches from the paint store."

Neil-in-the-mirror ran his tongue over his front teeth. "I can't stay."

"You could if you wanted."

"Then I don't want to."

She let out a huff of air. "You're impossible. I don't think I'm that demanding."

"I haven't said you were."

"Delivery pizza. Is that too big a commitment? Do you realize you've never taken me out to dinner?"

Neil-in-the-mirror made the unhappy face again. The skin scrunched up at the corners of his eyes.

"Sheila, I'm married. I can't take you to dinner."

"Why not?"

"Someone might see us."

"We could meet somewhere, out of town."

"I'm not going to sneak around on my wife."

She laughed. A high-pitched laugh, not at all throaty.

"Neil, what do you think you've been doing?"

"You know what I mean."

"I know. You mean you can't take chances. Not for me. I'm not important enough."

"I don't know what you want."

"I'm not important," she said. "Not as important as your wife. And that's pitiful. Because I've never had the impression that you care very much about her."

"Of course I do."

"You never talk about her."

Neil turned away from the mirror. Directed the unhappy face at Sheila Cotton.

"Why would I talk to you about my wife?"

Sheila leaned forward in the water and hunched her shoulders. "Now you're just being mean," she said. "I don't know why I put up with you. Serves me right for dating a married man."

Neil stared at her back. Her skin wasn't as flawless as he remembered. He saw small blue veins just under the surface. He noticed a mole.

"We're not dating," he said.

"Again—mean. You know, you'll have to choose eventually. Me or her. I've been waiting for you to come here one day and tell me that you're choosing me. That you're ready to treat me the way I deserve. How long do you expect me to wait?"

"I'm not leaving my wife."

"No. Why should you? You get to have it both ways. Maybe I

should go see Megan. That's her name, right? Maybe I should tell her where you've been spending your time the last few months. That would stir things up, wouldn't it? That's what you need."

Tension gripped Neil's shoulders. He tipped his head from side to side, trying to relieve it.

"You don't want to do that," he said.

"I don't. But maybe it's the only way to make you see what's in front of your eyes. To make you appreciate me."

She reached for the chain to pull the plug, to let the water begin its slow drain. In a few seconds she would rise up. Neil visualized it. She would sweep her wet hair back. The water would flow down her body in a rush. The bottom of the tub would be slippery. She could lose her footing, crack her head open on the hard, rounded rim of the tub. He would see her blood turn the water pink. Her head would sink beneath the surface.

It would be perfect. He'd be done with her and she would never talk to Megan.

He thought about it. If he thought hard enough, maybe it would happen.

Sheila stood up in the water. Brought her hands up to her head. As Neil watched, she leaned back slightly, squeezing the water from her hair. Her feet shifted; she started to lose her balance. She threw her arms out. Managed to steady herself.

So very close.

Neil rose from the straight-back chair and gave her a shove. She let out a startled cry and jerked backward. Bounced off the wall behind her. Her feet slid in the direction of the drain; the rest of her went the other way. She fell hard but her left arm and shoulder absorbed most of the impact. She groaned and pushed herself up out of the water, and he snatched a handful of her wet hair and slammed the side of her head against the rim of the tub.

The impact knocked her out, long enough for Neil to push her head underwater. The level was falling, but he thought he had enough time. She came to—her eyes snapped open—and she gasped reflexively. Water filled her lungs.

Fear in her eyes. Her body thrashed. He held her down by the shoulders. Felt the spasms tear through her, each weaker than the last. And in the end, stillness. He knelt by the tub as the water drained away. It left her skin pale and slick, her dark hair a seaweed tangle.

The last of the water ran away through the pipes and the world went silent. Neil pulled himself up into the straight-back chair. He watched Sheila Cotton, expecting her eyes to blink, waiting for a tremor of life to pass through her. Nothing happened.

Sound reentered the world: footsteps on the floor above. Neil knew he should be worried. People lived here. Someone might've heard, might've already made a call. At any moment there could be sirens. Cops pounding on the apartment door.

Neil went to the bedroom and found his clothes, his shoes. He put them on. Patient, calm. He tucked his shirt in. No sirens. He opened the bottom drawer of Sheila's dresser, because he had seen her stash money there once, when she thought he wasn't watching. Under a stack of sweaters he discovered an envelope that held a little over fourteen hundred dollars. He tucked it in his pocket.

Returning to the bathroom, he spotted the remnant of the joint on the sink. He dropped it in the toilet and flushed. He found a small towel and wiped the handle of the toilet. He wiped the straight-back chair. He moved around the room and then around the apartment, wiping everything he remembered touching.

His cleaning spree ended with the shoe box under the couch. He wiped it down and started to push it back into its hiding place, then reconsidered.

At the apartment door, with the shoe box clutched under his arm, he listened for sounds out in the hall. He pictured the hall empty, thought about his route down the stairs and into the lot. Imagined it devoid of people. When he was ready he used the towel to open the door; he twisted the lever in the knob to engage the lock. He pulled the door shut behind him.

He moved through the hall and down the stairs unseen. Out into the sunlight.

His car had been baking in the July heat. He dropped the shoe box and the towel on the passenger seat and turned the key. He felt sure the engine wouldn't start. It started. Hot air blew from the vents. He pressed the button for the air-conditioning and made himself wait—wait for the air to turn cool. No one came for him. No one rushed from the building to stop him.

The air was blasting cold when he drove away from Sheila Cotton's apartment.

On Monday morning, Sheila Cotton's apartment manager knocked on her door to collect the rent, which was overdue. He tried again on Tuesday. On Wednesday he used his passkey to let himself in, because he'd had tenants skip out before and he was losing patience. When he got inside, the smell led him to the body.

The story topped the news at eleven on Wednesday night. A spokesman for the police declined to say whether the death was an accident or the result of foul play. Neil watched the report on the TV in the bedroom, with Megan beside him, reading a book. He hoped the book might distract her. It didn't.

"Did you know that woman?" she asked him.

"No," he said. "Why would I?"

"They mentioned she worked as a sub. I thought you might've run into her at school."

"I don't remember her," he said. "Maybe I'll ask Gary."

Gary was always good for a distraction these days—Gary and his infidelity.

"Don't talk to me about Gary," Megan said.

And Neil obliged her. He clicked the remote to switch off the TV. Rolled over onto his side. But she didn't let it go.

"You haven't said what you think."

"About that woman?" he asked.

"Yes."

"I told you, I didn't know her."

"You can still take a guess," Megan said. "Was it an accident, or foul play?"

When a week passed without any visit from the police, Neil Pruett began to hope he might be safe.

He'd been careful never to give Sheila his home phone number, and he didn't own a cell phone. He'd first made contact with her the previous fall, when he spotted her in the teacher's lot at the high school, lighting up in her car at lunchtime. They'd done their communicating one-on-one, in person. People might have seen them together at school, but not recently. After their arrangement began, he'd made a point of staying away from her in public.

He supposed she might have kept a list of her customers, but he didn't think so. She wasn't in the kind of business where you kept lists. She might have talked about their relationship with a friend, but it wasn't really the kind of relationship you talked about.

Which left one person who could draw a connection between them: Luke Daw.

In the evenings of those days in mid-July, Neil found himself stepping out onto his porch in the fading heat. He'd watch the passing cars. Sometimes he'd walk up and down the block. It took him a while to realize he was waiting for Luke.

On the eighteenth of July, a Thursday, nine-thirty, the black Mustang stopped at the curb in front of the house. Luke Daw leaned over and opened the passenger door. Neil went down from the porch, slow and deliberate as a sleepwalker. He got into the car.

He didn't worry about Megan. She wouldn't see; she wasn't home. She had gone to console Cathy, because it looked like Gary was starting up his affair again—the one with the eighteen-year-old.

Luke pulled away from the curb, driving with one hand on the wheel. The other hand held a popsicle stick. He spun it around slowly with his fingers.

"Kev," he said. "You don't look happy."

"Why don't you tell me what you want?" said Neil.

"I thought we should talk. Things have been happening."

Neil leaned back in his seat and waited.

"Crazy news about Sheila," Luke said.

"I don't know what you're looking for."

"You're always wrong about me, K. We're on the same page."

"What does that mean?"

"I get it. I know what she was like. There were plenty of times I felt like drowning her too, believe me."

"I didn't drown her."

"I know. That's the first thing I thought when I heard the news. *I'm sure K didn't drown her.* They found her on Wednesday and she'd been dead a few days. So figure she died sometime around Saturday afternoon. And you were there every Saturday. I bet it's surreal for you, thinking how she must have died right after you left."

"I had nothing to do with it."

"I know. It had to be an accident. She was a gorgeous girl, but needy. She was bound to have an accident sooner or later. I wish it hadn't happened. I wish you had let me look out for you. If I'd known you were bored with her, I could've found you another. Then you wouldn't have been around—when she had her accident."

Luke pulled the Mustang to the curb. Neil looked through his window and saw that they had driven in a circle and arrived back at his house.

"Here's the problem," Luke said. "She made me money. Now that money's not coming in. You see where that puts me."

Neil tipped his head back against the headrest and braced himself for what he knew was coming.

Luke Daw laughed. "Honestly, K, you should see your face. Always thinking the worst. This isn't a bad thing, it's a good thing. You just have to trust me. Here's what we're gonna do."

Two days later. Saturday. Five o'clock. Neil Pruett rounded a curve on Humaston Road and saw the trailer. He slowed and made the turn onto the gravel, his tires throwing pebbles up under the car.

He had five hundred dollars in his pocket, part of the money he had taken from Sheila Cotton's dresser. He had it ready when Luke stepped out of the trailer. Luke took the money carelessly, as if it meant nothing.

"K," he said. "Take a walk with me."

They passed along a lane overgrown with weeds. There were ruts in the lane that would have been muddy in the spring, but the mud had baked in the sun. Neil saw the roofline of a barn in the distance, a matchstick structure open to the sky. He was aware that they had moved out of sight of the road.

"I can't stay," he said.

Luke kept walking. He pointed out the pond on their right, and the barn. He said something about his grandfather. He guided Neil up the slope of a hill toward a heap of timber that had been a house. They stopped near a wagon wheel half-sunken in the ground.

"This is it," Luke said.

"What?" said Neil.

"What I wanted to show you."

"I don't understand."

"You will."

Neil saw a black moth in the grass by the wheel. Watched its wings rise and fall.

"I gave you the money," he said. "Now I need to go."

"You won't go yet," said Luke. "And when you do, you'll come back. Next Saturday. You'll bring me another five hundred."

The moth flitted from one blade of grass to another.

"I can't," Neil said. "You have to realize—I don't have that kind of money. I can't go on paying you. Not week after week."

"You will, though. I know you, K. We're the same. That's what you need to get through your head. You think I'm threatening you, but I'm not. I won't make you come back. You'll come back on your own."

The moth fluttered over the grass and landed on an iron ring.

"Why would I come back?" Neil asked.

The moth flew away. Luke bent to take hold of the ring. He lifted it with an effort, and the ground came up with it.

"You'll see," he said.

44

should feel bad about this," said Neil Pruett.

No one heard him. Megan's heart had stopped beating. He touched the shaft of the arrow in her chest. It no longer shivered.

Outside, lightning flashed. Neil saw it as a thin, bright line in a gap between two curtains. The boom of thunder came five seconds later. Which meant the lightning strike was about a mile away. Basic physics: the speed of sound versus the speed of light.

Neil took a candle and went to find the things he needed. Paper towels, a blanket, scissors, a roll of twine. He came back and opened the blanket on the floor. He started to move Megan onto it and realized the arrow would be a problem. He broke off the shaft and left the rest inside her.

He rolled her onto the middle of the blanket. Used the paper towels to wipe the blood from the floor. Lightning struck again and automatically he counted down to the thunder. The bloody paper towels and the arrow shaft went into the blanket with Megan. He tossed her shoes in as well. Then bundled everything together and tied the bundle with lengths of twine.

He touched Megan's cheek through the blanket.

Said, "Tell me again how I was never much for housekeeping."

He should feel bad. He knew. Just as he should have felt bad about Sheila Cotton—and about the time he spent with Jana Fletcher in the wooden room at the farm on Humaston Road.

He had one regret about that time. He wished there'd been more of it.

That first Saturday, he spent an hour with her. When he came up from underground, the sky was brighter than any sky he had ever seen. The world was in sharper focus.

Luke Daw was waiting for him.

"See?" Luke said. "I told you."

Neil didn't respond.

"K, I swear. You should look in a mirror right now. See what you look like when you're happy."

Smug satisfaction in Luke's voice. Neil tried not to let it bother him.

"Who is she?" he said.

"Do you really want me to tell you?"

Neil decided he didn't. "But how did you—"

"None of that matters, K."

Neil gazed at a white cloud in the too-bright sky.

"She saw my face," he said.

"Don't worry," said Luke. "The stuff I'm giving her—she won't remember."

"But she looked right at me."

"Trust me. When are you gonna trust me?"

Luke told him he could come back in a week with another five hundred. Neil didn't think he could wait. He arranged to come back Wednesday—and again the following Saturday.

That second Saturday, the twenty-seventh of July, it all went wrong.

Blame it on Megan. Megan, who trailed Gary to a hotel like a cheap private eye and caught him with Angela Reese. Megan, who couldn't keep it to herself, who had to tell Cathy. Did she think Cathy would be grateful? Anyone should have been able to predict how that would turn out.

But to be fair, Neil hadn't predicted it. He never thought Cathy would follow *him*. Afterward, when he tried to work out her motive, he came to believe that she'd done it out of spite. As if to say: *You spied on my husband? Fine. I'll spy on yours.*

Neil could only guess what Cathy must have thought when he drove to Humaston Road and met up with Luke Daw. Maybe she thought she'd struck gold. *Neil has a gay lover.*

She didn't recognize the danger. It was a few minutes past five in the afternoon. Still daylight. How much danger could there be?

She drove past the trailer, parked her car on the roadside. Doubled back and followed them at a distance. When they turned toward the ruined farmhouse, Cathy made for the barn. She hid herself there. And watched.

Luke opened the door in the earth and Neil went down. Luke waited above—which wouldn't have fit with the gay-lover hypothesis. What would Cathy have thought then? Would she have started to worry?

She'd be safe in the barn, out of sight. But how long could she stay still? She'd want to move around, maybe find a better view. There were plenty of holes in the barn wall.

Luke didn't hear her moving. But there were swallows in the barn, and the swallows heard. Four of them took flight through the empty frame of the roof.

Luke saw the swallows.

Neil had no clue to what was happening. But after he'd been down with Jana Fletcher for ten minutes, he heard shouting from above. Luke's voice yelling, "K!" A woman's scream.

Up the stairs and out under the blazing sky, and he sees Luke Daw dragging Cathy from the barn, shoving her to the ground. Luke's hand dips into his pocket and comes out with a knife. The blade folds out, liquid silver in the sunlight. Cathy scuttles away like a crab.

She spots Neil. Pleads, "Help me!"

Luke says, "What the hell, K? How'd she get here?"

Then she's up and running, and Luke is tackling her, rolling her onto her back. The blade sinks into her stomach.

It happens so fast that Neil thinks his eyes are cheating him, until she screams.

Luke seems dazed. He lets go of the knife. He's on his knees, leaning over her. She tries to push him away. When she starts to scream again, Neil is there. He claps a hand over her mouth.

She squirms in the grass. Slaps at his arms. Luke pulls the knife out and holds it up for Neil to see. Bright red on silver. Neil takes it and tosses it away.

"Hold her down," he says. He uses his take-charge voice, the one he brings out when he needs to control a rowdy classroom.

Luke obeys. He grabs Cathy's wrists, pins them to the ground.

Neil has a hand over Cathy's mouth and it's not enough. Two hands. He bears down. Her eyes are wide and wet with tears. Neil looks away from them, but then he's drawn back. He wonders what he looks like from her perspective. She's staring up at him and seeing his face upside down.

He bears down harder as she writhes in the grass. Her eyes are full of life. She's still breathing. He takes one hand from her mouth and pinches her nostrils shut. She writhes more desperately and almost throws off Luke Daw. But it's only temporary. Neil holds fast and Luke recovers. Cathy closes her eyes. If there's a moment when she dies, Neil misses it. He's thinking about how uncomfortable it is, kneeling on the hard ground.

That was the twenty-seventh of July, 1996. It would be months before Neil Pruett returned to the farm.

He let Luke deal with the body. It made sense. Neil was the more vulnerable one. Cathy was his sister-in-law; he was more likely to fall under suspicion.

He thought trusting Luke might be a problem, but once the shock of the situation wore off, Luke seemed to return to his old self.

"Leave it to me, K. I've got it under control."

"If you want help, I can help."

"No. I've got all the help I need."

He was referring to his cousin, though Neil didn't know it at the time. In September, when he heard about Eli Daw's death, Neil began to put things together. The news reports took for granted that Luke had shot Eli. Neil knew there could be a different explanation.

He waited till November to drive out to the farm. He climbed the slope of the hill on the Saturday after Thanksgiving. The hidden door was covered over with a blanket of autumn leaves. He opened it and went down with a flashlight. The light sent things scurrying into dark corners. Neil aimed it briefly at what was left of Luke Daw's face.

He knew then that Jana Fletcher had gotten out—though at that point he didn't know her name. It didn't worry him. He didn't think he would ever see her again.

He saw her more than a year later. A snowy day in March. By then, Gary had been convicted. Neil had stood by him all along, playing the role of the loyal brother. He had no real compassion for Gary, but it was useful to pretend he did—mainly because it alienated Megan, and he was tired of her. He was glad to have an excuse to leave her.

So on that day in March, he was living in Gary's house on Bloomfield Street. He was shoveling the walk in front. A lazy snow falling. Jana approached him, bundled up against the weather, wanting to talk about Gary. Neil didn't recognize her until he invited her inside, until she took off her winter coat and hat and scarf.

Everything left him then: his breath, his voice, his balance. He would have fallen over, but he caught himself against a counter. His heart must have been racing, but at that moment he thought he had no pulse at all. Open him up and there would be nothing inside.

Somehow he made it through their first conversation—Jana telling him how she hoped to see Gary set free. In the weeks that followed, she came back, once to ask him questions, another time just to reassure him that she was committed to seeing the case reopened. Neil convinced himself that she was playing a game with him. She knew him. She knew the truth. Then he decided he must be wrong. It didn't matter that she had seen his face. Luke had drugged her.

One night in April, Neil couldn't sleep. He lay in bed thinking about Gary getting out of prison, about the police taking another look at Cathy's murder. He worked himself into a dark state, convinced himself it was only a matter of time before Jana remembered him from the wooden room.

He didn't despair. He got angry. He was turning into a cliché.

He rolled out from under the covers and went to the bedroom closet. The highest shelf held a shoe box with a dusty lid. He took it down and opened it. Nothing inside but a few empty zip-lock bags. A memento of Sheila Cotton.

Holding it reminded him of who he was.

That was the night he decided to kill Jana Fletcher.

Megan had parked her car directly in front of the house. Neil sat in the driver's seat and listened to the patter of the rain on the windshield. His clothes were wet through. There were beads of rain on Megan's purse. He'd brought it out and tossed it on the passenger seat. Her key was in the ignition. Her body was in the trunk.

The hardest part: moving the body from the house to the car. The darkness helped. The power was out all along Bloomfield Street. But there was a full moon. And lightning.

Nothing he could do about the moon.

But he had stopped the lightning.

He had stood inside the front door, ready, Megan's bundled body slung over his shoulder. And he had thought about the lightning, willed it to hold off. Thought about his neighbors too. There'd be no one on the street, but there could be people looking out their windows at the storm. He concentrated. Pictured them turning away.

Then out the door, down the porch steps, to the car. He dumped the body in. Closed the trunk. Easy.

Now, in the driver's seat, Neil saw the sky light up. He counted three seconds before the thunder.

He knew what he should do. Take Megan to the farm and put her in the wooden room, where no one would find her. But he didn't want to.

He had other plans for the wooden room.

What if he put Megan in the canal, like Jolene? He would have to do it right this time. Weigh her down. There were landscaping bricks in Gary's backyard. They would do the job. Neil would need to devise a way to attach them to the bundle. A straightforward problem. He knew he could solve it.

But it would be dull work. Neil stared at the rain-blurred windshield. Outside, the lightning flared again. The wind raged. He imagined his neighbors huddling in their houses, timid. But Neil felt charged, like the lightning. This was not a night to be timid. Not a night for dull work.

He squeezed his right hand into a fist and felt the pain of the cigarette burn. It was meant to remind him to aim higher.

Megan could wait.

He got out of her car, got into his own, and drove off.

45

The traffic lights were dead along Erie Boulevard. Emergency crews had put up temporary stop signs at the intersections. The rain battered them and the wind threatened to topple them over. We made slow progress heading east toward Bloomfield Street.

Warren Finn had kept to himself ever since I told him about Neil Pruett. But when we pulled up to one of the stop signs—wipers slapping at the rain, a lost umbrella blowing through the street—he broke his silence.

"We should have the gun," he said.

He meant the Makarov pistol. I could think of lots of reasons why we shouldn't have it: Warren might be a little too eager to use it. Neil Pruett could be innocent. Even if we had it, we'd be foolish to rely on it. I'd never tested it. I didn't know if it would fire.

On the other hand, if Pruett was guilty, then he had a gun of his own—the one he took from Simon Lanik. The mate of the one that was resting in the middle drawer of Jana's desk.

"We can get the gun," I said to Warren, "but I'm holding on to it."

"Whatever you say."

I turned north at the next intersection and we made a detour to Jana's apartment.

Twenty-five minutes later, when we came at last to Bloomfield Street, a strobe of lightning lit the sky. We rolled past the pale blue house and there was a car at the curb in front, but it wasn't Neil Pruett's.

The time was well after midnight. I parked the truck down the block. Warren and I walked calmly through the wind and rain. We had our flashlights and I had the gun in my pocket. I also had a steel pry bar from the bed of the truck. I carried the pry bar for the same reason I carried the gun: just in case.

Dark houses all around us. Windows like empty eye sockets. We climbed onto the porch of the pale blue house and knocked on the door. Waited. Knocked again.

"He could be sleeping," I said.

Warren looked skeptical. "Do you think he's sleeping?"

"I think he's not home."

Warren reached for the pry bar and I let him take it. He worked the end into the seam between the door and the jamb, just above the level of the lock. One hard shove was all it needed.

Inside, we turned on our flashlights. There were pillar candles on a coffee table, recently extinguished. Their blackened wicks floated up from pools of liquid wax. I motioned for Warren to keep still. We listened. No sound but the storm.

Warren aimed his light at a mirror leaning against a wall. The beam shifted higher and found a series of small holes punched in the drywall—arranged in three lines to make a letter K.

"That's not normal," he said.

I noted the bow on the sofa. Two wineglasses on the coffee table. I beckoned to Warren and we moved together through the house, keeping our flashlights aimed at the floor.

Dining room. Kitchen. Dirty dishes overflowed the sink and filled the counter. We moved upstairs. Three bedrooms. Two abandoned, one in use. An unmade bed. Clothes tossed around carelessly. I looked under the pillows, felt under the mattress, opened the drawers of the night table, thinking I might find Simon Lanik's pistol. I didn't find it.

We went down to the basement last. Boxes and old furniture. A file cabinet. No torture chamber. No evidence that a killer lived in this house.

We returned to the first floor. Warren drifted away from me. I aimed my light around the living room, thinking. The candles on the coffee table suggested that we had missed Neil Pruett by mere minutes.

He must have had a good reason to venture out on a night like this.

I wandered into the kitchen and found Warren snooping through the drawers and cupboards.

"You're leaving fingerprints," I said.

He sighed a put-upon sigh. Grabbed a dish towel and started wiping down knobs and handles. I looked around for something that might tell me where Pruett had gone.

Warren finished with the towel and tossed it over the back of a chair. His flashlight beam played across the kitchen table. He aimed it at the refrigerator door, at the trash bin.

I stood by the counter and the soles of my feet hurt. The small of my back too—the place where the bull had gored me. I thought I'd left the bull behind, but I had a feeling he wasn't very far away. He was here, in this house.

Warren had left one of the drawers half open. I pointed my flashlight inside and saw silver: knives and forks. And something not silver.

I opened the drawer all the way. Removed a small cardboard box. Emptied it onto the counter.

Popsicle sticks.

"It's him," I said quietly.

Warren didn't hear me. He was shining his light into the trash bin. He reached in and pulled out a slip of paper. A receipt.

"Pruett went to a hardware store today," he said.

The bull was very near. I remembered talking to Neil Pruett late that afternoon. Hearing him tell me he had used my truck to run errands. It seemed like a lifetime ago.

"What did he buy?" I asked.

Warren handed me the receipt and I read it.

The bull ran the tip of his horn along my spine.

"No," I said. "Son of a bitch. No, no, no."

Darkness everywhere.

Neil Pruett stepped out of his shoes.

He had a penlight that fit in his pocket. He clicked it on and let the narrow beam lead him to what he wanted. He listened to the muffled sounds of the storm, and streaks of rainwater trickled down from his hair, along his temples, to his neck. The beam found a row of drawers.

The first one he tried held rolls of tape. Scotch tape. Masking tape.

Packing tape.

Exactly what he needed.

He trailed the beam along the floor: kitchen tile and then white carpet. A shimmer of lightning came through a pair of sliding glass doors. The thunder boomed as he crossed the threshold of the bedroom.

He clicked off the penlight and stood silent beside the doorway.

His eyes adjusted to the dark. He could make out shapes. The solid mass of the bed. A quilt spilling onto the floor. A sheet covering a sleeping form.

He could hear her breathing.

The bed was a queen, big enough for two, but she was sleeping alone, in the middle. Neil walked around to the far side. He put the roll of packing tape on the night table. He laid down the penlight and sat on the edge of the bed. Pulled the Makarov pistol out of his sock.

Sophie Emerson stirred and rolled onto her back. She touched his arm.

"Dave?" she said.

Barely awake.

Neil picked up the penlight and clicked it on. He wanted to see her. He'd never been this close. She had beautiful skin, like Sheila Cotton. She had chestnut hair that flowed in soft waves over her pillow.

She squinted into the light. Waking up fast. Neil returned the penlight to the night table, standing it on end so the beam shone on the ceiling. He covered her mouth with his left hand and pressed the muzzle of the Makarov against her forehead.

"I'm not Dave," he told her.

Sophie Emerson tried to scream.

"Don't," he said.

He watched her realize what was happening. Gave her a chance to catch up.

"You have questions," he said. "There's no time now, but later on we'll talk."

He watched her debating whether to struggle or give in. He pulled the gun back a few inches, to give her a better view of it. To help her decide.

"It'll be fine," he said. "I know a place we can go."

Keys.

I still had the keys to the old apartment. Sophie's apartment.

We drove there in five minutes, Warren Finn and me. I didn't pay much mind to stop signs. I swept into the lot in the beating rain and the truck's headlights showed me Sophie's car, in its usual space. My heart sank. I'd been hoping to find the space empty—hoping she was at the hospital.

I remember a squeal of wet brakes and sprinting through the rain. Warren following. I remember coming to the building's outer door and using one of my keys to open it. Then charging down the hallway and up a flight of stairs, flashlight beams bouncing wildly over the walls. Then another key to let us into the apartment.

Unnatural quiet. Nothing out of place. But everything looked wrong in the roving beams of light. I broke the quiet, calling Sophie's name. No answer.

I crossed into the bedroom. White sheets. Empty bed. Still nothing out of place except for a lamp on a night table with its shade askew. As if it had been knocked over and put back carelessly.

And one other thing: Sophie's cat's-eye glasses on the floor.

"He's got her," I said.

Warren joined me. "Are you sure?"

I pointed my light at the glasses. "She wouldn't leave them."

Pruett had her, and I was the one who gave her to him. I let him in. I had given him the keys to my truck that afternoon—I had given him all my keys, because they were all on the same key ring. And he had taken them to a hardware store and made copies.

"He walked right in here," I said. "She never had a chance."

Warren picked up the glasses. "She'll want them when we find her."

I had my cell phone out, but there was no reception. The storm. I punched 911 anyway and watched the screen. CONNECTING, it said. And then: CALL FAILED.

Warren spotted the landline on the night table and picked up the receiver. I watched him hold it to his ear and shake his head. No dial tone.

"It's just us," he said. "Where would he take her? Back to his house?"

No, I thought. All those neighbors. Why risk it? Especially if you knew about a better place. A ready-made prison.

"The farm," I said.

Pitch-black.

Sophie Emerson listened to the tin-roof sound of the rain, to the hiss of the tires on the wet road.

He had taped her wrists together behind her back. Her captor. She didn't have a name for him. He had taped her mouth too, but not her legs. He had left them free and marched her down the darkened stairwell and out of the building—in nothing but the scrubs she'd fallen asleep in, no shoes—and he had forced her into the trunk of his car.

No one on the stairs or in the hallway or outside. No one to see.

She lay on her side and twisted her arms against the tape. Twisted them until they hurt.

The tape held.

The car began to slow down. Rolling onto her back, Sophie used her bare feet to push against the lid of the trunk. It didn't budge. The car accelerated again.

She was breathing fast through her nose. A raspy sound. She didn't like it. The air was stale and the trunk smelled of spare anti-freeze and motor oil. She thought she might pass out. A bad thought.

But breathing was something she could control.

She turned onto her side again. The floor of the trunk had a wet-carpet smell. Not so bad. She focused on her breath. Felt it slow.

When she had it under control, she went to work on the tape over her mouth. She rubbed it against the carpet. Tried to peel it off.

We sped west on Erie Boulevard, driving into the wind. The traffic lights were still dark; all the intersections were four-way stops. I honked the horn as we tore through them.

We passed a minivan driving slow and left a spray of mist in our wake. Warren Finn eyed the road ahead and braced one hand against the dash. The minivan flashed its high-beams, angry.

Half a mile on, we hit a puddle that spanned two lanes. Black water boiling in the rain. The truck hydroplaned. It spun a hundred eighty degrees, three sixty; it jumped the curb of a convenience-store parking lot. I watched us heading for a pair of glass doors. I turned the sluggish wheel, hit the brakes hard.

The front end of the truck jerked to the left. The back end snapped around and slammed through the glass.

The wind vanished and the rain hung motionless in the air, and there was nothing but the truck rocking gently side to side. A few long seconds passed. Warren Finn drew his hand away from the dash and twisted around in his seat to survey the damage.

"You're good," he said.

The truck still swayed. I swayed with it. Left right, left right. The minivan pulled into the lot—the one with the angry high-beams. The driver climbed out. I thought he looked worried.

"Time to go," Warren said.

He sounded confident and sensible and levelheaded. I decided to take his advice.

When I pressed the gas pedal nothing happened.

"It stalled," Warren said.

I pushed the pedal some more. The minivan driver came closer.

Warren shifted the truck into park and reached over to turn the key in the ignition. The engine roared to life. The minivan driver stopped in his tracks.

Someone said, "Let's go." Warren again.

The world came roaring back like the engine. The wind blew and the rain fell.

I shifted us into drive and hit the gas.

Sophie felt every curve in the road, every crack and pothole. She knew the moment when the car drifted onto the shoulder, when it moved onto gravel. She felt it rumble to a stop.

The motor went silent. A car door opened and shut. Footsteps. A key slid into the lock of the trunk.

Neil Pruett raised the lid of the trunk and was met with a burst of movement—the girl kicked out at him with both feet. One of her heels struck the burn on his right hand, his gun hand. The Makarov pistol went flying.

He whirled around to find it in the dark, slipped on the wet gravel and fell. A flash of lightning revealed the pistol, just out of reach. He scrambled for it, snatched it up.

Turned back to see the girl on her feet, out of the trunk. The tape gone from her mouth, but her arms still bound behind her back. She stepped toward him and launched a kick at his face.

He twisted to catch the kick on his shoulder, crawled knees and elbows on the gravel to escape her, rolled onto his back and brought the gun up. She kicked it away again, but the kick left her off-balance. He grabbed her ankle and pulled.

Then she was down with him, down on the ground. A bolt of lightning ripped through the western sky. Neil spotted the pistol lying on an island of wet grass amid the gravel. The girl saw it too.

She tried to roll toward it. He got there first. She kicked at him as he lifted it from the grass, and when he stood up she was still kicking at him. He aimed the gun at her head, then shifted his aim a few inches and fired once. The shot raised a spit of mist and mud from the ground.

The girl stopped kicking and let out a wail of pure despair.

The wind carried it away.

We came around a bend on Humaston Road and the storm threw a tree branch in our path. I drove over it and it caught on something under the truck, and we dragged it all the way to Luke Daw's trailer.

I slid to a stop in the gravel and felt the bull's horn along my spine again. I didn't see Neil Pruett's car. I thought I'd made the wrong call; he'd taken Sophie somewhere else.

Warren Finn was out of the truck with his flashlight. I followed him. He ducked inside the trailer and came out a moment later, shaking his head. I snapped on my own flashlight and felt the weight of the Makarov in my pocket and the beat of the rain against my neck. We went around to the back of the trailer and there was Pruett's car. A dull sedan.

No one in the car. No way to make out footprints in the gravel. But we knew where they must have gone. There was only one place.

We found the lane and followed it through the trees.

The full moon hid behind the clouds above the barn: a blurry wash of pale light.

The light guided Neil Pruett up the slope of the hill. He pulled the girl along with him. When he came to the farmhouse and the wagon wheel, he put the gun in his pocket and took out his penlight. He used it to scan the ground until he found the iron ring.

He pushed the girl down to her knees, then hauled up the heavy door. He let it stand open, resting against the wheel, and aimed his penlight into the void. Saw the familiar stairs leading down. And saw something wrong: mud on the steps. Shoe prints.

Someone had been here. The wooden room was no longer a secret.

"There's no way I'm going down there," the girl said.

Neil clicked off the penlight.

"You'll have to shoot me," the girl said.

He traded the light for the pistol. Touched the muzzle to the top of her head.

"Shhhh," he said. "I'm thinking."

Change of plans. He couldn't use the wooden room. He would go back to the car. Take the girl to Gary's house.

He pulled her to her feet and lightning struck. Close. Just the other side of the pond. The thunder made him flinch.

His eyes adjusted in the wake of the strike. He looked down at the pond—a gray pool amid the darker gray of the surrounding fields. He blinked.

There were two spots of light advancing up the slope of the hill.

I saw them first as silhouettes: two figures at the top of the slope, against a sky of night and cloud. Then the lightning turned the sky to daylight and I saw them clearly: Neil Pruett holding Sophie's arm, with the Makarov pistol in his free hand.

The sky turned to night again. Warren and I raced up the hill, flashlight beams jittering over the uneven ground.

A shot rang out.

I dropped my light and drew the gun from my pocket. The rain slanted sideways through the air. I saw it in the beam of Warren's light.

"Turn it off," I told him.

Too late.

A second shot cut through the night, and I dove to the ground. Warren dove too.

His flashlight rolled over the drenched grass. I crawled to it and worked the switch. The light went out.

A third shot sounded from up the hill. I raised my gun and fired twice, aiming wide. I didn't want to risk hitting Sophie. The shots rang loud. My eyes closed reflexively. When I opened them again I saw the two silhouettes running—one dragging the other—heading in the direction of the barn.

I went to Warren. He was lying facedown. I shook his shoulder and heard him moan. I rolled him over onto his back.

I could see the blood on his white shirt, even in the dark.

Neil Pruett took the girl to the far end of the barn. The broad door stood open. He pulled her inside. The rain still fell on them, pouring through the bare frame of the roof. But the walls kept out most of the wind.

He could still get out of this.

He only needed to reach his car. Nothing stood in his way except the two men on the slope—and he had hit one of them, he was sure.

They weren't cops. If the cops had discovered the wooden room, there'd be swarms of them, not just two.

No, the cops didn't know about the farm. But David Malone knew. Malone had been here before. So that's who he was dealing with: Malone and a friend. And one of them was already down.

The rain streamed from Neil's hair into his face. He wiped it away with a damp sleeve. The girl was talking to him. She'd been droning on in a dull and patient voice, the kind you might use to talk to a foreigner. He'd been half listening. She wanted him to let her go; that was the essence of it. She had money and her parents had money, and they would pay him if only he would let her go.

Neil brought the Makarov pistol up and aimed it at the bridge of her nose.

"Shhhh," he said.

Out of the corner of his eye he saw movement at the other end of the barn. Someone stepped into the open doorway there—a dark shape against the night-gray sky.

———

S ophie?" I called.

    She answered in a wavering voice. "Dave?"

The rain faded back. I could still hear it falling; it tickled the mud of the barn floor. It sent ripples through a puddle midway between us. I could see the ripples in the light of the moon: concentric circles spreading out into one another.

"Is he there?" I asked Sophie.

"He's here," she said. "He's got a gun in my face."

"Yes, I'm here," said Neil Pruett.

"I think he's crazy," Sophie said.

"I know," I told her.

"Put your gun down," said Pruett.

I watched the circles in the puddle. I didn't do what he said. I didn't intend to do anything he said.

"The police are on their way, Neil."

No reply. Not at first. I heard movement at the other end of the barn, and a gasp from Sophie. I could imagine what Pruett was doing: moving her in front of him so he could use her as a shield.

"You're lying," he said.

"You're right. I'm lying. But Warren Finn—he's the one you shot—he's not dead. You winged him. I sent him to get the police. So they're not on their way yet, but they will be."

"You're lying," Pruett said again.

I thought I could see him, down at the other end. He was just inside the doorway. Seventy feet away from me, maybe a little more.

I stood sideways with my head turned toward him, trying to present as small a target as possible. I had my gun arm extended in front of me.

"Warren must've reached my truck by now," I said. "He'll go to the police and bring them back. There's nothing you can do."

"They won't get here in time to save you," Pruett said.

I tossed my shoulders. "It won't matter. Not to you. He'll tell them all about you. They'll track you down. I'm giving you a chance to get away. A head start. Let Sophie go."

Quiet in the barn. Just the patter of the rain in the puddle.

"What if I want to keep her?" Pruett said.

"That's not the deal I'm offering."

Pruett stepped into the square frame of the doorway, pulling Sophie with him. She cried out softly. I could make out the shape of them. He had his gun against her temple.

"Here's the deal *I'm* offering," he said. "Put your gun down or I'll kill her right now."

Neil Pruett pushed the muzzle of the Makarov into the side of the girl's head.

"Right now," he repeated.

Malone didn't move. "You're making a mistake, Neil," he said.

"I'll kill her."

Nothing. Then Malone lowered his arm. His gun dropped into the mud.

"Now kick it this way."

Malone kicked it. It landed in the puddle.

"Now turn around and put your hands on your head."

I didn't turn. I didn't put my hands on my head.

If Pruett wanted to shoot me, he could shoot me in the front, not the back.

Seventy feet between us. He was a schoolteacher, not a soldier.

Not a marksman. He'd managed to hit Warren, but that was a wild shot. Dumb luck. I didn't think he could hit me.

He seemed to have the same idea. He moved a few steps closer, pushing Sophie in front of him. He took the gun away from her temple and aimed it at me.

She butted the back of her head against his chin and tore away from him.

I reached my hand behind my back, fast, and brought it out again.

Neil Pruett fired his Makarov at me. Four times. I felt the first one like a bee buzzing by my sleeve. The other three I felt not at all.

I didn't shoot him. My gun hand was empty. I didn't even have my cell phone. I'd dropped it in the mud and kicked it into the puddle.

Pruett lowered his spent Makarov and turned to run. Warren Finn met him in the doorway of the barn and shot him in the gut with the second Makarov.

46

Weeks went by before they found Neil Pruett's body.

The storm passed before dawn on Saturday, and by Sunday night most of the city had power again. There was still a lot of cleaning up to do. Roofs that needed repairing. I managed to keep busy.

When Megan Pruett missed school on Monday and didn't call in, some of her fellow teachers worried about her. Two of them drove to her house on Tuesday and found it empty. They tried to call her husband and got no answer. Finally they drove to the house on Bloomfield Street and found her car parked in front. They went onto the porch and in through the damaged door and saw the letter *K* on the wall. They called the police.

The police discovered Megan's body in the trunk of her car. Killed with a bow and arrow.

That's when they started looking for her husband.

The manhunt for Neil Pruett began with a statewide bulletin and soon expanded through the northeast. There were sightings as far afield as Harrisburg, Pennsylvania, and Bangor, Maine. One woman swore she had seen him in Niagara Falls, crossing over into Canada.

People see what they want to see, and there are plenty of forty-year-old men in the world with plain faces and sandy hair.

The police caught a break in July, when a retired state trooper and his wife pulled off on the side of Humaston Road to hunt for wild blackberries. The trooper had been following the case, and he recognized Pruett's car when he spotted it behind Luke Daw's abandoned trailer.

The Rome P.D. found Pruett three days later, with the help of a cadaver dog on loan from the county sheriff. They found him in Luke's underground room. Right where I put him.

T he night of the storm. Warren in his blood-soaked shirt, standing over Neil Pruett with the Makarov pistol. Sophie running toward me. I sloshed through the puddle and caught her up, spun her around, asked her if she was hurt, told her I was sorry.

I used my pocketknife to cut the tape that bound her wrists.

We turned to see Warren firing another round into Pruett's stomach. Thunder drowned out Pruett's scream. Warren pointed the gun at Pruett's head and pulled the trigger again.

Nothing happened.

Warren didn't let it faze him. He stepped around to Pruett's right side and stomped his heel down hard on Pruett's hand. He did the same on Pruett's left side. He brought his flashlight out of his back pocket and used it to break Pruett's nose. There was no thunder to mask the screams.

We went to him. I took the pistol away—gently—and flicked on the safety. He kicked the side of Pruett's neck.

"It's enough," I said.

Warren drew his foot back for another kick, but all the exertion had left him unsteady. He swayed. I caught him and helped him down to the ground.

"I'm fine," he said.

I opened his shirt. The bullet had struck his shoulder. We looked at the wound in the beam of his flashlight. Sophie leaned close, squinting. I remembered her glasses; Warren had them in his pocket. I gave them to her.

"He needs to go to the hospital," she said.

"No hospitals," said Warren.

Neil Pruett tried to sit up. I pushed him back down into the mud.

"I'm good," Warren said.

He looked better than he had a right to.

"What if you drove him to the apartment?" I asked Sophie. "Could you treat him there?"

"No," he said.

"Maybe," said Sophie.

I handed her my keys. "The truck is down by the trailer. Come back for me when you can."

"I'm not leaving," Warren said, nodding at Pruett. "Not while he's alive."

I got down on my knees so I could look Warren in the eye.

"I'll take care of him," I said. "I promise you."

I stood by the side of the barn and watched Sophie lead Warren down the hill. I tracked their progress in the moonlight and in the occasional flare of lightning. Warren did okay. He kept on his feet.

When I returned to Neil Pruett I found him standing, trying to get a broken finger onto the trigger of his empty pistol. I grabbed it away from him.

"Come on," I said, taking him by the arm. "We're not finished."

I led him toward the farmhouse, and when he staggered I helped him along. The door in the ground stood open. Pruett didn't want to go down. I didn't give him a choice.

I switched on Warren's flashlight. The stairs were wet from the rain. Halfway down, Pruett slipped. Or pretended to slip. He fell back against me. Maybe he was trying to knock me over. I fended him off. Pushed him. He tumbled the rest of the way down the stairs and I'm afraid he made a hard landing at the bottom. He broke his fibula, one of the bones of the lower leg.

The bone came through the skin and tore through his left pant leg. I could see it jutting out, like the splintered tip of a spear.

There was shrieking.

I dragged him through the doorway into the room.

He lost consciousness and I got some relief from the noise. I laid him on his back on the mattress and wrapped the chain around his neck. I fastened it in place with the padlock and took the key.

I tore the tail off my shirt and used it to wipe my fingerprints from the chain and the lock.

Pruett woke. Hazy. He brought a swollen hand up to touch the links of the chain.

"You can't leave me here," he said.

I went looking around the room for Luke Daw's bones, the larger pieces, the ones Warren might have handled. When I found them, I wiped them down.

Pruett touched his broken nose and groaned. He trailed his hand along his left leg until his fingertip found the jagged end of his fibula.

"I wouldn't touch that," I said. "It's what you call an open fracture. It'd be easy to get it infected."

He moved his hand to his stomach and it came away bloody. He brought it up to his face so he could see.

"This is bad."

"I know it seems that way."

"I need help."

"Maybe you'll pull through."

I found Luke Daw's wallet and driver's license and wiped them down.

"You have to get me out of here," Pruett said.

I went to stand over him. "Maybe you'll make it out on your own."

"This is serious."

I still had Jana's quarter. I showed it to him. "She got out with just this," I said. "So we know it can be done." I put the quarter away. "You got any change in your pockets, Neil?"

He didn't answer. He was quiet for a while, and I went back to wiping Luke's bones. Five minutes went by, maybe ten. I heard Pruett breathing hard. I put the light on him. He was trying to sit up.

The effort did him in and he fell back.

"This is a cruel way to die," he said.

"I know."

"You don't have to do it this way," he said. "You could shoot me."

I had the Makarovs in my pockets. I laid the flashlight on the floor and took them out.

"These guns are junk," I said. "They're counterfeits. It's a wonder they worked as well as they did."

"Just do it. Shoot me."

"I don't really want to."

Neil Pruett struggled again to sit up. Managed to brace himself on his elbows.

"I'll tell you something about Jana," he said.

I returned the empty Makarov to my pocket. Kept the other one out.

"She remembered me at the end," Pruett said, "when I had her on the floor."

He straightened his arms, pushed himself up.

"She remembered me," he said, "and I've never seen anyone so afraid."

No thunder above us. No lightning. Just the sorry sound of the rain falling on the stairs. I flicked off the safety of the Makarov, then pulled back the slide and released it. The unfired round dropped onto the mattress and a new one entered the chamber.

There were eight bullets in the clip to start. I'd fired two and Warren had fired two. And one on the mattress, which left three.

Pruett's arms trembled. I pointed the gun at his head and squeezed the trigger.

Click.

"I told you," I said. "Junk."

He closed his eyes. "Try it again."

I worked the slide. Squeezed the trigger.

Click.

"Jesus Christ," he said. "Again."

One last try. Slide. Trigger.

Click.

"That has to be fate," I said.

He didn't say anything.

I tucked the gun in my pocket. Collected the bullets and the flash-light from the floor. And I left him there.

When they found his body the story made national headlines. UNDERGROUND DUNGEON IN UPSTATE NEW YORK. The cable news shows covered it for days. It gave them a lot to work with: the Pruett brothers, Gary and Neil, and their two murdered wives. Luke and Eli Daw, the pot-dealing cousins who came to a bad end. Wendy Daw refused to be interviewed, but plenty of others were eager to talk—people who had grown up around the Pruetts or had a story to share about the Daws. Gary Pruett himself sat for an interview in a prison rec room up in Dannemora, proclaiming his own innocence and his brother's too.

The coverage started to lag at the end of July, until a reporter tracked down Luke Daw's mother in a small town in Nebraska. Maggie Daw had spent the last nineteen years moving around the Midwest, waiting tables in diners. She was a haunted woman, a picture of wasted beauty, with streaks of gray in her hair and dark faraway eyes. She broke down on camera, crying for her dead son and describing the abuse she had suffered at the hands of her father.

In August there was a school shooting out west, and a pretty young blonde went missing on her honeymoon. The cable channels lost interest in the Pruetts and the Daws and Rome, New York.

The Rome police pursued the investigation through the summer and into the fall. The lead detective was not Frank Moretti; it was a gruff cop named O'Keefe, a balding man who wore suspenders and smoked cigars. O'Keefe theorized that Neil Pruett had been killed by drug dealers, unidentified associates of the Daws— the same unidentified associates who had killed Luke and Eli. On this theory, Megan Pruett was collateral damage, murdered by her husband when she found out about his involvement in the drug trade.

In September, traces of blood recovered from the underground room were tested and matched by DNA analysis to Cathy Pruett, and people began to wonder whether Cathy might also have been a collateral victim of violence among drug dealers. The *Rome Sentinel* ran an editorial arguing that the new evidence justified another look at Gary Pruett's conviction in the murder of his wife. Roger Tolliver announced that he would take up Pruett's cause and work toward getting him a new trial.

I spoke to Tolliver a few days after his announcement. He sounded determined and optimistic. He believed he was doing something Jana would have wanted. I wasn't so sure. If Gary Pruett was anything like his brother, maybe prison was the place for him. He hadn't killed his wife, but maybe that was because he never got around to it, because someone else did it first.

I could understand the value of helping him—in the abstract. Because everyone deserves a fair trial and the whole system suffers when justice is denied. But I couldn't say if it was what Jana would have wanted.

In September I was still living in Jana's apartment. The nights were growing cool, and for the first time since she died I wanted to build a fire. Her fireplace had gone untended for months, and when I swept out the ashes I found something I'd been looking for: a few fragments of paper, charred around the edges. On one of them I could make out part of a heading: *Oneida County Coroner.*

It was from a copy of the autopsy report on Cathy Pruett.

I was looking at what remained of the green file: Jana's notes on the Pruett case.

Ashes.

There'd been a time when I thought that Frank Moretti had taken the contents of the file—and later I decided that Jana's killer must have carried the papers away with him. But now I believe that Jana disposed of them herself, that she burned them at some point in the days before she died.

I think she did it because she realized she wasn't responsible for Gary Pruett's fate, because she was ready to let the case go and move on. Ready to live her own life.

I'd like to think she did it because she was happy.

I'd like to believe I had something to do with that.

In July and August, after the police discovered the underground room, people were drawn to the farm on Humaston Road—people curious to see a place touched by death.

But when the police had collected their evidence, the county sent workers to dismantle Luke Daw's creation. They took it out board by board. They filled in the root cellar and hauled away the wreckage of the farmhouse. They bulldozed the barn and hauled that away too. They towed Luke's trailer to a junkyard.

By September hardly anyone went to the farm anymore. There was nothing to see.

I drove out there several times, especially after the weather turned mild. I saw Angela Reese there once, with a stool and an easel set up on the hill. She was branching out from acrylics to oils, from abstracts to landscapes. She had rendered the pond in blue and green, and the forest of cattails on the far shore. She told me she had an exhibition scheduled for the spring, at a gallery in Syracuse. I told her I would come.

A week later I pulled onto the gravel lot that once held Luke's trailer and was surprised to see Frank Moretti's black Chevrolet. Surprised and not surprised. I walked back through the trees and up the hill and found Moretti sitting on a blanket on the ground. He wore a gray suit and had his shirt collar unbuttoned. His tie lay coiled in the grass.

"I've been expecting to see you," he said as I sat beside him.

"Have you?"

"I like coming here. Maybe because it's quiet." He paused, to demonstrate how quiet it could be. "But I knew I'd see you eventually."

"Why?"

"Because people don't learn. No matter how smart they are. They always return to the scene of the crime."

Moretti pulled a clump of grass from the ground at the edge of the blanket. He kept the longest blade and tossed the others away. He wound the blade around his finger.

"It could've been my case," he said wearily. "When we found the wife with a broken arrow in her heart, the chief offered to let me take the lead. I didn't want it. So he gave it to O'Keefe. And when we found the husband, that one went to O'Keefe too."

I looked off at the distant birch trees. Their leaves had just started to turn.

Moretti said, "I went down in that room, though. Just about every detective in the department went down there. Whoever killed Neil Pruett did an amateurish job. They got some things right. No shell casings left behind—that was good. But other things they screwed up. If you're going to kill a man, you kill him. You don't leave him to die."

He played with the blade of grass, winding it and unwinding it.

"The M.E. couldn't say how long Pruett lasted, down there alone in the dark," Moretti said. "Maybe a few hours, maybe a day. But before he died, he tried to scratch a message in the floor. He used a key. That was another rookie move, leaving him his keys. He didn't get very far, just one letter, an *M*. O'Keefe thinks he was trying to name his killer."

"*M* could mean anything," I said. "*M* for Megan. Maybe it was a message for his wife."

"Maybe he was crying for his mother. But I thought you'd want to know: O'Keefe has his eye out for an *M*. He's curious about the keys too. So am I. There were a lot of them. Some of them—O'Keefe doesn't know what they open. But he'd like to know."

I wasn't worried about the keys. I'd changed the locks at Sophie's apartment. At Jana's too.

"There's nothing I can tell you about keys," I said.

Moretti held up the blade of grass and let the wind take it. He draped his tie around his neck.

"Do you have time for a walk?" he asked.

We strolled down the hill, Moretti with his blanket folded under his arm. As we approached the pond he said, "Warren Finn's wife had her baby."

I knew. I'd already been for a visit. They had a boy, seven pounds. I noticed that Warren tended to cradle the kid with his right arm. His left was still a little stiff around the shoulder.

"I drove there the weekend before last," Moretti said. "They seem happy. Lydia too. She loves the boy like he's her own grandson. I think that's good."

We came to the pond and Moretti picked his way through some tall weeds and led me to a dock I hadn't seen before—the wood weathered and bleached by the sun. We walked out almost to the end.

"Lydia has questions, about Jana," he said. "She asked me about these new murders, if I thought they were connected in any way with Jana's death. I told her no, I didn't see how they could be."

Warren and I had told her the same thing when she asked us.

"I don't like lying to her," Moretti said. "But I don't want her to know the truth. I wish I didn't know. When I went down in that room, I saw the gap in the wall, the missing board. I know what it means. I've got that piece of two-by-four sitting in evidence—the candleholder from Jana's apartment. O'Keefe hasn't made the connection. Maybe he never will. He's about as dense as you could hope for. But there are other things that might give it away."

We watched a heron flying low over the pond.

"I've spent some time with Lydia," Moretti said. "I've listened to her stories. Jana's trip to New York City, and how she came back on the bus because she had to sell her grandmother's car." He rubbed the nape of his neck. "What do you think happened to that car?"

"I don't know."

"I think it's here," he said, looking out at the water. "It never turned up anywhere else. It's somewhere under the surface, maybe under the lily pads out there. But if we have a dry spell and the water goes down far enough, somebody might find it. And then everything comes out in the open. I won't be able to keep it from Lydia," he said, turning to face me. "So should I tell her now? That's the question that's been troubling me. I want to do the right thing."

He was looking for an answer and I didn't have one. I had something else, something that had been building inside me for a long time: a pressure, white-hot. I was thinking of the chain of events that began with one bad decision by Frank Moretti: if he hadn't framed Gary Pruett and sent him to prison, then Jana wouldn't have needed to save him, and she never would've gone to see Neil Pruett, and she would still be alive.

I thought the desire to do the right thing had come to Frank Moretti a bit too late.

The pressure had been building. It needed to go somewhere.

I made a fist and punched him in the jaw.

The night of the storm, after I gathered all the shell casings and retrieved my cell phone from the puddle in the barn, I waited for Sophie in the shelter of Luke Daw's trailer. She came for me around four in the morning and brought me back to her apartment, where Warren Finn, stitched up and bandaged, was recovering on the sofa.

Sophie checked on him, and then she and I went into the bedroom. We lay together in the darkness and she told me about waking up with Neil Pruett in the room. She asked me what I'd done to him and I told her.

"I would've put the bullets in the other gun," she said.

At dawn she fell asleep. I stayed with her.

I spent a lot of time with her that summer and fall. I didn't move back into the apartment—she never asked me to—but she called me when she needed me. She didn't feel safe alone at night, especially in those first few weeks after the storm.

Our engagement was called off by unspoken agreement. The wedding invitations never went out. We'd once scheduled the ceremony for a day in late September. I didn't hear from Sophie that day, but she called me the day after—the day I punched Frank Moretti.

We watched a movie on TV that night, something with Meg Ryan or Tom Hanks or both. I kept an ice pack on my hand; the knuckles were scraped and swollen. The punch had caught Moretti off-guard. It knocked him down. If the dock had been narrower, he might have gone into the water.

He sat rubbing his jaw and his expression showed me everything: shock and betrayal and regret. I wanted to help him up. He got up on his own.

"I wish I hadn't done that," I said.

Moretti turned away and walked back along the dock. I watched him go. His feet shuffled and he looked tired. He had always looked tired.

I never talked to him again.

When Sophie asked about my hand, I told her the truth. She said I should keep icing it and it would be fine. It wasn't what I wanted to hear. I wanted her to tease me about it. I wanted to go back. I wanted her to say, "Dave, promise me you'll stop punching policemen."

Later in the fall she started seeing someone—another intern at the hospital. Not Brad Gavin. A different one.

There's one last thing to tell. It happened in October, on a Sunday afternoon. I was walking on the hill at the farm.

In another year everything would be grown over, but on that day I could still see the long rectangular footprint where the barn had stood and the square plot that had held the ruined farmhouse. I paced back and forth between them, my shoes dragging through the grass.

Moretti had come here looking for quiet, and if I wanted to fool myself I could say I hoped to find quiet too, and a measure of peace. But what I wanted was to find Jana.

There were nights in her apartment when I woke up and lit the candles on the mantel and walked out onto the patio and into the grass, and if the moon was out I could almost feel her there. Almost.

I'd had the same feeling here on the hill. Once. I stood at twilight and watched the first stars appearing in the sky. I closed my eyes and she was next to me, as real as a touch on my shoulder.

Now I came to the footprint of the barn and turned back, and in the distance, at the edge of where the farmhouse used to be, I saw a crow.

It was on the ground, but it hovered over the grass, as if it didn't weigh anything, as if the tips of the blades of grass could hold it up. I walked toward it. I thought it would fly, but it stayed. As I got closer I realized it was perched on something: the wagon wheel.

The wheel had been torn from the ground, but no one had hauled it away. It lay on its side in the grass, and the crow sat on the rim.

I stopped a few feet short of the wheel, not wanting to startle the bird.

It took off.

It flew a circle in the air and headed for the pond. I followed, jogging down the slope through a scattering of autumn leaves, red and orange.

The crow made its landing on the dock.

I lost sight of it until I stepped through the weeds and onto the sun-bleached planks. Then I saw it: shaking out its black wings and hopping over the boards to the end of the dock. It looked down into the water.

I walked out to join it. Slow, careful steps. It let me get close. I got down and crossed the last distance on hands and knees. I stretched out along the dock on my stomach. I looked into the water.

I heard the wind stirring through the cattails on the other shore. I saw the blue-gray sky below me. I saw my own face in the water and the crow beside me.

The crow leapt into the air.

I watched it fly through the sky's reflection until it passed out of sight.

I reached down and my fingers broke the surface of the water. It felt cold. The ripples spread. They passed through the image of my face. And that's when I saw her. Jana. She was there in the water, only for a moment. I saw those brown eyes looking up at me. Those high exotic cheekbones. She had no bruise. Her mouth looked like it was laughing.

In that moment, I reached for her, even though I knew I could never touch her.

I knew.

But I could swear she was reaching back.

ACKNOWLEDGMENTS

When I was a kid growing up in Rome, New York, hardly anyone ever got murdered there. Things are a little different in this book.

In the course of setting this story in my hometown, I've gone beyond tinkering with the crime rate; I've sometimes altered the geography of the place to suit my purposes. People familiar with Rome will recognize the many liberties, large and small, that I've taken in describing the city.

That kid who grew up in Rome had a moderately wild imagination, but he never would have guessed that he would one day have the good fortune to work with people like Amy Einhorn and Victoria Skurnick. I'd like to thank them on his behalf, and mine.

Thanks also to Tom Colgan, Ivan Held, Leslie Gelbman, Ashley Hewlett, Glory Plata, Elizabeth Stein, Tom Dussel, David Chesanow, Melissa Rowland, Lindsay Edgecombe, Elizabeth Fisher, and Miek Coccia.

This book is dedicated to my brother and sister, but I'm grateful for the support of all my family: the Dolans in New York and the Randolphs in Michigan. And always, especially, Linda.

READERS GUIDE FOR

THE LAST DEAD GIRL

by Harry Dolan

DISCUSSION QUESTIONS

1. *The Last Dead Girl* features many strong women, most notably Jana and Sophie, who both make the first move with David, rather than the other way around. In what other ways are these women similar? How are they different? What does their confidence say about both of them, and how does it shape their stories?

2. Do you think David's lack of control in his two relationships—both in their beginnings and their endings—serves as a catalyst for him to pursue clues in Jana's case so thoroughly? Or is this curiosity a facet of David's character?

3. Initially, there seems to be only the slenderest link between Gary Pruett's case and Jana's death. Why, then, do you think David researches Pruett's case so passionately from the start?

4. The young painter Angela Reese tells David that she's okay with Gary's current situation—because he's not her problem, and she's not responsible for him. How do other characters in the book

contradict this train of thought, the idea that we only take care of ourselves? Who feels the most responsibility for others in this story? Who doesn't? Why?

5. Both David and Roger Tolliver are interested in Jana romantically. After what happened to her, why do you think Jana is so much more comfortable with David, a stranger, than she is with Roger, her admired professor?

6. What do you think of Sophie's confession, when she ultimately tells David the real reason for her infidelity? Do you think they would have been happy if he'd known the truth before he met Jana? Or do you think that David needed to meet Jana, no matter what?

7. Discuss Angela Reese's idea of duality. What are some of the different sides that each character shows throughout the book?

8. Discuss the relationship between the brothers Neil and Gary Pruett. Do you think they're both beyond saving, as David seems to think? Do you think there's any real compassion left, on either end?

9. Why do you think the author chose to tell this story in alternating narratives, and with an irregular timeline? Did it add to the atmosphere of the novel?

10. Most of the characters in *The Last Dead Girl* have secrets, both good and bad, and no character seems to be purely good. Do you feel this is an authentic portrayal of human nature? Who do you relate to most in this story, and why?

ABOUT THE AUTHOR

Harry Dolan is the bestselling author of *Bad Things Happen* and *Very Bad Men*. He graduated from Colgate University, where he majored in philosophy and studied fiction writing with the novelist Frederick Busch. A native of Rome, New York, he now lives in Ann Arbor, Michigan, with his partner, Linda Randolph.